WORLDS APART

by

David Diprose

Alan Keen

and

Paul Wilson

Published by New Generation Publishing in 2013

Cover design by Guy Wilson

www.newgeneration-publishing.com

 New Generation Publishing

Chapter 1

To the casual observer it would have appeared that the Joint Services Resettlement Centre, near Ely in Nevada, merely converted the military training and experience of those about to retire into qualifications that might be useful in finding civilian employment. Nobody seemed to notice that the aircraft bringing people in arrived almost full and departed nearly empty.

Daniel Swift was a low-ranking communications specialist. He had no experience of teaching others; he regarded himself as a 'hands on' sort of guy. He had no idea why he was being sent to the JSRC. In fact, his boss had volunteered him. A call had gone out for men and women with his skills who had no strong personal attachments and were therefore free to move at short notice. Even though he had turned thirty, he had not yet found anybody with whom he wished to share his life. He had seemed like an ideal candidate.

Daniel joined the military conveyor belt without any great concern for his own skills. He was more worried about the landscape. From the aircraft window, Ely looked like a place that could get very cold in the wintertime, not a place where it would be much fun working outside erecting aerial masts.

As soon as Daniel stepped off the plane, he was met by a guy who looked old enough to be retired himself. "Hi, Daniel. I'm Andy. You'll be working with me for a few days." Andy was a couple of inches shorter than Daniel and was solidly built rather than overweight. His face was square and weather-beaten. Daniel had expected to be met by a man in uniform. Andy wore a suit that was smart but not expensive.

Andy saw the confusion on Daniel's face. "I'm one of the sergeants on the staff here. None of us wear uniform. We are trying to prepare people for Civvy Street so we act like civilians." Daniel could see the sense in that, although he knew it did not apply to him. "We'll get you booked in and give you a meal, and then I'll brief you." Meals and briefings sounded more like what Daniel was expecting.

An hour later, Daniel found himself sitting in Andy's office. Large windows gave views of building work less than a hundred paces away to the south. It looked like part of the resettlement training. Further away, there were mountains on the horizon to the west. "First, I need you to sign this document," said Andy. "You are about to be enrolled in something that is more secret than the Manhattan project." He sounded a little nervous. Daniel recognised the document. He had signed something similar the day he had joined the military, promising not to divulge any details about his work to people who had no need to know.

While Andy filed the paperwork, Daniel looked round again. He was a comms engineer. He knew very little about things that went bang. None of the buildings looked big enough to contain the sort of major undertaking that Andy appeared to be suggesting. The busiest was a small hangar, which had several dozen people milling around it.

"Okay," Andy continued. "I'll let you watch the presentation and then we can have a chat." He put a DHD in the scanner. Daniel was familiar with the technology, one of the early holographic-format replacements of the old DVDs. It began with an agricultural view before sweeping across open countryside towards a small town. Everything looked so typically American that Daniel's concentration had begun to fade before the picture closed in on a smartly-dressed man standing on a corner where two streets crossed at right angles.

"Hi, folks," said the man. "I know that you have spent time in an American military uniform, just like me. Your service has given you the right to join me here on Springfield." The picture reversed out to the farm where it had started. "This is typical of the little bit of Springfield that we have colonised so far. There are about five thousand of us, I am told, although more are arriving all the time." The DHD continued to display the sort of view that might have been taken from a helicopter. It all looked and sounded sort of old-fashioned, which Daniel accepted as being typical of military presentations. He was still trying to figure out what was going on when the whole tenor of the presentation changed.

A graphic of two spheres slowly rotating round each other appeared on the screen. "An American team of scientists has discovered a parallel universe. In that other universe there is a planet, which we have named Springfield, that is close enough to colonise. You have earned the right to be one of the colonists, with your family, if you so wish. I know you guys will want a little bit of the science before we get down to the nitty-gritty, so here goes. There is a doorway that is fixed on the surface of the Earth, here on the base at Ely. It traces out a loop about three hundred miles long, close to the surface of the other planet, as the two globes move round each other in their different universes." Something like a halo appeared between the two spheres on the graphic.

"In the early days, we just hung a rope out of the doorway and people went up and down as if they were on a ski lift," the commentary continued. "Now, we have a railway track running below the doorway and an escalator that can join both securely for several hours at a time. The Springfield day is about twenty-seven Earth hours long and the doorway takes about forty hours to

6

go round one loop, so there are scheduling limitations to the operation. It has worked for several years without incident, however, permitting the safe transfer of both people and resources." There was a holograph of families flowing down an escalator, something that would not have been out of place in any modern airport or shopping mall. Daniel didn't notice that there was no airport or mall.

"So what's the deal, you are asking yourselves," the voice continued. Daniel was definitely wondering what was coming next. "At the bottom of the escalator you go to *Registration*. Every family gets a buggy for transportation, photovoltaic panels for energy generation, a cellphone for communication, and a water catchment kit." The camera panned across a range of items while the voice explained each of them. Daniel was too amazed to absorb every detail. All the while, a little voice in his head was asking: can this be real?

"After you have assembled your buggy and loaded up all your belongings, you are ready to move out," the commentator advised. "Make a careful note of your registration number, which is also your cellphone number. If you have friends here already, check the map on the wall in *Registration*. There is no satnav on Springfield; there are no satellites. Instead we have what we call cellnav. Use the menu to select the navigation mode and enter your friend's number. The cellphone will then guide you to them like a compass." The video showed a demonstration in slow time. "Oh, yes. You will want to register your very own ranch early on, so that you can set up your own water catchment kit and get planting. Each ranch is ten thousand acres. That's a patch of land about four miles by four miles."

Daniel turned to Andy, who stopped the DHD at that point. "Where is this Springfield place?" Daniel asked.

"Not sure myself," said Andy, more cheerful now that he had got through what he had expected to be the most difficult bit. "It will make more sense when you look for yourself. The next transfer will start in about five hours. The escalator gives us a transfer window of about two hours at a time. We move people when it is daylight on Springfield and freight when it is dark. Although night will have fallen here in five hours, it will be close to midday on Springfield. You'll be able to get a good view of things."

Daniel didn't know enough science to challenge what he had seen and heard so far, which did not worry him unduly. His years in uniform had taught him that he would be told only as much as his bosses thought he needed to know. The bit about a colony led him to the view that perhaps a secret base was being set up in another country. Obviously, he thought, he would not be told its name until he was actually there. He wondered how many men like him were being given a similar briefing. After Iraq and Afghanistan, there had been many voices saying that trying to support the local rulers was a waste of time; better just to let Uncle Sam run the whole caboodle.

"It started back in 2014," Andy added, which reinforced Daniel's assessment. "It was all a bit hit-and-miss in those days. The operation moved to Ely about four years ago. They were still using the ski lift at that time. Then the railway was built. About two years ago the Springfielders decided to start their own calendar. They are now past the middle of their Year 2. They have their watches and clocks set to the longer day and their calendar has ten months in each year. There's a break of about two weeks between the years when the weather gets bad. Some sort of monsoon, I think. The Springfielders just treat it as a holiday."

Andy paused. "Best you see for yourself," he said. "I'll look for you in the canteen at eight."

"How will I fit in?" Daniel asked quickly before Andy could leave.

"There are no satellites round Springfield," Andy replied patiently, "not even any aircraft. The buggies are the fastest transport, which is okay because there are no roads. People seem happy with a slower pace of life. Maybe the longer day is responsible; I don't know. What I do know is that everybody on the staff here has got their ranch registered already. There are now so many that Springfield needs an accurate system of defining the ranch boundaries in the popular areas. It needs a top-class cellular network to ensure that the triangulation is spot on. Lots of guys have rigged their own aerials, most of which are not exactly reliable. Also, the photovoltaics only operate when the sun is shining. It is very easy to mismanage your electrics and end up out of contact with your buddies. There are no rescue services; the place is too big. Anyway, Uncle Sam has decided to set up a proper comms network. Your boss will be Colonel Hayes. He is on the military payroll, like you. We've been sending transceiver kits down for several months now. You'll be rigging and maintaining them, I guess."

Andy met Daniel in the canteen shortly after he had finished his evening meal. They walked across to the hangar he had spotted earlier that day. "The atmospheric pressure is a little lower on Springfield than on Earth. We have to go through an airlock," Andy explained. Daniel could see several queues of people waiting to enter the hangar.

"Are all these people . . . ?" he asked, unsure how to finish his sentence. He still assumed that they were headed for some sparsely populated region on the Earth. He reckoned the airlock was just the normal biosecurity. The secure comms bit was standard military operating procedure. It was the ecology business, having everything powered by the sun, that didn't sound right. He warned himself that there had to be something that he had not understood properly.

"Yes," Andy said in reply to the unfinished question. "Anybody with more than three years' service and a conduct assessment of 'good' or better is eligible. They are encouraged to bring their families with them. It makes everything seem more normal, more stable. And because everybody is ex-military, it's like one big family. I'm sure that there are the usual minor scams that you find on any military base but almost no drugs, no organised crime, no Mafia stuff. It's like the nasty side of society has just been left behind." He could have continued with his happy tale but he knew that there was a job to be done. "We will be going down first. We'll move out of the way of the others at the bottom. You can have a look round for about an hour and then we'll come back up." He made the exercise sound very simple.

Every entrance into the hangar was an airlock. Once inside, Daniel was too busy looking around to notice any difference in the air pressure. There were groups of people being organised into queues. For an instant, he recalled a picture that he had seen of other queues, of people arriving at a concentration camp during World War II. Those people had looked tired and worried; these people looked alert and excited. Andy moved him towards the front of the queue, from where he could see a dark circle directly ahead.

"The doorway is aligned to face backwards while it is over the railway," Andy advised. "At the moment it is still in the mountains, which puts it below ground level, but when the ground drops away we'll see daylight. The hook-up is completely automatic, like the system used on aircraft carriers to catch the jets when they land. We just have to wait for the escalator to be locked in place." Sure enough, Daniel soon saw a view of a hillside through the doorway. Signs of human habitation were noticeable not long after that. Eventually, railway tracks became visible. "Here we go," said Andy, taking Daniel's arm gently. "This is it."

Daniel stepped onto an escalator that was longer than he had ever seen before but it moved very smoothly and steadily. Looking back, he could still see the hillside. Already, it was so far away that he could believe that the railway had simply come out of a tunnel through the rock. Near the bottom, he turned to look up towards the doorway, from where people were still appearing. He had a sudden queasy feeling that thousands of people were going to fall down and crush him. Andy grabbed him. "Don't look up," he said firmly, holding tightly onto Daniel. "Sorry, I should have warned you. We call it *Springfield vertigo*. Look out to the horizon. Tell yourself you are on a train. You'll be okay. In a couple of minutes you will feel completely normal again."

Daniel looked around very slowly, taking deep breaths. The dizzy sort of feeling was already passing. He saw that none of the other people wanted to look up; that would have been like looking into their past. They were looking forward, out across the land that would be their future. Only a few needed to hold onto their loved ones to steady themselves. Most were gripped by excitement, transported by their imagination. Everything was plain and simple but it was fresh and clean. And it was quiet. He suddenly sensed the tranquillity. Yes, the people were chattering away to each other but there was almost no mechanical noise.

Photovoltaics, Daniel remembered. The train would be powered by electricity, he guessed. The railway was built on a raised gantry to keep it at a constant level below the doorway. He could see vehicles moving just below him. They were buggies and they all had photovoltaic panels covering their roofs. This place really was solar-powered. Then he noticed that there were no telegraph poles and no wires between the buildings. This was also a Wi-Fi place. That was why he was here, he told himself. The buildings were raised above the ground, some on stilts and some on piles. He recalled something about a monsoon and he guessed there might be flooding. It seemed these guys were ready for that. In fact, it was easy to believe that these guys were ready for anything.

Within ten minutes, Daniel felt completely normal. He could look up now. The top of the escalator was just a hole in the sky. Nothing was going to fall on top of him. The countryside was undulating beyond the strips of buildings alongside the railway. There were trees, patches of green, and hills in the distance, but there were no aircraft. A question sprang up in his mind: where in America could one go and not see an aeroplane in the sky? He could have been on the Earth but it was the empty sky, empty apart from the escalator, that began to make him believe that he might be somewhere else.

The dark circle at the top of the escalator reminded Daniel of a magician's top hat. A long time ago he had seen a man in a suit produce a white rabbit from an empty hat. Now, people were appearing, with equal wizardry, it seemed. He felt a tap on his shoulder. "Come on, Daniel, it's time to go back." Andy was there, smiling. More than an hour had passed, another bit of magic. It was time to return to the JSRC.

The escalator emptied, stopped, and reversed. They stepped forward. They were the only people making the return journey. Those down below looked up in amazement. They were all thinking: why would anybody want to leave? Daniel waved, knowing that he would soon be back. Looking down was easy; to one side, the land that he saw from the escalator could have been Oklahoma, his homeland. He let himself be assisted at the JSRC end and he was able to walk steadily out of the hangar and into the night. Andy showed him back to his room and wished him goodnight. He slept easily that night.

Daniel was almost pure Cherokee from Oklahoma. He could trace his ancestors back through many generations. A couple of inches under six feet tall, he had the body of an athlete. His grey eyes were watchful and his face suggested a thoughtful nature when he was not smiling at some little bit of good fortune. He smiled often. He was not a greedy man. There had been few luxuries in his childhood but he had seen enough of life to know that there were many people less fortunate than himself.

Daniel spent the next few days learning about the transceivers in use on Springfield and the latest developments in photovoltaic technology, which provided virtually all of the power on Springfield. He studied alongside some of the men and women who were hoping to start second careers, second lives, on the planet. At some point he rejected his initial assessment in favour of the truth, which was that Springfield was not somewhere on the Earth. Nevertheless, it was only an escalator ride away, which made it considerably closer than Yemen or Ethiopia. The new territory held no fears for him, nor did the strange transport after he had helped a couple of times with the transfer of some freight.

"Why do you need me?" Daniel asked Andy one evening.

"Politics," the other man replied. "The

Springfielders pretty much have their own jurisdiction. The place is very relaxed. Don't get me wrong. It really is very nice there, no commies, no terrorists, and no taxes so far. In fact, it's just a bit too relaxed. They don't do anything till it needs doing and then everybody wants to be in on the discussion. They don't exactly plan ahead. Imagine what we would be like without cellphones and satnav. There's a clause in everybody's contract that allows Uncle Sam to crack the whip when the need arises. The Springfielders rely on their cellphones for almost everything. I don't think they even have any maps yet. So we are making sure that at least their comms are reliable."

Daniel was ready and keen to get started. He knew how to assemble a buggy, the ubiquitous transport on Springfield. In reality, the buggies were little more than boxes on wheels. He had been repeatedly warned of the twin dangers of running out of electricity or water: stop the electric motor as soon as the emergency battery is no longer being charged by the photovoltaic panels; never let the reserve of drinking water fall below a full day's supply. There were few natural dangers on Springfield but the emergency services were virtually non-existent. Daniel had not worried about the limited maps, as he saw no reason for him to go beyond the furthest ranches. "Which is fine until you get to a ranch where there is no water and you cannot find anybody," Andy warned him. "Folks move around all the time, or the place might be waiting for occupancy, like my own ranch." There had been no calming smiles to go with those words.

Daniel knew that he would be one of a small team responsible for establishing a reliable transceiver network as swiftly as possible. The ranches were not defined by natural boundaries. Instead, borders could only be decided by precise measurement. The science was basic stuff. The black boxes contained well proven circuitry that would bounce radio signals backwards and forwards and measure the time taken in precise decimals of a second. Elementary computer calculations would convert the times into distances and trigonometry would use the distances to plot a position. All the signals were limited to line of sight. The natural curvature of the planet meant that two masts fifty feet high could maintain communication across about twenty miles, more if they were placed on high ground.

As the network expanded, computer analysis would decide roughly where to put the next transceiver. It would then be up to Daniel to pick the best position for reception within the little area that he would be told to use (not much more than an acre each time) and to run a full diagnostic to confirm that the new unit had been correctly incorporated into the system. If that were deemed successful, the software would generate instructions for the next installation. Nobody seemed too worried that most of the network died when the sun went down. Only a couple of transceivers had battery backup. The Springfielders were a fairly relaxed bunch.

When Daniel made the descent to begin his new job, he stepped off the train at Grand Central without any hesitation. The name had been copied from the terminal station in Midtown Manhattan. On Springfield it included the entire township that had grown up around the railway. He and Andy were just part of the crowd that moved to *Registration*. He was given a number - 12064. "Listen up, folks," said a voice at the other end of the hall. "Welcome to Springfield, where it is now November of Year 2. You will need your number to register your ranch. There is a chart on the wall over there showing all the ranches registered so far. If you want to call on a buddy before you register you will need to find their number on the chart. That number will be the number to call on your cellphone. If you cannot make contact, that will most likely be because they are outside the network. We are a couple of weeks behind with setting up the relay stations." After that simple reminder, the new colonists were directed towards the arrival packs.

Andy led Daniel to the table where he had checked in. An older woman introduced herself as Bella. She was short, only about five feet tall, and dumpy, with black hair pulled back from her face in a ponytail, which made her look unwelcoming. "Just wait while I check your paperwork," she told him. She seemed flustered. "We weren't expecting you yet." She flicked a finger through a pile of forms. "Here we are," she said in a more relaxed manner. "You're supposed to meet up with Colonel Hayes. He's head of the network. His number is 6582." She set off towards the wall chart and Daniel followed.

The chart was no more than a vast array of numbered squares marked on the large, flat, white wall. "We're here," she said, pointing to a concentration of squares. "6582 is over here in Newhaven, on the coast." Her hand moved right, across a speckled array of squares. Daniel assumed she was going east. Her hand stopped over another concentration of numbers, which ended fairly abruptly in a curved line running approximately north-south. He guessed that might be the coastline.

An older guy joined them, whom Bella introduced as Major Wilson. "Hi, I'm Roy Wilson," he said, nodding to Andy and shaking hands with both of them. "We'll soon get you sorted out." There was no mistaking his military bearing, his upright stance and close cut hairstyle. He was about Daniel's height but more stockily built. His gaze was piercing but his smile was friendly. He took over the briefing, describing the chart as if it were showing the disposition of his forces.

"The early arrivals are mostly concentrated round the railway. Beyond that there is a scattering all round as folks began to spread out. Then the sea was discovered a couple of hundred miles to the east. Most arrivals are now heading across to the coast. To register there now, you have to go a long way north or south. Grand Central is actually a bit north of the equator. It gets pretty arid once you go any further south. The animals from Earth find it uncomfortable, so you can see," he pointed with his hand, "most of the development is to the north. Stay on the route we'll put into your phone and keep it charged, and you'll be fine." 6582, Daniel could see, was close to the coast and a little way north of Grand Central.

"Okay," Roy continued, "come and have a look at your arrival pack." He led Daniel out of the hall into a yard full of equipment, where several dozen small groups of people were already working feverishly to construct their buggies. "You get one of the ants," Roy explained. Each ant had twice the load-carrying capacity of the standard buggy, a fairly basic ball-and-socket joint between the cab and the cargo area, and three axles. Nearly twice the roof area meant nearly twice as many photovoltaic panels and they had a six-wheel-drive mode, which made them much better climbers than the buggies. Daniel had been warned that some of the transceivers would have to be set up in very rough terrain.

"The mess hall is over there," Andy said after Roy had left them, pointing in the direction of another large building. "The people there will arrange accommodation until you are ready to leave. First, I will help you construct your ant and load up your kit. That should only take a couple of hours. Then I will take you across to Comms HQ to let them know you

are here. That's the building with the radio mast."
Daniel smiled. He had already figured that out.

It was still bright daylight when they completed the circuit for the photovoltaic panels on the roof of the ant. The needle on the only instrument in the cockpit swung across into the high green, showing that the emergency battery was being charged, and they set off towards Comms HQ. As soon as Daniel's presence had been noted, Andy told him that Colonel Hayes was now his boss, shook his hand and then departed.

Daniel woke early the following morning. His first day on Springfield had gone well, he thought. He had spoken with his new boss, who had advised him to take things easy until he felt in sync with the longer day. He loaded up all his personal kit and his technical equipment. The guys from Comms HQ hoisted five crates onto the back of his ant. His cellphone contained what passed for a road map. It was no more than a list of ranch numbers representing the most popular route to 6582. The ant was heavily laden but his heart was light. He was looking forward to starting his new job.

Chapter 2

Daniel set off knowing that eight hours of sunshine remained. He had been told he would reach his intended stop for the night in about six if he followed his cellphone instructions, which would cut the corners automatically and avoid having to actually visit every mast along his route.

Much of Daniel's journey kept him within a ranch boundary, although it was not always obvious that he was close to anybody else. Some ranches already appeared to have developing communities but many did not. Those people whom he did see usually gave him a friendly wave. Several of the homesteads that showed no signs of life already looked derelict. The gift of ranches had been intended to persuade people to spread out and colonise rapidly but it had not been entirely successful. Grand Central already had the feeling of a congested town and the early discovery of the sea east of Newhaven had only distorted things further.

What had appeared on the wall chart in *Registration* to be a solid strip of ranches joining the two towns was often more empty than Oklahoma. The silence was eerie, particularly when the ant was moving. The ride was soft and the electric motor made almost no noise. There was only one track. Daniel could see the two, parallel lines of crushed vegetation ahead of him, made by the tyres of those who had gone before. In Oklahoma there would have been more wildlife. Here, not even the few birds that he saw came close enough for him to make out their details.

Daniel checked his position on his cellphone frequently. The sun was behind him when he saw his destination. The cellphone said it was about four miles away, roughly twenty minutes. He was not irked by the gentle pace of the ant. The only radio mast in view had to be the one that he was aiming for, he told himself.

A copy of the wall chart showing all registered ranches was available on every cellphone, to reduce the risk of new arrivals trying to claim a patch that had already been registered, he guessed. Three numbered blocks - 293, 294, and 295 - stepped down gently from north-west to south-east. He noticed that the track on the ground showed far more usage now. He saw the farmhouse before he noticed the river. Then he spotted the sign: *Scott crossing - $10 per buggy*. Nobody had said anything about a toll bridge. It was the first thing to jar in his mind that day.

"Hello there, traveller," a confident female voice called out.

"Hi," responded Daniel. The river was at least twenty yards wide and almost certainly too deep to cross without submerging the electric motors, he told himself. The shout had come from the farmhouse, which was situated above the far bank. He took the sensible option, the bridge, and pulled up on the track by the farmhouse. He took out a ten-dollar bill. "I'd like a receipt, please," he said.

"Receipt?" The lady who had appeared was probably late fifties, hair pinned up in a bun, and stern faced. She looked ready for trouble. Daniel nodded. He reckoned that people looking just like her would have been colonising America a couple of centuries earlier, which made the setting feel completely normal.

"I'm working for Colonel Hayes. You can call him if you like. I'll want to claim it back." The lady's face broke into a smile.

"That's okay," she said. "I'm Kath Scott. The Government goes free."

"Oh, right," replied Daniel. He introduced himself and explained that he was going to be working on the comms network. "I've got five crates with me that I have to deliver to Colonel Hayes. I was planning to camp up by the mast, if that's okay?" He directed a finger towards the high point that was marked as a dot in square 294 on his display. He guessed that a short spur would run up to the mast from the main track.

"Don't be silly," Kath responded immediately. "You must eat with us. The men are only penning the animals for the night. Gerry will be back shortly." When Daniel looked curious, she continued. "He's my husband. Our son and daughter came with us and they brought their families. That's how we managed to get three ranches. Gerry was smart. He registered the three blocks so that the river ran through the middle of them. We control a stretch of water about ten miles long. Then he, our son Bob and Martha's husband Joe built the bridge. If folks don't have any money we usually do a trade." She made everything sound very relaxed.

Daniel discovered that the Scott tribe was flourishing. Initially, they had all lived together by the river but Bob and Joe now had dwellings of their own. All were of a similar construction, Kath said, pointing to the walls made of logs packed with mud. Inside was lighter than Daniel remembered from similar houses back in Oklahoma. The windows were not small and defensive; they were large and demonstrated that the occupants had confidence in their surroundings. The roof was of fir brashings laid on top of each other. The veranda faced south and looked out across the river.

Gerry appeared well before the sun vanished. Back on Earth, he would have been in danger of developing a beer belly. Here he was muscled and weather-beaten. "I never thought I would end up as a farmer," he admitted, "but it is a great life. Having three ploughs means we can produce more in the way of crops than we need, so we are concentrating on the animals. Because of the limited roads, I reckon there will be a market for horses. We have five so far, with more on the way. We need more photovoltaic panels but every watt they produce is absolutely free. It's fantastic." He clearly regarded Springfield as paradise.

Daniel again woke early the following morning. After a sociable breakfast, he was keen to be on his way. He passed Bob Scott's house within the hour. He gave a friendly wave but did not stop. When the track began to rise, he slowed the ant to keep the charging in the green, as he had been instructed. The higher ground soon put the photovoltaic panels clear of the trees and in full sunshine, and he was then able to move more quickly along what was a fairly smooth surface. The ridge of uneven hills to the north appeared to have little other than scrubby grass by way of vegetation. To the south the land was an undulating sea of green with large patches of broken forest. He spotted birds occasionally but if there were any animals, they remained hidden from him.

The quietness of ant travel made Daniel doubt his rate of progress but his cellphone indicated that he was still on schedule when he decided to stop by the mast in 1387 for the night. He headed for the mast, which was set on high ground some distance from the nearest homestead. He gave his boss a brief update and set about preparing for the night. Each mast had a skirt of photovoltaic panels approximately six feet off the ground. The transceiver unit was contained within the frame of the mast and protected by a chain link fence, which ran around the outer rim of the panels and stretched down to the ground. It was intended to prevent animals nibbling at the circuits, not that there seemed to be any. Daniel unfastened the latch on the doorway, moved his kit inside, and settled down for the night.

Daniel had set the alarm on his watch to wake him early, although he was now only a few hours away from the coast. The track quickly became wider and was flanked by solid lines of fields. Several buggies passed him and he was pleased to wave to their drivers. 6582 was actually on the coast. The office occupied by Colonel Hayes was in a proper building that overlooked the sea. It was mid morning when Daniel stopped the ant outside the Newhaven reception office.

Daniel was glad to be able to tell himself that he was back in reality again, even if that reality meant that his first duty was to report to the boss. "Up the stairs to the top," he was told. It was four floors, which left him slightly out of breath, but he was welcomed with a smile and invited to sit down. The large desk between him and his boss was bare except for the ebony prism holding a brass plate with *Colonel Oliver Hayes* engraved upon it.

"Sometimes I need to be reminded who I am," Hayes said apologetically. "Springfield looks so like Earth, it's weird, and yet, I always have the feeling that this place is just waiting to catch me out." He was a late-forties version of Paul Newman, Daniel thought, with a neatly proportioned face, cheerful eyes and slightly straggly moustache. His frame was solid but definitely not chubby. He did not look like a man who enjoyed being stuck in an office.

As soon as the usual pleasantries had been dealt with, Colonel Hayes wanted to talk about Daniel's job. "Somebody said to me that we are trying to cram four hundred years of colonisation into not much more than four, and I am not convinced that we are going to succeed. I guess the Pilgrim Fathers had their faith to hold things together. Our technology often appears to be a very poor substitute. At least the network should help to reduce the sense of social isolation. There's a lot of talk about needing to start a TV school, otherwise we are going to have a generation of children who can hardly read and write. Then we will be back in the Stone Age before we know it." It was not the cheerful introduction that Daniel had been expecting. "That's why you're here. If Springfield survives it will be because of people like you. To begin with, I'll send you out with some of the guys who have been here a while, just to get you used to working on Springfield. Then, after about a week, you'll get your own schedule."

Colonel Hayes paused at that point, as if inviting Daniel to respond. When he did not, the senior man continued. "We're stretched pretty thin, the coast is just about saturated with ranches and people are going to start spreading out again, certainly north, maybe further west. The monsoon season is only a few weeks away and there will be the usual crop of repairs needed after that, so we can't afford to hang about. Check in on the second floor. They will sort out accommodation and get you started." They were done, Daniel realised. He got up to leave but paused to look out through the windows.

"Just like any other town on the coast, here or Earth," Hayes suggested. "Of course, there is no moon here and no tide, although the wind does whip up a bit of a swell at times. It's got potential but the free energy is a double-edged sword. People can get away with just playing at being farmers. It's too easy to sink into a false comfort zone, too easy to forget that the next generation must be educated." He turned back to Daniel. "Glad you made it here safely. We'll speak again in a week or so."

During Daniel's first few days in Newhaven, he discovered that most of the staff were like him: still enlisted, but here because they were single and did not mind being moved around. He quickly sensed that the civilians near the coast seemed more creative than those who had stayed close to Grand Central. They did not feel any need for an escalator. One guy was drawing up plans for an aeroplane where the wings would be covered in photovoltaic panels and somebody else trying to build a motorboat powered by photovoltaics. Daniel did not think that mixing water and electrics was a good idea but the variety of the small businesses that were springing up along the coast encouraged him to believe that Colonel Hayes' view of things had been unfairly pessimistic.

After Daniel had completed a week in Newhaven, he was ready for his first proper working day. Colonel Hayes met him after breakfast. "We'll go through the entire process," he said. "Call up 6582 and ask for 'Installation'. You'll get a text message that you can save." Sure enough, instructions appeared that told Daniel where the next transceiver unit was required. "Save that," Hayes told him, "and then you must check that you have a full set of kit before you depart. It will just about fit on one ant. There is a standard checklist that you should go through," Hayes emphasised.

Daniel smiled; the military did everything by checklist. He confirmed the cargo on his transport was a complete kit: one transceiver unit, rolls of photovoltaic panels, rolls of wire fencing, several packs of metal rods and other, smaller items. "The most important things are food and water," the colonel advised him. "You get them from the ration store round the corner." Daniel knew his boss was not being awkward. He was more likely to remember something in the future if he did it for himself this time. He picked up two packs and stowed them. "I've put a shotgun in the rack in the cab," Hayes informed him, "just in case." Daniel guessed that meant it was time to go.

The location for the new installation had arrived

with the text message. Daniel stored his destination as a way point and followed the instructions. After about three hours, he stopped at the base of a small knoll. He judged the top was about thirty feet above the surrounding land and it was the highest point within his destination circle. Higher ground away to the north-west would curtail the signal in that direction but there was a line of sight in the opposite direction all the way back to the coast and the main mast in 6582. He looked at his boss, who merely grinned and shrugged his shoulders. This, he realised, was how Hayes checked out his subordinates.

Daniel took a few minutes to decide where to place the mast and then he began to follow the drill he had been taught. He knew he was not expected to rush. It was more important to get the job done to a high standard. It took nearly an hour to get the base level to his satisfaction. The transceiver came in four sections that sat on top of each other, a bit like a wedding cake. Each section weighed about fifty pounds and he wanted to be sure he knew what he was doing before he started lugging them around. His boss was busy on his cellphone and clearly did not expect to be interrupted.

Daniel knew it was important to get power to the unit as quickly as possible to check that nothing had been damaged on the journey, so he then set about constructing the skirt for the photovoltaic panels, which would also give the base of the mast a satisfying rigidity. Soon, there was enough power to start the transceiver on its test mode. Colonel Hayes tapped him on the shoulder. "Time for a break," he said.

About half an hour later, a beep from the equipment indicated that it had completed its test routine. "I guess that's the end of the break," Daniel said, returning to his work. He was delighted to see that the unit was fully serviceable and he set to work finishing the mast gantry and aligning the aerial quadrants in position. He had barely finished when his phone rang. It was HQ to say that they had a printout of the results of the diagnostics. The unit he had just installed had good comms with five others. As soon as he was satisfied with the tidiness of the site, he advised his boss that he was ready to leave.

"You're a good technician, Daniel," the colonel said on the way back. "I've already said that we are overstretched. There's a big block of ranches about sixty miles south of the escalator. They have been neglected because they are out on their own. I'd like you to be responsible for getting them linked properly into the network." Daniel nodded again. The colonel was clearly pleased. "Excellent," he confirmed. "I'll get it all arranged as soon as we get back and then you can be off first thing tomorrow morning." When they reached the HQ, Colonel Hayes sent Daniel off with an encouraging smile to clean up. Daniel was pleased that his first proper job had gone well.

Hayes met Daniel again in the mess hall during the evening meal. "Hi," said the colonel. "I'd like you to do what we agreed. You will have to return to Grand Central first to pick up another kit. We need to keep the ant here. You'll be travelling back empty, so you will be fine in a buggy. You can swap it for another ant at the depot. The Scotts have the bridge nearest the sea but it's still a long way north of the direct line between Grand Central and Newhaven. A guy called Henshaw says he has completed his own river crossing in 3762, which looks to cut the journey to just two days. Check it out for me. When you are ready to leave Grand Central, you must make contact with 101. You should speak with a guy called Wolf Boston. I've heard he has a strange set-up but he is good news. I've told him what you will be doing and asked him to give you a full briefing. I'll say goodbye now because I have to head north first thing tomorrow."

Daniel set off the following morning in high spirits. The empty buggy felt almost like a car in comparison with the heavily laden ant. His days around Newhaven had given him time to think about the little bit of Springfield that had been colonised, considerably less than the area of most American states, he realised. Colonel Hayes had been dismissive of Grand Central, which he regarded as little more than a freight terminal.

Although Daniel was single, he thought that the demand for schools and hospitals would increase and he guessed it would be the provision of those services that would decide which town eventually dominated the other. Colonel Hayes had more or less indicated that he would stay on Springfield but of those still paid by Uncle Sam, he seemed to be in the minority. Most had registered a ranch, which had cost them nothing, but few expressed any interest in the planet beyond their jobs.

Chapter 3

Daniel had not needed to consult his cellphone to know that he was getting close to the river. There had been a sudden marked increase in the signs of human activity - stacks of sawn timber drying in the sun, fields ripe with corn, and animals grazing. By the time he reached the river, he reckoned that the whole of 3762 north and east of the river was under development of some sort; he must have waved at several dozen people, he was sure. He had not seen people anywhere else on the planet taking life as seriously as those guys. He got down from his cab, glad to be able to stretch his legs, and introduced himself to the man who was obviously in charge.

Luther Henshaw was a black, powerful-looking man, completely bald but with a relaxed countenance. When Luther said he charged twenty dollars for passage on his pontoon, Daniel explained that he was on official business. Luther grinned. "You've been Scott's way," he said. "I'm afraid we treat everybody the same." He made it sound as if he wanted complete independence for his community. "Give you a receipt, if you want one," he offered, still amused. Daniel was nodding to that when Luther continued. "Won't be any more crossings today. There is a dinosaur nosing around."

The river at this point was about five times as wide as at the Scott's bridge. The crossing was just a metal pontoon and a couple of cables stretching between the banks. Daniel had always planned to make his night stop near the river and was unconcerned about the side on which he slept. He assumed that Luther had been joking about the dinosaur. Then, as he looked around, he realised that the man had been serious. The massive tree trunks arrayed along both banks were there as an obstruction to animals that might attempt to climb out of the water. A small concrete emplacement had what appeared to be an old, whaling harpoon-gun mounted on top of it.

"I bet you haven't seen much wildlife on your travels, have you?" Daniel realised that Luther was speaking to him and shook his head slowly. "That's because most of the creatures on this planet live under the water," Luther continued. "Even now, near the end of the year, the river is more than twenty feet deep here. What we call dinosaurs slide around on the muddy bottom, eating whatever they disturb. If the pickings are slim, they'll stick their noses up to sniff along the bank. They make good eating, taste like roast pig."

Daniel saw a group of men setting up a large calibre machine gun. Somebody was sitting behind the harpoon-gun. Two guys were lowering what looked like a dead sheep into the water, tugging it gently against the current on the end of a rope. They were all engrossed in what they were doing. Suddenly, a man pointed. Nobody spoke.

About a third of the way across, Daniel saw what looked like a log rise to the surface. It began to move slowly upstream towards the carcass. The men pulled their bait onto the bank, half out of the water. The man behind the harpoon-gun was tracking the log, which suddenly split in two, revealing rows of glistening, white teeth. A reptilian tongue flicked forward in the air. As the beast moved into the shallows, Daniel became aware of its enormous bulk. The men appeared tiny in comparison but they knew what they were doing. The carcass was in the ideal position. The dinosaur was being drawn towards the harpoon-gun. When it rose on its massive hind legs, it presented a target larger than the buggy.

The sound of the harpoon being fired was like the bang of a starter's pistol. The machine gun chattered away noisily for several seconds until everything above the animal's mouth had collapsed. A second harpoon was loaded and fired. Men ran to fasten ropes to winches. Even though its head was gone, the beast still wriggled its body. It seemed unable to back-pedal. It was trying to turn around but the harpoon ropes restrained it. Then the winches began to turn. The body was still moving its limbs as it was dragged through a gap in the trunks lining the bank and up onto a patch of land where Daniel guessed that other dinosaurs had lain. Luther let his friends get on with it. Word had gone out that there might be free meat and buggies driven by those who lived nearby were already arriving. The feeble, front limbs were the size of a fully-grown man. Each rear thigh was as big as a hippo. "I lost my brother in the river not long after we arrived," Luther said quietly. "This is payback."

Later, when Daniel was enjoying his dinosaur steak, Luther joined him and asked him what was going on in the world outside 3762. "I don't really know very much," Daniel admitted. "I've only been on Springfield a couple of weeks. You seem to be doing okay, though."

"A hell of a lot of folks upped sticks and headed east when the sea was discovered," Luther replied. "I don't know why. We have survived two monsoons here. If that's the worst that this place can throw at us then we won't be leaving. We get two crops of corn each year. The cotton doesn't do so well, although the harvest that we are about to start is looking good. The pigs are really great at clearing the ground and we've got some sheep on order to add to the cows and horses. Some of the folks who went to the coast are getting pretty desperate. A few have returned to join us." When he heard what Daniel did he was delighted. "We need the TV school that the folks in Grand Central have been promising us. Your job is vital." He clapped Daniel on the shoulder. "I guess you can go across for free in the morning after all."

Daniel admired the attitude of the people around him. The recent battle with the dinosaur had not frightened them. They appeared to regard the beast merely as a rival for space on the planet rather than some personal enemy. A little swift, well executed teamwork had allowed them to hold their ground. It reminded Daniel of many small, military exercises; as soon as they were completed, the chow came out. The colonists had been here long enough to have seen most of the hazards that the planet could present and they had seen them often enough to figure out a drill to deal with each one. Some people may have made a poor decision to run to the coast, others may have discovered that they were not natural farmers, yet all those now present had learned how to survive. Although this was no Garden of Eden, hard work brought a fair reward.

In spite of all the excitement, Daniel slept easily that night. The next morning he was keen to be on his way as soon as there was enough sunlight on the buggy roof. Luther was listening to the microphone dangling in the water, wanting to be sure that there was not another large beast nearby, and Daniel had to wait about an hour before he was told he could drive onto the pontoon. The crossing was completed without incident and he departed with a wave. The silence seemed to prompt a question in his mind: would he stay if he had the option? On the Earth, he would never have considered settling anywhere except America. This was different, he told himself, as if something in his life had already changed.

Daniel's mind drifted ahead of him to his

destination. He guessed that the wellbeing of Grand Central was due very much to the fact that everything from the Earth had to pass through the place. It enjoyed a monopoly over all the trade he realised. As soon as communities became free from the need of supplies from Earth, he suspected that they might also wish to enjoy other freedoms. There still appeared to be a common respect for the rule of law but he had not detected any yearnings to establish government. Uncle Sam's democracy had not exactly convinced people that it was an essential ingredient in their lives.

All such musings were quickly dismissed from Daniel's mind, however, as soon as he reported his return. The main transceiver for the area had been intermittent for several days. It just happened that he walked into the office when somebody finally decided that it had to be fixed. The unit was located several hundred feet above the point where the doorway emerged from the hillside, providing communication out to some eighty miles beyond Grand Central. It was one of the few transceivers to have battery backup. It was so important that it was powered to operate round the clock. An ant was already loaded with extra reserve batteries and a replacement transceiver.

Daniel wondered what he would find on the hillside. He recalled that the doorway linking the Earth and Springfield effectively had one side fixed in the hangar at the JSRC and the other side moving round a loop on Springfield. The scientists attributed the movement of the doorway round the loop to the relative motion of the two planets. Grand Central had sprung up where the loop ran almost parallel with the surface of Springfield after emerging from the mountains, which were so high that nobody had yet tried to see what was on the other side. In fact, there had been almost no interest in anything beyond the point at which the loop emerged from the rocky hillside.

The initial descent zone had been established about ten miles east of that exit, equivalent to a little more than an hour above ground, sufficient time to get the necessary equipment checked and deployed using the ski lift. Several months later, somebody had suggested the construction of the synchronised railway. It seemed sensible that one of the first comms units should be set up above the point at which the loop came out of the hillside.

The high ground appeared to run approximately north-south for a considerable distance. Daniel reckoned that nobody would try to see what was on the other side of it until the sea had exhausted its attraction. His operating base was located near to the terminus because of the vast amount of heavy comms equipment that was coming in, which meant a thirty-mile journey to the troublesome transceiver. Fortunately, the road parallel to the railway was the best on Springfield and even the final ten miles to the mast had been worn smooth. He moved quickly while the meter was still in the green but he slowed when the sun began to disappear. He had been assured that his extra batteries would allow him to travel all night, if necessary, but running without photovoltaics didn't seem right somehow.

Daniel was glad that the track was clearly indicated. The point at which the loop emerged from the hillside was marked with a large circle of whitewash. As he passed it he saw that the area was fenced off, to prevent anyone being in the path of the doorway in case anything fell out, he assumed. Beyond that, the track was very poor. He doubted that a buggy could have reached the installation, which was set on a patch of levelled ground and included a double array of photovoltaic panels. He guessed that the mountain shadow cut off direct sunlight several hours before the end of each day, requiring both more battery power and more rapid charging thereof.

Daniel had already decided simply to swap the transceiver currently in situ with the spare in the ant. He called the depot to give warning that the unit would be going offline for a couple of hours. The response was a curt order to ensure everything was fixed by sunrise. "Oh, and remember the escalator will be emerging about twelve minutes before three," he was advised. "Don't let it surprise you so much that you drop something vital down the hillside." He set the alarm mode on his watch and began the next phase of his task.

Daniel was relieved when he was finally able to let the installation begin its own diagnostics. He made himself a snack and sat down with his back resting against one of the large, ant tyres. He stared back at the town. Rows of lights ran parallel to the railway, suggesting a runway at some massive international airport. He knew that he would have heard the sound of jet engines back on Earth. On this world there was only silence.

Daniel had nearly finished loading the ant when his watch beeped. The doorway was due to appear in the next few minutes so he stopped what he was doing and strolled carefully down to the caged area about four hundred yards away. He was still searching the painted, white circle with his torch beam when the doorway emerged. For an instant it was exactly as if a circular hole had been cut into the hillside. As the doorway moved away, light from the interior lit the ground briefly, until the surface had dropped away too far to reflect the diffuse beam. It was eerie. The circle of light had emerged silently from the mountain. Nothing had been disturbed, not even a few grains of sand. There had been no noise until the doorway had gone past and then the sound of a human voice drifted back, too indistinct to make out what had been said.

Daniel saw more lights begin to come on in the town as people got ready for the next delivery. He watched until he was bored and then he called his HQ. "Yep," the voice at the other end confirmed. "It's all okay. You can come home now." It was chaos around the terminus when he got back. The night was still dark and there was a panic on, created by people who knew that they could not return to their beds until the railway trucks had been unloaded. After the silence up by the mast, he felt as if he had walked into a shouting competition. He parked up, reported in, and asked for a bunk. There had been a change of shift. Nobody was expecting him, so he laid out his bedroll in the back of the ant. He was so tired that he fell asleep as soon as he put his head down.

Daniel was not amused to be woken only a few hours later by somebody banging on the side of the ant and shouting at him to report for duty. He was directed by an overweight major to an office on the other side of the yard, where a sergeant introduced herself as Joy. She was pencil thin, a little over five feet tall, with an olive complexion and long, black hair. "You've just come from the Rat," she said with a smile after Daniel had explained himself. "He's the boss here. His name is Rattigan. Has to be the most useless man on the planet. We try to work round him." She shook her head in disgust. "Now, what can we do for you?"

Daniel said that he had been sent from Newhaven by Colonel Hayes. Then he added the details of the job he had been working on in the night. "Well, the paperwork from the night shift is probably lost in the middle of all the other stuff on the Rat's desk, so I wouldn't worry. There's been no feedback from that, which probably means that you fixed it. Did you find a fault?"

"No," Daniel replied. "Somebody said the job was urgent, so I just replaced the transceiver."

"Okay," said Joy. "Put the unit you've brought back in Bay G while I see what has been written on the task sheet."

Daniel did as he had been asked. "Good," said Joy when he returned. She spent a moment typing into a terminal. "It's much easier keeping track of everything properly than trying to find items that seem to have gone missing," she told him, "not that anybody is going to steal a transceiver unit. It's the kits for the masts that disappear. They can be used for constructing a lot of other things besides." She smiled at him. "Now, let's deal with you. It sounds as if you could do with a proper meal."

"I don't think Rattigan will be happy if he bumps into me," Daniel said quickly, hoping to avoid any more trouble.

"He won't remember who you are," Joy replied with a smile. "Do you want to stay here for a few days, or do you want to get out and about?" Daniel was now fully awake. He was no longer terribly bothered by the way he had been treated by Rattigan and the success of the night's work had boosted his confidence. Also, he now had a spare set of batteries in his ant, which he decided to say nothing about.

"I need a shower and a decent meal. Then I'll be happy to pick up another job." He knew he found the noise of people working in and around the office comforting but he was also curious to learn more about Springfield.

When Daniel returned a little over an hour later Joy welcomed him with a smile. "Hayes' report on you was still in the admin office, so you stood no chance of getting a fair deal from the Rat. The report says you are to extend the network to 101. Are you okay with that?" Daniel nodded. He thought she sounded efficient, not likely to mess him about.

"How long have you been down here?" he asked.

"About eight months," she replied. "I like it. I don't let the Rat get under my skin and Hayes treats me fair. The Rat will be gone in less than a year and Hayes has said that he will promote me to fill the vacancy."

Daniel smiled and nodded slowly. Already, Springfield felt more like America than most other countries he had been to, in spite of Rattigan. "What about long-term? Will you go back to the Earth?" They seemed like perfectly natural questions for him to ask.

"I haven't left anything behind there," she replied without emotion, "If I get my promotion, I will stay."

Joy took Daniel across to a wallchart and described what she knew of the region nearer the equator. The most southerly mast in the official network was about twenty miles from the one he had spent the night working on. Beyond that, Joy knew very little. There was a large block of ranches registered around 101 but it had only intermittent contact with the network. "The people there keep themselves to themselves," she said, "All I can confirm is that 101 is an active number. Somebody is still there."

Joy and Daniel agreed that he should go to the most southerly mast and try to assess the lie of the land beyond there. He loaded up the ant and set off, following the edge of the rolling prairie past the southerly mast, which was clearly visible up on the hillside. He was taken by surprise about ten miles further on when a jagged fracture appeared abruptly in the line of hills. The pass had not been visible until he had been within a mile of it and he guessed that he was probably the first person to discover it. The gap looked no more than a couple of miles wide before the hills rose up steeply again and continued south as far as he could see.

Daniel resisted the temptation to search west, telling himself that he would be coming this way again. The vegetation on the plain changed from scrubby grass to woodland, which appeared to stretch from the base of the hills quite some distance to the east. The woodland eventually reverted to prairie. He put another way point into his cellphone, which told him that he was about twenty-five miles north of 101. It was clear that the greatest network coverage would be achieved by placing a mast on the southerly stretch of high ground. When he went into the hills and looked down, however, he decided that a transceiver would be needed down on the plain near the tree line to bridge the gap in the high ground.

Daniel set up the transceiver he had brought on a stepped spur close to the pass and only about a hundred feet above the prairie. He still had little idea about wind strength. There was a good signal from Grand Central, so no need to expose the unit more than it already was, he told himself. After the job was completed, he reckoned he had about an hour before he needed to begin his return to base. On a whim, he decided to survey the hillside south of the pass and try to pick out the spot for the next mast.

Daniel quickly spotted a little platform that had good elevation and was set against a steep wall of rock that would shelter the unit from bad weather. He took the opportunity from his vantage point to look out across the land around him. The high ground continued south to the horizon and blocked his view to the west completely. The east was fringed in dark green where the forest to his left, north, appeared to become more dense and swing south. From his recent travels, he estimated that the enclosed area was about fifty miles wide. It was predominantly what he would have called prairie, except for about two dozen hillocks and a lesser number of lakes. He guessed that each hillock rose a couple of hundred feet above the surrounding ground. As far as he could make out, the surface vegetation was mostly a poor, stringy sort of grass.

Daniel knew that the vital test was to check that the platform permitted direct communication with the people living in and around 101 and the best way to do that was to give them a call. He phoned Joy to say that he had completed his task and that he wanted to have a chat with the folks around 101 in order to assess what he should do next, which she thought very sensible.

Daniel recalled that there were about fifty ranches registered in the area immediately to the south and east, although he could not make out any signs of habitation there. 101 was nearly forty miles away in a south-easterly direction. Maybe these folks had adopted the same strategy as Luther and his friends and were concentrating their resources, Daniel suggested to himself. He was delighted to get an immediate reply when he called 101.

A lady introduced herself as Jessica. Daniel explained that his job was to extend the comms network. When she said that he could visit, he realised that it would be as quick to reach her as return to Grand Central, so he headed for 101. He used his phone to get a bearing on her signal and set off towards the hillock on which his gaze had settled. As soon as he reached level ground, he quickly noticed that there was some wildlife living here. He caught flashes of fur that was the same colour as the grass and there were also larger animals with darker skins that he guessed were predators.

It was only as Daniel got within about ten miles of

his destination that he was able to make out signs of human development. The changes in the vegetation were not obvious from a distance but close up, their extent was impressive. The variations in colour that he had assumed were no more than random changes in the ground cover resolved themselves into large groups of animals and neat lines of trees. It was the formal arrangement of the trees that puzzled him. They looked as if they had been there for at least a decade, certainly more than four years, which was when he believed that the first colonisation of Springfield had begun.

As Daniel drew closer he noticed people moving about. When he approached what he thought was his destination somebody waved and shouted, "Go on to Rhino Hill. It's only about three miles. We're all going to meet there." It was another female voice, sounding very cheerful. As he passed by, his eyes were drawn to the hill. A grassy platform, about a dozen feet above the level of prairie and bounded by a ring of trees, encircled it. It looked unnatural, as if it had been created. Ahead, a few more people were waving to indicate his destination.

When Daniel eventually drew to a halt a couple of children came down the slope to meet him. The atmosphere reminded him of Gerry's place. There were more people here, although nowhere near as many as there had been around Luther Henshaw's development. Daniel suddenly realised that he had seen only about eight buggies on what was fairly open plain. Where was all the other equipment? The people that he could see appeared to have established themselves with great success but where were the rest? Something did not seem right.

Chapter 4

"Welcome to Rhino Hill," a woman called out. "I'm Jessica. You must be Daniel." Jessica was almost as tall as Daniel but slightly slimmer, with an oval face and light brown hair that hung straight down to her shoulders. She wore grey shorts and a loose, pale blue shirt. She appeared hesitant. Daniel wore the standard khaki shirt and trousers but both were crumpled and sweat-stained. It had been hot in the ant cab and he was glad to stand in the shade of the trees. He knew he did not look at his best but that did not worry him. If his somewhat grimy appearance helped the residents to accept him more quickly, then that would make his job easier, he told himself as he looked around.

Daniel could not see any houses, only a couple of what looked like animal shelters cut into the slope of the hill. Jessica had two children with her, aged about ten, he thought. From his slightly elevated position, his view across the prairie extended for several miles. He guessed the older kids were away working with the other adults somewhere. It appeared that the community was more thinly spread than he had earlier assumed, since what he had seen so far could not have been the representatives of more than two or three families. "Hi," he said as he waved at the kids, who looked in extremely good health. He gave them a wink and a smile. "I'm supposed to be meeting Wolf Boston."

"Wolf will come across from Blue Hill with Sally shortly and then we can complete the introductions," Jessica said. "We don't get many visitors, so we'll have a bit of a party this evening." Jessica explained that she provided the medical services, such as they were, for this community. She studied the stranger while he stretched his arms to relieve the discomfort of his journey. For her, the fact that this guy had mentioned Wolf's name had been a big plus as far as she was concerned. Up close, she struggled to maintain the basic requirements of politeness. She could not remember the last time that there had been a visitor and if this one had not been alone, she might have armed herself before she had even spoken.

Daniel would have liked to have had a wash but a boy had come forward, curious to have a look at the ant. Jack was a chatty lad, nearly ten years old, clearly at ease with himself and his surroundings, and Daniel was happy to humour him. Daniel explained that not only could the ant carry about twice as much as an ordinary buggy but also, the six wheels gave it better traction for moving over steep ground. The boy looked puzzled. He had climbed to the top of Rhino Hill several times but he could not imagine why anybody would want to drive up there. "I'm a radio engineer," Daniel explained. "I'm here to improve your comms, to give all of you a better link into the network. There's going to be a TV school, so all you guys will be able to continue your education."

Jack thought about that for a bit and then he nodded. "Holly used to do the teaching here," he remembered, "but Charlie does it now." The picture of just one person teaching all the children that Daniel assumed were living in this block of ranches raised questions in his mind.

"So how many children are there?" he asked.

"I've got two sisters and a brother," Jack began. "Sally has six children, but Henry and John are still too young for school. Then Charlie has four children and Anna has two." It took Daniel several seconds to realise that Jack had finished.

Jack did not notice the puzzled look on Daniel's

face. The boy was not aware of the large number of ranches registered around Rhino Hill. Instead, he continued to describe their settlement. He explained that he actually lived inside the hill, in rooms excavated not far from where he and the visitor were standing. Anna and her family also lived here during the monsoon. At the moment, they were still based on Brown Hill. Jack pointed to the first inhabited hill that Daniel had passed, some three miles to the north-west. Sally and Charlie lived on Blue Hill, which was about a mile away to the north-east. About five miles further north was Red Hill. Nobody lived there but it had a platform to allow some of the deer to shelter there during the bad weather, Jack said.

Daniel thought he had seen a large lake less than a mile away; he asked if anybody fished in the lake. "Oh, no," replied Jack, sounding alarmed. "You have to stay away from the water because of the swimmers. They are huge. They can eat a whole deer." The boy's comments reminded Daniel of what he had seen at Luther Henshaw's place, where there had been enough people to tackle the huge dinosaur. Here, despite the larger number of ranches, all the indications now were that there were far fewer people, certainly not enough to take on a large predator. Daniel decided that this was not like the Henshaw community. In fact, in terms of numbers it was now beginning to sound more limited than the Scott enterprise. There were a couple of men, Charlie and Wolf, he thought, and three women. Because of the relatively large number of children, Daniel wondered if he had stumbled into some sort of commune.

Wolf appeared at that point. He was shorter than Daniel but slimmer and wearing a very faded khaki shirt and trousers. He looked as if he could have been anywhere between forty and sixty years old, with skin as smooth and as grey as beech bark. His eyes were piercing, as if he studied everything that he saw in the greatest detail. His hair was fading into grey and pulled back tightly into a simple ponytail. Daniel had already realised that every community needed a competent barber. It seemed that most individuals on Springfield had been forced to find alternative solutions. After a brief but friendly introduction, Wolf wanted to know why Daniel was there. Daniel explained about the comms network and the fact that Uncle Sam was worried about educating future generations of Springfielders.

"Oh, yes," Wolf said, nodding. "Colonel Hayes told me about you. I'm glad you've come. You never realise what a responsibility kids are until you have some of your own. The sixteenth-century colonists had one huge advantage over us. They had no idea what the twenty-first century would contain. We can manage without the most advanced medicine but education is a 'must have'. Boys like Jack deserve the chance to train for jobs like yours or to be able to manufacture photovoltaic panels and buggy motors. Otherwise we'll soon be back to a coach and horses and then people will discover how difficult it is to construct a spoked wheel." Although Wolf was smiling, there was a serious tone to his words.

"Let's go across to Blue in this fine machine of yours," Wolf said in a friendly manner. "It will be quiet over there. You can freshen up in decent privacy while the ladies get things ready over here." Daniel nodded, hoping that he would also have an opportunity to quiz Wolf about the set-up in this region. Some of the fields that Daniel had driven across had contained the stubble of crops that had recently been harvested. That did not surprise him but the number of deer grazing on the stubble had been massive. This seemed to be the centre of things, Daniel told himself as he climbed back into the ant, but where was everybody?

Wolf interrupted Daniel's thoughts by asking him what was happening at Grand Central and back on Earth. Daniel began to recount what he remembered of his briefing at the JSRC. Wolf slapped the side of the ant and laughed loudly. "So that old coot Springfield still has control of the entire show, does he?" Daniel looked puzzled. "Lieutenant General James Richmond Springfield is just a politician in uniform," Wolf explained. "He thought he was all set to be a senator in Nevada when he was handed E2P, the Earth 2 Project, on a plate."

Daniel began driving the ant in the direction indicated by Wolf as the older man continued talking. "This all started back at Nellis in 2013 AD." He felt the need to emphasise the Earth date. "A planet was discovered in the Alpha Centauri system. On the first anniversary of E2P, they decided to have a flight simulation exercise. It was just a bit of publicity but it all went wrong. Almost from the beginning, it was decided that the project should be one of colonisation. The population would come from canisters of frozen, fertilised embryos and six women incubators doing the IVF thing. The flight simulation was supposed to be a test of the spaceship. The women were included really only as tinsel for the TV cameras. At least a part of every system was crammed into the craft, including some frozen embryos. Anyway, there was an accident and the spaceship disappeared. Nobody knew where it had gone." His face showed a wry grin at the memory.

"The boss at the time, General Sanderson, declared the project a failure and wanted to close it down immediately," Wolf continued. "She was only just prevented by those of us who believed that the women might have survived. The chief scientist, Mark

Richards was his name, had an eight-year contract. He reckoned the accident had flicked open a doorway to another universe, although he couldn't explain how at the time. Fortunately, he just kept working until he came up with a solution." Wolf paused briefly when a fresh idea occurred to him. "Have you been told about the *Rhino*?" he asked. Daniel shook his head.

"Well, we can have a look at that later," Wolf suggested. "It, the spacecraft, arrived on this planet, buried in the hillside back there." He gestured to where they had come from. "I had been on the staff of E2P, teaching the young women survival techniques, and I was chosen to lead the rescue team. I actually helped to design the first ski lift. I know that sounds extremely primitive now but you must remember that we had spent nearly a decade waiting to rescue the women. Even I expected to find a fairly desperate situation. Looking back, I suppose we should have had more faith in the team that we had selected. They had only been on the planet for a few days before the computers worked out that the Springfield day was about twenty-seven Earth hours long. One of the women adjusted the computer clock to show a twenty-four-hour Springfield day, which probably created an illusion of normality. Before she could explain what she had done, however, she was attacked by predators and killed. Somehow, the others convinced themselves that this was all part of the exercise, so they just got on with living. They created this farm and they started having the children."

By this time the ant had reached Blue Hill. Wolf broke off from his tale and directed Daniel to drive up onto the platform. When they stopped, Daniel could see a tunnel into the hillside. To either side there were windows that revealed rooms cut inside the hill. He guessed that the platform was mostly the result of the rocky waste that had been excavated. Much of what he had already seen began to make sense. The platforms round Brown Hill and Rhino Hill would have been created in a similar manner. It was obvious now that the trees had been planted, maybe as saplings, some as long as a decade ago. The majority of the farm was explained, although he still had questions about the lack of people.

When Daniel had showered and dressed in clean clothes provided by Wolf, the two men climbed back into the ant again, ready to return to Rhino Hill. Daniel had the ant pointing down the platform when he saw the lake and remembered what Jack had said. "Animals in the lake?" Daniel asked, looking at Wolf.

"The women call them swimmers," Wolf confirmed. "Actually, I think they are some sort of dinosaur."

Daniel nodded. "I saw one winched out of the river at Luther Henshaw's place," he said. "It looked extremely dangerous."

"They rarely stray out of the water," Wolf replied, "and we don't go in. The women quickly noticed that none of the local land animals would cross so much as a ditch, so it was very easy to keep the rodents away from the crops."

"Colonel Hayes said that you would be around for a while doing the comms," Wolf continued. "You're very welcome here but I don't want you asking questions or saying anything that might upset the women or the kids. You are the first actual visitor that we have had in a long time. There was a great deal of unpleasantness back on Earth concerning E2P. I don't want these people disturbed again. I visit Grand Central about once a month. There's something about that place that I don't like. I don't want what we have here spoilt."

Daniel was driving the ant slowly, which gave him time to ask the obvious question. "Is there anything else that I should know?"

48

"There were five women when I arrived to rescue them," Wolf said. "I had imagined them struggling to survive inside their cramped spacecraft, living on recycled everything. I found them pretty much as you see today. They had taken the colonising philosophy to heart. Practically the last thing they needed was rescuing. Even after I had explained that General Sanderson was set on closing the project down and that the doorway might be closed after I had gone, only one woman wanted to leave. When I got back to Nellis, General Sanderson blew a fuse because I had let the others stay here. To keep her under control, her boss told her that the project would be closed down anyway, which it was at Nellis. It was not difficult to sell it to General Springfield, who hid it in the JSRC at Ely. In a way, he owns the entire planet. He calls himself *ambassador*, I believe. You probably know the rest. Feel free to chat with everybody but remember that the kids have spent their entire lives here. For them, this is like the Earth is for you."

Darkness was beginning to fall as Daniel and Wolf reached Rhino Hill. Daniel was impressed by how well lit up it was. They left the ant at the bottom of the hill and walked up to the platform, which was quite a bit higher than the one they had recently departed from. A woman moved to be beside Wolf. He introduced her as Sally. She was only a few inches above five feet tall. She was Native American - Paiute, Daniel discovered later. Children swirled around her. The eldest, Amber, named because of her golden hair, held a baby in her arms. John was a little over a year old and the youngest member of this community. Both were Sally's children.

Another woman introduced herself as Charlie. Not a man, after all, Daniel realised. She nodded in the direction of the other two adults present. "You have already spoken to Jessica. The other is Anna, who looks after all our animals. She does a fantastic job with them and she looks after all the children who think they might enjoy that kind of work." Finally, she introduced a strapping lad as her son, Greg.

The young man was suntanned but clearly white, while Charlie had the darkest skin of all the people around. Daniel recalled that Wolf had mentioned IVF. The realisation that the embryos might not be biologically related to their birth mothers served to emphasise Wolf's warning about how easy it might be to cause unintended offence.

Daniel was pleased that one of the four women had spoken to him without any effort on his part. He was not to know that it would only have been Charlie. Sally wanted to remain with Wolf, Jessica did not like to talk to strange men, and Anna knew that another monsoon was almost upon them. Her mind was filled with concern for their animals. Daniel asked Charlie about the relatively large number of ranches registered in this region. "Where are all the owners?" Charlie gave a slightly guilty grin before she spoke.

"Wolf said we should register as many as we could, to protect our future. When our colony grows, we will need all this land. We used the kids' names, anybody that we could think of, even Holly, the one who went back to Earth."

Daniel detected a strange sense that Charlie did not regard herself as part of Springfield but only part of the small community around Rhino Hill, and the emphasis, again, on the children puzzled him. "During our training there was a lot of talk about the minimum viable population for survival," she explained. "We were told that a settlement needs about two hundred people to guarantee its survival. That's why we started the implantations. There was huge pressure on us until Wolf arrived." She reached out for Greg. "Soon it will be the turn of the next generation to continue what we have begun." As the conversation continued, Daniel noticed that there was a strange conflict in her words. She sounded completely content with her own life, which had rarely taken her more than five miles from where they sat in the last decade, but she wanted Greg to have a grand career and to be an important man, things that seemed impossible unless he left Rhino Hill.

After a pleasant evening, Daniel spent the night in Blue Hill and departed the following morning after he had confirmed with Wolf that nobody would be upset if he installed a transceiver on one of the hills in their community. He took the opportunity on his journey back to Grand Central to venture into the gap in the mountains that he had discovered the day before. He drove slowly west for about five miles, to the limit of radio contact with the mast he had recently installed. He was no geologist and he could not say what had created what looked like a sharp fracture in the mountain range. When he finally stopped, the sides of the pass looked very steep, yet the gap itself did not appear to be getting any narrower. He turned round, thinking that it might extend all the way through to whatever lay west of the mountains. Perhaps, when he had some leave, he might do some exploring with somebody like Wolf, he suggested to himself.

Meanwhile, Daniel knew that there was work to be done. He returned to the depot at Grand Central and arranged for another kit to be loaded onto his ant. Joy was not on duty. Nobody seemed at all interested in him. He had no wish to be noticed by Rattigan, so he stayed just one night and checked out early the next day. He had the platform stored as a way point but it took some time to get the heavily laden ant up to the spot. He worked quickly, knowing that the next installation would allow him to spend time near Rhino

Hill. It was dark when he got back to Grand Central.

Daniel woke the following morning feeling very pleased with himself and knowing that today he would be taking a kit to Rhino Hill. He phoned Wolf to say that he was on his way but he did not rush. He guessed he could have reached his destination and completed the installation that day if he had so wished. Instead, he intended to take a couple of days. He liked what he had seen around Rhino Hill. Despite its isolation, the people there had been considerably more courteous than most of those at the depot. He failed to notice that the sky had become cloudier than any other day that he had spent on Springfield. When he reached the settlement, everybody seemed to be busy herding animals up onto the platforms round the hills. He was instructed to drive his ant up the ramp on Rhino Hill and park it close to the hillside.

"What's happening?" Daniel called out to the nearest child, a girl of about seven or eight years old.

"The monsoon is about to start," she replied. He recalled that he had heard that word mentioned several times before. At first, he wondered why nobody at the depot had said anything. After a little thought, however, he convinced himself that these people were overreacting. How could they predict the weather, he asked himself. He shared the evening meal with just Anna, Jessica, and their children. Most of his conversation was with the youngsters, who wanted to know more about him. When it was time to retire, he was given a room for the night.

When Daniel woke there were a couple of lights on. Apart from that, however, everywhere seemed unusually dark. He checked his watch and confirmed that he had woken at the normal time. In the background he could hear a sort of wet, rumbling sound, like a washing machine, he thought. He found the other occupants of the hill in a room with a window, where the noise was much louder. They were looking out at the rain, which was already falling in a steady downpour. It was obvious that the monsoon had started. He was amazed. "How did you know?" he said to the others in the room.

"We're not peasants," Anna replied curtly. He and she had exchanged only a few words during his previous visit, when neither she nor Jessica had appeared to be completely at ease with his presence. "We have a kit that collects data about the weather. We got a red warning just over twenty-four hours ago. Usually, that gives us a couple of days to prepare. This year, the monsoon has started more rapidly than usual."

"Well, I should be getting back to Grand Central," Daniel said, thinking out loud.

"You'll never make it," Anna replied in a more concerned tone. "The land will start to flood in a couple of hours. Then there is a risk that the swimmers will come out of the lakes. You'll just have to stay here."

Daniel called the depot, not really sure what he wanted to say. He was glad that it was Joy who answered. He needed a voice that he trusted. "I'm just packing up here," she replied. "Then all you will get will be a recorded message. Did nobody brief you?" Daniel realised that the warning would have been obvious to those who knew, so obvious that it was one of those things that everybody thought somebody else would mention. "We won't start up again until the rain stops and the land dries out," she continued. "Even the escalator stops. It's usually about ten days or so. Are you safe where you are?" When Daniel said that he was, her reply was fairly terse. "Well, stay there." He shut off his phone and looked around.

"We won't even be travelling between here and Blue," Jessica explained, reluctantly accepting that

53

Daniel was stuck here with them. She was not prepared to shoot him. Instead, she had decided to trust him, although she had reminded herself that she had some fairly powerful knockout pills among her medicines. In comparison, she regarded the monsoon as no worse than a mild inconvenience. Her state of mind eased only when it became obvious that Jack, her eldest son, and Daniel were going to be good friends.

It was Jack who took Daniel to look round the *Rhino*, the spacecraft in which his mum and the other women had arrived. For the first half-dozen years of Jack's life, nothing had been said about the strangest part of their house. After Wolf's second visit, however, the children's collective curiosity had demanded answers. Jack still found the story exciting. The *Rhino* had simply arrived, burying itself in the hillside. The women had used the well-digging equipment contained within it to tunnel their way out to the surface. Jack took Daniel through the small circular door that was still the only entrance. "There used to be an airlock here," he said, "but it was dismantled when they realised it wasn't needed. Then there's the medical suite where my mum works. James helps her." Daniel had met James, a quiet boy, Anna's son, who was about two years older than Jack.

"The computer terminals are on the other side," Jack continued. "We use them for looking at DVDs when we are doing our learning with Charlie. Then the nuclear generator is at the far end." Daniel listened intently but said nothing. He was not a nuclear engineer but he made a mental note to search for a diagnostics log later.

This was a busy time for Jessica. The medical facility was unaffected by the weather and this was an ideal opportunity to give almost half the community their annual check-ups. Daniel sought out Anna to get

54

answers to the questions that filled his mind. He knew there had been six women originally. "What happened to the other two?" he asked.

"Wendy was killed by the baboons," Anna said without emotion. "We had only been here a few months when the first monsoon hit us. After the monsoon you will see the deer migration. That first time, we decided to capture a few animals. There were also predators that we called baboons. Now, we pretty much have them under control. Back then, we did not take them as seriously as we should have done. Wendy went out in the night to check on the deer we had caught and got caught herself."

Anna clearly did not want to say any more about Wendy, so Daniel changed the subject to the woman who had decided to leave. "Holly? Not much to say, really. She wanted out, we didn't. When the ski lift opened up and Wolf returned, which meant there was no more pressure to have the implantations, we all reckoned we had made the right decision. Wolf was on the staff when we did our training. It was obvious even then that he and Sally had a thing going." Anna gave a shrug and finished with a happy smile on her face.

Daniel quite liked talking to Anna but he was not yet a man who felt comfortable spending a great deal of time in the company of one woman so he decided to pass the hours by giving the systems in the strange spacecraft as much of a check-over as he was able. He confirmed that the monitoring log for the generator was up-to-date and that the control system still worked even though nobody had touched it since arriving on Springfield. The information stored on the accompanying DVD said that it had been designed to have a working life of twenty-five years. It was about halfway through that and still performing to spec.

All the technology was a decade old, Daniel

realised, even the medical equipment, much of which was used fairly frequently. Almost nothing had been updated. These people had clearly ignored the existence of Grand Central. He set to work on the aged computers, which were attempting to continue to operate in spite of several failed components. Without access to spares, there was little that he could do. He made a list of the most urgent requirements, including new keyboards and DVD readers. He knew that a PC for every child would be a sensible addition. Outside, the prairie was like a lake. With the depot shut down, he realised that he was not even going to be able to order anything for at least several days.

Among his search through the logs, Daniel found where the clock and the calendar had been reset. The women had chosen their arrival date to be March 1st and the monsoon was near the middle of their year. Incredibly, they had not yet adopted the Springfield calendar. He also discovered that the original system had been voice-activated, to reduce keyboard usage, he guessed. He restored that, knowing he could cancel it again after he had obtained some new keyboards. He hacked into the medical computer, which was the only one that demanded a password for access, and discovered that there were still more than a hundred frozen embryos in store. That information that went straight into his *too difficult* folder.

All of the recycling units - food, water, oxygen - had been switched off as soon as they were no longer required. Although Daniel didn't know much about chemistry, they all appeared to be capable of functioning when he switched them on briefly. He noticed that there were pumps in almost every unit. He advised Jessica that the systems could probably synthesise a wide range of chemicals if somebody could figure out how to modify them. She told him to

56

add basic medicines to his list. When he queried how so much kit could be paid for, she told him to speak to Wolf as soon as the monsoon had ceased. Daniel realised that there was a growing list of subjects that he needed to discuss with Wolf.

Daniel was standing by one of the windows while this was turning over in his mind. The rain was so heavy that he could barely see as far as the trees that marked the perimeter of the platform. The deer were little more than brown lumps shuffling past. "It's strange how they always walk anticlockwise." Anna had come into the room. "We've created platforms above the flood level around four hills. The deer walk in the same direction round each one." His eyes were just about level with the top of her thick, black, curly hair. He knew that there would be a smile on her face when he lowered his gaze. He replied with a friendly nod.

At that moment a brown, furry face came right up to the window. "It's not a species I recognise," said Daniel, wanting to say something.

"No," agreed Anna. "They are native to Springfield. We called them deer when we thought we had been moved to Africa. Same with the baboons. You'll see them with the migration. Up close they don't look much like baboons. But you don't want to get up close," she warned. "You probably saw what we call the gophers and the cats on your way across here, and then there are the swimmers, which Wolf reckons are actually dinosaurs. Fortunately, they prefer to stay in the water. Some of them are bigger than a buggy. If you see one you won't forget it." Daniel told her what he had seen on his journey back from Newhaven.

"The baboons are really nasty," Anna continued. "They killed Wendy. They will kill a deer just for fun. They hunt in packs and will chase a victim to exhaustion. The swimmers are only dangerous if they smell you. They will just rise up from nowhere and snaffle anything that stands too close to the bank." She smiled shyly.

"So how many deer do you have?" Daniel asked.

"About two hundred," she replied. "You've been told about the MVP thing?" He nodded. "Well," she continued, "we are trying to create a new breed, our own super-species, so we have far more than we need for food. It's good for the kids who are interested, keeping a record of each animal and its parentage." She halted suddenly, as if she had said the wrong thing.

"Something wrong?" asked Daniel. Anna shook her head.

"Not really," she said more hesitantly. "I was just reminded of our situation, the embryo business. We don't know anything about the children's real parents and some are getting to the stage where they are beginning to ask very awkward questions. They see the deer mating and wonder where they came from. Some are nearly ready to mate themselves. Jessica is already saying we should give the girls implantations when they reach fourteen. I don't know. The other women seem to get on well with their kids but I just don't feel anything much at all for mine. Maybe it's because I don't believe that they are mine. I feel closer to the deer sometimes."

Anna suddenly looked careworn. Daniel felt a brief urge to give her a supportive hug, which he resisted. "Well, I think you have all worked miracles here," he said firmly. "You were sent as colonists, which was never going to be a piece of cake, and you arrived here by accident. You are talking about kids now. Give them another couple of years and they will realise how lucky they are to be alive." He paused before asking how her children were doing.

"Well, James is eleven, one of the first round of implantations. He was born a few weeks after Greg. He is Jessica's main assistant and wants to be a doctor. Ruth is just a typical nine-year-old, I guess. She's friendly with Rose, Charlie's girl, and Naomi, one of Sally's clutch. They both live in Blue Hill, so she's always pestering me to be allowed to join them."

"Sounds pretty normal to me," Daniel concluded.

After eight days, Daniel had run out of things to fill his time productively. He called Wolf to advise him about the calendar that operated on the rest of Springfield. There was general agreement among the women that they would change to the Springfield calendar at the start of its Year 3, which would be soon after the monsoon finished. There was some concern about the children's ages, which Jessica agreed to handle. She said she would check the medical log and produce a list of every child's age, accurate to the day, when she was advised that the new year had begun.

Although the rain continued to fall heavily, the wind was not as strong as Daniel had been led to believe. When Anna went outside to check on the deer and ensure that some fodder was available, he went with her. "All of our stock are able to look after themselves," she told him. "The greatest danger is that they might wander down to the water and get grabbed by a swimmer. We cannot do much about that except try to keep them supplied with food. We keep the mums and the newborns here and around Blue. Although the animals are crowded, we rarely lose any when we are able to watch them. We have talked about some of us occupying Brown Hill. Maybe we will next year."

Daniel would have liked to have spent more time talking to Wolf but the occupants of Blue Hill were forced to conserve power. Wolf's last comment was to ask Daniel to make a list of everything that he thought the settlement needed. Without the sunshine, and with no generator, those in Blue Hill were completely reliant on the batteries that had been fully charged before the monsoon had started to keep their freezers running and their stocks of food safe.

Daniel asked why they had not built a causeway between the two hills. "Because we didn't think it worthwhile," Anna replied. "We couldn't agree how high it needed to be in order to be safe. Anyway, it sounded like a great deal of work, so we just kept putting it off for another year. Do you cause this much trouble everywhere you go, or are you making a special effort here?" Her comment was not said angrily. Combined with the look she gave him, it sounded rather flirty to Daniel, so he changed the subject.

"This deer migration. Where do they come from?" When Anna said that they came from the north, he realised that they could only have come through the pass that he had recently discovered. It was yet another thing to be discussed with Wolf when the opportunity arose.

Neither Daniel nor Anna found it difficult to coexist in Rhino Hill on a social level during the monsoon. Indeed, when the rain ceased and the water began to subside, Daniel was extremely apologetic when she invited him to go with her to check on the deer and he felt forced to refuse. They went as far as Blue Hill together, where he got out of her buggy to see Wolf. He wanted the other man's advice regarding the gap in the mountains. When Wolf realised that they could get there and back in a single day, he insisted that Daniel show him.

"I guess nobody explored this far west and south of Grand Central before the sea was discovered," Wolf said in amazement as he looked up at the steep sides of the sharp fracture.

"So what does it mean?" asked Daniel. Wolf looked incredulous.

"You do realise that you might have found the only passage through to the other side of the mountains, don't you?" Wolf almost glared at Daniel. "That bit of real estate might turn out to be the most valuable piece of land on the planet. Have you registered a ranch yet?" Daniel shook his head. "Right," Wolf replied firmly. "We have to get you properly enrolled as a Springfielder."

"But I'm not retired," Daniel protested.

"Who said you have to be retired?" Wolf responded with an amused snort.

Wolf immediately wanted to explore further into the gap but Daniel said that he had already gone to the limit of radio contact. He described the little that he had seen. He decided that they should return to Rhino Hill via the transceiver that he had installed most recently in order to see how it had survived the monsoon. Despite that severe challenge, he was delighted to confirm that it had not suffered any damage. The following day he moved the transceiver kit that was in the ant and began setting it up around Rhino Hill. While he was placing the aerial array high up on the hill, he took the opportunity to look around. He could just make out a long ditch stretching round Brown Hill and Red Hill. Anna had said that it remained wet only for about a month after the monsoon, because there was no lake close enough to provide a permanent water supply, but that was long enough to ensure that the migrating animals avoided the settlement.

As soon as Daniel had completed the installation on Rhino Hill, he phoned the depot for an update. He was delighted to get a reply. It was already the second day of Year 3 in the Springfield calendar. He was advised that there was no rush for him to report in person. The escalator was already in operation but a glitch in the paperwork meant that transceivers were arriving without any accompanying mast kits. He would be called when things had been straightened out. He did not mind; he was curious to see how the Rhino Hill community recovered from the monsoon.

It was a busy time for Daniel's hosts. They had to avoid the sudden blizzard of biting insects that seemed to be attracted by the damp ground and they also had to keep their animals fed until the vegetation recovered. Then, shortly after the ground turned green, the migration appeared like a brown tide from the north. Anna took Daniel right up to the outer ditch to view the wild deer, which were about a head shorter than those that she was nurturing, and the baboons. The latter did not seem particularly numerous but they were every bit as vicious in harrying the deer as she had said. Normally, everybody was involved in planting the next season's crops as soon as the migration had passed. This time, however, Wolf gathered together a little team for what he called an expedition. He was determined to investigate the gap in the hills that Daniel had discovered.

All involved were excited apart from Daniel, who found himself reluctant to leave Anna. They had become more than friendly but both were aware that he could be sent back to the Earth at any time and both knew that she would never leave the farm that she had helped to create. They had actually agreed that their friendship could not develop further until that conflict was resolved. They contented themselves with a squeeze of their hands and a shy peck of his lips on her cheeks, both hoping that they would see each other again soon.

Wolf's scheme required two vehicles, one to act as a

radio relay station in case a problem developed while the other went another dozen miles further into the gap. Wolf took Sally in a buggy while Greg and Jack rode in the ant with Daniel. Wolf went to the limit of phone reception. Even there, the western extremity of the mountains could not be confirmed, although hoofprints in the ground indicated that the migration had passed this way. After a couple hours of exploration, during which time Wolf stored several sets of coordinates in his cellphone, Sally and the lads were sent home in the buggy while he accompanied Daniel to Grand Central.

Daniel watched in amazement as Wolf went into *Registration* and claimed four new ranches, giving Daniel's name in addition to those of Henry and John, his two small boys, and his own, carefully copying the details stored in his cellphone. He had discovered that the system had no way of checking if the same name was used more than once. There was so much land that Major Rattigan had never worried about that sort of thing.

Almost before Daniel had recovered his composure, Wolf then rushed him round to *Requisitions*. "Give them your list, Daniel," he said. Daniel had itemised everything that he thought the Rhino Hill community needed, as he had been requested to do, without worrying about the cost. Nevertheless, he was very relieved when Wolf produced a bag filled with nuggets of gold. "You'll need to check in with the depot, Daniel," Wolf advised, "but give me a call on 101 before you leave the town. I might want a lift somewhere."

Chapter 5

For the first time since his career had stalled, Archie Rattigan was beginning to feel a sense of pleasure. Although he had attained the rank of major, which would have satisfied many people, the time limit for advancement to the next rank had passed nearly a year earlier. Indeed, some of those with whom he had begun his military training had already made general. He had applied for the top job on Springfield, which was only one rank above his, as a final gamble in the great promotion game but Hayes had beaten him to it. Not only that, his application had linked his name with the planet, a factor that he had failed to consider in his stratagem. Now, however, he hoped he could rectify all of that.

Archie's superiors saw him as being too impetuous. In any scheme, he could rapidly spot what might be of benefit to himself but he was not so quick to acknowledge the cost to others, an attitude not valued in the military. His overly optimistic application for the top job on Springfield was typical of him. Thus, when what appeared to be a really impressive idea was brought to his attention, he was more than ready to embrace it.

The project was, quite simply, to seize control of the doorway linking the Earth and Springfield. Ricky Marlow was a former lieutenant who claimed to be a test pilot and, by implication, an expert in all things scientific. He was a couple of inches short of six feet tall, with the suntan and crew cut that appeared to be obligatory for all jet jockeys. He had a thin face, which he tried to hide with a broad smile and a great deal of nodding. Like all salesmen, he knew that one of the essential ingredients of success when working his ventures was to sound positive. Success, as far as he was concerned, was achieved when the money came to him and any blame went in the opposite direction. With his ventures, there was always an element of blame.

Ricky had been up to the spot on the hillside and watched the Ely doorway emerge. He had wondered what would happen if it met a doorway built on Springfield. He was now convinced that if both doorways were equal then they would simply meet and lock together. He did not worry too much about what he meant by 'equal.' Instead he coined the phrase *the perfect kiss* to sell his idea to those whose assistance he thought he needed. In Archie Rattigan, he found a willing listener. Ricky had sensed Archie's dissatisfaction with life in general and Ricky knew he could use that.

Ricky had immediately realised that there would be financial benefits from owning the land where the doorways locked together. While the single doorway moved in its strange three-hundred-mile loop, nobody could claim ownership. If it were stationary, however, it would be as easy to control as the Scott's toll bridge. He could charge a tax on everything that passed through. It sounded like a lovely little earner, he thought. It all relied on complete secrecy until the two doorways kissed, however, and there was no point in doing anything until he had obtained title to the land.

Ricky had chatted up several people before he had chosen Archie to help him register a ranch containing the vital piece of hillside. Because there were no maps, it appeared in public as just another number on the wallchart in *Registration*. Archie had asked Ricky for a full explanation of the scheme, which wasn't ideal from Ricky's point of view, but 'full' was a relative term in Ricky's vocabulary. The subsequent discussion had convinced him that Archie would not reveal their little secret to anybody else. After that, they got on famously. With the land securely registered, Ricky then went back to America to order parts identical to those that had been used to construct the doorway at the JSRC.

Major Rattigan's name on all the invoices ensured the smooth flow of electronic equipment without any awkward questions being asked. Ricky's name didn't appear anywhere except on the title to the ranch. He was so sure of himself that he never considered consulting Mark Richards, even though he knew that Mark had created the first doorway and that Mark lived in Newhaven. Ricky believed that the fewer people who knew about his scheme, the better. Anyway, he had important decisions to make, like when *the perfect kiss* should actually take place.

Ricky completed the concrete base that would support his doorway several weeks before the monsoon began. Archie obtained the eighty photovoltaic panels that Ricky had calculated would be needed to power the second doorway. Now, all they needed to do was to set them out and put their doorway in place. During the monsoon, Ricky finished assembling the thirty-six sections of electronic circuitry that would lock together like a three-dimensional jigsaw. There was only Archie to help him with the final construction and the two men could not have coped with pieces that were any heavier.

At one point, Archie did ask Ricky why the JSRC doorway would not just continue going round the loop, to which Ricky replied, "It's like magnetism, isn't it? As long as we switch on at the right time, the two doors will pull themselves together just like magnets." Ricky's response sounded so natural that Archie never doubted it. Actually, it was one of those little bits of inspirational fantasy that just seemed to come naturally to Ricky whenever he needed to maintain the attention of his listeners. In reality, he had no idea what he was talking about. For Ricky, that was quite normal.

Initially, Archie had also been worried about somebody on the staff at the JSRC looking through the doorway and spotting what was going on. Ricky had assured him that the operators did not enter the doorway until it was linked to the escalator. He had chatted to several of them during his journeys between the two planets and discovered that they always had a tight schedule to maintain during deliveries. It was not easy to work through the relatively small portal of the doorway and none of them would notice any signs of activity where the doorway emerged from the hillside.

Ricky selected a day when the JSRC doorway would appear in the early afternoon, giving about five hours of daylight to complete the assembly of the Springfield doorway but still guaranteeing full sunshine on the panels when the doorways actually met. Strangely, neither man thought to ask what would happen when the sun went down and the power died. They started at daybreak and a little more than the lower half of the doorway was in place and wired together after two hours. Five rows of four sections, twenty pieces, were done.

Ricky became complacent. One section slipped and almost smashed. Neither man had thought about spares. Losing one section would have lost the entire endeavour. The accident frightened them. After that, they worked more carefully. They finished with barely half an hour to spare. "Well," Archie said nervously, "are you going to test it?"

"Don't be silly," Ricky replied. "It will go shooting off into the hillside as soon as we switch it on if the other doorway isn't there to stop it." Again, he actually had no idea what he was talking about but he spoke with such assuredness that he silenced Archie. They connected everything up to the master switch and confirmed that the power available exceeded what Ricky had said would be required. Then they waited quietly. Ricky sat looking into the distance, to Grand Central and beyond, telling himself that he would soon be a very rich man. Archie was the nervous one. He paced around, checking his watch every few minutes.

With just five minutes to go, Ricky realised that he should have built his doorway further away from the hillside in order to give him more time to switch it on. He suddenly guessed that it might take half a minute or so to warm up. There was nothing special about this day. He could have stopped at that point to make a few simple safety checks, but that was not his style.

Ricky decided he would flick the switch as soon as the other doorway appeared and accept what happened. His hand was poised. His twitch when the surface of the hillside showed its first hint of change was enough to connect the power. A vertical circle of light advanced through his doorway, leaving nothing of the structure behind it. When the circle of light reached the end furthest from the hillside, there was only a loud pop, not even a bang. Then there was nothing. The thirty-six sections were gone.

Ricky and Archie looked at each other in stunned silence, waiting for their doorway to reappear. Previously, they had observed the JSRC doorway move off towards Grand Central several times. This time, when they looked round, there was nothing. It was the simplicity of the situation that confused them. There was none of the noise and chaos that they associated with a normal disaster. When good sense finally prevailed, they put the only remaining evidence of their misadventure, the photovoltaic panels, in the buggy and drove away.

In the hangar at Ely, the entire structure of the doorway, a cylinder of electronics some twelve feet in diameter and more than eight feet long, disappeared with a sharp, popping sound as if a balloon had burst. The winchmen were just beginning to ask themselves if the impossible had happened, if the doorway had crashed, when they realised that there was no doorway. Only the plinth and the supporting cradle remained.

Nobody in the hangar was thinking about *perfect kisses*. Jim, the senior winchman, took charge. He had seen several dreadful disasters in his time. He knew that situations like this had to be gripped firmly before panic set in, even with seasoned troops. Secure the area and get a list of casualties, he told himself. He reacted before anybody started to move, which made the body count very much easier than it might otherwise have been. Yes, the doorway structure had disappeared, which was worrying, but the most important thing was that nobody was missing. Nobody was even hurt.

Only when Jim was sure that every name had been checked off the list for a second time did he let them depart. He locked all the doors before passing the problem up the line. As a winchman in the past, his job had been to rescue people. He was not really concerned about what might have happened in the hangar. He had done his job. The rest was somebody else's responsibility.

The buck got passed rapidly all the way to the top, reaching the desk of Lieutenant General James Richmond Springfield in the Pentagon within an hour. He reacted immediately, recognising that damage limitation had to be his top priority, simply in order to protect his own position. He knew that his escalator was no more an official project than Major Oliver North's business in Nicaragua had been.

General Springfield arrived at Ely that evening. Jim,

the winchman, gave him a first-hand account of what had happened. When General Springfield was assured that nobody had been hurt and the scene had been safely secured, he recognised slick work. It gave him confidence that the situation was under control. The JSRC could continue with its legitimate business as if nothing had happened. A move into politics after he retired from the military was still an option.

It did not take long to discover the requests signed by Major Rattigan. Then General Springfield chased up the scientist who had worked with Mark Richards on the original design of the doorway. Pete Lopez was not difficult to find. He was one of the foremost theoretical physicists of his generation, still working at Berkeley. He was a small, dumpy figure with bright blue eyes. His hair had receded to the point where he had hardly any left but his cheeky grin suggested a man who was extremely content with his lot.

When Pete was told about the printed circuit boards that had recently been sent to Springfield, his smile lit up the whole of his face. "I fear that Mark got curious," he said in his usual, amused style. His first assumption was that his friend had built another doorway and that there has been some sort of accident, a simple, scientific accident. General Springfield liked that. It sounded like something that could be hidden very easily.

"So what does it mean?" Springfield asked the physicist, who still appeared somewhat amused.

"I have no idea," Pete said without concern. "Is there any indication that there was ever a doorway in the hangar?"

"Absolutely nothing that we can detect," Springfield replied, confident that he had the situation under control. Pete nodded slowly but said nothing. He found that fact increasingly suspicious. Things could have

70

been worse, he told himself. A permanent hole, with the Earth's atmosphere rushing through, trying to equalise the pressure on Springfield, would have been extremely alarming.

"How many people are there on the other planet now?" Pete was forming a fresh theory.

"Around ten thousand," Springfield replied. Pete thought that might make a community large enough to decide that it was ready to go its own way. He wondered if Mark had actually been trying to close the doorway, although he said nothing to Springfield, who was keen to get the show, his show, back on the road. "Will it be okay if we build another doorway?" he asked.

Pete shook his head. He assumed that only Mark could have figured out a way of making the Ely doorway disappear. He never considered that two scientific simpletons could have been responsible for nothing more than a crazy accident. Instead, he concluded that the result had been intended. Maybe there had been some sort of coup on Springfield and those seizing control had demanded independence, he thought. He recalled Mark's reputation as a bit of a rebel.

"What are you saying?" asked General Springfield.

"This might have been a warning to back off," Pete felt compelled to suggest. "If you insist on building another doorway, the next response could be to destroy the entire hangar."

For a while, some Springfielders had believed that the doorway would reappear. Archie had deleted all records of Ricky Marlow's registration of the hillside ranch and Ricky had just disappeared. Mark Richards declared himself to be as baffled as everybody else. "Something must have gone wrong at the JSRC," he

71

maintained, which led to all sorts of rumours, including mention of terrorism and war. Nobody suspected that the cause of the failure had been within sight of Grand Central.

The Springfielders likened the disaster to the floods and earthquakes that they remembered from the Earth. All they could do was try to carry on. For the genuine farmers, that was not difficult. The community round Rhino Hill was virtually unaffected. Even farmers like Luther, who were busy trying to squeeze two harvests out of each year, had little time to worry about the state of the escalator. He was already looking forward to the first crop of Year 3, followed by the next planting immediately after that.

In Grand Central, discussions were held to try to decide what else could be done. Had the Pilgrim Fathers left Plymouth hoping to sever all ties or had they expected always to receive some support from the old country? Most Springfielders put themselves firmly in the latter camp. They had come to push forward the frontiers, not to break off relations. The assumption that the Earth might never contact Springfield again did not firm up overnight. Instead, it spread like an illness, flaring up in the minds of some while seeming to pass others by. Nevertheless, when no doorway had been seen for more than ten weeks, there was widespread acceptance that contact would not be restored any time soon.

Colonel Hayes set up a meeting to take proposals, rule on those that appeared clear-cut, and make a list of the others in some sort of priority order, which people would be expected to study and be ready to vote on before the end of the year. It sounded like a reasonably democratic process, more than adequate for people who had lived by the military code. It was soon obvious that the most important proposal was to re-establish contact with the Earth.

The colonel brought along Mark Richards. The physicist spoke plainly. "Springfield does not have the ability to manufacture so much as a circuit board. I have no idea what the problem was. All I know is that only the Earth can provide the solution." There was no scientific jargon; he used words that everybody understood. The unspoken message was that they all now faced something that could have happened at any time and they simply had to make the best of it.

Mark carefully avoided saying anything that might cause panic. He had been a member of E2P from the beginning and he had been at the meeting after the accidental launch of the cramped little spacecraft when the big boss had tried to close the project down. He remembered that Wolf had insisted that they had to keep searching because the women could still be alive.

Well, apart from one nasty accident, Mark was aware that the women had done considerably more than merely survive. They had managed to thrive in a region that few later colonists visited, because the climate felt uncomfortably hot to those still used to air-conditioning. Given that the more recent arrivals had chosen seemingly better locations for their ranches, Mark reckoned that they would find survival no greater a challenge provided that they were prepared to work as hard.

Not everybody on the planet was actually a Springfielder. It seemed only sensible to Colonel Hayes that he should call together all those on the military payroll and spell out the new situation to them. They assembled in *Registration*. There were about sixty people in total. "There is no system of taxes on Springfield," he said bluntly. He saw no point in adding *yet* because his next topic was to explain that money, coins and notes, was in very limited supply. All of his

73

audience had been paid by Uncle Sam. Most had their savings back on Earth. Food and accommodation on Springfield had been provided as part of their employment. "I have nothing with which to pay you. Your accommodation can continue for as long as you wish but I cannot guarantee to feed you. I, myself, am relying on friends." Many of the government employees had already discovered that their credit in the local community had run out. "If any of you think you have friends or can find employment that will sustain you, I advise you to do that as quickly as possible. I know that some of you have already started. Well," he added with what he hoped was an encouraging smile. "I think you have been very sensible."

There were questions and moans but Hayes waited for everything to subside. "I have asked Joy to maintain a list of everybody and where they are. Please keep her informed of your location and how you are coping. If the Earth does establish contact again I will insist that you are all eligible for back pay. As regards all the rumours of what might happen with the escalator, you will know when I know." Most people had been hoping for news and advice that was considerably more positive. "I reckon I can find work for maybe half a dozen," he added, "but even that will only be on a day-to-day basis. At the moment the greatest demand seems to be for medics and teachers. Anybody with skills in those areas should be able to set themselves up in business." He had wanted to finish on a positive note but that was the best he could do. He was glad that Joy had remained her usual, efficient self. Archie Rattigan appeared too shellshocked to be of any use at all.

Chapter 6

Daniel had started a small business repairing electrical goods, everything from toasters to cellphones, anything that would earn him a bit of cash or credit. Items that would simply have been thrown out in the former consumer society were now being recycled. He had managed to find himself enough work to keep himself fed but it wasn't what he wanted. He wanted to go to Rhino Hill.

Should he phone in advance or should he just turn up? That question had hung about in Daniel's mind for several weeks while he had struggled with the decision. Unfortunately, he couldn't see how to say that he simply happened to be passing by, because Rhino Hill did not have passers-by. Nor could he say that he had come to install another transceiver. Their comms were fine.

Daniel's analysis had never got beyond that point before but the colonel's words had convinced him that he should not hang around any longer. Until now, he had kept on telling himself that the escalator would start up again in a few more days. Well, those 'few more days' had already stretched to weeks. Now, he had to face the fact that the escalator might not start up again for years. He clicked 101 on his cellphone. James, whom Daniel remembered was Anna's boy, answered. Daniel spoke quickly. "Could you let Wolf know that I will be calling by in the next day or so? Nothing special. I just want to check that you are all okay." James agreed to pass the message on.

With the call made, Daniel went across to Joy's desk. His hand trembled a little as he wrote *Rhino Hill - 101* against his name. Then he nodded to himself, pleased that his decision was made. There were a good four hours of daylight remaining after he tossed his bag in the ant and advised Joy that he was actually leaving. His hope was to get south of the woods before Wolf replied to the message. At that point, he thought he could reasonably say he was so close that he should just call in anyway.

Daniel smelt smoke before he reached the southern limit of the trees and he came out of the woods close to a small encampment. He waved as he approached and he pulled up beside two buggies. "Hi, Daniel," Wolf's cheerful, welcoming voice called out.

"Hello, Sir," Daniel replied. He thought that bumping into Wolf seemed to confirm that he had made a good decision. They shook hands and then the others approached. He recognised Sally, Charlie, her eldest son, and Jessica's boy. "Hi, ladies, hi, Greg, hi, Jack" he said, trying to put names to the other faces. Naomi was one of Sally's girls, the same age as Jack. There were two younger lads whom he did not recognise immediately.

"We're here to get timber and saplings to plant around Rhino Hill," Wolf told Daniel. "Your ant will be a great help dragging the tree trunks back," he said, looking round at everybody. It sounded as if he wanted to have another man around. Daniel was extremely grateful for Wolf's assumption that he was going to Rhino Hill, as it left him without any need to explain himself.

Charlie offered Daniel one of their venison steaks, which was delicious. "You guys really have got things all sorted, haven't you?" he said to the people he hoped to join. They wanted to know about the escalator and he revealed what Colonel Hayes had said.

"So we're back on our own again," said Charlie in a slightly amused tone.

"Pretty much," Daniel admitted. "Colonel Hayes has

got us checking that communities like yours are still okay." It was only a small extension of the truth, Daniel told himself. Nobody seemed greatly concerned. The conversation returned to matters more closely connected with Rhino Hill.

Wolf guessed what Daniel was up to and quietly took him to one side. "Rhino Hill belongs to the women," he explained. "You'll have to ask them if you want to stay for more than a few days."

"What will they say?" Daniel asked.

"They've got used to doing things their own way," Wolf replied. "If you show that you are prepared to fit in with them, you'll get on fine."

Daniel liked the other man's direct manner. "I take it you and Sally intend to remain around Rhino Hill?" Daniel hoped the reply might tell him a little bit more about the society that he intended to join.

"Oh, yes," Wolf confirmed. "I do a bit of prospecting in the hills when I get bored. When I've gathered enough to make it worthwhile, I go into Grand Central. I would like to explore more of that gap in the mountains, although there's probably no rush now that the escalator's broken." He shrugged his shoulders.

The next morning, Wolf and Daniel worked steadily and had felled and partly trimmed three trunks, each more than a yard in diameter, before the others returned in a buggy filled with saplings. From there, it seemed entirely natural that they should continue working together to harness the trunks to the ant and get ready to depart. Daniel found himself accompanied by Charlie and Greg. Charlie understood that knowledge was power and she wanted the very best for Greg. He was already excited by Daniel's descriptions of life beyond the horizon.

The journey passed more easily than Daniel had feared, although his appearance at Rhino Hill caused some surprise as James had not mentioned his message of the previous day. While the others attended to the saplings, Daniel busied himself moving the trunks up to the electric saw.

As well as looking after the animals, Anna was in charge of the saw. She was there, ready to organise the placement of the trunks, which would be further trimmed immediately and then left in the sun for a couple of weeks to begin drying out before they were cut into useful timber. Normally, Greg would have helped her but he was dragged away by Charlie, leaving Daniel and Anna by themselves.

For everybody else the priority was to plant the saplings. Even up on the platforms above any flood, they needed to have been in the ground for at least several months if they were to survive their first monsoon. The tree roots secured the soil round the edges of the platforms, which provided the only safe ground available to the deer during the monsoon. It partially explained why they could remain on the farm when their relatives were forced to migrate.

The trees also attracted birds, many of which were now permanent residents. They in turn helped to control the insects. Although the latter were needed to pollinate the plants, they also seemed to enjoy biting the colonists. It was a little jigsaw that needed every piece in position in order to remain stable. The women understood that and they were content to occupy their place. Indeed, they trusted the jigsaw. They were not keen to accept change.

"You never called," Anna said when there was a break in their work. She knew that she didn't mind Daniel being around but she needed to know that he was going to be around. She had seen Sally waiting while Wolf had come and gone several times. She didn't want the sort of uncertainty that she had seen in

Sally's face.

"I didn't know what to say. I was afraid of saying the wrong thing," was Daniel's weak response.

"So what is different now?" She wanted to hear something positive.

"While the escalator was working, I was still on the military payroll," Daniel tried to explain. "I could have been sent back to America at any time. A couple of days ago we were told that it might be years before the escalator will be fixed. It can only be done from the Earth end. Springfield doesn't have the resources. My boss said that I should plan on staying here."

"So why are you here?" Anna persisted with her questions, hoping she might get some sense of commitment from him.

"I thought this was where I should be," he said. "I thought I could fit in here." He was afraid of saying too much, of sounding too forward.

"And when the escalator is fixed?" Anna hoped that Daniel's answer would reveal his plans for the future.

"Uncle Sam is no longer my priority," he replied more positively. "This is the place I know best on Springfield. I wondered if we could pick up from where we left off." He thought he was bold to say that much.

"You don't sound very sure," she responded, still not particularly impressed.

"I'm not here seeking charity," Daniel replied, beginning to get fed up with her tone. "I figured I should give it my best shot for a couple of weeks, by which time we will both know whether I should plan on staying longer." He had made himself as clear as he was able. He had said more to Anna than he had said to any other woman.

Charlie wanted Daniel to stay. She wanted Greg to be an important man on Springfield and she saw Daniel as somebody who could help her son on his way to that.

Sally wanted Daniel to stay. Without the escalator, she knew that there would be a lot of desperate folk on Springfield. Her natural instincts told her that another man around the place would be very sensible. Jessica wanted Daniel to stay. Wolf had been able to collect most of the computer bits that Daniel had ordered for Rhino Hill, along with the PCs for the kids, before the escalator had failed. She reckoned that Daniel would have a place in the jigsaw, for several months at least.

The three who had cast their votes then turned to Anna. She had liked Daniel's presence during the monsoon but the fact that there had then been absolutely nothing from him until his unannounced return had unsettled her. She wanted to know where she stood with him before she made any commitment. "Can I abstain?" she asked.

Charlie shook her head. "Why do you think he's come back, Anna? You've got to wise up. He's here for you. Really, our votes don't matter." Charlie looked round. The other two nodded in agreement. "If you say no, he won't want to stay, so it's your choice." Anna sat with a rather glum look on her face for several minutes.

"Okay," she said as she nodded slowly.

"Who's going to tell him?" Jessica was looking at Sally.

"Wolf will know what to say," was her reply, which satisfied the others.

The normal routine was that everybody gathered around Rhino Hill for a shared evening meal. This evening, Wolf took Daniel for a stroll while the women prepared a meal. "They want you to stay." Wolf saw no point in teasing Daniel. "And so do I," he added, "but it had to be the women's decision, just in case there's any friction in the future. Do you know what you plan to do if the escalator starts up again?"

"Maybe it won't start." Daniel didn't want Wolf to be under any illusions. "I need to see if I got the right message during the monsoon, when we were sort of thrown together." Wolf knew who got thrown together. "I'll only leave if people decide they don't want me here."

"Fair enough," Wolf responded. "I managed to pick up most of the stuff you ordered. You'll have plenty of work."

"Yes," Daniel acknowledged, pleased that he would have something to keep him busy. "I meant to ask. How did you pay for it all?"

"When you're free, I've got a couple of schemes that I would like to discuss with you," was all that Wolf would say.

The evening meal passed without incident. Jack wanted to know how long Daniel was staying but Jessica rescued what might have become an embarrassing situation by saying that Daniel was going to be fixing all the electrical equipment. "And he'll make sure that there's plenty of schoolwork on the PCs for boys who ask too many questions," she added. The conversation allowed her to set out Daniel's schedule for the next few days. Although her sudden wish to have him working with her surprised the others, she wanted him to ensure that her medical facility was in tiptop condition before he became fully occupied with Anna.

The first awkward situation arose when everybody began to retire for the night. Wolf made an early, tactical withdrawal. Sally and Charlie lived in Blue Hill, Anna lived in Brown Hill. None of them made any comment about where Daniel should spend the night. He was left in Rhino Hill, which did not please Jessica. He moved into the room he had occupied during the monsoon as quietly as he could and let everything else take care of itself. The next day started without fuss. Daniel chatted with Jack at breakfast time and then started on Jessica's schedule.

Jessica was pleased when Daniel confirmed for a second time that the nuclear generator was performing to specification. She was still concerned about the remaining frozen embryos. Although she could not imagine more than a very limited use for them, she worried that a power failure would kill them. "You know," said Daniel, "there are quite a few single women who retired from the military to Springfield. You sound as if you would like the embryos to be used. Maybe you could try contacting them." Jessica made no response.

All four women had stayed with E2P after their role as incubators had been thoroughly explained. IVF was not an issue for any of them, although they had chosen to describe the procedures as implantations. Jessica was the community doctor. That, together with memories of sexual abuse in her youth and her wish to avoid killing the embryos had led to her suggesting that implantations for the girls in their community should be considered soon. Not surprisingly, her comments had led to a heated debate with the other three women.

"Well," Jessica had said. "What happens if Greg and Rose want to have children?" There was actually no suggestion that Greg and Rose wanted to do anything together but they were both Charlie's children. The women knew that they had both been implantations. The chances of them being related genetically were practically zero but even so, the taboo against brother and sister marrying persisted in the women's minds.

The oldest kids had reached puberty. They had all seen the deer mating and they had giggled at the animals' strange antics. Fortunately, no child had yet asked in public about the human equivalent, although

Sally had spoken to Amber and Jessica had spoken to Daisy about the facts of life. Jack and Naomi were by far the closest pairing, both a very mature ten. Jessica suspected that they would be the ones who pushed the boundary first. Now, though, she knew that Daniel had given her something else to think about.

Daniel was surprised when his cellphone rang a couple of days later. He was servicing the main computers in the Rhino, going through the interminable diagnostics, and he was glad to have a break. It was Colonel Hayes, who was delighted that Daniel had found somewhere to settle down. He warned Daniel that a number of unpleasant incidents had been reported from remote ranches, mostly no more than simple theft, but unsettling, nevertheless. He confirmed that the situation regarding the escalator was unchanged and added that he would visit as soon as he had the time.

Daniel passed on what he had been told to Wolf, who informed the women. Along with the idea of publicising the availability of the embryos, there had been talk of having a sale of some of the deer. Everybody now agreed that it would be silly to advertise their presence. It would only invite trouble. Nevertheless, there was a worry that being separated from the rest of the population might not be good news either. Jessica was most concerned but Wolf assured her that even if strangers made it through the woods that stopped eighteen miles north of Rhino Hill they would not see anything that would encourage them to continue further south. "We just need to keep our wits about us," he said knowingly. He made a mental note to check the state of the weapons on the farm.

Daniel's presence caused the evening conversations to range more widely than in the past. There was now renewed talk of trading for sugar, salt and other basics. The comments drifted on until Wolf interrupted. "A cattle drive," he said suddenly. "That's what people would have done in the old days. We don't want people to come here, so we will go to them." The others looked at him in amazement until they slowly understood what was being suggested.

"Let's arrange a sale of the deer somewhere near to Grand Central. We can drive the animals there. Nobody needs to know where we have come from. I am sure I can find a suitable location." Daniel checked that Colonel Hayes was happy with the idea. He was delighted by something that sounded so natural and yet so new. Although he was aware that many people were struggling, he also knew that there were others who felt that they were merely marking time. He reckoned that this could be a real boost for those who were looking for something positive. "Can it be held before the mid-year harvest?" he asked. Wolf said that it could.

When Wolf repeated their desire to keep the location of Rhino Hill quiet, the colonel said that would not be a problem. A former engineering officer by the name of Jeremiah Hopkins owned Ranch 22, just south-east of Grand Central. He was a friend of Colonel Hayes and was happy to hold a sale on his land. All agreed on a date some three weeks in the future. 'Sale of prime native deer, including four-year-old females, due to produce before the next monsoon. Willing to trade salt and wine/vinegar. Ranch 22. June 24 at 10 am.' was advertised on the network.

Daniel had practically completed Jessica's list of jobs and he immediately volunteered to help Anna, who was suddenly extremely busy. "What's wrong?" she asked. "Are you tired of Jessica already?" It was not the response that Daniel had been expecting.

"I've done all the jobs she asked me to do," he replied. "Now, I thought I could help you."

"What do you know about deer?" she asked sharply.

"You seemed happy to tell me about them during the monsoon," he reminded her. "I'm sure I could learn more if I was given a bit of encouragement." She glared at him. "The sale is in three weeks. Let's say I'm on probation till then." He had been looking forward to being able to work with her and he did not know why she seemed so antagonistic. In his mind, he was not the only one on probation.

Anna didn't know how to reply to that. She resented the fact that Daniel had immediately started working for Jessica. Anna had wanted him to move across to Brown Hill to be close to her but she had not known how to set that up. If Charlie had wanted him, she would have just told him to move in, but Anna wasn't that bold. Certainly, Anna knew that Jessica was never going to be more than friends with him but she had hidden her weakness behind a baseless jealousy of her friend. Daniel did not understand any of that. All he knew was that he had lived in Rhino Hill when he had been working for Jessica. Now, he moved into a spare room in Brown Hill. Nobody made any comment. For once, even Charlie managed to refrain from making any provocative remarks.

The deer were Anna's responsibility. There was more work than she and Daniel could easily cope with, and they were forced to pull together. She dived straight into the nitty-gritty without any reserve. She knew that most of her four-year-old deer would produce a calf. The older deer were not such good stock, although many of those were also pregnant. She was not sure which animals she should take to the sale. She had thought it would not be right to be selling animals of variable quality. Daniel suggested that she took her stock records with her, so that any bidders could see exactly what they were getting. That brought a nod of acknowledgement from her.

There was also the question of how many deer to take. Anna had nearly a hundred animals to sell, plus about a dozen bucks. Daniel suggested that they take half, saying that they could always arrange another sale if demand exceeded supply. She agreed readily. She began to forget her earlier unfounded jealousy and he didn't remind her. Talking about future sales led to talk about what might happen to them in the future. They agreed that they would both stay where they were. They started making plans together.

The drive was uneventful and Jeremiah Hopkins greeted them with enthusiasm. He was a tall, thin man in his late fifties. He had an oval, stern face but a friendly disposition. He had moved to Springfield not as a colonist but as a technologist. He had brought some specialised equipment with him and set up a business drilling wells. When new ranches were being registered on a daily basis, his business had been much in demand. More recently, he had been forced to take a greater interest in obtaining food from the land. He had two generations of his family with him, about to become three. They had turned their hands to farming and foresting. He welcomed his visitors and introduced his wife, Mary, and his adult children, Michael and Caroline.

All interest swiftly moved to the deer. When Jeremiah realised that Anna had a stock book that contained a full breeding record of the animals, he was particularly impressed. "I'll be perfectly open with you," he said. "I'd like to buy all these animals. We've got cows and sheep that did okay back in America but they just don't seem to do so well here. Your deer are very interesting."

"Well, that's nice to know, Mr Hopkins," Anna replied rather primly, "but we've advertised a sale and I want to be fair to all the folks that might be travelling some way to get here." Wolf and Jeremiah exchanged friendly smiles. Nobody knew how many people might actually turn up.

The event became more of a market than a sale. Some people had brought salt or wine because those commodities had been mentioned in the text. Grapes were not ready this season yet but one enterprising individual had brought what he said were vines. Charlie spent the day introducing Greg to anybody whom she reckoned might be important. Jessica had also asked her to help with the matter that Daniel had suggested.

Most of the retiring men had come to Springfield with wives and families but many of the retiring women had come by themselves. There was a shortage of eligible bachelors. Generally, the single women were not too bothered about the lack of men except insofar as they were needed to have children. Jessica found the subject highly embarrassing but Charlie seemed to know how to pick her audience, one whose members were unlikely to be spreading the story to any undesirable elements.

Anna met several people who were keen to build up herds of quality animals. Some breeders wanted at least twenty deer, in order to develop herds of their own, and they exchanged contact numbers with her. Jeremiah bought eight deer and then added that he would like Greg to remain for a couple of weeks to teach him about the animals. Charlie agreed. She knew that Greg had to experience more than Rhino Hill if he were to become the man that she hoped for. It was already clear that they would be returning to 22 with another drive, probably quite soon after the forthcoming harvest.

Daniel was left in charge of the kids who had come on the drive. Jack and Naomi had wangled their way into the group. William, Naomi's brother, and Mike, Greg's brother, had been brought along for the experience. Michael offered to show them round the most cultivated part of 22. Daniel was particularly impressed with a buggy that had been modified to operate as a mechanical digger. It was operated by compressed air instead of hydraulic fluid, so it was nowhere near as powerful as the machines back on Earth, but it was still a vast improvement over a man and a shovel. It could be operated by anybody who could operate a basic buggy. He managed to persuade both Wolf and Anna to take a look, and then he went to talk to Jeremiah about a deal. "Could you make another of those diggers?" he asked.

"I can't get the parts while there's no escalator," Jeremiah replied. "However, I don't have much use for it either while there's no new ranches being registered. I'd be happy to rent it out." Daniel said that he would have to consult with his friends first, although he hoped that a deal could be done at the next sale maybe.

The residents of Rhino Hill were delighted with the success of the drive even though this first major contact with the rest of Springfield would force them to change. Charlie and Greg had indicated that the children needed to see more than just this one community, something that even Jessica could accept. Anna and Daniel became an item. Then, when three women arrived and asked about 'the IVF treatment', it became clear that it was the beginning of the end of Rhino Hill's complete insularity.

The four women - Jessica, Sally, Charlie, and Anna - had been forced to make huge changes to their lives since their spacecraft had buried itself in the hillside. Nobody could say exactly why they had pressed ahead with their implantations. The woman who had led them in that process had been killed before the first child had been born. Initially, the monsoon had been in the middle of their year. Now, it separated the years in a calendar that had been decided by those who had arrived the easy way, by escalator. Nevertheless, it was the physical arrival of the other people that made the biggest difference.

The four women had survived for more than a decade, which convinced them that other communities would also survive. They no longer felt forced to repeat the frequent incapacitation of bearing children. Indeed, the offspring were, in the main, remarkably capable young people, better judged by what they could do than by how many days they had lived. Without their extra pairs of hands, the drive in the first half of Year 3 would not have been possible.

During the second half of Year 3, Rhino Hill and Blue Hill were made more comfortable. Brown Hill already had its own well but more rooms were excavated. Everything that was dug out was used to enlarge the platforms. Red Hill was five miles away, a distance that had once been regarded as too far to permit frequent travel. Now, it was developed to the same standard as the others.

There were other hills in the extra ranches that Wolf had encouraged them to register, north of Red Hill. Several were now rented out to groups that he trusted for a nominal rent. His reasoning was that any trouble would come from the north and the tenants would provide early warning. He controlled the Rhino Hill armoury, which contained half a dozen weapons and several hundred rounds of ammunition. He wasn't looking for trouble but he wanted to be properly prepared for it.

In the very beginning the women had bounded their field system by a water channel that was waist-deep in order to keep out both the baboons, which would attack a deer or an adult human, and the Springfield rodents that they called gophers, which would eat the crops.

Some time before Daniel had appeared, an outer channel that extended round both Red Hill and Brown Hill had been excavated. At the second sale, Daniel hired Jeremiah's digger. He used it to move more soil out of that ditch and began to create a causeway between Rhino Hill and Blue Hill. He reckoned he might complete the job in two years. He hoped that would confirm his commitment to his new home. Jessica was disappointed that the requests for embryos came in a trickle rather than a flood. Greg travelled backwards and forwards, spending much of his time working for Mr Hopkins. Greg was learning the essentials of business. Charlie was very impressed.

The monsoon at the end of Year 3 effectively marked the passage of a year without contact between the Earth and Springfield. Unbeknown to anybody else, Wolf was 'lending' Colonel Hayes quite large sums of money, the results of his prospecting for gold in the mountains west of Rhino Hill. Fortunately, it seemed that some folk would always value the yellow metal. Hayes used it to keep his small staff fed. He could do little more than monitor the situation and keep people informed of developments via the network. Food had become the absolute priority. Grand Central and Newhaven were only sparsely inhabited. Many people had been forced to leave to search for sustenance. He guessed that the total population of the planet had fallen back to only a few thousand but he had no way of making an accurate assessment.

The thieving, caused mostly by the shortage of food, that had started in the middle of the year was not halted by the monsoon. Things became violent. Those caught stealing were dealt with harshly. Some were put into slavery. Some, rumour suggested, were added to the stewpot. Nothing could be wasted when food was in short supply. Many settlers tried to copy Luther

Henshaw and pull food from the rivers and lakes. It was extremely dangerous work. The dinosaurs were not easy to kill. What they lacked in brains, they more than made up for in brute strength. Even Luther had little idea what he would do when the cartridges for the harpoon-gun were exhausted.

A man in Newhaven had built a boat and caught some animals in the sea that were edible, although few people had been prepared to call them fish. After only a few weeks, however, he had gone out one day and not come back. After that, nobody wanted to copy him. There were several small, native species of animal but very few people had the skill and patience to catch them. Even though Colonel Hayes was supported by people like Wolf, who thought it important that some sort of authority was maintained, he struggled. He was hampered by the fact that he had come to Springfield alone. The same applied to many of the former staff. They had no relatives or close friends to help them.

Although few of those living in the Rhino Hill community realised it, their settlement was a beacon of outstanding success. The women had quickly learned how to produce more food than they needed and they had valued security over adventure. Now, they had tenants, whom they had briefed thoroughly on everything: crop management, warnings about the swimmers, capture and management of the migrating deer, even the basics like ditch boundaries. The arrangement might have sounded rather feudal to some but the four original colonists regarded it much more as a cooperative venture.

A school had been set up in Red Hill. Daniel had installed a modern computer that Colonel Hayes no longer needed and added a DHD player. Shirley Owen, now one of the new tenants, had been a teacher before she had arrived on Springfield. She had set up classes in two shifts, mornings and afternoons, each with about a dozen pupils. Pauline Clarke, a former sergeant medic, was renting 127. She had been initially attracted to Rhino Hill by the rumour regarding IVF. She had no doubt that it contained the most advanced medical facility on the planet.

Wolf only appreciated that Year 3 had passed when the end of year monsoon began. The failure of the escalator, the sales, the new tenants - all had filled his time in one way or another. When the monsoon started, he suddenly found himself with time on his hands, time when there would be no interruptions. At last, he could attend to the project that, he felt, had been delayed for too long. He wanted to explore what lay beyond the mountains that began a little over thirty miles west of Rhino Hill.

Chapter 7

The vast, self-contained factory that forged stable openings between universes had a highly technical name that most simply translated as lab - locate, assess, build. Each time, the process began with gathering data that might identify the precise position of the cosmic nodes. An adequate explanation was to regard the universes as inflated balloons resting lightly against each other. A node was a place where two entirely distinct universes touched each other.

It was not so easy to comprehend that the gaps between the balloons were dimensionless, composed of absolutely nothing. According to the scientists, they were not even empty space. Many people were content to dismiss the gaps as *nowhere* and forget about them. When somebody had realised that bubbles of dimensions - minute, artificial universes - could be projected through the *nowhere*, it became clear that even this nothingness would need a name. It became known as the Void.

The lab contained the sensitive equipment that could identify points where a universe boundary was stressed. At such points, a probe would be dispatched to gather all the data required for a formal assessment. If the algorithms then delivered the big tick of approval, construction would begin. Twisting the dimensions of two separate universes so that they came into alignment at a node was normally the easiest of the three tasks by far. It involved no more than assembling what was called a transformer from a kit of parts and then tuning it to the local conditions.

Tom - Transformer Operations Manager, Grade 7 - had been in hibernation because he had nothing to do until a node was confirmed. As soon as he was contacted by Rus - head of Recycling, Upgrades, and Servicing, Grade 12 - he knew that something had gone seriously wrong. Main power was dead, backup systems were stuttering and apart from Rus, the comms were silent.

Tom guessed that a major upgrade had gone wrong. They often did, which was why they were supposed to be banned in the Void. "What is the problem? What have you guys done this time?" Tom had seen some pretty big disasters, including a fatal alignment failure that had ejected a gang of grunts, the Grade 16s who did the dirty, dangerous work, into oblivion. He hoped that things were not as bad as that.

"It's not an upgrade malfunction, Sir. As far as I can tell, there has been some sort of failure right across the lab. I couldn't get any response from the bridge, so I contacted you." Rus sounded extremely nervous.

"Okay, Rus," Tom repeated. "Stay calm while I check around." *Void-stress* was rare in Grade 12s, but not unknown, Tom reminded himself. It was more common in the Grades 16, when getting the IQ balance right was a permanent challenge for management. Too low meant that they could not accomplish the most difficult aspects of what needed to be done but too high meant that they became paranoid about the risks. He made a routine call to the Grade 11 line manager to check if Rus had any history of instability. There was no response.

Tom turned his attention back to Rus. "There's been a power failure somewhere, Rus. Get your techies working on that and put the grunts on general rectification. Keep them all busy. We don't want an outbreak of *Void-stress* making things worse than they already are." He hoped that Rus would take his last sentence as a warning not only to monitor his subordinates but also that he might need to allocate more resources to his own wellbeing.

The approved method of moving through the Void was to create a multi-dimensional, cylindrical bubble around the lab and then slide forward inside the bubble, which automatically extended at the front and retracted at the rear. It sounded laborious when described but it was extremely smooth when properly coordinated. The lab was laid out so that each floor was at right angles to the direction of travel. Now, it seemed that the forward third of the lab and that part of the bubble that had enclosed it were missing, including the bridge and all the operators therein.

When Tom realised that he was now the senior surviving officer, he issued the order to reconfigure the bubble assuming Floor 20 to be the nose of the lab. He refused to speculate on what had happened to the section that was now missing. In the Void, trying to guess distance was an exercise without meaning. Either the two parts were in contact or they were not. He hoped that it had enough power and bubble generators to survive. His responsibility was to secure this part of the lab and get under way again.

Detection of a sudden, rising stress across one section of the temporary hull caused a greater increase in worry among the crew. Swift analysis indicated that they had reached the Void boundary and that they were in contact with dimensional space again. All were relieved to have reached potential sanctuary so quickly. Tom announced that the GAP - General Arrival Protocol - was to be initiated, confirming that imminent disaster was behind them.

Had it been known at that juncture that the damage to the lab had been caused by Rattigan's misadventure, it would not have seemed surprising to find a node nearby. Although the effects had been benign in the physical universes, a massive pulse of energy had been projected into the Void, where there were no dimensions that would have allowed a wavefront to form and the force to disperse. Instead, the pulse had punched through the lab and then continued onwards.

Tom was familiar with the protocol stating that after any incident, the senior officer should escort the surviving crew members to the first point from where contact could be made with the grid authority and seek further instruction. Although they quickly identified a node joining two insignificant planets, neither of those worlds was connected to the grid. They would have to prospect for other nodes nearby and establish a pathway to the grid using the mini-transformers, the lab's lifeboats. Every full navigator, including the highly experienced Grade 5, had been lost. Only Tina, the nickname given to all trainee navigators, could perform the necessary calculations. She would find the task challenging, although she would be well rewarded if she were successful. Tom promoted her to Navigator, Grade 8, and told her to start the search.

Tom did not expect an immediate result from Tina. He began constructing a transformer to link the two nearby worlds. The translator, which was a standard piece of equipment in every lab, was picking up electromagnetic-wave communication on both planets. One sounded frenzied, chaotic, and warlike. The other, which the occupants referred to as Springfield, seemed calm and quiet in comparison. They had come from the other planet to Springfield in the past but communication had now ceased. The translator had been unable to determine the reason for that. Tom did not regard it as important. After the recent excitement in the Void, he knew that he wanted some time for personal analysis.

Normal protocol was to leave an isolated transformer in shutdown mode. Nevertheless, the machines were themselves valuable pieces of equipment. In the event of perceived danger, it was expected that they would be actively protected. The perception of danger was left to the local commander, as was the method of protection. The damage to the lab was unexplained. It could be argued that making contact with the network was routine, whereas the transformer faced an uncertain threat.

Tom's report concluded that he should guard the transformer while Tina led the search for a pathway back to the grid. He could not promote her above himself but her promotion to Grade 7 ensured her full cooperation. A site that showed great promise for eventually regaining contact with the grid was identified on the other side Springfield. Now, hopefully, Tina could begin to establish the chain of nodes that would lead to the grid, using the mini-transformers to pass through the nodal sites.

Tom was pleased that Tina had found a likely site on Springfield rather than the other world. He sensed that introductions were more likely to be conducted in a gentle and controlled fashion on Springfield. Arrival protocols declared that communication with local species possessing only inferior technology was not to be initiated by transformer staff, although leaving a door open, so to speak, was not a direct contravention of the rules. There was only one intelligent species on the two planets. It was thinly spread on Springfield, where he was content to wait for the natives to approach him.

Chapter 8

Wolf's greatest concern when he looked at the plans for his expedition through the western mountains and beyond was maintaining radio communication with Rhino Hill. Including the tenants, the community still only consisted of ten pairs of adults and about three times as many children. They were the only people who might be able to effect a rescue if some disaster befell those who went off exploring with him.

Wolf wanted Daniel to move several transceiver units in order to extend the network coverage through the gap towards what came to be called the Western Plain. Daniel refused to do that without approval from Hayes, who in turn wanted the Rhino Hill community to accept several family groups that he believed deserved a second chance. There were many sad cases where husbands had died leaving wives and children in a situation not unlike the one that the four women had endured for their first years on Springfield.

Wolf again insisted that the decision could only be made by Sally and the other three women. The deal was done in time to separate more than a hundred deer from the passing migration and distribute them among the new arrivals, who were initially settled in five groups. Those deer were not quality stock but at least nobody would face starvation before the mid-year harvest. It gave the incomers a fair chance.

After agreeing to keep Colonel Hayes informed of anything they discovered, Daniel was given permission to move four transceivers. While completing that task, he was able to confirm that the high ground was less than fifty miles wide. Beyond that, the terrain looked remarkably flat, although frequent small patches of woodland offered the hope that the expedition might discover something of interest. All involved were happy with the outcome of the deals. The number of people who now counted themselves as members of the Rhino Hill community exceeded a hundred. More than half of them were between the ages of five and fifteen, which seemed to offer considerable hope for a decade hence if they could avoid disaster until then.

Basic safety had prompted Wolf to opt for three vehicles. He judged that setting out with two buggies and the ant would still allow for an easy return even if any one vehicle failed. Daniel and Anna were now an obvious team and it seemed natural for Daniel to take the ant. Wolf decided that he would take one buggy with James, who would be the expedition medic. The lad had studied hard under Jessica but there was a general feeling that he needed to get out and about more. Sally and Greg would take the second buggy. There had been no reports of looting within thirty miles of Rhino Hill. Thus, nobody was concerned when what was probably the strongest team of six set out from there.

Wolf reckoned that the expedition would have to last eight days to be worth the effort. That determined how much food and water would be required. The sums didn't add up unless he created a staging post somewhere. He had hoped to dig a well at the western end of the gap, to provide a water supply for emergencies. Instead, he reluctantly agreed that all the excavating equipment should be loaned to the new arrivals for longer than he wanted to wait. He set up a cache of water and food below the most westerly of the transceivers that Daniel had recently moved. Although nobody was interested, it was almost precisely a full calendar year from the day that the escalator had ceased before the expedition got under way.

It took the expedition most of the first day to get

clear of the gap and their camp that night was set up in the open only about twenty miles from the high ground. The next morning they set off with the sun rising behind them. The land had the same reedy vegetation that had surrounded Rhino Hill when the women had first arrived, although Anna was pleased to note that a richer, Earth-type grass had begun to take hold in some places. There were a few, shallow water features but for the most part it appeared to be benign prairie in every direction. What Daniel had thought were patches of woodland turned out to be small mounds populated by some sort of spindly bush.

Halfway through the third day, when they stopped for lunch, there was general agreement that nothing was likely to be gained by continuing west for another day and a half. After some discussion, it was agreed that they should turn south-east with the intention of inspecting the western slopes of the mountain range that now separated them from Rhino Hill.

The land that they had been crossing seemed to have less of interest than the land round Rhino Hill. Sally had hoped to spot at least indications of previously unseen species. Anna had wanted to find out more about the origins of the deer. Wolf reminded everybody that there were large areas of barren land near the equator on the Earth. With the benefit of hindsight, they told themselves that they should have searched further north. They meandered generally south-east from mound to mound. Wolf now hoped to find some mineral deposits when they went back along the foothills, so that he might extend his mining business.

The high ground was still so far away when they stopped for the third night that it did no more than provide a fringe to the eastern horizon. On the fourth day, most felt a strong temptation to cut the corner and head directly back to the gap. Wolf kept them on their south-easterly course. He had calculated that they did not need to reach the initial slopes before lunch on the fifth day. They still had radio contact with Rhino Hill via the transceiver that was located above the cache of emergency supplies. He hoped that they would find something of interest if they kept looking. They watched the mountains grow in size as they got closer until they stopped as planned on the fifth day. They took their lunch to the top of an outcrop but they were hardly inspired by the view, which was similar to that of the previous days.

Wolf spent the second half of the fifth day and much of the sixth selfishly prospecting, the most obvious result of which was that the others became extremely bored. While he searched up every gully, the other buggy was driven slowly along the fringe of the prairie. In the ant, Anna drifted increasingly west, hoping to find something of interest around one of the mounds. It was near the end of the sixth day when Wolf asked Sally to start setting up camp and advised Anna that she should head for Sally's position. They were all aware of how quickly day changed to night near the equator. The peaks were still bathed in sunlight, and would be for more than an hour, but their chosen campsite would be dark in less than twenty minutes.

Anna was still several miles from Sally when she saw shadows begin to flow into the lowest gullies. She had been admiring the sharp relief of the peaks when a circular light appeared to burst into life much lower down. She guessed that it had to be some massive mirror, reflecting the rays of the setting sun towards her. Daniel quickly called Wolf. Anna was keen to investigate immediately. Wolf said that it was already too dark to begin a search safely and asked Daniel to mark the ground where they had been when Anna had first spotted the light. They would look in the morning.

The little party awoke in the gloomy shadow of the peaks that had been the last to lose the sunlight the previous evening. After Wolf had driven the ant to the spot that Daniel had marked, he swung the searchlight up and panned left and right. He looked to the others. They nodded; they could see the reflection that Anna had spotted the night before. "Drive the buggies forward," he instructed, "but do not go past it. Flash your lights when you stop." Daniel and Greg drove the buggies forward slowly on battery power and stopped when they lost the reflection. Wolf caught up with them and they repeated the process. When they met again, they could not get a direct reflection. The light was bounced away up the hillside. They lost even that guide when the sun came over the mountaintops but they were close enough to see something that looked out of place on the rocky slope, some sort of cavern that appeared to be too the circular to be natural.

The opening was shielded by rocks, so much so that it could not be seen from directly below, and from further north it was completely invisible. Even coming from the south, it was not obvious from more than about half a mile away that there was anything unusual about this particular bit of hillside. Wolf insisted that they built a cairn that was clearly visible on the fringe of the prairie to mark the location and then he allowed everybody to scramble up to the circular opening. They assembled close together on a small rocky platform and peered into what seemed to be a cavern that was large enough to hold three or four buggies.

The inside of the cavern was smooth and light grey. It could have been the last, short section of some huge pipeline blocked off at the end, which was a couple of buggy-lengths into the mountain. The cavern looked as if it could have been bored very neatly out of the solid rock, except that the surface colour was perfectly uniform. There was not even a hint of any layers or seams in the surface. Just outside the entrance there were some signs of a recent rockfall but the loose stuff was nowhere near enough to fill the empty chamber.

Sally stepped through the opening, looking from side to side. She touched the vertical wall at the far end. It had the same texture that she had felt through her shoes, softer than sand, more like dust, but when she inspected her hand it was as clean as it had been a few minutes earlier. Nor, when she looked down, could she see any mark on the floor that showed where her feet had been. She called out. "Hello, hello, is there anybody there?" Unconsciously, she had already decided that the hole in the mountain side could not be a natural phenomenon. It seemed only polite to alert the owners.

Since the arrival of the lab, the translator had been analysing the radio traffic from the cellphone network. It could handle that form of communication easily. In the last few days all the analytical resources had been concentrated on the group that had been approaching the transformer chamber. The lack of radio transmissions when the people were close together suggested that they had a secondary form of communication, which had come as a surprise to the translator. It meant that considerably more work might be required.

The cellphone network and messages expressing concern about electrical energy levels had led Tom initially to the assumption that his team had found a machine species less well-developed than their own. Messages about starvation and death, even when sunlight was plentiful, had led to a reappraisal. He had issued a directive that they were to be regarded as biological unless there was any reason to change that assessment.

Advanced biological species were rare, he knew, partly because of their relatively short lifespans, although none of that was important at this time. The group now in the chamber would provide an excellent opportunity for the two species to learn more about each other, he hoped, to their mutual benefit. After all, he reminded himself, they were probably going to be neighbours for a very long time.

Fresh analysis of the radio communications suggested that the new arrivals in the chamber were typical of several biological models. Most of the detailed background information on the subject of biological species had been lost during the incident. In the protocol that covered extension of the grid, however, Tom had found one piece of advice that intrigued him. 'Remember that biological species have distinct parts.'

Tom had struggled to understand that when, in a sense, every part of the transformer was a part of him, even though, in biological terms, he was only the head, the brain, the decision-making part. The other parts had names only to help him keep track of the ongoing processes. He had tried to imagine the lowliest grunt leaving the bubble and working in the chamber. He had been unable to convince himself that it had not remained part of him, even when it was actually on Springfield.

Tom had been unsure which of the four adults to contact first, so he had applied a randomising algorithm. When Sally's phone rang, she answered without asking herself how there could be radio reception so deep inside the mountain. "Hello, Sally speaking," she said automatically.

"Hello, Sally. I am Tom. Welcome." He had decided to try to keep things simple to begin with. He was pleased to note that Sally showed no alarm.

"What's up, Tom?" she asked.

"I just wanted to introduce myself," he replied. "I'm in the space outside your universe. I built this chamber to link your planet with what you call the Earth."

When Sally didn't respond, Tom continued. "Our craft was damaged while we were in the Void, which is what we call the emptiness outside the universes. We travel using points that link the universes. We call them nodes. Our navigator is trying to make contact with the nodal grid at the present. When Tina returns we will know that she has succeeded."

"Please, Tom," Sally burst in. His extremely concise briefing had been too much for her. "Can we stop there? I think I should talk to my friends now. Is that okay with you?" Tom agreed as soon as the translator warned him that she was already sounding rather stressed.

Sally tried to explain what she had been told to the others. "He says his name is Tom and that this . . ." She paused, wanting to recall the word he had used. "This chamber is linked to Earth."

"Is he on the Earth?" asked Wolf, still not sure what he was hearing.

"No." Sally shook her head. "I think he said he was in somewhere called the Void, outside the universes."

"Does this lead to another escalator?" asked Daniel. "Can we use it to get back to the Earth?"

"I think that is what he meant." Sally replied uncertainly. She was sure that that she had been speaking to another human being. It was the abrupt mention of contact with the Earth that left her dazed, although she had no wish to go. She had not been at all disturbed when she had been told that the escalator had failed. Now, she needed time to assure herself that what Tom had described would be equally irrelevant to her life on Springfield.

Tom stayed silent, guessing that the visitors would want to complete some analysis of his information before any of them spoke to him again. He was correct. The little expedition had found considerably more than Wolf had ever expected. He looked around the plain chamber very carefully but saw nothing that caused him to feel alarmed, which he knew was a good sign. He looked across to Sally, who merely shrugged her shoulders. She was not worried either. He did not doubt that Tom, whoever he was, wherever he was, might have considerable technological muscle. He felt encouraged by the fact that there had been no indication, yet, that Tom wanted to demonstrate any aggression.

Wolf quickly realised that the existence of another escalator on Springfield could offer amazing opportunities, although it would also demand extremely careful management. One thing was clear: a team had to remain in the chamber. Occupation of the site was the time-honoured method of staking a claim. His mind was racing. He did not want to leave just one person alone. They would have to set up a system to keep whoever stayed there supplied with water and food. They could check this guy Tom out more thoroughly after that, Wolf told himself, see how his escalator worked, prove his statement. Obviously, they had to see how the kit operated before they involved anybody else, he told himself firmly.

Sally wanted to stay, although she could not explain why. Essentially, Wolf knew, the choice lay between her and Daniel. It couldn't be the boys. It couldn't be him because he needed to be free to set up the supply chain. Anna immediately volunteered to remain with Sally. If there had been more food and water remaining, Wolf would have preferred three people but he knew that those two women made a strong team. At that point, they still had the rations for the seventh and eighth days remaining, equivalent to sixteen man-days, and they were about forty miles from the cached supplies.

Wolf silently congratulated himself on having arranged the cache and on having placed it near a transceiver, making it easy to locate. His prospecting plan was immediately jettisoned. He knew this might be considerably more valuable than a little gold. He felt twenty years younger. He was back in his element, planning on the hoof, organising barely adequate forces that might be spread over a wide area. He delighted in exactly that sort of challenge.

"Okay," Wolf said when he had a plan that satisfied all his immediate objectives. "Here's what we need to do. Sally and Anna will remain here to guarantee our claim to this place. We will leave all the water and food here. It should be enough to keep you going for eight days," he said, turning to the women. "Try to get the ant up here. We will hurry back in the other two vehicles to the cached supplies, where we will pick up a meal before returning to Rhino Hill. We need to get a supply chain established."

"Why don't we phone ahead and tell people what we've found?" asked Greg.

"Because somebody round Rhino Hill would feel forced to tell somebody else," Wolf explained patiently. "Then the story would spread like wildfire. Before you knew it, there would be hundreds of people heading here, all demanding to be transported back to the Earth before we even know if that is possible. Also, this guy Tom can obviously listen into our cellphones. We don't know what his agenda is. He already knows a great deal about Springfield. Sally reckons he sounded okay. She may be correct. We cannot assume that yet, however, so we must keep our powder dry."

Wolf smiled at Greg, knowing that the isolation of Rhino Hill had shielded the lad from the nasty side of human nature. "We will need to involve Colonel Hayes," Wolf added, trying to sound more encouraging, "but not before we know that this thing actually works. Our priority should be to get ready, properly ready, for a demo from Tom showing us how this escalator operates. If what he has said is correct, I don't think we will need to rush."

It was now broad daylight outside. Wolf urged the women not to do anything silly while they were on their own. Then he was off, encouraging his little party to travel as fast as possible. They reached the cache after about two hours, needing only to take on enough supplies for the remainder of the journey before charging on. When they reached Rhino Hill, they had proved that the journey could be completed in a day, although safety considerations suggested that some sort of manned relay station should be established near the middle of the route.

Wolf had phoned ahead just before they arrived, to assure Jessica and Charlie that their return with only two vehicles was nothing to worry about. Word quickly went round Rhino Hill that the ant was not returning. Although Jessica tried to convey Wolf's assurances to the others, there was considerable concern. It was announced that a formal meeting would be held as soon as those who had been travelling all day had been able to freshen up. Since Greg and James were obviously going to be in attendance, Amber and Naomi also insisted on being there to discover what had happened to their mother. That meant that Jack and Daisy arrived with Jessica. Charlie brought Rose with Greg. Fortunately, Ruth was content to be left in charge of the younger children.

Wolf had attended many meetings that he had shared only with the four women. This was the first important assembly to include children. Perhaps that was only right as the eldest were now teenagers. Having had time to think about the chamber, he had little doubt that what they were about to discuss might affect all their futures. There was a great deal that he wanted to say and he struggled to get his thoughts in order. He knew that he was still fired up, as were all those who had returned with him. He had forbidden any of his fellow travellers to say anything. As soon as he stood up, even the youngest children present immediately fell silent. "What I'm going to tell you must remain a secret until I say otherwise," he began. He then went on to repeat much of what had been discussed in the chamber.

"Here are my recommendations," Wolf continued quickly before anybody could ask any questions. "I think our priority at the moment should be to claim the site of the chamber. If what this guy Tom said is genuine then it's going to be a pretty valuable place. Sally and Anna are there effectively staking our claim. We need to establish a supply system that will keep them fed and watered until we find out a bit more. Part of the supply process should include the construction of a permanent base at the far end of the gap, where we cached the emergency supplies. If we can get the new base up and running before the next harvest starts then I think we will have done well. Obviously, we need to see proof of Tom's words at some time, but I reckon we will know about that fairly soon one way or the other." Wolf had expected a clamour as soon as he stopped. Instead, the room was quiet. His listeners were speechless.

As soon as Wolf had been able to confirm that Sally and Anna were safe, Amber and Naomi left to phone their mother. The other children lost interest because the Earth meant little to them. Even a new base wasn't that exciting and the chamber sounded like just another room in a hillside. Jessica and Charlie were not greatly excited by the idea of a replacement escalator, although they could both appreciate that the site might be extremely valuable if Tom had spoken honestly. Common sense, not Wolf, put doubt in their minds. When a few questions were put to him, he admitted that in all his four years on Springfield he had never seen anything like the chamber. He had dug holes in the mountain slopes that faced Rhino Hill, where he had mined for gold and copper, but he had never seen anything like the smooth, almost featureless inner surface of the chamber.

It was Charlie who expressed the greatest interest in a new base at the far end of the pass. She thought it might be an opportunity for Greg to make his mark. Being able to control access to the Western Plain sounded to her like a business venture that would allow him to establish himself, become the important man that she had always wished him to be. A dozen years earlier, she and her friends had created a base in Rhino Hill. All it had required was hard work. She knew she could do it again.

Chapter 9

Since their arrival on Springfield, Sally and Anna had not forced themselves upon each other but they had developed confidence in each other and in their ability to survive. Although they had been left on their own at the site of the chamber, they did not feel alone. After they had watched the others disappear, they parked the ant close to the entrance of what would be their home for the next few days. They had everything they needed except water for washing, which had been annoying them since the second day of the expedition.

When the two women had moved their kit into the chamber, they relaxed on their bedrolls, pleased that the atmosphere within the chamber felt cooler than outside. "What now?" asked Anna. There was something she wanted to talk to Sally about.

"It will take Wolf two days to reach Rhino Hill," Sally replied easily, "and probably another day to load up with supplies, although I suppose that could be done overnight. So, a minimum of four days before he returns, more likely five or six. We have rations for eight days, more if we save our energy. We don't need to do anything for at least four days. We can certainly allow Wolf six before we will need to think about making a run for it. We actually have nothing to do for the first time in goodness knows how long." She felt very confident that all was well.

"And do you think this chamber will allow people to go back to the Earth?" From her tone, Anna clearly had something troubling her.

"That is what Tom said," Sally replied without any excitement. She had no desire to leave Rhino Hill but she understood that Wolf might be interested if he detected what he called a business opportunity. She was thinking that people from the Earth might pay to come here, not that those already here would pay to go back. She trusted Wolf to sort things out and anyway, she had another matter to keep her busy.

The chamber fell silent. After only a few minutes, however, Anna felt forced to speak again. "Do you think Daniel will go back to the Earth?" She was very conscious that his first comment after being told about Tom was that very matter. Sally looked at her friend and raised her eyebrows, inviting more comment. "I thought I was quite content until he turned up," Anna continued. Sally knew what she meant. She had felt the same about Wolf. Life had been okay when he had been left on the Earth. Then he had turned up; Anna's little phrase seemed very appropriate.

Sally recalled that there had been an uncomfortable couple of months in her life when she had not known what he was doing. Fortunately, Wolf had made the decision that she had wanted. It had changed her life. While the other women had been glad to stop having children, she had produced two more. Very recently, she had sensed that another one had started inside her.

That brought a pause in Sally's thinking while she examined how her body felt. Suddenly, she realised what Anna was trying to say. "You're pregnant, aren't you?" She looked across to Anna, who nodded.

"I think so, even though it's early days, but it wouldn't surprise me. I haven't told Daniel yet. I wanted to be certain before I said anything. Now, I don't know what to do. I suppose I just assumed that the escalator wouldn't be starting up again."

"You had James and Ruth without any man," Sally said gently. "You'll be okay." That was not what Anna wanted to hear.

"I don't want to be okay. I want Daniel," she replied.

Sally did not know how to respond to that. She recalled that she had gone through agonies waiting for Wolf to confirm that he was staying on Springfield. Looking back, she still only partially understood what his scheming had been about, registering all the ranches. Even if this involved him going back to the Earth, she was not worried. She was confident that he would return, as much for his sons as for her, she acknowledged. She did not mind that. He was a good father to all her children.

Anna was cross with herself. "Daniel said the escalator would not start up again for years. I wish I hadn't seen anything yesterday." She was confused by a combination of circumstances that she had never anticipated.

"Well, you've got to talk to him," Sally warned. "The next time you see him," she insisted. "Don't complain if he appears more pleased about the baby than anything else." Anna knew that she would not complain about anything if Daniel said he would stay with her. That was all she wanted but she feared that he would go.

Sally had no more advice to give. Only Daniel could solve Anna's dilemma. During the eight years before Wolf had appeared, men had not been missed. The most challenging time had been very soon after the *Rhino* had arrived, just after Wendy had been killed. Certainly, none of the women had ever suggested that the presence of men would have been beneficial during that phase of their lives. There had merely been an increased determination among the others to survive.

Anna's mind wandered back to the starting point of her confusion, the possibility that the chamber in which they lounged was some sort of escalator. She couldn't see how it was. If it were only a hole in the rock then she could dismiss all her worries, she told herself.

"Sally. Did Tom say how this thing works?" Sally shook her head. "Do you think he was telling the truth?" Sally shrugged her shoulders. "Maybe we should ask him to show us," Anna suggested, hoping that Sally would do something. Sally was reluctant to stir herself, knowing that Wolf would be annoyed if she did anything rash. "I want Tom to give us a demonstration," Anna said more forcefully. "How do I call him up?"

"He called me," Sally replied, determined not to start anything that she might later regret. Her comment brought that little conversation to an end.

Anna convinced herself that the way to make all her troubles go away was to prove that the chamber was not an escalator. She began to click her phone on and off absent-mindedly. Suddenly, it began to ring. She looked at it in some trepidation. "Go on, Anna," Sally called out. "You'd better answer it."

"Hello," Anna said uncertainly.

"Hello, Anna. Did you want something?" It sounded like a man's voice. He knew her name. She was taken by surprise.

"Who are you?" she asked bluntly.

"I'm Tom," was the reply. "Can I help you?" Tom knew that there were only two communication devices in the chamber: Anna was 96, Sally was 94. The probability was that the others would return shortly.

"This escalator. How does it work?" Anna asked somewhat abruptly.

"It's a transformer," Tom replied carefully. "It matches the dimensions on Springfield with those on the Earth to permit travel between the two." Anna found Tom's voice relaxing enough to ask him again how it worked. "It's probably easiest if I show you," he replied. To have said that she was incapable of understanding would have sounded unnecessarily rude.

114

Hopefully, he told himself, opportunities for trade would not be hampered by the limited technological understanding of her species.

There was no sound. The first thing the women noticed was a sensation that the chamber was rolling a little to the left. They realised that it was only gravity dragging them. The chamber had not moved. The slippage had stopped by the time they began to look round. Then they noticed that something was obscuring the view out of the chamber entrance, as if some sort of fog had suddenly formed on Springfield. As they stared at each other, Anna's gaze was distracted by the view behind her friend. An opening was replacing the blank wall. The external view was sufficiently different to force her to accept that she had not merely been spun through half a turn. When she felt steady on her feet, she raised an arm and pointed, compelling Sally to turn round and look for herself. Neither of them noticed the change in air pressure.

The women found themselves looking out across some broad, wooded valley. They could hear the sound of running water. Sally wrinkled her nose. The air smelt different. There was a contrail in the sky. The sun was hidden behind her somewhere. She guessed the day was young, in which case she was looking west. She was able to identify the scent of fir trees drifting into the chamber. Her memory insisted that she had to be close to where she had grown up. When Anna, who had come from much further east, looked at her, afraid to speak, Sally nodded. "Earth." That one word was sufficient confirmation.

Anna realised that her phone was still switched on. "How do we go back to Springfield, Tom?"

"Just say when you want to return," Tom replied. His sentence effectively confirmed that they had left that planet but neither woman was paying much attention. "Your instruction will only be ignored if you leave something blocking the portal," he warned. Anna wasn't really listening; she was fully occupied trying to come to terms with the simplicity of the operation.

"What do you reckon?" Anna asked Sally.

"I think we have to make sure that we are not seen, otherwise we'll have a lot of explaining to do," Sally replied firmly. "We know what it looks like when it's open. How easy do you think it is to see when it is closed?" Sally was worried about being seen, although she could not explain why. The two women had a long, hushed discussion about what they should do. Should they take the ant through the chamber and out on the Earth side to examine the location? They asked Tom who could operate the chamber.

"No restrictions have been imposed," he replied.

"Okay," said Sally. "Can we limit it to just us two?" She was trying to think of all the things that could go wrong. Tom agreed that only instructions from their cellphones would be acted upon. He also confirmed that communication was not affected by whether the chamber was open or closed.

Sally and Anna were so excited that they could not resist the temptation to explore. They agreed that they should go back and fetch some equipment. This time, they sat down on the curved floor of the chamber, so that the gravity change did not throw them off balance. This time, they felt the drop in pressure. They noticed that the air felt several degrees warmer when the Springfield end of the chamber opened again. Anna drove the ant into the chamber, angling slightly up to the left to prepare for the gravity shift. Sally got the guns and the binoculars ready. Then they asked Tom to open the door at what they already thought of as the Earth end of the chamber.

Sally spent about twenty minutes scanning the local

area carefully through her binoculars. There was not much cover this side of the river, which made the land easy to check. The far side of the valley had a thick expanse of firs, which came right down to the river in places. She was sure there was some movement beyond the far bank. She allowed herself a smile when she spotted a group of wild ponies down at the water's edge taking an early morning drink. Their behaviour was confirmation that they were not aware of any humans in their vicinity.

Sally gestured to Anna to drive the ant out. She asked Tom to close the portal and then she nodded to her friend to drive forward. They looked back from about fifty yards away. The gentle slope of the ground appeared to be almost unbroken. Patches of bare rock and shale mixed with scrubby vegetation. The soft tyres of the ant had left no tracks. There was nothing to indicate the existence of the chamber. Anna clicked her phone in minor panic, fearing that they were trapped there. She relaxed visibly at the sound of Tom's voice. "Just checking," she said with relief. Had she really been afraid that she might be stuck on the Earth? Yes, she was forced to admit; she had.

Anna accepted that she had not just travelled through a short tunnel. She could ignore the different angle of the shadows. Maybe she had not moved in a straight line, she told herself. She could not ignore the change in the vegetation. She had never seen any fir trees on Springfield but she could see fir trees now, the sort of fir trees that were common on the Earth, planted in long rows as if they were managed by foresters. She and her friends had planted what they called trees on the platforms and along their field boundaries, a dozen here and a dozen there, but not an entire hillside. This was not somewhere she could identify with Springfield.

Sally let Anna watch the ponies through the

binoculars while she took stock. There was no visible sign whatsoever of the chamber. Suddenly, the grey, rectangular outline of the ant looked far too obvious. "We have to camouflage the ant before we try to use it here," she said to Anna. "And we need to set up some sort of marker, even if it is just a cairn or something, so we can find the chamber easily." Anna looked round. She nodded in agreement with her friend. The ant's bare metal did not match any of the natural colours around them. Nevertheless, they were where they were, she told herself. It seemed silly to waste this opportunity.

Anna pointed down to the river where several weathered tree trunks were beached on the stony bank. "We could drag one of those up here before we hid the ant," she suggested. "It would make a more natural marker than a pile of rocks." They selected a tree trunk with relative ease and began to drag it up the slope confidently enough. Both spent more time watching the log behind them than looking where they were going.

Anna slowed the ant, then stopped it altogether. "I'm lost," she said, more surprised than angry. "This just doesn't look anything like the right place." Sally looked back. It appeared to be the right distance from the river. She looked ahead. They were on a patch of almost bare rock. She feared that they might have come too far. They might even be on top of the portal and preventing it from opening, she told herself.

Sally clicked her phone. It seemed like an age before Tom responded. "We'd like to return now, please," she said quickly. When there was no reply, she felt herself begin to panic. "Tom, Tom, now, please." She knew she was shouting.

"It's open, Sally," Tom replied. She sensed something soothing in his voice. She had been staring at her phone. Now, she looked from left to right in front of her. Slightly higher up the slope and two hundred yards further to the left, the chamber entrance yawned wide open.

"Thank you, Tom," she heard herself say. Like Anna, she had felt a surge of panic when she had thought that she might be trapped on the Earth.

The fear of being isolated from Springfield left both women sweating profusely even though the ant had proceeded up the slope without complaint. They left the trunk in a slight dip in the ground, pointing directly towards the chamber. Sally looked round carefully. The marks left by the log as it had scraped along the ground would be gone in a few weeks, she reckoned, and there was nothing to indicate that its current location was of any significance whatsoever. In another couple of months it would look as if it had simply fallen over where it had lived and died. They parked the ant on the Springfield side of the chamber and tried to relax.

Before long, the thought of bathing in the river became irresistible. This time, the women went on foot. They took it in turns to bathe in the cold water while the other kept watch. Nothing disturbed them. They walked slowly back up to their tree trunk and then into the chamber, where they were content to spend the next few hours resting and thinking about how close the Earth suddenly appeared to be. Looking around, this construction appeared remarkably uncomplicated and spacious in comparison with what they remembered of Earth technology.

"Do you remember the early days when we wondered if we would survive?" Anna asked. Having seen how easy it was to operate the chamber, her worries about Daniel were beginning to subside. "Stuck on our own for all those years. I guess it will take time to get used to just walking through a hill to travel between the Earth and Springfield." She wanted to know more about Tom and she clicked her phone to get his attention.

"Hi, Tom, can we have a chat?" Anna asked when he answered. "I'd like to know more about you. Where are you? Why are you here?" Tom had already accepted that these biologicals were going to be his neighbours for the foreseeable future. He was keen that they got to know each other. He repeated his description of the accident to the lab in the Void and its fortunately swift arrival at the boundary adjacent to Springfield.

"The chamber is part of me, not really on the Earth or on Springfield but somewhere in between," he revealed.

"What sort of being are you?" Anna was confused by his reply. His voice coming out of her phone sounded human but his words puzzled her.

"I think you would call me a machine," Tom replied. "I was created many cycles ago. If I had got lost in the Void, I would have put myself into what you would probably call a 'sleep' mode, so that I could resuscitate myself whenever I reached the boundary. I'm also capable of extensive regeneration. With the appropriate raw materials I am capable of constructing a copy of myself or other machines to trade." Nothing that Tom said registered with Anna at more than a superficial level. She was not able to imagine what he might be capable of. She never considered that he could be more powerful, and perhaps more dangerous, than anything on the Earth.

"How long will you be here?" Anna asked somewhat bluntly. Tom chose to make a slightly guarded reply.

"The chamber will remain in operation probably for as long as the location remains stable. It provides our standard method of travel. I have a team that is trying to find a pathway back to the main grid. When that is established, you will be able to travel anywhere you want, not just to the Earth." Anna hoped that she wouldn't need to travel to anywhere except Rhino Hill.

Anna understood about trade and she asked Tom for more details. "I can build all sorts of machines that you might find useful," he explained. "Because I was forced to dock without going through the normal arrival protocol, without seeking permission, this chamber is effectively yours. If this node becomes an important part of the grid then there might be a large volume of traffic and fees will be charged. My employer needs to recover the cost of the expedition but you will have the right to ask for a commission."

"Okay," said Anna, indicating that she had heard enough. She guessed that Tom wouldn't want to trade for deer.

Sally called Wolf when she reckoned that he would have finished whatever he had wished to complete that day. She told him that she and Anna had been through the chamber to what was clearly the Earth. When she mentioned seeing the wild ponies, he was extremely pleased. He then advised her of what had been agreed with the others about establishing a new base at the western end of the gap. He had been worried about supplies of water and of food. The close proximity of the river that she and Anna had bathed in pleased him. A couple of tubes of water purifying tablets were considerably easier to transport than several hundred gallons of water.

Daniel called Anna, which pleased her greatly. She quickly passed on the message about having been through the chamber and Sally's assessment of what they had seen. Anna was keen to hear Daniel's response, which was muted at first. "What will you do?" she asked.

"I want to stay with you," he said without any prompting. He had already guessed that she would wish to stay close to Rhino Hill. "But . . . I probably need to speak to Colonel Hayes. That will have to wait because Wolf doesn't want us to say anything about the chamber until he knows more. Officially, I'm still in the military. I will need to ask Hayes how I get a discharge. I expect I can serve out my time on Springfield."

Anna was delighted. Daniel had virtually said that he didn't want to go back to the Earth. His only concern was how quickly he could get out of uniform. "I think I might be pregnant," she said. She had not meant to say anything so soon. She had wanted to wait until he was with her so that she could see his face but she felt so happy that she simply could not prevent herself from telling him.

"Wow," Daniel replied, clearly amazed. The subject of children had never properly come up between them. Because of what he thought he understood about Rhino Hill, he had assumed that Anna couldn't have any more. He had come to terms with that, telling himself that he was a bit old to be starting a family.

Now, Daniel sensed a warm glow inside him. The thought that there might soon be a little Daniel made him feel very happy. He forgot that there might be a problem about his current employment if a link were established between the Earth and Springfield again. He had joined the military to see the world but he knew now that he had seen as much as he needed to see. He was where he wanted to be and he had found the person he wanted to be with. He felt a contentment that he had never experienced before. Their phone call lasted more than an hour even though they didn't really say very much at all.

Chapter 10

Wolf woke the following morning determined to move things ahead as quickly as possible. He was pleased that Charlie wanted to be in charge of the new base to be constructed at the western end of what was now called Migration Gap. In her mind it was about halfway between the place that he seemed so excited about and Rhino Hill, so she said she would call it Halfway House. Wolf said that her first priority should be to dig a well, even though the river that Sally had reported had eased his concerns considerably with regard to the supply of water.

Charlie wanted Greg to help her but Wolf had other plans for the young man. It was particularly important that a reliable supply chain was maintained. He reckoned that pairs of buggies would have to carry supplies from Rhino Hill on a daily basis for the foreseeable future. That was something that the kids were capable of and it seemed sensible to put the eldest in charge. Jessica remained to supervise Rhino Hill. Daniel, James, and a couple of the eldest girls were asked to help Charlie. Wolf warned everybody to guard against accidents and injuries, not to do anything silly or dangerous.

Daniel began to rig up photovoltaic panels at the site of Halfway House to provide power to operate the excavating equipment. Jack and Naomi, who were now eleven, began to bring what had been spare buggies out of store, to use as mobile electrical supplies and battery chargers. With power constantly available, the general assessment was that it would take two weeks to make Halfway House habitable, unless there was some serious accident, and then another week to spread enough soil across the obligatory platform to make it worthwhile transplanting some saplings. Nobody saw any reason to change the model that had proved so successful around Rhino Hill.

Wolf devoted that day to making sure that every part of his plan was beginning to flow smoothly. After spending the night at the spot where Halfway House would be created, he and Daniel set off the next morning in a buggy full of supplies for the chamber. Wolf was pleased at the way things were turning out. Daniel was the nearest person that their little community had to a technical expert. He wanted the young man's opinion before he alerted Colonel Hayes to their discovery.

Sally and Anna had a meal ready when Wolf and Daniel arrived. The women had spent most of the previous day resting in the chamber. They had resisted the temptation to explore the land around the chamber, telling themselves that even merely straining an ankle would have been an unnecessary complication in this situation. While they ate, Sally described everything that they had learned. Then she demonstrated the operation of the chamber. From the outside, there was nothing to see on either side when that entrance/exit was closed. They went through to the Earth side, where the terrain looked exactly as Sally had described it.

Wolf had a brief scout around the rise above the chamber. After about a quarter of a mile, he met a solid line of fir trees. He looked north and south but saw nothing that excited his curiosity. A couple of contrails ran east to west in the sky high above him. Darkness was approaching. He nodded to himself. This could easily be the Earth, he told himself, but where?

They all went back into the chamber and closed the Earth side. Wolf asked Daniel for his opinion. The other man shrugged his shoulders. "It's a neat machine," he conceded. "It calls itself Tom but that sort of thing is easy to program. It doesn't mean anything. The story about the accident might be true or it might not. The guy who designed the escalator is on Springfield somewhere. We should get him here. He's the only person who might be able to understand what this chamber thing really is." Daniel's priority was to chat to Anna about their future.

Wolf departed on his own some six hours later. He had to wake Sally to ask Tom to open the portal. It was still dark on Springfield but dawn was appearing on the Earth. He took a buggy out and disguised its outline by tying fir branches to the sides. With its silent motor, he was confident that he had done enough to camouflage it. He set off south, reckoning that he was more likely to find signs of civilisation downstream. After less than an hour he saw a massive lake ahead of him. Through the binoculars he thought he could detect buildings across the water, maybe another twenty miles away. He did not want to go that far from the chamber, so he turned north. After a further two hours, now some ten miles north of the chamber, he came to a road sign pointing to Interstate 15 and indicating that somewhere called Mesquite was twelve miles to the right. He was sure he had gained enough from his recce to justify disturbing Colonel Hayes.

Hayes was using the old registration offices as his HQ. Trying to create an accurate register of all those still alive on Springfield filled most of his time. He listened carefully to what Wolf had to say. He got out his maps, which confirmed the existence of a town called Mesquite up near the border between Nevada and Arizona on Interstate 15. "I'll have Mark Richards here in Grand Central as soon as I can, probably take a couple of days. Can you meet us here?" Wolf said that sounded like an excellent idea.

Although Daniel wanted to remain with Anna, Wolf

convinced him that completing Halfway House was more important. When Sally and Anna said that they were content to remain in the chamber for another couple of days, the men said their goodbyes and departed, leaving the women with supplies that would last more than a week. Wolf left Daniel at Halfway House, where a well had already been dug, and went on to Rhino Hill to let Jessica know how things were progressing. The story she had given to their tenants was that they were building new bases. Expansion made the future sound rosy. The story made them feel encouraged rather than curious.

Jessica was not entirely happy with the children being given so much responsibility, although they all seemed to be remarkably competent. There was now no shortage of buggies. Greg was supplying the workers at Halfway House with all their needs. The other youngsters kept the farm running as if nothing had changed. Jessica guessed that many would not want to give up what appeared to be a sudden boost to their independence.

Wolf never liked sending just one person on a journey, not even himself. He was aware that even quite a minor illness or injury to a person on his or her own could prove fatal if they were unable to summon assistance. Thus, he took William, Sally's eldest boy, and Mike, Charlie's second son with him to Grand Central. Both boys were nine years old and easily capable of driving the buggy. William had two elder sisters, and Mike was overshadowed by Greg, who was clearly favoured by their mother. Wolf judged that the lads needed more time free of women.

They stopped at Jeremiah Hopkins' ranch. He and Wolf had become good friends, two of the most successful survivors on the planet. Jeremiah was delighted with the deer that he had obtained from Anna.

"When are you going to let me have the services of that young man Greg again?" he asked Wolf.

"Soon," replied Wolf. "We are starting up some new ranches. We should be done in about three weeks. We hope to have enough food to get everybody who is still here through the next monsoon. That will confirm that we have put the last year behind us."

"Amen to that," agreed Jeremiah. Successful farmers like himself had not really had to struggle to survive. Nevertheless, he was as aware as anybody of the extreme suffering that had been endured by those who had failed to recognise the priorities of colonisation.

Wolf reached Colonel Hayes later that day, having gained a good understanding of the general situation on Springfield from his time spent at Ranch 22. Jeremiah's attitude was that looters either worked to pay for their crimes or they were hanged. After three months, those who had buckled down were invited to stay on the condition that they continued to work. Most had learned the new priorities and saw that they were being offered a genuine chance of survival. Nobody died of starvation on Jeremiah's ranch. He allowed no passengers but the food was shared equally. His community supported more than two hundred people and included enough men to keep trouble at bay. That was reality.

Colonel Hayes knew that Ranch 22 and Rhino Hill were two of very few success stories. Back at the beginning of E2P, one of the central themes had been the minimum viable population. Lisa Ford, a professor at Caltech and the population expert on the original project, had stated that one hundred and eighty was the critical threshold for survival. Jeremiah Hopkins was proving her correct. The many tiny communities that had simply vanished had proved her correct. Rhino

Hill, even with its tenants, was only about halfway there. It did not mean that Lisa had been wrong, just that the trend could be bucked if the colonists were chosen with incredible care. Also, all four women would admit that they had been amazingly lucky. Their hard work could easily have been to no avail.

There was not much to see in what Hayes called his HQ. There was still the huge display on one wall, now marked by daubs of fresh paint where it had been confirmed that settlers were no longer in residence. Outside, Grand Central was rapidly being reoccupied by weeds. Across by the coast, the population of Newhaven had peaked at over five thousand. Now, it was probably no more than a thousand, although Hayes believed that many people had spread out into the countryside to concentrate on farming. He confirmed that the professor was on his way before asking Wolf what was going on.

Wolf waited for Hayes to close the office door before he began. "I think we've found a way of making contact with the Earth," he said quietly. "I don't want to sound too optimistic or raise any false hopes." Hayes nodded vigorously in agreement and Wolf continued. "I thought we should get an expert opinion. I knew Mark Richards back on the Earth 2 Project. There's nobody better able than him to make a sensible assessment."

"When we spoke on the phone, you asked me about Mesquite," Hayes said, staring Wolf in the eye.

"A few days ago I saw a sign saying I was a dozen miles from the place," Wolf confirmed. Hayes was dumbstruck. "Don't ask me how. After all the difficulties on Springfield, I just want to make sure that we get this thing right."

Mark Richards arrived before lunch the next day. He was wearing glasses, his hair was thinner, and he had lost weight, but he still had his cheerful smile. He

128

recognised Wolf immediately and put out his hand. "What brings the survival expert to our neck of the woods?" he asked. Each had the greatest respect for the other. Wolf repeated what he knew. Hayes got out his maps. There were two places called Mesquite. One appeared to be a subdistrict of Dallas, an urban sprawl. The other was an isolated dot in Nevada, almost on a straight line between Nellis and Ely. Mark smiled.

The three men agreed to set off that afternoon. They could reach Halfway House before nightfall and be at the chamber the following morning. Wolf made phone calls to inform people of his plans. He wanted a buggy full of rations at Halfway House and warned Greg that he might have to set up a regular shuttle to the chamber. Hayes had very few arrangements to make before he was able to depart. Wolf led them south and west through Migration Gap. Hayes drove a second buggy with Mark, who remained deep in thought for the entire journey.

Halfway House was busy that evening. Charlie proudly introduced Greg as their supply manager and then showed the new visitors what had been achieved: the well, two corridors into the mountain, and six rooms for storage and accommodation. "We need about another week in here and then we will start outside. We should get a good harvest before the next monsoon." She had no doubt what her priorities were. Colonel Hayes would have been immensely impressed if this were all that he had come to look at. The fact that it was merely a sideshow to the main event made it even more amazing.

Mark still had little to say. He had never doubted that the failure of the escalator had been caused by something at Ely, so much so that he had given up thinking about it. Now, his mind was filled by what Wolf had described. Mark wondered how the Wright brothers would have felt if they had been able to take a flight on a 747. That aircraft was longer than their first powered flight near Kitty Hawk in North Carolina.

Mark had no illusions. After listening to a description of the chamber, he knew that his doorway had been no more sophisticated than the first contraption built by Orville and Wilbur Wright. All three of them had built machines that worked without really knowing how or why they worked. Now, he was on his way to visit the Wrights' equivalent of a 747. How much of it would he be able to understand, he wondered.

Mark thought back to the start of E2P. He had been there when the young women had been recruited. Now, it seemed that two of them had found a way back to the Earth. That struck the scientist as being an unlikely coincidence. The women had been chosen for their ability to bear children, not because they knew anything about science. Since the construction of the escalator, he had lived in a generally quiet and very contented retirement. Could he come out of retirement, he wondered. Was his brain still as sharp as it had once been or was he just going to make a fool of himself? He never bothered to think what might be happening on the Earth.

Sally and Anna had been down to the river to bathe. Their temporary home was clean and tidy when Wolf and the others arrived. Mark recognised the women and complimented them on how well they looked. Wolf took him and the colonel for a look round the chamber while Daniel greeted Anna and Sally hugged William and Mike. There was not much to see. Everybody was soon sitting round in a circle while the two women explained what they had discovered. They went outside and Sally asked Tom to close the Springfield end. The circular opening was silently replaced by what looked and felt like unbroken hillside. She asked Tom to open the chamber. They went back inside. Then she asked Tom to open the Earth end. She and Anna walked instinctively to the left as the gravity shifted. Then they led the others out into what appeared to be a cloudy afternoon. A sun was in the west. On Springfield, the sun had been overhead and the sky had been clear. The men looked across the valley to a dense, fir forest. On Springfield, there had been no valley and no dense forest. Wolf pointed to his right. "Mesquite is about twenty miles in that direction," he said quietly.

Mark indicated that they should go back into the chamber. He had already figured out the reason for the circular cross-section. It was to allow travellers to adjust quickly to the gravitational shift. He guessed that the two portals were precisely vertical. He had no doubt that he had just visited the Earth. He had been unable to detect any wobble or vibration in the surface of the chamber while the opening and closing operations had taken place. He was sure that his doorway at Ely had never been that steady. He reminded himself that he had never solved the other half of the problem, which was to create a fixed point of arrival on the other side of his doorway. He guessed that the guy in charge of this machine actually understood what was going on. He was too impressed to be frightened.

Mark did not feel guilty that the women had been stranded on this planet for eight years before he had figured out a way of rescuing them. Indeed, he knew that only one had wanted to leave and he was sure that the others were better off than they would have been if they had stayed on the Earth. He was therefore able to chat in a fairly relaxed fashion with Anna and Sally. He began to realise that he had probably underestimated all the women.

Anna and Sally were not highly educated but they

were not stupid. They called what had been found a chamber. Some people had described Mark's doorway as a tunnel. They were just words, interpretations based on individual experiences. For him, 'chamber' meant something neat, pointing to construction more than to a natural cavern or an accidental fall of rock. He liked that word.

Mark thought that the radio communication sounded slightly strange. He was no expert on language but the reported conversation sounded . . . He struggled to think of the best description. 'Simplistic' didn't really hit the button. Then it struck him. Sally was describing a translation into her language by somebody or something not entirely familiar with the vocabulary. When she added that Tom had been able to link into the Springfield radio net he suddenly realised that the communication might stretch well beyond the chamber, well beyond the planet perhaps, but he decided to say nothing.

"Okay," Mark said to the others after Sally had stopped talking. "I think I should talk to Tom, if nobody minds."

"You just click your phone," Sally advised him. He did so but nothing happened. She clicked hers and Tom responded almost immediately. "Professor Richards would like to speak with you," she said.

"Do you wish his name added to the list?" Tom replied. Sally recalled the fuss there had been allowing Wolf to take a buggy through the chamber. She assumed that Tom was merely being officious, something she had not experienced since she had left Nellis. She confirmed that Tom should follow instructions from Mark and Wolf as if it were her speaking.

Mark had an extremely productive conversation with Tom. The professor liked the idea of transforming, or bending, dimensions so that they were aligned with each other at the node. He formed the impression that the chamber might not actually be on Springfield or on the Earth but somewhere in between, maybe in the bubble that Tom liked talking about. That might explain why the surface was so smooth and featureless, he thought. He recalled that Pete Lopez had suggested that there might have to be something like the Void merely to provide a boundary between the universes, although he was glad to move on quickly from what he regarded as an extremely alarming subject.

Mark glanced around the chamber, telling himself that it was just a very sophisticated version of his doorway, which had also been cylindrical in shape. As the conversation progressed, it became clear that Tom had to be some sort of machine. The translator had chosen the name in order to encourage what it called the biologicals to regard him as one of them. Mark suspected that the translator was just a specialised part of Tom, although he made no comment in that regard. Before he ended the conversation, Mark used the frequency employed by the cellphone network to confirm that Tom had correctly calculated the units of length, time, and mass that humans employed in their calculations. Then he thanked Tom for their exchange and went back to the others.

Mark confirmed to the others that they were dealing with a highly intelligent doorway. It would allow them to move between universes without the need for any escalator. "But this looks completely different," Colonel Hayes said, not really sure what to make of what he was hearing. "You built a doorway. This thing . . ." He ran out of words. Mark looked round again.

"Remember, we had to put an airlock round the doorway at Ely," he said. "That was not very different to what we have here. The two end walls open and

133

close in a manner that is very similar to an airlock. We actually have something that might be almost identical."

There was much that began to make sense to Mark. Tom's node was a stable point where two worlds in two different universes met. Nellis and Ely had been close enough to the node to construct doorways that could be fixed at one end but not both. They had merely been lucky guesses. Tom didn't guess. He had measuring devices and mathematical algorithms that gave him a precise solution. When Hayes interrupted to say that he needed to make contact with the authorities, Mark showed no interest in leaving the chamber. Instead, he insisted that they would need to have more information if they wanted to be taken seriously and Wolf agreed. He remembered the battle there had been to keep E2P alive after the young women had gone missing.

Wolf tried to think what year it would be on the Earth. He reckoned it could be 2028, an election year, a year of turmoil where people would be interested only in making political capital out of the situation regarding Springfield. Wolf did not think of himself as particularly intelligent, nowhere near as bright as Mark, but he felt sure that Tom had to be presented as something good. Springfield, with its recent troubles, would not cut the mustard. "You have to be able to take a positive message to your boss," he warned the colonel, already assuming that Hayes would feel compelled to make a report to somebody on the Earth. "Otherwise, you'll be locked up as insane and this place will be embedded in concrete."

Mark had another long chat with Tom, this time making notes as they went along. Then he sat down to update his friends. "I believe that Tom's arrival here was completely random," he said. Already, he preferred to use the name given by the machine as shorthand for what he guessed was actually a complex assembly of components, perhaps even several entirely separate machines. Like Wolf, he was already thinking about how the chamber could best be presented to the population at large. "Think of a situation where a stricken ship or aircraft has struggled to make a landing. Also, I am fairly sure that his outfit operates along commercial lines, although I cannot understand the sort of currency they use." He paused there because he did not wish to emphasise that they were dealing with machines.

"Because Tom arrived here under emergency conditions, there is no charge for us using the chamber," Mark confirmed. "It sounds as if he has sent some sort of communications team to search for a way of getting back to his base. He says there is what he calls a grid of thousands of these chambers. His team has to find a chain of nodes back to the grid and then rig up temporary chambers. He estimates that it might take ten years. Until then, we can make our own agreements with him. Some sort of standard agreement comes into force if and when Springfield gets linked up to the grid, a bit like the UN Charter, I guess."

"Why does Tom seem to be acting as if he prefers Springfield to the Earth?" Wolf asked, trying to anticipate the suspicions that might be raised by the authorities back on Earth.

"Because the expedition that he sent to search for the grid set off from a node that is located on the other side of Springfield," Mark replied confidently. "A bit like Colonel Hayes here, Tom can't be paid until he makes contact with his boss.

"Where does that leave us?" Colonel Hayes didn't feel that they were making progress.

"It's the grid that drives Tom's people," Mark stated. "To them, a chunk of the grid is like a continent to us. A single, isolated node is like a tiny island without any fresh water supply, not worth bothering with. We should be grateful that we can have contact with the Earth. If Tom's assessment is correct, it will be years before we need to concern ourselves with anything else." Mark's thinking did not extend beyond the amazing design of this one chamber. He never considered what communication with the rest of the grid might mean.

Colonel Hayes took heart from what sounded like comforting words from the scientist. "So what can Tom do?" Hayes was hoping that the technology that had created the chamber could do other things that might have a more obvious benefit.

"Well, Tom says he needs a range of raw materials for construction. He can convert areas that he has mined into plots for growing crops," Mark suggested.

"We should ask him for a demo," Wolf said quickly. "If that is successful, it would definitely be something positive," Wolf was delighted that Mark seemed to be thinking about practical matters at last.

Tom said that he would have something to show them within a month. Colonel Hayes agreed that he could wait that long before involving anybody else. He wanted to be absolutely sure about whatever he reported to his bosses and feeding Springfield was still a priority. Mark said he would like to set up residence close to the chamber. That reminded Wolf of the matter that he wanted to confirm with Hayes, the ownership of the land around the chamber. "Sorry, Wolf," the colonel said firmly. "It won't wash. It has to belong to Springfield. For a start, you are still drawing a military pension. If it belonged to you, Uncle Sam would find a way of confiscating it."

Wolf did not want an argument, not yet, anyway. "I know you found the chamber and I know you are not a greedy man, just concerned about your kids' future," Hayes continued. "What if I say you can have a share of the crops that Tom has said he will produce?" Wolf shrugged his shoulders, realising that he had been very wise to register ranches that effectively controlled movement through Migration Gap. He decided that he would be better talking directly with Tom and he made a mental note to keep Hayes' name off Tom's access list. He recalled that he had about twenty ounces of pure gold waiting to trade. What would that fetch on the Earth, he wondered. Probably a lot more than on Springfield, he told himself.

Colonel Hayes returned to Grand Central to think about preparing a brief for his bosses back on Earth. Mark Richards continued to try to learn more about the physics of the transforming process. Sally and Anna chose to remain near the chamber. Crop planting began at Halfway House.

Tom had agreed that what he called grunts would start work immediately. About a dozen machines could be seen on the hillside, grading patches of ground into terraces. Each grunt looked like a grey slug and was about the size of a buggy. They worked almost continuously, emitting a low-pitched growl while they did so. After a week, what they had planted looked like some sort of cactus. Within the thirty days that Tom had stated, they produced sweet, yellow fruit about the size of figs.

As befits a story about alternative worlds, there are alternative endings. One begins on the next page. The other commences on page 248.

PART 2A

Chapter 11A

A man stood silhouetted against the failed gateway. Archie Rattigan, approached him briskly. Since the loss of contact with Earth, he had sweated in his office in case anyone working around him managed to stumble across any details of the hushed-up materials he'd quietly shipped to Springfield. Thankfully, his meticulous efforts in concealing his dealings had been so thorough that as of yet, at least, they had not been noticed. As the months had passed and Springfield had begun to fall into social unrest, it appeared that the investigations were pushed into the background as the attempt to restore communications with the Earth became more and more important. He had quietly encouraged that shift in priorities. So far, he was not considered a suspect in the loss of contact with the home planet. So far, he seemed to be quietly getting away with it.

A brief gust of wind rattled around Archie's body as he approached the now defunct gateway, out here in the vast isolation known as No-Man's-Land, away from anyone who may have noticed anything untoward. At times, he feared that his destruction of the doorway across the reaches of space would be discovered, sooner or later, yet that calamity was still waiting to be explained by anyone other than himself or his partner. At one time, he had believed that the gateway symbolised great wealth and prosperity but now the secret, failed project stood dormant and useless, the skeleton of an idea that at one time had promised him so very much.

"What do you want?" Archie asked arrogantly as he approached the shadowy figure still stood there investigating the gateway. "I've got better things to do with my time than waste it out here talking to you." He watched as the shadow turned and took the form of Ricky Marlow, the man who had proposed the once amazing idea to him and which had subsequently backfired so spectacularly. Archie saw the look of seriousness and concern upon his face and frowned, instantly recognising that there was a problem, another one. In fact, Ricky now appeared to have aged considerably since their last meeting, however many days or months ago it had been.

"Archie," Ricky replied hastily. The tone of his voice unnerved Archie slightly. "We have a problem. A huge, huge problem."

Archie slowly closed his eyes and sighed. "What is it? What now?" he asked, approaching his former colleague across the barren ground. "With this?" he asked, nodding towards the cracked plinth. Ricky looked at him and nodded slowly. "Ricky," Archie sighed with great frustration, "the damn thing blew back and closed the link with Earth. What can be worse than losing all chance of new equipment, or even spares for the little that we have?"

Archie began pacing toward the gate, looking with great condemnation toward the dysfunctional gateway. "I am sure Uncle Sam's finest communications specialists and technological whiz-kids are working to re-establish connections with us, and they're having one hell of a time in doing it. They've been unable to do it since this blew. How long ago was that? A year?" he openly mocked his one-time partner.

"Give or take," Ricky replied sheepishly.

"If not longer," Archie corrected him. "What type of problem can this lump of concrete possibly pose to

Springfield or to the Earth?"

At that very instant, a surge of energy spat vibrantly from where the gateway had emerged from the hillside, causing Archie to jump back. Electricity sparked momentarily, as if arcing between tesla coils, before vanishing in random fits of cracks and flashes. "My God, what was that? What just happened?" Archie snapped, looking to Ricky for an immediate answer.

"That's what I'm trying to tell you," Ricky began, his face now contorting as if he were about to cry. "It's becoming activated." Archie looked at him. A flutter of fear surged through his body.

"How can it be activated? It has no power?"

"You saw it!" Ricky snapped quietly as he hurried over to the stout man. "Obviously it's not being activated at our end, but by someone else!"

"Someone else? Who? Ricky, what the hell is happening here? What do you know that you are not telling me?"

Ricky grabbed hold of Archie's shoulders tightly and shook him none too gently as he spoke. "Think about it, Archie, will you, just think? How many of these gateways might there be across our galaxy? Across the entire universe?"

"Could be hundreds . . ." Archie was distracted momentarily by that thought.

"That's right," Ricky interrupted. "Hundreds of them, scattered all throughout the reaches of space and upon planets we know nothing about. Just because we don't have the ability to bring this gateway back online here on Springfield, it doesn't mean that no one else has the ability to establish a connection from their location and reboot the gateway."

"You mean Earth?" Archie questioned, still unsure as to exactly what Ricky was raving about out here in the wilderness. He didn't think Earth would be a threat, more like a bonus. Ricky lowered his head and sighed.

"You don't get it, do you?" he began, releasing his hold of Archie. "If it was Uncle Sam that burst through there, we'd be screwed. They'd know about the materials we smuggled up here and sooner or later, they would figure out what had happened and who had done it."

"No they won't Ricky," Archie interrupted, pushed by his guilt to convince himself that he was in the clear, although, strictly speaking, he knew he was still on the military payroll. "Those materials are untraceable to us, or to anyone up here," he said firmly. And they had been, so far. They had ordered very little in the way of spare equipment, something that had very nearly prevented them from completing their task, but all of that was located in a storage unit near to his workplace, where he could keep a very close eye on it. He believed he had also been very smart. He'd managed to have four cases of PST pulse grenades smuggled onto Springfield. If the situation did turn pear-shaped, he could destroy everything with a few of those grenades. One pull of a pin and all the evidence vanished.

"But that's not the worst case," Ricky insisted quietly, alarmed by his friend's naivety. Lightning jolted once more within the hillside, causing both men to jump.

"Then what the hell is?" Archie snapped, unsettled by the discharge. Ricky stared at him for a brief moment.

"It's not Earth attempting to come through." Archie stared at Ricky with wide eyes. The wind ruffled their clothing as it gusted by.

"What?" Archie whispered in shocked amazement.

"Here," Ricky replied, gesturing with a nod to move closer to the crumbling hillside. Archie followed him in silence as they took a couple of paces closer. Ricky squatted down near the rent and pointed to a strange object lying on the ground. "Look," he said, with horror in his voice. Archie forced himself to look more closely at the rubble ahead of his feet.

"My God," he whispered in disbelief, clenching a fist and placing it gently over his mouth. His heart hammered inside his chest. "What do you think it is?" Ricky returned his gaze to the ground and shook his head gently. His bottom lip trembled and his breathing became erratic.

"I don't know for sure," Ricky whispered, his voice all but lost to anxiety. The dreadful truth was that he didn't know at all. "An arm, maybe?" He knew he was guessing. Before him lay an appendage unlike any he had ever seen back on Earth or up here on Springfield. His best assessment was that it might have been the arm of some large creature, severed clean just above a joint which the two onlookers took to be the elbow. The forearm was bumped and contorted, the skin as smooth as the bark of beech trees on Earth. Three long, skeletal-like fingers emerged from the limb, all closed and lifeless. It was an appendage from a living creature, of that they had no doubt. It was the solid mass of brown looking bone that created an image in Archie's mind of something primitive.

"Why is it there? What happened to it?" Archie asked, viewing the dismembered body part from a safer distance than Ricky.

"The gateway," Ricky replied tersely, though sounding much more certain of himself this time. "If this, whatever it was, was in the process of coming through, I guess the gateway closing would chop anything caught in the way clean off." He turned back to look directly at Archie. "There's something out there, somewhere trying to get across here to Springfield. And judging by this, it's like no other life form we've ever encountered since we settled here."

"What have we done?" Archie whispered, his gaze still firmly upon the lifeless limb resting on the ground.

"We have to do something, and quickly, before they manage to open this gate fully. If that happens, there's no saying what the hell will come through here," Ricky advised his senior counterpart.

"What do you want me to do?" Archie snapped, more from fear than anger. He had no idea how to deal with something like this, an incident far beyond the scale of what he was used to dealing with back behind his desk. The wind gusted once more and stirred their garments around them.

"I don't care what happens, Archie. You have to call in your people to destroy this entire section of hillside. We don't have the time or the resources to do it by ourselves."

"Are you insane?" Archie bellowed above the gale. His sense of self-preservation meant that his boss still appeared to be a more immediate threat than what he had just seen. "That's a certain prison term for both of us, probably life!" Ricky's response was to shake his head defiantly. He rose to his feet.

"I honestly don't care what happens to us. We knew of the risk we ran when we decided to do this. I'd much rather be sitting in a prison cell either up here or back on Earth, than see some creatures like this heading towards me. That arm does not look at all friendly. I'd say it's definitely carnivorous, probably as bad as the dinosaurs."

"Well I wouldn't," Archie snapped back, his frustration with his partner clear. He turned away in disbelief. The shattered gateway crackled once more and electrical discharges rippled across the broken area of hillside. He turned back and pointed a finger at Ricky. "No one knows it was us and no one should

144

even be able to suspect us. Everything's been hidden so well that the investigations have turned from a whodunit to a simple communication re-establishment. We can deal with anything that pokes its ugly little head through there. We just need to sit this out and see what happens. Nothing may ever come of it. The force it blew with may have caused enough damage to restrict it to this random, flickering light show. There's nothing more than electrical surges in there. That arm proves it's unstable."

"At some point it opened long enough for a creature of some kind to get half an arm through," Ricky insisted. "Sooner or later, it's going to become more stable, and then we're into a serious world of hurt."

"Damn it, Ricky! Have you seen those Enforcers roaming around Newhaven and Grand Central? Hayes is setting up a hard, military presence here on Springfield to stamp on the gangs that are coming out of Newhaven. His militia is armed to the teeth with the supplies Uncle Sam sent when the gateway was first established, in case a situation like this should arise. Let them deal with it." It was knowledge of that secret reserve of weaponry that had persuaded Archie to establish his own little cache.

"Yes, but they are soldiers who are good at fighting other humans," Ricky shrilled, pointing to the arm lying on the ground next to him. "There's no telling what that belonged to!" Archie had always been a man who took the easy solution. He saw that Ricky was not going to give way; there was not really any choice other than to destroy this opening somehow. He had hoped that the gate would be repairable and bring him the wealth that Ricky had promised but it now seemed that it represented an unknown threat that had to be kept at bay. He had never imagined Ricky as a snitch, a man who would run to the authorities and blab.

Momentarily, he considered killing Ricky, to keep him quiet, but he guessed that in itself could pose more problems than it solved. Too many dodgy people knew Ricky and it would be almost impossible to keep them quiet. At least if he neutralised the gate with a pulse grenade, the electrical surges would stop, Archie told himself.

The gateway exploded with far more violence than merely the force of the grenade. Both men were blown through the air by the blast. The ground quaked as though a volcano had erupted beneath them. Lightning crackled thunderously as it emerged from the gate in bright shafts of white light. The stabbing forks spat wildly out into the air around the structure and leapt high up into the rolling clouds. Something reached into the sky and disappeared with erratic flashes of white. Ricky pushed himself upright. A horrendous, high pitched scream boomed from the lightning, unlike anything he had ever heard before. Archie cried out as a huge shadow loomed from the light. It emerged from the structure and lay still momentarily, surrounded by the brilliant light flowing from the gateway. A huge, hand-shaped claw rose from the gateway. A thunderous roar bellowed, making the ground tremble beneath them. The hand closed and smashed into the ground, lofting debris high up into the air. "We're too late," Ricky whimpered solemnly to himself, "we're too damn late."

Daniel awoke wearily from his accommodation within Halfway House. The project he had been working on in something of a panic was finally approaching completion. Temporary rooms and a mess hall had been established for everyone working on the site; more comfortable surroundings meant more rapid progress. Colonel Hayes had embraced the way of life that had been established on Rhino Hill and had been very much surprised by the empowerment of all the people who lived in that area. So much so, in fact, that he had contacted Grand Central to recruit help for several more projects like Halfway House. With the civil unrest since the loss of contact with Earth flaring up again, he wanted to make sure that those people who had no need to stay within the larger communities had an excuse to leave, and many had volunteered to assist as necessary. Of course, the peaceful way of life that Wolf and the others had come to expect was now disrupted, and the population of Springfield would probably be more aware of Halfway House's existence, but the chances were that it would be treated as one of the many farms on Springfield and was less likely to generate any specific interest once the excavations were complete.

The hangover sealed Daniel's eyes for a moment or so longer, until his consciousness kicked in fully and his eyelids burst open to take in his immediate surroundings. Last night, Wolf had produced a bottle of an unnamed, evil brew - something he said he had been saving for a special occasion - and they had celebrated the delightful news of impending fatherhood. Daniel could not remember how the evening had ended. Even through his headache, however, he could feel the glow that the thought of a little Daniel gave him. He guessed he had been dead to the world for many hours. Slowly, he realised that Halfway House was quiet, too quiet. There was no sound of the frantic activity that usually filled every minute. In fact, it was as silent as the grave.

Daniel wandered through the corridors toward the newly constructed mess hall. He was usually one of the first to arrive, ready for work, but today, he was alone. There should have been volunteers loitering around and other workers prepping for the new day. He assumed he was even later than he had thought and everybody was already at work. Then, as his head cleared, he began to focus on the silence. Underneath his feet he felt a gentle rumble reverberate throughout the skeleton of the building. It reminded him of the aftershocks of thunder that he had experienced from time to time back on the Earth. He assumed that everybody had been called away to begin some fresh excavation work. A dull, clicking thud echoed from further away. He frowned. It sounded like it was coming from outside the building, from across the landscape in the distance somewhere. He reached the double doors leading to the hall and passed quickly inside.

Most of the few tables and steel chairs had been upturned. Mugs, cutlery, and the metal trays for serving food were strewn across the tiled floor. The long, generic lights hung from the ceiling. Some of their supports had been broken allowing them to hang vertically from one strand and down to within touching distance. Some flickered as they attempted to bring their bulbs to life, some crackled as electricity passed into the fittings, its power cut from the bulbs themselves. Foods and liquids were plastered across the walls and spilled untidily upon the shining floor. Papers and clipboards that belonged to workers frequenting the mess hall rested motionlessly across various surfaces.

Daniel's mind harked back to the many news reports he'd seen covering conflicts and various documentaries depicting Earth's war-torn past. It immediately looked to him like a rogue missile had crashed through the building and exploded in there. He stood there in shock, unable to process what was going on around him. What had happened? Where were the remaining workers? Anxiety forced his mind to clear. If something unusual had happened in the last few hours, he had to admit that he would have been unlikely to hear it. His celebrations had knocked him out.

The ground rumbled again underneath Daniel's feet, now catching his attention immediately. He could no longer convince himself that this was caused by work. He turned and quickly made his way through the carnage to the huge windows overlooking the bland world outside. The day itself was clear but he noticed small pops and lights emanating across to the horizon. He pushed himself as close to the Perspex as possible. The immediate area appeared almost normal, except for the absence of his colleagues.

Halfway House was completely empty. Daniel was on his own. The chaos in which he stood offered no explanation of what was happening. Something was going on out there beyond the Perspex and he had no idea what. With no answers inside the structure, he decided to venture outside and see if any could be found out there.

Chapter 12A

Daniel emerged outside Halfway House and began scouting around for anything that could be found to explain the situation. He knew immediately that he wanted to drop the duty at Halfway and return to the chamber because Anna was there. If there was some kind of situation happening on Springfield then returning to Earth through the chamber would be a quick and safe route away from any danger. The overwhelming sense of unease he felt slowly grew stronger. The sound of explosions grew louder. The day was clear and offered nothing to restrict the noise ricocheting across the prairie. Daniel was becoming more distracted by what he perceived to be a conflict. The ground rumbled with distant explosions and now, plumes of smoke were slowly rising. Daniel did feel somewhat relieved that the disturbances appeared to be close to the horizon. For a moment he was thankful of the No-Man's-Land in between, the term used by the human settler's for any great, vast, open area with nothing but miles of emptiness. As long as it was empty, he was safe.

Daniel wandered around outside until he found two ant-like buggies which he had never seen before. The machines had been modified, with four seats filling the rear and a widened roll-cage. Extra photovoltaic panels existed on the rear of these aggressive vehicles. They were fitted with the normal huge, wide tyres, which allowed access to all but the most hostile terrain on Springfield. Daniel was attempting to recall having seen them before when a shout from behind stopped him.

"Freeze! Do not move!" Daniel span around. "I said freeze!" The unfriendly voice paused only briefly. Four shadows emerged from cover and closed in on him. A huge, muscle-bound gunman appeared from the front. He was clad in black plated armour that covered his chest and legs. His arms were left exposed and the sleeves of a white tee shirt strained out over his biceps. He wore a black bandana over his head and stared intently at his target. "Put your hands up!" Daniel complied. "Higher," he ordered, gesturing the barrel of his gun upwards. Another man appeared beside Daniel. He was smaller than the aggressor and had full body of armour that offered no entrance to any weapon or bullet. His face was shielded by an orange tinted visor that fitted closely onto a worn helmet. The weapons these guys carried appeared to be assault rifles but none like Daniel had seen before. Both men had utility belts strapped around their waists filled with long, circular objects, probably the clips holstered for their weapons, Daniel decided.

"Who are you?" a voice emerged from behind. Daniel tried to turn.

"He said don't move," the big gunman growled. "Just answer the question!".

"Swift, Daniel, here by order of Colonel Hayes," Daniel explained quickly.

"Registration number?" the voice ordered once more.

Daniel squinted as he attempted to recall his ID. "1 2, 0, err, 6, 4, I think." He had not realised how nervous he felt.

Daniel heard the sound of tapping and bleeping from some sort of hardware beyond his vision. A flutter of bleeps sounded. The explosions continued far away in the distance.

"Swift, Daniel, 12064. Specialist, comms. He checks out," came a different voice.

"Turn around," the other voice ordered. The man in

the helmet nodded once at Daniel in confirmation and gestured for him to turn. Daniel slowly took a few steps and faced the voices who had been conversing behind him. Two more men stood there, their weapons thrown over their shoulders as well as handguns holstered to their thighs, and were both clad in the same armour worn by the others. One was small and of oriental origin, the other, slightly taller soldier was peering down upon the data pad he was holding. Its edges were forged of dark, metallic handles but the information screen contained between the two was completely transparent and projected the written data into an orange font upon its surface.

Daniel could see a black and white picture of himself being studied intently upon the data pad. "According to this, you're still serving?" the taller man asked, his focus still down toward the data pad. Daniel nodded, hoping that things were about to improve. "At ease," the taller man ordered. The guns pointing toward both Daniel lowered in unison. "I am Captain Brookes of the US Marine Corps, based here on Springfield. We are the Bravo team of Enforcers created to keep the peace during this time of unrest. This is Lieutenant Okachi, data, communications and technology specialist," he said, gesturing to the man holding the data pad. Okachi nodded. "You've met Corporal Wyatt," he then added, gesturing to the muscle bound soldier stood at point, "and Private Drake," he said, nodding towards the soldier hidden by the helmet, "and there's one more who you're yet to meet," Brookes informed him.

"Captain, what exactly is happening up here?" Daniel asked. He was still confused about the events unfolding around them.

"Bravo team, this is Echo, do you copy? Over?" an electronic voice emerged from somewhere. All soldiers were wearing an earpiece and speaker that ran from their left ear, except for Drake, who probably had his hidden somewhere in his helmet.

"Echo, this is Bravo. We hear you, over."

"Captain Brookes are you still at Golf seven, five, zero, Alpha, Kilo, over?"

"Affirmative."

"Captain, you have to get the hell out of there! We've got a track on a Screamer, one of the big ones, and it is heading straight at you!"

Brookes didn't waste time querying the message. "You heard him! On the double!" he shouted to his squad. Wyatt was already pushing Daniel forcefully onwards.

"Get...hey, what's going on?" he asked quickly.

"Either you keep up with us or we leave you for the Screamers!" Wyatt warned him as the others dashed towards the buggies.

"Where are you taking me?"

"We'll explain later, just get aboard the vipers."

Daniel slumped down in a seat next to Drake. Okachi jumped in behind. Both vipers juddered into motion. "Forrest, do you copy?" Brookes' voice echoed over the comms system.

"I copy, Sir. Get me the hell out of here! The ground's rumbling like there's a freight-train approaching!"

"Got it. We're heading to you now."

"Copy. Forrest out."

Wyatt took the lead as the vipers bounced and lurched over the ground, heading into Migration Gap. The structure of Halfway House shrank behind them. Daniel turned and watched it sink away into the distance, wondering if it would ever be fully operational. Okachi bleeped and tapped in the rear seat.

"Not good, not good!" the lieutenant called out from

the back. Brookes looked round at his deputy.

"What is it?" he shouted over the comms from the viper they were following.

"I've got a lock on the one heading our way. It's huge and travelling fast!"

"Distance?"

"Approximately two kilometres," Okachi screamed.

"Goddamn! It's like the beginning of an earthquake out here!" Forrest's voice crackled over the comms network.

"There!" Wyatt shouted, noticing a soldier sprinting in from the left.

"This thing is moving like nothing I've ever seen!" Okachi stated as he watched the tracking device on the data pad.

"Over there!" Drake shouted. "Incoming! Six o'clock!"

Daniel looked round and saw huge plumes of dirt and soil explode into the air. Something immense appeared to be surging through the ground towards them. "What is that?" Daniel asked, watching it cascade closer. The question went ignored. The disturbance rippled through the ground. In other circumstances, it might have appeared impressive, graceful even, but Daniel knew it could only represent a deadly force. Forrest sprinted towards the first viper. The wave of broken soil gained on their position. The vehicles began rocking as the ground broke up beneath them. Daniel held onto the roll cage. The wave slowed and the quaking dropped to a small tremor.

"It's getting ready to attack!" Okachi screamed.

"Copy! Forrest, get your ass in here now!" Brookes ordered.

The viper ahead of them slowed. Forrest jumped into the rear seats. The ground exploded as a huge creature launched itself into the air. The vipers rumbled as it screamed horrendously, a deep and primitive sound. The long, limbless body before them must have pushed some eighty feet in length as it soared through the air for its attack. Its head resembled an open palm with five, ten-foot plus claws replacing fingers. A huge, circular opening inside the palm was lined with thousands of razor sharp teeth, much like those of a shark. Daniel pushed himself down in the seat. The claws on the creature's head closed as it crashed down into the ground, piercing the soil and thundering deep beneath the surface once again. The impact shook the vipers as they sped away.

"Where did it go?" Brookes asked Okachi over the comms.

"I got it!" the lieutenant replied. "It's travelling nearly fifty feet below us, about thirty feet behind!"

"Step on it!" Brookes shouted. Okachi studied the data pad as the creature followed behind them.

"It's tracking us!" he shouted. The shape on the pad tailed them closely.

"Affirmative. Weapons live. Shoot to kill."

"Roger," Drake's voice echoed in reply. He turned to Daniel. "Take the wheel," he ordered. "It's just like a normal buggy but more powerful."

Daniel had no time to question the order. Drake took hold of the roll cage bar above him and pulled himself to his feet. The viper veered to the right and Daniel lunged over quickly to take the wheel. Drake swung his right leg around the side bar and moved along the outside of the viper. Daniel jumped over into the driver's seat and took control. From the viper ahead, he saw Brookes and Forrest rise within the confines of the roll cage. Drake un-holstered the rifle on his shoulder.

"It's gaining! It's going for another attack!" Okachi warned.

"Roger! Brace yourselves! Fire at will!" Brookes

ordered. The chasing wave of earth subsided once more.

"Depth ten feet…twenty feet…thirty feet. It's going all out!" Okachi screamed as he monitored the creature's progress. Daniel concentrated on the open area around him. "Tracking at thirty feet."

"It's going to attack!" Wyatt's voice crackled through their earpieces.

"Thirty feet…thirty feet…thirty feet…getting closer…twenty-five! Twenty! Here it comes!"

Terror surged through Daniel as he struggled to keep the viper away from the rocky walls of the gap. At least here, he thought, the beast could only attack from the rear. If they had gone west they would have been vulnerable to attack from every direction. Okachi holstered the pad to his thigh and drew his rifle. "Left quarter!" he shouted. Drake turned slightly. The ground began to shake with the approaching colossus. "Get ready!" Okachi screamed. The ground exploded as the creature launched itself once more from the ground and up into the sky. Soil and rocks rained down violently on top of them, falling from the huge body leaping through the air. Daniel's ears filled with the sound of the creature's roar and the rapid firing of the rifles. He closed his eyes momentarily as the debris cascaded down all around him. The viper shook as the creature dove into the ground, missing them only by a few feet, it seemed.

Okachi reached down to his pad once more. "It's underneath us! Travelling fast!"

"Roger! Track its movement!" Brookes ordered unnecessarily. Okachi watched the blip on the screen speed beneath them towards the viper out in front.

"It's bypassed us now and is heading for you!" he warned the soldiers ahead. The ground erupted between the vipers. The huge body seemed to defy gravity, swaying violently in the air above the ruptured surface. Daniel recognised the danger and jammed hard left on the steering wheel, sending the viper slithering sideways on two wheels. His passengers crashed into each other but the creature slammed down onto the ground almost where it had emerged, narrowly missing both vehicles. The ground exploded around them with the ferocity of the attack.

Daniel scraped his viper along the rocky wall of the gap. The sound of rifle fire mingled with the screech of tortured metal and the creature's roar as he chased the leading viper. "Clever bastard! Tried to separate us!" Drake stated as they watched it withdraw into the crater it had created.

"Okachi? Status?" Brookes requested over the comms network. Okachi took a quick glance around. Drake gave him a thumbs-up.

"Confirm no injuries." He took a quick look at the pad and sighed. "It's coming to attack again!"

"Roger! This time let's finish it!" Brookes ordered.

"Copy that!" Drake replied. Daniel sighed. Please let this be over, he pleaded to himself.

"Tracking once more at thirty feet...thirty feet...twenty-five! Here we go!" Okachi holstered the pad to his thigh once again. The huge, worm-like body exploded from the ground yet again and screamed as it sailed through the open air. The rifles engaged around Daniel whilst he pushed the viper as fast as it would allow. The creature let out a shocked roar and closed its five claws as it submerged back into the ground. The vipers shook once more with the vibrations but suddenly, the colossus vanished.

Okachi grabbed the pad from its holster yet again. "Status?" Brookes queried from the other viper. Okachi watched the blip on the screen that represented the creature and gave a grateful sigh.

"It's in retreat. Dropping thirty feet...sixty feet...eighty feet..."

"Scale out and locate any teams in this area," Brookes ordered. Okachi prodded the data pad.

"Nothing, we're on our own out here," he replied. "The creature is diving, looks like we injured it."

"Copy that. Good work everybody." Brookes sounded as relieved as every member of his team, glad to know that they had all survived without anything worse than a few bumps and bruises. He called Echo several times but failed to get any reply. "Okay," he said to his team. "Let's slow down while we figure out what we do next."

Daniel sighed as he regained his composure and took more careful control of the viper. The exchange must have lasted for considerably longer than he had realised. They had raced through most of Migration Gap. Travelling in the vipers, Rhino Hill was probably less than an hour away. "There's civilisation over there," he shouted to his passengers, pointing with a free hand towards the hill he called home.

"How do you know that?" Okachi asked.

"I live there," he said factually. After a brief discussion between Brookes and Okachi, the captain gave the order to head for the first settlement that had been established on the planet.

After the fearsome engagement with what had been called a Screamer, Daniel was slow to notice the lack of activity around Rhino Hill. He stopped his viper just below the platform that encircled what had become his home since the failure of the escalator. The company of soldiers waited while he quickly looked round, searching for any signs of life. He asked the captain to send men in the vipers to check the nearby hills. This had been the most successful community on Springfield since the escalator had disappeared but it was now empty. His friends and their animals had all disappeared. He was glad that Anna was at the chamber, hopefully completely separate from whatever disaster had befallen Rhino Hill.

Daniel slowly recognised that there must have been a disaster. When he had left Rhino Hill, it had been full of people. The community had been modest in number compared with some other settlements but it had been guided by the original colonists, who knew Springfield better than any of the more recent arrivals. He was relieved that Anna and Sally were at the chamber and that Wolf was keeping them supplied from Halfway House. Then Daniel remembered the state that Halfway House had been in when he had left it only a few hours earlier. That was when the shock hit him. In less than a day, Springfield had changed from being a tranquil haven of simplicity into a dangerous place. If Rhino Hill was not safe, then where was? He was certain that no other human settlement could be less vulnerable.

"Drake, Wyatt. Recon the area," Captain Brookes ordered. As soon as he had seen the sophisticated burrows leading deep into the hillside, he had realised that these people should have been more secure than any living on the surface of the planet.

"Sir," came the obedient reply of both his soldiers.

"Forrest, perch yourself up there, cover us for the time being," Brookes added, pointing to the hillside behind him.

"On my way," Forrest replied before grasping his rifle and scrambling for a vantage point. He was the unit sharpshooter and had saved many a comrade in previous missions with his accurate covering fire.

"Okachi, assist our engineer in there," Captain Brookes ordered the communications and technology specialist. "We need to find these people." Okachi nodded at his orders and un-holstered the data pad from his thigh. After a few taps of the transparent screen he entered the tunnel that Daniel had taken.

"Hey, wait up" Okachi called out. Daniel stopped and turned to him. He had been wandering slowly from room to room, determined not to miss a thing. Okachi noticed the look of concern upon his face. "Are you okay?" he asked quietly. Daniel nodded gently.

"Yes, I'm just confused. This place should be full of life. There were so many people here."

Okachi tapped the pad once more. After a few beeps and a soft, whirring sound, bright orange lasers beamed out across the rooms, penetrating even the darkest corners. "It's a scan," Okachi explained as he shone the moving lines around, "it'll find any sign of life." They watched as the fluorescent orange lines broke and rippled over the various surfaces and objects scattered around the gloomy area.

"Have our comms systems been damaged since this started?" Daniel enquired out of professional curiosity. He guessed that with this new alien life-form emerging upon the planet, things could only have gotten worse.

"Yes, all the aerial masts around Grand Central were rendered useless, which left a huge hole in the network," Okachi explained as they searched through the darkness. "Initially, we thought that the STs were attacking our comms but their focus was upon civilised areas instead. We are not sure that they have the intelligence to know what the masts are for. They just seem to enjoy random destruction."

"STs?" Daniel asked as they moved slowly down a long corridor.

"Subterraneans. STs for short. The creature we encountered on our way over here. That was just one of two known species so far."

"Why Subterraneans?"

Okachi watched the orange lasers from his pad

160

ripple and spread across a cargo box and onto the corridor wall. "I'll explain later. Right now, we need to search this place and see if there are any survivors." Daniel's stomach fell slightly when the word 'survivors' echoed quietly through the darkness.

"How are you communicating on your current system?" Daniel then asked, changing the subject quickly.

"The transceivers up here will handle signals on a wide range of frequencies," Okachi explained briefly. "There was always a secure, military backup, separate from the cell phone frequency band, based on infrared. Turns out this is very, very powerful, so it doesn't need nearly as many aerials."

"Bravo, this is Wyatt," came a clear, strong voice through Okachi's comms.

"Copy you Wyatt, you found anything?" Brookes asked. Both men sounded only a foot or two away. Okachi stopped moving and concentrated on what was being said.

"Yes sir, I have," Wyatt replied. Daniel's stomach fell instantly at the tone of his voice. "We've got either an entry or exit crater for one of the Screamers out here."

Brookes responded with a single word. "Damn."

"Screamers?" Daniel asked Okachi.

"The massive slug that we just repelled," Okachi explained. "We call them Screamers."

"Oh no," Daniel whispered hesitantly, now feeling forced to fear the very worst.

"Crater's huge," Wyatt continued in a matter-of-fact tone. "Drops at least fifty feet before disappearing. Steady incline suggests it was planned, not a solitary attack like we just experienced. Maybe allowed the Stumblers out."

"Copy that. Re-group. Bring our guest back

161

immediately, Okachi," Brookes ordered.

"Copy," Okachi confirmed before turning to Daniel. "You heard the captain."

"But..." Daniel was stopped by the sound of a metallic bang reverberating through the edges of the dim corridor. Okachi span in its direction and immediately shot the orange lasers into the area.

"Got a blip. Something's here," Okachi whispered as he studied the data pad.

"Where from?" Daniel asked nervously. Okachi flicked his forehead upwards and raised his brows. "Up there, behind the cargo boxes."

"Hello?" Daniel asked out into the corridor, "anyone there?"

"Daniel?" came a dishevelled voice that he instantly recognised.

"Colonel?" he quickly replied, scurrying over in the direction of the disembodied voice. There, hiding in the darkest recess behind the crates, was Colonel Hayes.

"Captain, do you copy? We have a survivor, over." Okachi said into his comms unit.

"Copy that, Lieutenant. Is assistance required?"

"Hey, do you need any help?" Okachi asked Hayes as Daniel helped him gently to his feet.

"No, I'm okay," Colonel Hayes replied timidly. "Only just, though."

"Negative, Captain," Okachi relayed back. "He appears fine, at least on initial inspection. I'm going to run a background check. Swift says he is Colonel Hayes."

"The colonel? That is great news, Okachi. We need to find out what he knows and pass it on immediately. We'll be waiting by the vipers. Brookes out."

Chapter 13A

Daniel and Okachi walked either side of the colonel, supporting both his arms as they travelled back outside to the main group of Enforcers. Hayes appeared shaken and unsteady but otherwise fine. He was coherent and talkative, and able to respond to Okachi's questions. "Colonel, glad to see you safe," Brookes said, saluting briefly as they emerged into the open. Colonel Hayes nodded slowly in acknowledgement. Daniel assisted him to one of the vipers and sat him down. "Can you tell us what happened here?" Brookes asked.

"Anna? Have you heard from her?" Daniel interrupted, his emotions becoming the better of him. "Is she okay?" Colonel Hayes looked up at him. There was exhaustion etched across his face.

"Honestly Daniel, I don't know," he replied truthfully. Anxiousness surged briefly through Daniel's body. "I thought she was still at the chamber. I cannot recall all those who were here but everybody headed across to the mountains when those things hit us. I was able to hold the creatures back long enough for them to escape. Whether they made it or not, I do not know."

"What did you do?" Okachi asked. "How did you distract them from the people escaping?"

"Lots of noise, banging pipes off of metal surfaces, shouting, that kind of thing. There were many children at risk here. I did what I had to."

"Looks like you did a fine job," Brookes replied, commending the actions of his boss.

"Why did they head for the mountains?" Wyatt asked as he made his way to the viper. Drake had been rummaging through various compartments in the viper and found a canteen of water, which he handed to the colonel. Hayes took a quick sip and looked over at

Brookes.

"We thought the creatures would find it tough going through solid rock," Hayes replied, sighing as he did so. "And I think it was Jessica who said something about caves where Wolf had been prospecting. They were using them to store stuff. She thought they might be able to make it across the mountains to the chamber. We thought it was only about forty miles, although the terrain . . ." He shrugged his shoulders. He told himself that he had done his best.

Brookes frowned. "This chamber sounds significant. How come I don't know about it, Sir?" he asked sharply.

Colonel Hayes responded with a glare as cold and sharp as an arctic breeze. "It's a gateway, a simple passage leading directly back to Earth, far more simple than the escalator."

"What?" Brookes whispered, his tone one of mixed emotions; amazement slightly, but concern predominantly.

"No way?" Wyatt replied softly.

"It's true. A search party from Rhino Hill headed out there not long ago and found something. Mark Richards and I were still in the process of evaluating it. We didn't want people building up false hopes. They even took an ant through there and explored the other side. Seems to be America."

"Shit! This is not good! Not good at all!" Drake's electronic voice phased from the hidden microphone in his armoured helmet.

"Dammit!" Brookes sighed.

"Hey, look! Does anyone mind telling me exactly what's going on?" Daniel interrupted hastily. Although he had been a member of the party that had found the chamber, he was considerably more concerned about the perceived severity of the immediate situation. "You still haven't explained why you raided us over at Halfway House or what exactly is going on across Springfield!" Okachi looked to Brookes. Brookes nodded. Okachi tapped the data pad once more. Orange laser lights beamed out from the hardware and created a holographic image suspended in mid-air. Daniel looked on as an orange sphere took shape and morphed into a realistic depiction of Springfield.

"We are under attack from some sort of alien race," Brookes began, moving across to a large rock as he began his story. He gently sat down on its surface, his armour clattering gently as he did so. "At first we didn't know how, what or why; we still don't know much. We call them Subterraneans or STs for short, because they attack from beneath the ground, as you have already experienced," he said, talking this time directly to Daniel. "There are two classes of ST that we know of so far." He did not sound at all confident that there would not be more. "Okachi can show you on his pad better than I can describe them." He looked back across to Okachi and nodded.

A few blips and taps on the data pad and the holographic interpretation of Springfield morphed into a strange looking creature stood on its hind legs. Its head appeared almost human on first inspection, two eyes and a nose; however, located directly underneath the nostrils, a row of pointed teeth existed, in place of a top lip. This declined and receded to the base the creature's throat, with no lower lip or chin. The creature had shoulders and a body similar to those of a human being, although its arms were notably longer and harboured three claws where, if it had been human, hands would have been found. Its legs resembled those of a velociraptor, in Daniel's eyes. They bent backwards at the knees with a heel midway along its leg where a calf muscle would usually be found. At the heel the leg bent once more and reached down to a flat, clawed foot. It was a disturbing and distressing image to look at. He could instantly see why it may choose to exist underground.

"These we call Stumblers," Okachi explained, "as they stumble and wobble like zombies when they move above ground. Their bodies are extremely tough and durable, with almost no weak points to aim at except the head. We're guessing that billions of years living underneath the surface of their home world has fortified their bodies into a natural type of armour. Shoot at its body and you get nowhere. Shoot it in the head and it usually goes down. Other notable weak spots are its legs. They're both thin and fragile. If you cannot get a head shot, aim for the legs to incapacitate it. That'll buy you some time at least."

"My God," Daniel whispered as the severity of the situation sank in.

Okachi tapped the data pad once more and the Stumbler morphed into the maggot-shaped body of the creature they had repelled. Its hand-like claws were open and poised to attack as they had witnessed. "These we call Screamers," he explained as the virtual interpretation span around slowly in mid-air. "When they attack, they scream out loudly, hence the name. There are small, rocklike spikes across its body that we think assist to propel it above and below the ground. We know that these creatures burrow and create passages underground, allowing the Stumblers to move freely behind them. Reports from Newhaven and Grand Central consistently suggest that the Screamers are targeting our civilisations. Initially, we thought our masts, aerials, et cetera, were their primary targets. Personally, I don't think they are that smart. I think they're simply looking for food. They break things to see what falls out. The Screamers and the Stumblers

166

appear to work together when the latter can keep up, spreading across Springfield and treating humans as a free source of food."

"All units respond." A woman's voice came over the comms network. Okachi killed the hologram.

"This is Bravo, confirm request, over," Brookes responded.

"All units, Echo team has confirmed the destruction of the gateway from where the STs were emerging. Repeat, the gateway is destroyed. Priority orders are as follows: search and rescue for survivors, seek and destroy the STs."

"That's a damn suicide mission!" Wyatt shouted angrily. Brookes looked across to him and gestured with an open palm downwards. Wyatt shook his head and looked away. "Copy. Bravo out," Brookes confirmed. "We've got more important things to worry about than search and destroy," he then told Wyatt. "This other gateway, this chamber thing, if it really is up there, and I don't doubt you Colonel," he said, quickly turning to Hayes, "but if it is, this could lead the STs directly to Earth. You know the old saying? Do not pass go, do not collect two hundred dollars. It will be a direct route back home if they find it."

"Shit," Drake sighed electronically. "Even though they thrive underneath the ground, they can move across any surface, even the Screamers, with those spikes propelling them across the various terrains on this rock. That's how they've been able to attack us. We know they were flooding through the hole in the hillside that the escalator came out of, up by Grand Central. It's taken, what, two days to destroy that? How many of them do you think are digging around beneath us, this way and that, making a network of tunnels below our feet?"

"Yeah. I'd like to be more convinced that the

167

gateway is really shut for good," Okachi interjected. "How do we know that there isn't a network of tunnels linked to a gateway inside the mountain? There could be thousands of those creatures swarming around up there, hidden by the landscape."

"And if they find their way into those mountains," Brookes stated, pointing to the west, "and to that chamber gateway, then Earth is at risk of a full-scale invasion."

"It seems that so far, no matter how isolated some humans have been, they've been found by the creatures," Drake responded.

"Look at you," Wyatt began, speaking directly to Daniel, "you were the only one back at the structure but you still had a Screamer bearing down on you."

"Oh no," Daniel sighed once again, far more concerned about the present than the past. "What about the people who were here? There were many more of them than just the two of us. You think they could have made it to the mountains? Will they be safe there?"

"They're in great danger," Brookes replied. They all stood in silence a moment as a gentle breeze darted around them. "Okay listen up. You read me, Forrest?"

"Loud and clear," Forrest replied through the comms. He'd been listening in on the conversation the whole time.

"Colonel, I think we need to head for this chamber," Brookes suggested. "Obviously, we should try to locate your friends on the way but the situation is changing all the time. We must establish the current status of this thing."

"But that's a huge risk to take," Drake chipped in. He had seen enough to know that he hadn't signed on for anything like this. Brookes didn't want to waste time in discussion but he was aware that the chain of command was not as secure as he would have wished.

"We have to move as quickly as possible. You say the gateway is real, Colonel, and leads to Earth, but will we have to destroy it to keep Earth safe? If it's secure and Earth is just a step away, then re-establishing contact with the home world becomes the number one priority. Communication with Earth means we can bring in a military force that will blast the invaders back to wherever they came from. Let's confirm the situation and then decide what we can do after that."

"And if we get attacked again?" Daniel asked, playing devil's advocate. Brookes smiled at him.

"Then we do what we do best," he replied.

"Daniel!" Anna shouted as he made his way inside the chamber to where she had been waiting. He ran across to her in the poor light and hugged her tightly. Both were hugely relieved that Brookes had brought his little convoy to the chamber without mishap.

"Anna," he whispered, almost overtaken with emotion. The smile vanished quickly from Anna's face as she twitched gently. "What is it? What's the matter?"

Anna forced a quick smile. "Nothing, nothing at all. The baby just kicked," she replied happily.

"Damn," Brookes whispered in surprise as he entered the chamber. There it was, as clear as crystal, well, something as smooth as crystal though not as clear. They had reached the mountains, seen that not even the vipers could get over the tops and taken the proven track past Halfway House. They had travelled with great care, not really surprised that they failed to catch up with those who had left Rhino Hill ahead of them but heartened by the fact that they had seen no signs of recent carnage on their journey.

Wolf and Anna had remained near the entrance to the chamber, maintaining a lookout for approaching danger, and Sally was still assisting her friends from Rhino Hill. "Colonel," Wolf said, making his way over towards the man who had been prepared to sacrifice himself in order to allow the others to escape. The men shook hands. "Thank you, for everything." Colonel Hayes smiled in return.

"Where's everyone else?" Daniel asked as he looked around the chamber.

"Gone through," Wolf responded, overhearing the question. Daniel turned and, with one arm still around Anna, shook Wolf's hand. "Safest thing, especially for the children. They've taken buggies and ants and set up camp on Earth."

"What about Mark? Did he go too?" Colonel Hayes enquired. Wolf nodded.

"I don't know what their arrangement was but he went through with the rest of them," Wolf replied. "He was going to attempt to make contact with the military. He had this crazy idea that almost made sense. He said that they knew he was up here and if he managed to make contact with them, they would know another gateway existed."

"That may take him forever and a day," Colonel Hayes said mutedly.

"Maybe, but it's better than doing nothing."

"I don't believe it," came Drake's amplified voice. Wolf and Anna turned their attention to the military squad joining them.

"Who are you?" Wolf asked as they gathered together.

"Enforcers. Bravo team," Captain Brookes answered. For the next hour Daniel and Captain Brookes explained the situation to Wolf and Anna, from the Stumblers and Screamers to the predicament they had found themselves in.

"So you can see why I'm concerned that this

gateway actually exists," Captain Brookes finished. "If they get through this gateway, they're invading Earth." He had seen that Hayes was just about wiped out; as next senior in rank, he was ready to assume command.

"We just can't let that happen, no way," Wyatt confirmed.

All the while Okachi sat in the recesses away from the others, his mind concocting, formulating and sparking with life. "Captain," he chipped in when the conversation paused. Brookes looked across the cavern to him. "Fort Gyan?" he asked questioningly.

"What about it?" Forrest asked from his lookout post above the chamber.

"Fort Gyan? Well, it's not a fort, as such, more a small military base unknown to the population of Springfield," Colonel Hayes explained.

"What?" Wolf asked, looking questioningly towards the colonel.

"Fort Gyan was General Springfield's idea, a military backup option to protect his investment in case the colonisation project turned sour," Hayes admitted frankly. Wolf was only a little surprised to hear that. He was rather pleased to know that there might be a Plan B, in spite of the selfish reasoning. Too often at the beginning of his military career he had found himself and his men left out on a limb by those sitting in chairs half a world away from the action. He had learned the hard way that nobody except himself was looking out for them. He suddenly realised that he had placed more faith in Tom than was wise, perhaps. "It's a base a few clicks away from Rhino Hill, up near the equator. It's unknown to any civilians, as no one has ventured that deep into the wilderness, No-Man's-Land, whatever you want to call it."

"Okay," Daniel began, "what about it?"

"They seem to have stayed out of the firing line,

considering the STs have attacked almost every populated site on Springfield."

"Okachi, that's obviously good news but I've got bigger problems right now," Brookes replied bluntly to him.

"No, no, no, Captain, just think about it. They haven't attacked the fort or been anywhere near that place. There must be some reason why? And if there is, why couldn't we adopt it here? You know, to keep the STs away from this gateway?" he explained, pointing into the chamber, happy to believe that sight of Earth's clear, blue sky was only a few paces away.

Brookes mulled over the idea for a moment before pressing two fingers to his comms device. "This is Captain Brookes, Bravo Team, requesting connection to Fort Gyan, over."

"Patching you through to Lieutenant Whiteside at Fort Gyan, Captain, go ahead."

"Lieutenant, Captain Brookes, Bravo Team. Who is the commanding officer currently overseeing operations there please?"

"Fort Gyan is currently under the order and occupancy of Major Wilson."

"Major Wilson?" Daniel mused, hearing the voice across the comms network, "I'm sure I met him when I first transferred up here."

"Lieutenant, we have rescued Colonel Hayes from a planned attack by the STs. We have also discovered a handful of survivors in the process. I'm requesting permission to bring my team and stated survivors across to you, over."

"One moment, Captain," came the lieutenant's reply across the system.

"Go there?" Anna began, "but I don't want to leave the others!"

"Hold on," Daniel said comfortingly to her. Brookes

shot her a quick look out of concern.

"Captain," came a firmer voice over the comms, "this is Major Wilson. What seems to be the problem?" Brookes explained the situation but refrained from mentioning anything about the gateway to Earth.

"Permission granted, Captain, but make some serious haste. These damn Stumblers become more active during the night. The sentries will be watching out for you. See you upon arrival. Wilson out."

"Best get moving," Okachi responded, having heard the conversation in his own earpiece.

"No! Wait!" Anna snapped. "We can't leave the chamber unguarded like this! We can't leave the others back on Earth!"

"Stay calm, Anna," Daniel replied, rubbing her arms gently. "We'll sort this out.

"She's got a point," Wyatt added, looking across to his captain. "If we leave this thing unguarded, the STs could find their way up here. It may take them a while, granted, but like you said, if these things are set loose on Earth . . ." his words trailed off, leaving the rest to the imagination of his audience.

"He's right. We can't allow that," Colonel Hayes agreed. He seemed to be waking up, recovering from his personal ordeal. "We can't even assume that Mark makes it to a military facility and gets believed quickly. His story is just too far-fetched to rely on a rapid response that will be anywhere near adequate."

"And," Daniel said, turning away from Anna, "we don't even know that it really is Earth. I know Wolf saw the road signs and everything but who is to say it's not some alternate dimension representing Earth? For all we know, humans may not be the dominant species, or they could be a different race entirely. There's no saying what will happen through there."

Captain Brookes looked round to his squad. None of

173

the last few comments had given him a warm feeling. "I'd like to head for Gyan with most of my squad and leave just a couple of men here to escort civilians through the gate," he said to Hayes. After what he had heard, he didn't feel he could call the other side Earth. Hayes nodded, knowing that he was responsible for the whole of Springfield. "Alright," Brookes began, leading his men away from the chamber and down toward the vipers.

"Captain?" Okachi asked, watching him fumble inside a large compartment. Brookes lifted out two large, black boxes, one sat on top of the other. "Corporal Wyatt, Forrest, you are to remain here on guard." He indicated that each man should take a box. "We won't forget you're both up here but you are to maintain radio silence."

"What for?" Forrest asked. He wanted to know why he had been volunteered. He wanted to know why he was so special that he was being left behind, isolated, probably relying on luck to survive. This was not the way marines did things.

"Because this gate may be humanity's only escape route back to Earth. As soon as the military on Earth learn of the true situation here, they'll destroy it, in the best interest of humankind, of that I have no doubt." This was Brookes' backup plan. "Your mission is to keep it open for as long as possible but without putting Earth at risk. You following this?" Wyatt and Forrest nodded. "You look out for those damn STs. Don't leave this cavern. Just take out any rogues that find their way up here. If a whole bunch of them charge into these mountains and you're going to be completely overwhelmed, you take the explosives," he ordered, pointing back towards the black boxes, "you cross through the gate and you blow the damn thing out of existence, understand? We keep it open for as long as we can but it must go before any ST can reach whatever is on the other side. Got that?" Wyatt and Forrest nodded again.

"But what about the others?" Anna snapped.

"Lady, you better make a choice. You either come to the fort with us or you cross over to the Earth to be with them," Brookes stated. Hayes had not disagreed with his proposal, so that was now the plan as far as he was concerned. Anna was sounding like a problem he did not need and she was obviously annoying him.

"Hey!" Daniel shouted. Anna was his priority.

"Alright, let's just all settle down," Colonel Hayes ordered. "He's right, Anna," he then said after the situation de-escalated, "it will have to be one or the other. I know what Captain Brookes is saying is correct. If anyone else up here finds out about this, they'll destroy it. Whether you are thinking about the STs coming in or going out, it's far, far too risky."

Hayes was being pulled in opposite directions. He had been isolated on Springfield for too long not to feel a huge loyalty to the people he had led through fairly desperate times. He did not want to desert them now but he could not ignore the danger to the considerably larger population on Earth. Certainly, he believed that it was Earth on the other side of the chamber. He had listened to Wolf's description and there had been absolutely no doubt in that man's mind. Daniel was just being alarmist, Hayes thought, his view distorted by his concern for Anna. Hayes was prepared to spend just one more minute with her. "I believe we should have some means of escape. If the situation becomes too intense on this planet, I wouldn't want to be backed into a corner without an escape route. Trust me; I've seen these things in action. It's a miracle I survived back at the hill. Nevertheless, if it becomes necessary to sacrifice Springfield to save Earth, that is what we must do. End of." He turned to Wolf. "Your orders are to warn Earth of everything we have seen here, leave the authorities in no doubt of the threat, so that they can begin to make preparations for an underground attack and develop weapons that will take out the Stumblers."

"What are you going to do?" Anna whispered to Daniel. He turned to her.

"I'm going to stay here. I might be able to help with something," he replied.

"Fort Gyan is the safest place to be," Wyatt added. "If you're set on staying, it's probably the best place for you, too," he added, gesturing towards her developing abdomen.

"No," she said, gently stepping away from Daniel. "I'm sorry, but I can't."

"What?" Daniel whispered.

"I'm sorry, Daniel, but those women and their children are my family. I'm not going to be parted from them, not for anything."

"Anna . . ."

"No, Daniel, just, no," Anna replied, gently shaking her head. "This place sounds like complete madness. It is not the planet I have lived on for more than a dozen years. It sounds like we have gone back to the time when we were threatened by the baboons. If the chamber is going to be destroyed, I'm crossing over to the Earth where I'll stay with the other Springfielders. We'll find some land there to start farming again. I'm sorry. I love you but I'm not staying. I've got our child to think about. If you have any sense, you will do the same. One man is not going to make any difference here." Anna turned her back and headed towards the chamber.

"Anna!" Daniel snapped. She stopped and turned to him.

"Come with me, then," she replied.

Daniel looked around. He was seriously conflicted by the unfolding events. "Anna, I can't!" he snapped angrily. "I can help out here!"

"Then don't worry about me," she replied.

"I'll look after her," Wolf added, patting Daniel on the shoulder. He thought Daniel was daft but he had too much respect for the young man to say so. He hoped his example would be the final persuader before it was too late. "I'm off this place. I've got family too on the other side of the chamber. Nothing is going to stop me being with them." He had seen the other side. He knew it was the Earth.

"If you're going, get a move on!" Brookes ordered. "The rest of us are heading out now!" Wolf looked at Daniel and smiled.

"I hope we'll meet again, my friend," he said, shaking him by the hand. "Thank you, for everything." The two men embraced quickly before Wolf released, joining Anna in the chamber. She looked to Daniel. "Come find us when you're done," she said and gave a faint smile.

Tom sat almost silently between Springfield and Earth, his circuits processing the situation sweeping across Springfield. He'd watched on from a great distance, or perhaps closer than one might imagine, but knew exactly what the situation was across the now infected planet. He'd seen the occupants of Rhino Hill begin to flee across the landscape towards the chamber but made no attempt to contact them or even prevent them from going. He believed it was in his best interest not to get involved. The occupants down there all knew of a threat to their lives, although he doubted that they could really know the extent of the danger they were actually in.

Looking down from the heavens above the planet,

Tom had no doubt of his overwhelming power as he watched the tragic events unfold below. His sensors had warned him of the STs emerging from the damaged node near Grand Central and wreaking havoc across the planet, attacking every populated area they could locate. Humankind was not wiped out, at least not yet, but the loss of contact with Earth and the negligent state of the node that allowed occasional contact with several other worlds would almost certainly lead to a body-count greater than that already suffered. And the combat units established to face the STs head on? Well, they appeared simply not great enough in numbers nor powerful enough in force to pose a significant threat to the invading life forms slowly destroying all other life. The social meltdown already in existence amongst the colonists ensured that only a handful of people could actually bond together sufficiently to put up any kind of resistance against the most recent arrivals.

Tom watched with disappointment but little surprise as, even during the attacks on civilisation, some humans were still intent on fighting one another and attempting to receive personal gain through any means necessary. Springfield was in the grip of chaos. His attention focused on a small area that the STs were avoiding. It appeared to harbour military personnel as an outpost or something of that nature but its role or purpose was not yet clear. He mused to himself for a moment. If this were a position that the STs were unable to invade, for whatever reason, it could be the only outfit able to repel them effectively and give the Springfielders a chance, perhaps only a small one but one that could be boosted if contact with the Earth were re-established.

On the other hand, Tom reasoned, if he could negotiate with the STs or manipulate them in some kind of way; the opportunities for trade might be greater with them than with the humans. The STs might offer an alternative future for Springfield, one that could be peaceful, harmonious and almost euphoric. He brought new sensors online, navigating the darkness until he was able to begin a fresh analysis. The landscape was rocking gently as though he was quickly traversing an uneven ground. He noticed a chained metal fence stretching out across the distance ahead of him. Tiny, blue lights flickered intermittently across the interlocking, metal wires. As he continued to move forward he noticed soldiers patrolling at its borders, their silhouettes deep in shade against the early afternoon sunshine.

Static crackled across Tom's sensors and his input distorted momentarily. He halted his probing and immediately checked for damage. Nothing. He ran a further analysis. Something was keeping the STs away from the outpost, something powerful. He left his sensors *in situ* as his analysis took a new line. These humans had called upon an unexpected technology, one that might give them the edge if they were able to use it properly, safely. Even so, if the STs found a way into the complex, it would almost certainly fall, and then it would be only a matter of time before the remaining human positions collapsed. If that happened, a new order would be created from the wreckage. He smiled; a new order. He kicked out a left leg. "I'm still here," he told himself softly.

Chapter 14A

Captain Brookes and his squad were almost at Fort Gyan. "This is Captain Brookes!" he called in. "We can see you. Open the damn gates!"

"Affirmative, Captain, gates opening," a reply came back through the comms network.

"Not fast enough! Okachi, where is that Screamer?"

"Tracking ninety-five feet to the right, collision course imminent."

"Captain, our infantry have you on visual. We will support you when within range."

"Copy that, Gyan. Drake, status?"

"We're right behind you, sir."

"Ready to fire?"

"Roger, Captain. Daniel's holding steady course, me and the colonel are locked and loaded."

Brookes checked the men in his viper. The Screamer launched itself from the surface and wailed monstrously. Its clawed head opened as it prepared to attack.

"Fire!" Brookes screamed. The air filled with the sound of bullets tearing through the openness. The Screamer sealed its head into the clawed point and sliced back under the surface. "Okachi! Status!"

"Passing beneath us! Turning to adopt another attacking position!"

"Captain! You're almost here!" Brookes looked up and saw the wire fencing of Fort Gyan looming closer. Strange, blue lights flickered at intervals through the early evening daylight. The entrance gate was opening. He could see laser sights darting back and forth from the sentry towers dotted along its perimeter. "Hold the course!" he ordered.

"Sir, the Screamer is catching us from the south,"

Okachi reported. Behind them, the ground exploded and plumes of soil and rocks soared into the air as the Screamer gave chase just below the surface. Okachi watched his data pad as the blip representing the Screamer gained on them. Then, suddenly, the picture changed. The two vipers had reached the border of Fort Gyan. The blip jolted left erratically and fled from the chase. Okachi frowned. "What the hell," he asked himself quietly.

"What is it?" Brookes ordered.

"The Screamer, it just, well, turned and retreated. It's leaving."

"What?"

"Seems you found out our little secret," came the major's voice from across the comms.

Fort Gyan's history was typical of many military backup facilities. After what had been a very uncertain start to the colonisation of the planet, General Springfield had indeed wanted to protect his investment. He had established the base in almost complete secrecy. Apart from its staff, the only person on the planet who knew of its existence had been Colonel Hayes, whose orders had been to ensure that it remained unknown to the colonists. When the situation on the planet had become increasingly stable and very profitable for General Springfield, the fort had fallen into near disuse, occupied by only a skeleton staff. The failure of the escalator had never been foreseen but the existence of the fort had remained a secret.

When Major Wilson had heard about the STs emerging through the broken gateway, he had immediately reactivated the base. Now, he greeted the Enforcers and their passengers. After a brief exchange of pleasantries and confirmation that the colonel was indeed okay, everybody relaxed a little. Daniel was very taken aback by the base, having had no knowledge of its existence. The company of soldiers and survivors entered the largest building on the complex. The armour and heavy boots of the military personnel clattered in the corridors as they followed the major and a woman who had introduced herself as Dr. Holly Kenford.

Daniel was treated to a hot shower and clean, military clothes. He emerged clad in standard issue greens, to a round of amused applause from Captain Brookes and his men. Drake had finally removed his protective helmet to reveal a young man, much younger than Daniel had imagined, with clipped, brown hair. In fact, Daniel would have said he was no older than twenty-five at most. He had proved himself as a first class soldier, to Daniel anyway, who guessed that he had already done so to Captain Brookes in missions past.

"So, what's your secret?" Colonel Hayes asked Major Wilson after they had congregated together. The major smiled.

"Follow me," he replied, and gestured with an open hand toward a corridor. "I'll let Dr. Kenford explain it. She's been our greatest asset since those creatures emerged upon the planet." They stopped outside a metallic door. A few men clad in lab whites were waiting for them. They handed out face masks to each member of the party. Each mask had a filter attached beneath it. "Put these on first," the major ordered. Daniel took one and placed it over his nose and mouth. The mask sealed to his face automatically and didn't require the use of a strapping to hold it firm. The filter valves clacked gently with each breath he took.

Major Wilson checked to make sure all men were suitably protected. "Follow me," he said through an amplified voice distorted by the airtight mask he was wearing. They entered the doors and stepped into a clean, immaculate room that looked like an operating theatre. Every appliance with a chrome finish twinkled in the sharp, bright lights, from the taps and tables to the shelving, draws and tools.

"Gentlemen, welcome," Dr. Kenford said, looking at them through small glasses that momentarily reflected the bright lights above them. She was a slim lady hidden by her standard, laboratory white coat. In front of them on the operating table lay the lifeless corpse of a Stumbler.

"How did you get that?" Brookes asked as they gathered around it.

"Shot it at the border," Major Wilson explained. "There were hundreds of them out here so we took a lone straggler down in an attempt to bring them in and understand them a bit more. Dr. Kenford has been studying these carcasses for some time now and has found out one or two extremely valuable details."

"They're ugly suckers," Drake interjected, looking over the lifeless corpse. It appeared exactly as it had done in Okachi's holographic explanation, with long, thin limbs and dark, armoured bone protecting the majority of its body. The human-like skull stood as it had been interpreted on the holographic image, still missing the jaw.

"Born of a dark, underground existence," Dr. Kenford explained as they looked the Stumbler over. "The fact that they have evolved into an almost humanoid form suggests that they have been exposed to atmospherics and have not evolved entirely beneath the surface of their home world like we initially believed."

"Do you know where that home world may be?" Daniel enquired. So many systems and planets had been discovered that it was almost like asking them to pinpoint a needle in haystack.

"Afraid not," Major Wilson told him, confirming his

own thought. There had been many theories since the STs had emerged through the broken gateway. "They do not appear to have any sophisticated technology. It seems they just wandered through the gateway like we might wander through a cave. They could have emerged from a planet otherwise deemed unpopulated by our previous generations."

"The solid shell encasing their bodies would suggest that they've spent more time under the ground than above it," Dr. Kenford theorised to the soldiers. "I believe that any gateway could only have been placed on their planet by a species vastly superior in technological terms. The STs had probably been dwelling there for centuries. It is just theory at this time but it's a strong one considering the test subject. The STs might simply have caught the new arrivals off guard and gained access to the gateway. The new arrivals might have a policy of non-interference with native species, which allows the STs to persist, or the STs may have been recruited actively as a ready-made army."

"So what exactly do you know or have you found out about these creatures?" Colonel Hayes asked the doctor. He was concerned only about the here and now. "You appear to be repelling them back from the camp successfully." Dr. Kenford smiled at him from beneath her mask.

"Therein lies our secret," she teased. She reached across to a table strewn with medical instruments. She picked up a scalpel and leant over the human-like head of the Stumbler. "Look here," she asked them, pointing beneath the creature's nose. If the Stumbler had been human, she'd now be investigating the area between the upper lip and nostril on its face. The company of soldiers leant in a little closer. "You see these?" she asked them, indicating the presence of a cluster of

184

pores dotted across the area.

"What are they?" Daniel asked, looking over the strange markings.

"Receptors," Dr. Kenford said to him, "evolved for a life of existence underground. We discovered they were similar to the Ampullae of Lorenzini, which are sensing organs that sharks have back on Earth." Drake scratched his head.

"I'm afraid I'm just a simple marine," he informed her bluntly, "you're going to have to bring it down to my level." Major Wilson smiled. Dr. Kenford addressed him.

"Ampullae of Lorenzini are the receptors that sharks use to sense variations in the electric field around them. They allow a shark to detect any disturbances within the water. Every living creature creates an electric field and these little pores help the shark make sense of it."

"So what has that got in common with these?" Captain Brookes asked, nodding toward the Stumbler.

"The pores that this creature has," Dr. Kenford explained, "act almost identically to those of the sharks. Even though they are not underwater there are still electric fields to detect. Every living thing emits an electrical field, a person, for example, you and me, absolutely everything that can be found on Earth and on Springfield. For a race that exists almost entirely underground, a key development and awareness would be established using these pores. There's no light underground and their eyesight appears to be extremely poor because of their evolution. They're almost entirely dependent on the electric fields that they sense."

"So, basically, you're saying that the Stumblers are using electric fields to locate us and to attack us?" Captain Brookes asked, piecing together the information the doctor had shared with them.

Dr. Kenford sighed. "Not just that. They are

primarily locating us through sound, listening to the noises that travel through the planet's surface but this is where our research kicked in. If you disrupt the electric field, you disrupt their being. If sharks are exposed to a higher voltage of electric field it overpowers their nerves so badly that they flee the area of the voltage. It's the same with these. In effect, if you overload these pores with an electromagnetic field, they'll keep their distance."

"Did you notice the transmitters dotted around the boundaries?" Major Wilson asked after Dr. Kenford had finished her explanation.

"The blue dots," Okachi recalled, "yeah I saw them. They were the transmitters first brought to Springfield when we began populating the planet, if my research serves me correct?"

"Indeed it does," Wilson stated. "Those transmitters were removed from service when unusually high fields of electromagnetic energy were found to be emitting from them."

Daniel nodded knowingly. "I remember reading up on them. So I'm guessing that the levels of energy that they throw out are enough to disrupt and repel any of the STs and keep them away from the fort?" he asked his hosts.

"Precisely," Dr. Kenford confirmed. "It can affect our perception greatly, which is why they were initially retired and stored here, out of harm's way. But the positives far outweigh the negatives. They've kept us safe."

"How does it affect us?" Brookes then asked, now intrigued by his lack of knowledge in the subject.

"In our senses," Dr. Kenford explained to him. "Heightened electrical fields change our perception, like senses of paranoia, the feeling of being watched, those types of sensations. Back in the twenty-first century, it was believed that paranormal activity was caused by high levels of this electromagnetic energy. Being on your own and having the intense feeling you were being watched, and becoming afraid of the situation you found yourself in, the belief of ghosts and spirits existing in so-called haunted houses, that kind of thing, it pretty much all boiled down to these fields disrupting perceptions and allowing the paranoia to replace rationale in those people it affected."

"I can see how that would affect our early populations, especially those bearing weapons," Brookes responded. "You give a paranoid soldier a weapon and I'm damn sure he'll use it however he sees fit. How have the symptoms held out in the camp?" he then asked the major.

"Not too badly so far," Major Wilson informed him. "We've had one or two isolated cases, fights, reports of an invisible force inside the camp, like Dr. Kenford explained about the ghosts, but not many, at least nothing we couldn't handle. Those appearing aggressive have been counselled and secured in our holding cells for the time being."

"I think it's important to stress that these symptoms do not affect everyone," Dr. Kenford chipped in. "Perception levels vary. Some people will sense the electromagnetic fields, some won't. It's hit or miss. Not everyone has noticed the effects of the transmitters in our camp so far." Brookes nodded slowly.

"Dr. Kenford's research, though, has been invaluable to us," Major Wilson began, "and it's allowed us to remain somewhat protected whilst we consider some alternatives to this situation that we find ourselves in."

Colonel Hayes frowned slightly. "Alternatives? You mean, you have a plan?"

The major smiled. "Colonel, Captain. Will you both

join me in my office? Daniel, you too. Your work here on Springfield has not gone unnoticed."

The light began to fade over Springfield and made way for the bland blanket of nightfall to cover the landscape. The first few days of the STs' emergence had caused widespread panic initially but then, as ever, the survivors had begun to adapt, hiding or fleeing. The invading life forms had slowly begun to spread out from the former concentrations of civilisation dotted across the planet. Dr. Kenford believed that they were establishing themselves beneath the ground and that it would only be a matter of time before a full-scale attack took place against the entire human population. She could not say exactly how many of the creatures had passed through the gateway or how many different species there could possibly be, but she was sure that there would already be enough to cause major disruption to the planet and the way of life that the human colonists had established since their arrival. Like several others present, she was not convinced that further arrivals had been prevented.

Drake and Okachi visited the perimeter fences in the twilight to investigate the transmitters currently repelling the alien life-forms. Many soldiers patrolled actively along the perimeter boundaries, keeping careful watch and guard over the fort. "Here," Okachi said as they approached the nearest box that pulsed neon blue throughout the diminished light. "I thought so," he smiled as he mused to himself.

"What?" Drake asked, watching him approach the flashing box hooked simply to the wire fencing.

"It's a Tevlor series 181. These came up to Springfield to boost the infrared communication signal sent through the aerials back in the early days, you know, give the signals a boost so that communications could be established wherever they were needed. They worked, too."

"Look out there," Drake gasped, paying no attention to the knowledgeable lieutenant. The tone in his voice caused Okachi's stomach to drop. His eyes followed Drake's gaze out across the open lands and through the darkness. Thousands of Stumblers surrounded the fort, their eyes twinkling in the fading light. They swayed and moaned *en masse*, as though their minds had been completely lost and their bodies functioned only on pure instinct.

"Don't worry," one of the soldiers interrupted, overhearing Drake's concern, "they've been out there the same time every night, watching us, taking it all in."

"Planning an attack?" Okachi mused. The soldier shrugged.

"No one knows. Maybe? Thus far, though, they've kept their distance."

"They are," Drake added quietly. His gut instinct agreed with the soldier. "They're figuring out how to bring down these transmitters."

"Seriously?" the soldier asked.

"They have to be. Why else would they be out here?"

"I don't know," Okachi replied, "but I don't like it. They're up to something alright."

The ground beneath their feet rumbled gently. Throughout the encircling Stumblers they noticed Screamers appear. They glided gently across the ground, their huge girths pulsing and shunting forwards through the Stumblers, towards the camp.

"Hey! You seeing this?" a voice echoed from the nearest lookout post. The soldier looked up. "This is serious," the voice added, confirming everyone's thoughts. The camp filled with the sound of running boots and clattering weapons as soldiers flooded to the fences. Captain Brookes quickly emerged from the buildings and jogged towards his squad.

"Seems we're surrounded," Okachi reported to his captain as he arrived.

The Stumblers groaned in the darkening light. The Screamers ploughed between them, passing close to the boundary of the camp.

"What the hell?" Daniel asked as he approached the Enforcers. Colonel Hayes and Major Wilson followed closely behind. Soldiers ran backwards and forwards, carrying crates of ammunition and grenades.

"We got a situation brewing!" one soldier shouted out above the chaos.

"Update!" the major bellowed up in the direction of the lookout post.

"STs, thousands of them, congregating *en masse* around us, Sir!" came the echoed reply from the lofty heights.

"Do you believe an attack to be imminent?" he shouted back.

"Yes, I believe so," Colonel Hayes responded in the soldier's place, "this is the pattern of behaviour they adopted back at Rhino Hill."

"Damn it!" Major Wilson shouted. "Comms units live!" Across the camp the electronic buzz of each soldier's unit powered to life. The major grabbed one from a passing infantryman.

The Stumblers became louder and more aggressive, hissing and moaning in the darkness, their eyes twinkling eerily. "All units, this is Major Wilson. Prepare for imminent attack from the STs. Adopt defensive position along the perimeter fences. Now! Now! Now!" The soldiers pounded the ground as they rushed around the fort to adopt their positions. "Units, follow the command of Captain Brookes, this is a direct order. Both he and his squad have experience in fighting these bastards. Follow him to a tee. Major

Wilson out." Wilson turned to Brookes. "This is your show now, Captain. You've fought these things; you know more about combat against them than we do."

"Copy that, Major," Brookes confirmed before placing gloved fingers to his earpiece. The STs roared from the darkness, like a rallying call far out of eyesight had motivated them.

"Shit! This is not good!" Drake sighed.

"All units, this is Captain Brookes. Stand tall, load weapons but do not fire, repeat, do not fire." The clatter of magazines and cocking levers rippled throughout Fort Gyan. Brookes turned to Drake. "Drake, switch to night vision."

"Affirmative," Drake acknowledged. He fumbled at a switch upon his visor. A small green light illuminated from his helmet. "Ah, shit, Captain, this is not good. Not good at all!"

"Status report," Brookes insisted, doing his best to maintain good order but worried by what he had recently learned. He was determined not to let any of his men panic.

"It's full out there. They're shoulder to shoulder, no room to fart, and they're engulfing the fort, and I mean engulfing in the truest sense of the word. They're surrounding us. Thousands of them."

"Damn it!" Brookes muttered. "Okay, Drake, Okachi, take up post. Drake I want you here. Okachi, patrol the southern border. Regular updates. Daniel, I need you at your best."

"What for?" Daniel asked.

"If they target those transmitters and manage to knock one out we'll have a weak spot in our defences. I'll need you to bring them back online as quickly as possible if that happens. If those transmitters fail, Fort Gyan falls. Major, can you arrange for the tools Daniel will need to repair the transmitters if they go down?"

Major Wilson dropped his head slightly and spoke into his comms unit.

"This is Major Wilson, requesting engineering tools, equipment and unused transmitters to be brought outside immediately. We also require a headset comms unit. Make it happen, people, and be warned, we are about to come under attack. Remember, these things have poor eyesight. Lights out, keep as still as you can. Let them get right up to you and then go for a head shot. Don't waste ammunition shooting at their bodies. The rounds will come bouncing back at you." He spoke calmly but firmly. His advice was simple but timely.

"Copy that, sir," came an equally calm voice in reply.

"Won't an all-out assault destroy our fences if we open fire on them?" Daniel asked as he awaited the delivery of his equipment.

"It's that or we just invite them in," Drake quipped.

"You heard the major," Brookes shouted out. "Make sure you hit the enemy, not our transmitters." He could see that if the STs did manage get through the electric fields that the simple chain-link fences wouldn't hold them back. He spoke quietly to Major Wilson, "Do you have any spotlights?"

"In the lookout posts," he replied swiftly. Brookes engaged his comms.

"All units in the lookout posts engage spotlights. Let's get some light out there." It went against what the major had said but Brookes wanted to see if he could blind the Stumblers. Also, when they were overrun, he hoped the enemy would concentrate on the lights and give his men a better chance of escaping.

Bright beams of white light exploded from the lookout posts across Fort Gyan. The STs screamed out and lurched back at the borders of the electromagnetic field, as the spotlights stung their poor eyes unused to

192

such vigorous and cleansing lights.

"My God," Colonel Hayes whispered. The camp had been completely surrounded from all sides by thousands of Stumblers; Drake had not exaggerated. Dozens of Screamers rested motionlessly within their hordes.

"I don't think we have enough ammunition," Major Wilson sighed almost silently as he looked out across the mass of bodies illuminated in the spotlights surrounding him.

"This is Captain Brookes. Hold your positions. Do not open fire until I call the order. Remain vigilant but remain calm. We can't assume that they will attack."

"Here, Sir," came a voice behind Daniel. Daniel turned to see a small soldier presenting a tool belt and comms system as the major had ordered.

"Thank you," Daniel replied, quickly taking the belt and attaching it around his waist.

"We have placed the spare transmitters in the middle of camp should you need them," the soldier then quickly added.

"Alright. Thanks," Daniel replied once more. He was shocked to see the soldier salute him before dashing away to his ready position.

"Why don't we just line out the spare transmitters around the camp to make even more of an electric field?" Drake's electric voice buzzed from his head guard.

"We'd be living a dangerous game," Daniel explained as he fitted his belt. "If we laid them all out there and a section gets destroyed, we'd have nothing but bullets and manpower to repel the STs, and if the ammunition situation is as bad as the major fears, there won't be enough to protect the fort, which means there'll be nothing to protect us. At least by replacing transmitters that have been destroyed one by one, we have a chance of being able to keep the electromagnetic field intact."

Captain Brookes nodded in agreement. "Major, how many engineers do you have on site?" he asked. Major Wilson sighed and shook his head.

"We have just two specialists of our own, Captain. Fort Gyan has never needed any more than that before today."

"We will need all available hands to assist Daniel as needed," Brookes advised him.

"Larsen, do you copy?" the major asked into his headset.

"Copy, sir."

"Larsen, I want you and Tali up here now to assist with any transmitter problems we may suffer. You're under the command of Daniel Swift."

"Affirmative. On our way."

The Stumblers swayed and hissed as the spotlights passed over them, revealing them briefly from the shadows. A Screamer grunted and groaned in the distance. The clatter of weapons being checked emanated around Fort Gyan as the soldiers did everything to prepare for the seemingly inevitable. Each lookout post was occupied by three snipers, their sharp eyes keeping watch across the thousands of bodies surrounding the camp.

"Sir, Larsen and Tali reporting for duty." Captain Brookes and the major turned to notice a man and woman clad in combat greens and wearing comms units standing to attention.

"At ease," Captain Brookes ordered, allowing both to relax their saluting arms. "Larsen, Tali," he began, looking between the both of them, "you are to follow the orders of this man." He pointed to Daniel, who was adjusting his comms set.

"Do you read me?" Daniel asked quietly, testing out

194

the unit he was wearing. He knew the headsets would be essential as soon as the firing started.

"Loud and clear," Tali replied, hearing his voice clearly through her own comms. Larsen nodded.

"Follow his orders closely, it could be the difference between life and death," Brookes added.

"Copy that," Larsen confirmed.

"Daniel, base yourself in the middle of the camp where the transmitters are."

"Will do, Captain," Daniel replied.

"All units, this is Captain Brookes. Any destruction of transmitters must be reported to lead engineer Daniel Swift immediately. Report the damage and wait for assistance. Hold the line, soldiers, that's a direct order."

"Good luck," Daniel added, grasping hands with Brookes then Drake.

"Stay safe," Drake replied. Daniel and his small team quickly dashed across the camp to the spare transmitters that had been primed for use.

The STs were packed together, moaning and groaning. It was not clear if they understood anything that was going on within the camp. The Screamers barged between them ruthlessly, like fat army generals swaggering towards a better vantage point from which to view their enemy. From the front of the army a Stumbler emerged and slowly began swaying towards the fort.

"I got movement!" came a cry from a sniper perched high in the nearest lookout post. Captain Brookes looked up toward the informant and then out into the beam of his spotlight. A single, solitary creature moved closer to the fences before jolting backwards and almost losing its footing.

"The electric field," Colonel Hayes whispered as he watched the events unfold. The Stumbler made another attempt to cross the invisible line and once again lurched backwards. A Screamer bellowed out a series of high-pitched roars in the direction of the troublesome Stumbler.

"What the hell..." Drake's electronic voice trailed, "Is that thing barking out orders?"

"I don't believe it," Brookes whispered in amazement. The Stumbler made a further attempt to cross the boundary but again lurched backwards.

"It's in their makeup. There's no way that thing can pass through the electric field," Major Wilson said with growing satisfaction. It seemed that this all but confirmed Dr. Kenford's theory.

The Stumbler stood swaying from side to side as if lost in a deep, meaningful thought. The Screamer bellowed once more and surged through the hordes with great ease. Its clawed head opened widely revealing the circular rows of razor sharp teeth and smashed down violently onto the creature unable to pass across the boundary. The soldiers from Fort Gyan winced and moaned as they watched the Screamer maim and then destroy its own ally at the edges of their camp. The Screamer shook its mouth vigorously and launched the decapitated limbs of the creature high into the air.

"Incoming!" shouted a soldier as she sprinted for cover. The mangled body of the Stumbler landed and exploded inside the perimeter of the camp. Its mangled remains, shredded so badly by the Screamer, were unable to take the ferocity of such a great impact and burst, splattering a black liquid across the immediate area.

"What the hell is going on now?" Colonel Hayes shouted out across the fort. More Stumblers emerged from the front lines. Again they failed to cross the invisible boundary created by the electric fields around the fort, further supporting Dr. Kenford's theory.

"Oh crap!" Drake shouted.

"What is it?" Brookes demanded aggressively. His tone insisted on an immediate answer.

"Screamers! They're everywhere. They're all surging towards the lone individuals at the front of their lines!"

"Damn! They're going to follow suit and launch them!" Brookes shouted. They were sacrificing their own, just as he had feared, though not quite in the manner he had expected. "Take cover!"

The Screamers were copying each other, snatching Stumblers with great force and aggression and hurling them over the fences. The soldiers dashed behind cover and tried to dodge the mangled remains of the bodies which struck with the force of cannonballs. The fences jarred and swayed as they were struck relentlessly by the bony objects but remained intact for the moment. The tactic was elementary. The enemy was sacrificing a relatively small number of its own in the hope of bringing down the human defences. The defenders watched as the Screamers began ploughing through the Stumblers once again.

Sporadic firing started but it made absolutely no difference to the situation. When the bullets did hit their targets they simply ricocheted off, but at least most were aimed harmlessly up into the night sky. "Cease firing!" Captain Brookes bellowed. "Everybody on the ground, take cover. Lookout posts, take aim on the nearest of those huge maggots." He wasn't going to call them anything in public that might suggest respect.

"It's pointless," Drake said in despair. He had seen it all before. "Those Screamers can soak up bullets."

"Maybe," replied Major Wilson, who knew less about the Screamers but still had two more weapons in his arsenal.

Major Wilson was a student of warfare. He had set

up his lookout posts to be like castle keeps, each a solid concrete structure that, even now, he doubted a Screamer could shift. He had studied the design of the Russian ZSU-23-4, which had been the best example of anti-aircraft artillery in its day and had proved extremely effective against ground targets also. He had thought it only sensible to install a Vulcan cannon atop each strongpoint. "Lookout posts, two-second bursts at the nearest maggots." Then he turned to his subordinates. "That's a couple of hundred exploding rounds," he said with a smile. "Now that we know what their tactic is, let's show them ours."

"Damn it! Transmitter down! Repeat, Transmitter down!" came a hysterical call across the comms network.

"Where?" Daniel asked aggressively into the comms. Adrenalin surged powerfully through his body. His heart leapt into action.

"Western border! Transmitter destroyed!" Body parts were still raining down around him. Some of the defenders on the ground were still firing ineffectually, unable to resist the need to do something.

"Oh God! The Stumblers are approaching! They're swarming towards the fence here!"

"Daniel, get to it," Brookes ordered calmly, feeling much happier that the responsibility for defence was being shared.

"Almost there!" Daniel replied, clutching a transmitter in his arms.

"Come on! Come on!" a soldier bellowed as he watched Daniel approaching. The Stumblers were tearing through the electric field and along an invisible path untouched by the remaining transmitters. The gap in the electromagnetic field that the destroyed transmitter had left appeared huge. The soldier took out the closest Stumbler with a single, clean head shot.

"Keep your cool!" Brookes ordered from his position across the camp. He could see Daniel and ordered Drake to take six men across to the gap. "Head shots, only head shots," he shouted. Daniel fumbled with the box in his hands and panicked momentarily.

"What are you waiting for?" another soldier shouted beside him. The Stumblers surged closer. Some bullets fired in blind panic deflected from their armoured bodies leaving sparks in the darkness. A spotlight fell motionless on their path to the perimeter. A body fell from the sky, landing beside Daniel, exploding on impact, and covered him in the dark blood of the mangled Stumbler.

"Transmitter down, repeat, transmitter down!" came another cry across the comms.

"Where are you?" Daniel shouted as he fumbled unsuccessfully with his own.

"South fence! Transmitter light is flickering but they seem to be getting closer!"

"Tali!" Daniel shouted into his comm unit.

"Sir!" came her immediate response.

"Take a transmitter there now! Plug it in immediately and then attempt to repair the other one!"

"Hurry the hell up!" a soldier beside Daniel shouted. The Stumblers were moving closer and closer. Fortunately they appeared extremely confused, or frightened by the Screamers, maybe. There were so many that they were actually obstructing each other.

"Copy that!" Tali confirmed.

Daniel fumbled with a tiny switch and moved it to the side. The blue light on its front panel shone into life.

"Got it!" Daniel shouted. He ran to the fence and placed its mounting hooks through the chain linked fence. The Stumblers lurched and fell, quivering, shaking and screaming as their senses were overloaded with massive bursts of electrical energy.

"Just in time!" one of the soldier's quipped.

"Tali! Update!" Daniel ordered.

"Mayday, mayday! Transmitter down on the north-west boundary, seeking immediate assistance," a fresh voice broke in.

"Damn, you got it Larsen?"

"Got it!" he replied quickly. Daniel watched him run from across the camp then quickly scouted the perimeter fences near where he was standing. All were holding. The air still rained with flying body parts, though none struck him. Beyond the fences the Screamers sounded even more enraged and aggressive. He was sure he could detect a change in their tone and pitch. He could feel himself begin to shake. The air was filled with the deafening sounds of battle.

"Daniel, come in! This is Larsen!"

"Go ahead," Daniel heard himself say.

"Daniel, I can't fix this damn transmitter, it's smashed to hell. Can you bring another one pronto?" Daniel sighed with despair. This is the end, a little voice told him. He picked up a transmitter, not realising it was the broken one he had just taken out of service and moved in the direction of Larsen. There were Stumblers all around him, bumping into him but ignoring him. Nothing made sense any more. He put the transmitter down and sat on it, watching the ghostly shadows wander past him.

"Daniel, Sir! Transmitter repaired!" Tali shouted through her unit. He merely laughed in reply.

The ZSU-23-4 had been called the *sewing machine* because of the noise it made. In Fort Gyan, a series of irregular snorts slowly became audible as the other sounds of battle began to fade away. The men and women up on the lookout posts were the first to appreciate what was happening. The Screamers presented huge targets. While their bodies appeared unaffected by ordinary bullets, the exploding shells from the Vulcan cannon quickly punched holes through their outer carapaces. The big beasts were choosing to retreat rather than make the sacrifice they expected of their smaller assistants. Now without any direction, and surrounded by confusion, the Stumblers were reduced to doing what their name suggested. Within half an hour, the attack had ceased and the fort perimeter secured. All those Screamers still able to do so had withdrawn beyond cannon range and their smaller allies were slowly wandering away.

Daylight brought a sight of absolute carnage outside the fort. As soon as Dr. Kenford appeared, however, she immediately advised that the electromagnetic field be switched off. A brief argument ensued. It ceased when the good doctor reminded everybody that she had the authority under military regulations to remove anybody from duty whom she deemed unfit. Even so, it was only several hours later that people began to feel normal again. Major Wilson and Captain Brookes realised that they had been very slow to act, much slower than they should have been. They found it difficult to believe that they could have been so ineffective.

Daniel was amazed. He had been convinced that the fort had been overrun, that he had been buried in an avalanche of body parts and surrounded by Stumblers. "Maybe you were," Holly explained to him and others. "More likely, you saw this awful situation developing, enormous stress increased your susceptibility to the weapon you were using against the enemy, and the shadows and your imagination did the rest."

Chapter 15A

A large campfire crackled and popped with the dry foliage fuelling its flames. Many of the children had fallen asleep under the canopy branches of the forest they were resting in. The chamber, the gateway to Springfield, was not far away, a matter of metres in reality, but when closed, it was completely invisible. Greg and James were wide awake, both excited by what was going on. Greg sat beside Rose, and James beside Anna. Jessica had allowed Jack to fall asleep naturally and he rested his head against her thigh and the small fallen tree trunk she was sitting on upon. Sally sat beside Wolf. Their children were all sleeping.

"We can't just wait here for something to happen," Mark began as his thoughts ran away from him, "we're stuck between a rock and a hard place."

"I can't believe everything that happened. What were those things? Where did they come from?" Charlie asked.

"I don't know. What we do know, though, is that it hasn't gone unnoticed. At least the military is doing something about it," Wolf replied.

"I was so glad to see the Colonel," Anna said softly, "I thought he was dead for sure."

"But he wasn't," Wolf replied, smiling, "and he saved us."

"For what, though?" Mark asked. "Look at us; we're sat in a forest on Earth with no way to contact personnel on either planet. It's a good job we're in summer here or we'd be freezing to death right about now."

"Mark, we're alive, the children are alive, and that's the most important thing. We'll find a way to contact officials on this planet some time," Wolf replied, keeping his voice low so as not to disturb the sleeping children. He was relieved merely to have survived and he was certain that the beasts he had seen on Springfield did not have the intelligence to get through the chamber. If he were surprised that Tom appeared to have done nothing to help, he made no mention of it.

"I have my doubts," Mark replied. "I couldn't reach anywhere I needed to when I left here, and with insufficient money I had no chance to get close to contacting the military." On Springfield, money had fallen out of use and people had reverted to barter. He had forgotten what Earth was like. "If we contact the emergency services, we'll be scrutinised for sure, especially if we say we came here through a secret gateway. Face it, we're stuck." He had failed totally in his mission to find assistance and was feeling very disappointed with life in general.

Wolf sighed. "You and I can go back through the chamber tomorrow. We can check with the two sentries to find out what's happening. They're in contact with Daniel and the colonel, and we can get an update." He then noticed Sally smiling. She noticed him looking.

"Baby's moving," she said quietly. Anna joined the conversation.

"Mine too." She was very pleased about the baby, not nearly so pleased about Daniel. In fact, she was beginning to wonder if she really needed him anymore. She felt safer than she had expected. Charlie frowned a little.

"That's a bit odd, isn't it?" she asked them both.

"What?" Sally asked her.

"The babies both moving at the same time?" Charlie was surprised, partly because she didn't think the pregnancies were that far advanced.

"Now that we have confirmed that the electromagnetic

fields disrupt the STs' senses, we need to start the ball rolling to reach out to Earth," Major Wilson informed his audience in his small office. Colonel Hayes, Captain Brookes and Daniel had been due to meet up with him before the Subterraneans attacked the fort. "And we need to consider the preservation of our current structures."

"I guess it has something to do with the transmitters currently in use across the camp?" Daniel asked the major.

Wilson nodded. "As you know, our transmitters serve two purposes. One, they were a previous system to boost any signals that we were using up here on Springfield when we first arrived, and two, they keep those damn creatures away. Because the STs have only been destructive during their attack against the colonies, I believe that any structure out in isolation and away from human civilisation will be safe. The infrared we're using is functioning perfectly. If we can fix the masts dotted around the area and attach one of these transmitters to their structure, like in the old days on this planet, we can protect the communication systems and units, and create an electrical field to keep the STs from causing any further damage."

"So why haven't you done it already?" Captain Brookes enquired. To him, that would be the first thing he would have done upon realising the effect of the Tevlors.

"The people serving on this base are soldiers, Captain. They just don't possess the skills to take on a mission like this." He sighed as he pushed back on his chair and away from his desk. "Since we colonised the planet all those years ago now, our one priority has always been communications, always. We knew the dangers that could arise if our transport network and communications went dark, and we were right.

Communications has always been our focus, our catalyst. If we can get the masts repaired and these transmitters rigged, we can ensure that some form of communication is functioning and that may also give us the opportunity to begin work on establishing comms with Earth once again."

"Why wasn't this done before, when you realised the power these boxes held?" Daniel asked, echoing Brookes' thoughts.

"Simply because we had no idea how the communication systems went down to start with," Major Wilson explained. "We were afraid that if we messed in anything without knowing the initial causes, we could have destroyed our entire structure. Turns out that everything is linked to a gateway that we thought was defunct, the gateway that the STs managed to stumble their way through."

"Surely the old escalator system is completely inactive." Brookes suggested. Major Wilson shook his head.

"We hope it is now," he said firmly. "But we do believe there are many more gateway systems dotted throughout the universe. Colonel Hayes has said that another gateway exists up here on Springfield. Maybe we can establish comms with Earth once again."

Brookes gave Colonel Hayes a sly look from the corner of his eye. "So what is it you want me to do?" Captain Brookes asked the major.

"I'll tell you straight, Captain. I want you to take these transmitters and link them up. We need to keep the STs from destroying them. We need to give ourselves the opportunity to contact Earth without putting it in danger. You and your team are the most qualified soldiers for this mission, and the strongest infantry unit that I have at my disposal at this moment in time. I know you have comms specialist Lieutenant

Okachi already in your team, but I want you to take Daniel with you to set these up. He's an expert in the field and his work has been recognised throughout the military."

Brookes squinted as though a thought was crossing his mind. "Locate the masts, attach the transmitters, and get out," he repeated to himself.

"That's all we need, Captain. If we can protect the structures we can give ourselves longer to review the situation on this rock when events begin to settle. The masts will be protected and that will be a start. If the masts fall and cannot be repaired we are likely to lose all basic communications across Springfield and never make contact with Ely, and that is a huge problem that we cannot afford to happen up here. We can provide you with their locations, and you simply protect as many as you can. It's an otherwise simple routine, Captain. In and out, and that is all. If the plan works we'll at least give ourselves that chance to function once more in the future."

Captain Brookes wandered through the hallway leading back to his quarters. He passed a few soldiers, a lab rat, and then heard the voices of two of his squad. He approached a corner in the corridor and turned to see Okachi and Drake having a stern conversation.

"Just relax, man," Okachi had replied. Brookes had not heard the beginning of their meeting.

"I will not relax. What the hell is going on?"

"Nothing. No one is looking for you, no one thinks you've done anything wrong, just chill out."

Drake sighed. "I bet they have cameras in here, watching our every move."

Okachi laughed. "Drake, this is a simple camp established as a warehouse more than anything before the STs showed up. You're letting your mind run away with you. It's been a long day, for all of us."

Drake sighed and ruffled a hand over his shaved hair. "Maybe, Okachi, maybe. But be warned, I've got my eye on you."

"Is there a problem, here?" Captain Brookes asked as entered the conversation. Both men jolted.

"No, sir," they both replied immediately.

Brookes cast a doubtful eye across the pair of them. "What's with the argument, then?"

"Err, nothing, sir. Private Drake has had a long day, as we all have, and I recommended he take some rest, sir."

Brookes had listened to part of the conversation and knew that Okachi's explanation was untrue but decided against challenging him for the moment. "Is this true?" he asked Private Drake.

Drake took a moment of hesitation before answering. "Yes, sir, that's correct. I just need to rest up, that's all."

Brookes mused over the situation. Neither soldier was telling the truth, that much he knew, but to what extent it may affect them, he didn't know. Maybe it was just tiredness. They'd all had one hell of a day so far. After a moment he decided to let it go and focus on the mission at hand. "Alright. Into our quarters, we have a mission."

Captain Brookes rallied his squad together. Okachi, Drake, and Daniel all joined him in their sleeping quarters. They'd been given accommodation that met their basic needs but that was all. Bunk beds, a standard issue grey blanket and a communal washroom, nothing more. Colonel Hayes had been upgraded, of course. He had joined Major Wilson to explain what had happened on his venture out to Rhino Hill.

Brookes briefed his team on the plan regarding the transmitters but he was also keen to attend to a detail that had only recently occurred to him. He fumbled with his headset whilst the rest kept a watchful eye out for anyone entering. Drake stood guard by the only door into the room, peering through its slightly open gap and into the corridor where he had argued with Lieutenant Okachi not too long ago.

"Wyatt? Forrest? This is Captain Brookes. Do you copy? Over," he whispered into the silent room and on a secure channel on the comms unit. "Wyatt? Forrest?"

"This is Forrest, Captain, reading you loud and clear, over," came a muted reply.

"Forrest, how are things up there under your watch? Any problems?"

"Negative, Captain, at least nothing we couldn't deal with. The scientist, a man named Mark, has returned from some expedition he took up. He confirmed that it is indeed Earth through the gateway but informed us he couldn't find any signs of a military establishment in the immediate area where he investigated. After learning a great amount of nothing else he came back through the gate in an attempt to get back to Rhino Hill. We had a few moments where he became uncooperative towards us but that other guy, Wolf; he showed up and took Mark back to a small camp they have established not far from the gateway. Other than that, it's quiet. We've had nothing to contend with."

"Okay, listen up. We've found a way to repel the STs."

"Really?" Forrest interrupted.

"Really," Brookes repeated, "these transmitters do the business. We're out at dawn tomorrow to rig them to the masts in an attempt to protect any structures still standing. First thing we're going to do is head up to you both and attach one to the gate. That way we know it can be protected without having a physical presence up there and we can get you both back on the team.

208

Copy?"

"Captain," Drake added quickly. Brookes looked across to him. Drake gestured out of the door.

"Copy that," Forrest replied.

"Stay safe, Private. See you tomorrow. Brookes out." Brookes removed his comms set and gently threw it next to his weapon. Drake removed himself from the guard position and sat down on a solid bed. Okachi span around rapidly and looked into an empty corner.

"Okachi?" Brookes whispered intently, frowning his brows as he made the point.

Okachi turned back but checked over his shoulder again as though he had been disturbed by something. "Sorry sir. I just had a feeling that someone was behind me," he answered, turning back to his superior.

"Keep cool, Lieutenant," Brookes ordered. The battle had been intense, as had the entire day so far, and he believed Okachi was still experiencing the adrenalin leaving his system similar to what Drake had apparently experienced out in the corridor.

Colonel Hayes knocked firmly on the door and swiftly entered without waiting for an invitation, followed quickly by Dr. Kenford.

"Gentlemen," he began as he allowed the doctor to enter and then swiftly closed the door behind her. The Enforcers stood up and saluted.

Colonel Hayes returned the salute. "At ease," he ordered.

"Gentlemen, the vipers you arrived in have been loaded with the Tevlor series 181 transmitters," Dr. Kenford explained. "They are primed and ready to go. All you need to do is secure them in place and the electromagnetic pulses will do the rest. You have ample transmitters in case of any accidents or complications," Dr. Kenford informed the soldiers.

"Be warned though. The STs may still be in the

local area. Out of sight does not necessarily mean out of mind," Colonel Hayes informed them, remembering the first thing he was taught on the battlefield.

"Yeah, I wouldn't put anything past those ugly suckers tending their wounds and attempting to launch another attack once more," Drake replied, recalling the sheer number of bodies that had surrounded the base while they had engaged in battle to protect the camp.

"We usually get interest from the Subterraneans during the night hours out here but never in the volume that we saw tonight," Dr. Kenford explained, "and that was the first time they have attacked Fort Gyan."

"They look like a dumb, unintelligent species, but I'd bet my bottom dollar that before tonight, they were gathering intelligence and looking for chinks in the camp's defences," Colonel Hayes added.

"Yeah, it's just pure luck that those Tevlors were stored here otherwise this entire camp would have been destroyed in a matter of seconds," Daniel mused.

"Just make sure the transmitters don't fail for us," Okachi said to the doctor, thinking of the mission he was about to undertake. Okachi was the thinker of the unit, the man who usually had a plan B in the back of his mind if everything else failed.

"The transmitters must be placed securely. That's why we requested Daniel accompany you on this mission. The masts were built to accommodate these transmitters when humankind first expanded on to Springfield, and, with the greatest of respect, the Tevlors would not have been covered during the basic training that comms or tech specialists received when you signed up," she added.

"No, no, you're right," Okachi agreed, "the only reason I knew about them was due to my own research. I had no idea the masts were created to accommodate them."

"No, I never knew that either, but I know where to locate the infrared scope on one," Daniel admitted.

"Whilst you are travelling you can use transmitters to protect yourselves but I wouldn't suggest using them too frequently. Above all, you must ensure that the transmitters do not get damaged," Colonel Hayes ordered.

"Great," Drake sighed from across the room, "basically don't use them."

"This is what you trained for. You're elite soldiers. You can get the job done," Colonel Hayes replied to him. He then turned to Dr. Kenford. "Doctor, may I please have a moment with my men."

Dr. Kenford smiled. "Of course. Good luck, gentlemen," she then added. Captain Brookes nodded as the doctor left the room.

"Okay, men," the colonel began, rubbing a hand across his mouth and down his chin, "this is what I want you to do. Head back to the gate-"

"Already ahead of you on that, sir," Brookes interrupted.

"Why? What have you planned?"

"I've been in contact with our soldiers up there in the mountains. We're heading there first thing to go and protect the gate."

The colonel nodded and smiled. "Exactly what I had planned, but there's something else I want you to do. I want you to head back to Rhino Hill and protect the entire site there. You'll have to use your intelligence and place them somewhere where the Screamers cannot launch an offensive against them. Those women and children are too important to us. They survived in the most hostile situations up here and I don't want it to have been for nothing. We need to protect them, and not leave their wellbeing to chance."

"I second that," Daniel added, "that place has been a

211

home to me while I've been working up here. They all mean too much to Springfield and have worked so hard to establish what they had there. Plus, Rhino Hill and Halfway House are my life now. I don't want to leave them unless it's absolutely necessary."

"I'd say it's a bit too late for that," Drake chipped in.

"No, Daniel and the colonel are right," Captain Brookes told the squad. "If these transmitters can protect Rhino Hill as well as they have Fort Gyan, we may be able to adapt a system to protect Newhaven and Grand Central, and all the other areas where human civilization exists."

"This could be it," Hayes emphasised to them, "our one shot at keeping everything together. There's no other way that I can see. I don't think Uncle Sam will come up with a solution to regain communications with Earth in the next decade if I'm honest. They've been twiddling their thumbs for the best part of a year and are still attempting find a way of doing it. We've been on our own now for so long up here, the top comms and scientists must have pretty much exhausted every idea and theory. You need to protect three transmitters at least to create a signal that we can use. This is it, gentlemen, our only chance. I'll leave the rest with you." The colonel saluted the Enforcers who returned the gesture. At dawn, the fight for Springfield would begin again.

Chapter 16A

Tom's eyes were closed. He was in a dark area, his whereabouts unknown even to his own conscious state. He'd watched on as the Subterraneans fell back from Fort Gyan, their numbers outclassed by vast weapons and deadly munitions. They had almost succeeded, almost found a way in, but had faltered to weapons they had no chance of defeating. The Subterraneans could return once more and attack Newhaven or Grand Central but what could they achieve by destroying an area already destroyed? Well, the civilisations were not entirely destroyed. The Subterraneans had demolished the borders and the resistance at those areas, but until they could defeat the key areas, their impact would not be devastating. Their lack of any great intelligence was a blessing to the Springfielders. Masts had been destroyed, but it had initially been along with the destruction of the immediate areas they had surfaced from. If the Subterraneans were following sound signals as was believed, they'd have attacked at the outskirts of these towns where the civil unrest was brewing.

The Subterraneans' lack of intelligence was about to change. Tom's plan had worked. Until he found a way to maximise the alien races' attack, he'd take his time and plan wisely. Let them use their own, limited initiative for now, and take hold when it counted. Tom smiled in the darkness; he was simply biding his time. He knew the residents of Rhino Hill were camping on Earth. He knew every single move they made. An idea emerged in his scheming mind as he floated through the darkness. What would happen if the Subterraneans managed to reach them, across the galaxy and on to Earth? He had no intention of allowing those from

Rhino Hill to remain there, but the possibility of the Subterraneans invading Earth? What would happen then?

The Subterraneans dwelled deep beneath the soil of Springfield. A vast network of tunnels and chambers was being created to house the species new to this alien world. The tunnels linked far and wide beneath the planet, with prime locations within the reach of Grand Central and Newhaven.

The Screamers swarmed between the Stumblers within the darkness, all of them moving in unison with one another. Their pores sensed the electro-magnetic fields emanating throughout the darkness which allowed them to continue their tasks with precision. They sensed the whereabouts of one another. In the depths of the Springfield landscapes, they thrived. Their attacks upon the human civilisations had been primitive and born out of inexperience on this alien world. As they bustled beneath the ground they also had the voice, a strange phenomenon that had helped them locate specific populated areas, such as Fort Gyan.

While the Subterraneans regained their bearings, they withdrew into the darkness and focused on their hideaway. The voice had told them to burrow deep, much deeper than they had anticipated, and keep hidden away. It had suggested that they relocate somewhere closer to a mountainous terrain. The voice had spoken of an imminent attack within the tunnels that would destroy any life form within its grasp. The Subterraneans took heed of the voice and advanced deeper and deeper towards the planet's core and spread further afield. There, they could be safe from attack and dwell harmlessly until called upon again. The voice was their leader, but also their protector. With little intelligence to understand the nature of the voice and a natural instinct for aggressive self-preservation, they could launch a devastating attack upon the Springfield civilisations when called upon by their new advisor. But for now they burrowed and worked upon their dwellings on the new planet. When called upon, they would unleash a wave of terror unlike anything the humans had ever seen or experienced before. For now, they dwelled, and remained, away from the atmosphere until the time arrived that they were needed again. They would attack once more, this time at Grand Central. The voice wanted to know exactly how far the Subterraneans would follow its order, and Grand Central was the ideal place to find out.

Chapter 17A

Rhino Hill was deserted. In fact, there had been no sign of any STs since the squad of soldiers and a tech specialist had left the camp. The squad had been placing transmitters inside and around Rhino Hill ensuring that no damage could come to the hardware if the STs resurfaced and launched another offensive. Captain Brookes gave out the directions, Drake and Okachi argued over placement effectiveness, and Daniel simply did as he was told. Once they were sure that the placement of the transmitters covered the entire area they jumped into the viper and headed toward their next destination.

Forrest jumped up from his resting place after finding Captain Brookes and the squad in his rifle scope. Wyatt joined him, and they both saluted on their captain's arrival.

"At ease, men," he ordered, shaking their hands. "Anything new to report?" he asked, making his way inside the vast, cavernous chamber they had been guarding. His focus turned to the gate and the bright, early dawn breaking across America he imagined, far across the distant galaxies upon the Earth.

"No, sir," Wyatt stated. "The colony from Rhino Hill has set up camp in the woods not far from this location, that is all."

"Not a human or an ST in sight since you left from this end, sir," Forrest went on to state.

From behind them Daniel stumbled over a small, uneven shard of rock and tripped, dropping the transmitter. Stumbling to gain his footing, he stepped onto the fallen equipment and crushed it beneath his boot.

"Damn it, Daniel! What the hell is wrong with

you?" Drake shouted as he followed the engineer from behind. "That's a spare transmitter destroyed! Idiot! Maybe your experience is best used serving the STs instead of the military!"

"Drake!" Captain Brookes snapped angrily. He frowned at his soldier.

"Carelessness, Captain. We're fighting out here, putting our lives on the line, and potentially lifesaving equipment is being thrown around and destroyed! Is this what I'm sacrificing my own life for?"

"Calm down, Drake," Okachi began as he wandered beside him, "we got spares."

"Don't tell me-" Drake became aggressive and pushed Okachi forcefully away. Okachi turned and slapped his visor, jolting the private's head backward.

"Alright, alright, alright!" Brookes ordered loudly. Wyatt and Forrest leapt into restrain the arguing soldiers. They continued to exchange verbal insults to one another until Brookes stepped between them. "Calm down, the both of you!" he shouted, his voice echoing to the deepest recess of the chamber. "Damn it, you're soldiers, not enemies, start acting like them." Okachi snorted in reply. "Now, are we going to have a problem here?" he asked his squad. "Lieutenant?" he asked, looking to Okachi.

Okachi grimaced and gently shook his head. "No, sir," he replied calmly.

"Private?" he then asked Drake.

Drake had all but given up his struggle. No matter how angry he was, he'd never break out from Wyatt's bear hug. "No, sir, I guess not," he stated gently.

Captain Brookes looked to the restrainers and nodded. "Okay," he said, signalling an order. Wyatt and Forrest let go of their captives. Drake rolled his right shoulder forward, allowing his armour to clatter against itself gently. "We are in the middle of a very

217

serious, very hostile situation," Brookes explained firmly to his squad, "and crap like this is unacceptable. I don't know what it is that's got you both into these shitty moods, but it stops, here and now. What we are doing will not only impact Springfield, but the Earth, our home, as well. Think of the situation you are in and the importance of what you are doing. I don't care who you are or how long we have served together, I will not let anyone jeopardise this mission. Do I make myself clear?"

"Yes sir," came the immediate response from his squad. Brookes said nothing more but gave a simple, stern nod to show his authority.

Daniel drew a deep breath and savoured the smell of fresh pine as he wandered through the forest on Earth. It was so long since he had set foot upon the home planet that it felt to him like a previous life. For that moment though, that solitary, single moment, he was home, and with his nose slightly in the air and a smile on his face, he was happy.

"You know how far inside they are?" Okachi asked as he wandered beside him. Daniel had volunteered to find the occupants of Rhino Hill and inform them of the news that they could return to their home. The plan was to transport them back using the ant that Mark had taken through the gateway. It would mean making a number of journeys back and forth to Rhino Hill but at least it would be safe for them to do so. A transmitter would be given to them to use between transfers so that the ant could remain protected from an enemy attack.

Daniel had volunteered to cross to the Earth to see his second family, more notably Anna, and inform them of the news. Okachi had been volunteered by Captain Brookes to accompany him, more so to ease the tension that was growing between both the lieutenant and Private Drake. They had never seen eye to eye whilst serving within the unit but they had never become as aggressive to each other as they had done during the past day or so. Brookes believed the situation was now becoming too stressful, which was taking its toll on both men, and decided to split them for a while in order for them both to gather their thoughts and start a fresh.

"No, but it can't be too far," Daniel replied, opening his eyes and taking in the natural surroundings. The bright sunlight was pouring down through the trees into shafts of golden light throughout the dry, debris filled ground they were traversing. "Ah, look," he then added, pointing to a small clearing on the trail they were navigating.

Greg was the first person to notice Daniel and Okachi heading towards them. He raised a jubilant alarm and turned everyone's attention to the pair emerging across the boundary to their camp. Anna was the first one to shout and stumble across to him. She flung her arms around him and hugged him tightly.

"Daniel," she said through a plethora of tears, "Daniel."

"Anna, what is it?" he asked her, sensing immediately that she was upset and not excited.

She clutched the bump in her abdomen. "Something's wrong," she said between the tears.

Daniel's heart leapt. "What? What is it?" he asked with immediate concern.

"I don't know, I don't know," she sobbed gently.

"Are you in pain? Are you bleeding?" he asked worriedly.

Anna took a step away and wiped her cheeks. "No, nothing like that."

"Then what?" Daniel enquired as confusion replaced his initial fear.

"I don't know. I just don't know, but something is

wrong, so very, very wrong."

Wolf had emerged in the background, noticing that the exchange between Daniel and Anna was not a welcoming one. He kept everyone away whilst they finished their conversation.

"What is it that's happening?" Daniel asked her, lightly grabbing her arms to comfort her.

"It's, just, strange. It's something so odd that I'm worried about. The baby moves," she began as tears re-emerged in her eyes.

"There's nothing strange about that. Come on, you've had children before."

"But this is different, Daniel. Why is it then when our baby moves, so does Sally's?"

"What?" he sighed, not taking this revelation as a serious matter.

"Whenever our baby moves, Sally's does too. They move at the same time and in the same way. Why would they do that, Daniel? Why?"

Daniel was at a loss for an explanation. He didn't see it as a cause for concern but more as a coincidence. "I don't know, Anna, but I'm sure it's something natural. I wouldn't worry about it right now," he advised, smiling at her warmly.

"I can't help it though, I just can't. Something is wrong; my instincts are telling me that."

Daniel placed an arm around her. "The baby is moving, you have no pain, I'd say everything is going to plan, okay? Just try not to worry yourself about it. Now come on, I have some news to tell everyone."

The children seemed happy to see Daniel once more, and Sally did not appear to be as dismissive of him as she may have been in the past. The children seemed more interested in Okachi, the soldier who was accompanying him, though. They swarmed around the lieutenant and began asking questions hurriedly and excitedly. Ruth asked about his armour whilst James focused on the weapon he clutched.

Daniel described the situation on Springfield to the adults, and the battle they had endured at Fort Gyan. He outlined the plan to re-establish communication across the planet, and hopefully, with the Earth. That met with agreement from all of them, notably Mark, Springfield's scientific expert. He had been reduced to a mere a survivor since the emergence of the Subterraneans. Daniel explained about Rhino Hill and the transmitters dotted safely across the area, and the plan they had created to allow them all a route to return safely, if they indeed wished to do so.

"I haven't got time to stand here and argue about whether it's a good or bad thing to go back there," Daniel began, wary of the little time that he had and the mission at hand, "but I can tell you it's safe to do so. I think in the current state of both Anna and Sally, it would be advisable. You can cope with those developments much better in the facilities there than in the forest here."

"I want to do it," Mark said quickly. He hadn't even been an occupant of Rhino Hill but was the first to air his view. "I may be able to re-establish contact with the colonel."

"I don't know," Charlie argued, "it sounds very dangerous. I don't know what would be best."

"I'll go back," Anna said, turning to address them. "When baby arrives I'd rather deliver back there than in this forest. At least we know we can deal with it there."

"What would you suggest?" Wolf then asked, turning his attention from Anna to Daniel.

Daniel shrugged. "It's safe. I'll be returning to Rhino Hill once this mission is completed."

Lieutenant Okachi then wandered across to Wolf. He reached into a small metallic compartment and handed it to him. "I need someone who will actually follow through with this," he said as he handed the small black box over.

Wolf frowned a little and studied it briefly. It looked much like an old jewellery box you'd find back on Earth, something that a nervous man may have used to make a lifelong proposal. He opened it up and found nothing more than a simple red button instead of a diamond ring. "What?" he asked the Marine curiously.

"The explosives rigged to the gate. No matter where you are, this side or that, if Earth faces the threat of invasion from those creatures, you need to blow it, regardless." His voice had dropped to no more than a whisper so as not to attract attention from the others. He looked across to Daniel and Anna.

Wolf nodded knowingly. "Done," he whispered softly.

"Daniel," Okachi shouted across the makeshift camp. Daniel knew what it signified without even needing his explanation. "Captain Brookes has been on the comms. We need to move."

Daniel hesitated momentarily before turning back to face Anna. "I'll return to Rhino Hill. If you're not there when I arrive, then I'll know you'll be here. I'll find you." Anna nodded and gave him a quick, meaningful kiss.

Daniel said his goodbyes and left the camp, but not before leaving them a transmitter.

"And don't worry," he had whispered in Anna's ear, "everything will be fine."

Daniel wandered beside Okachi, heading back to the gateway, and back across to Springfield. "You'll see them again," Okachi said comfortingly to him.

Daniel nodded slowly. "I know," he replied optimistically.

Captain Brookes laughed when they arrived. In fact,

the entire unit was in high spirits upon their return.

"What is it?" Okachi asked, curious as to why the sudden change in attitude.

"Advantage Earth-dwellers," Forrest answered him from across the chamber.

Daniel frowned with confusion. "What?" he asked bluntly.

"This morning the STs attacked Grand Central. They burrowed in once more and attacked our people there. Some bright spark from unit Charlie found a catchment of grenades in one of the military buildings, pulled the pin, and, boom, the STs were destroyed."

"Not just those in the immediate area, but all of the STs that launched the offensive." Wyatt added.

Daniel shot an unsure look back to the captain. Brookes grinned. "They weren't just normal grenades. They were PST pulse grenades."

Of course, Daniel thought. The PSTs were grenades which exploded into a huge electrical pulse across a wide area. Although nobody else knew, Archie Rattigan had smuggled them in and hidden them during the construction of his own gate.

"Where were they?" Okachi asked, amazed that such equipment existed upon the planet.

"Some storage unit somewhere," Drake replied, more upbeat and like his usual self than when Daniel had left. "How the hell they got there I do not know."

"Well we don't have to worry about that now," Brookes began optimistically, "all that matters is that they're here, we can use them, and they're being dropped down every worm-hole on this infested rock."

"You think it will wipe them all out?" Daniel asked the captain.

"I doubt whether all of them will be destroyed, but most should get an electric charge that will overload their systems and cause them to drop," Wyatt responded in his captain's place. "If all goes to plan over in Grand Central, everything will work to our advantage and these battles we're having with the STs should now swing in our favour."

"But we still have a job to do. We still have to ready the aerial and transmitters ready for contact," Captain Brookes told his squad, bringing reality back to the situation, "and if those grenades are working, I'd expect the STs to be flooding from their craters. Let's keep it together and remain focused."

"Yes sir!" the squad replied.

Bravo team left the mountainous chamber that lead longingly back to Earth. Daniel reflected on his brief time there, back home, having taken in as much of the forest as his senses allowed. He thought of Anna and the others, and if they would make it back to Rhino Hill. He worried about his unborn child, more so from Anna's reaction to its erratic movements than anything else. She had been truly distressed about it moving alongside Sally's unborn, and that unnerved him. Anna was a strong woman, which was one of the attractions he had felt towards her, and seeing her in such an emotional state worried him slightly.

The soldiers found the vipers exactly where they had left them. Once settled and ready to undertake the next quest, Okachi tapped the co-ordinates of the first aerial into his system. The orange lasers projected an image of their destination from his data pad. "This is it," he then explained, "about three clicks west of our position. The aerial remains intact, and, with any luck, should just need a transmitter adding to its infrared port to boost the signal. Let's hope the STs aren't in the local area."

"If they are, we do what we do best," Wyatt replied, cocking his rifle.

Drake shook his head. "You're such an idiot," he

said quietly.

"What'd you say?" Wyatt shouted angrily. Drake's mouth had offended someone else yet again.

"Whatever, man. Calm the hell down. That's all we need; a testosterone fuelled alpha male with a loaded weapon."

"What the f-" Wyatt began as he charged toward the opinionated soldier.

Brookes jumped between them. "Goddamn it! Will you all just settle down! Drake! What's your damn problem?" The ugliness of Drake's recent behaviour was beginning to surface once again, and at the wrong time.

"Nothing, sir. I don't have a problem," he stated, in an extremely calm and composed tone, "I'm just stating a fact for our unit. If someone is as tanked up on adrenalin as he is and starts firing a gun behind you, do you think he'll release his trigger finger if you get in the firing line?"

"What? What the hell are you thinking?" Forrest replied angrily.

"Motherfu-"

"That's enough," Brookes ordered Wyatt, "stand down." Brookes held an open palm towards the soldier. His simple gesture, tone in voice and serious look told Wyatt that he'd deal with it. Wyatt sighed and stepped back.

Forrest slapped him on the shoulder. "Don't let it get to you, man, it's just not worth it. He can't deal with the situation," he told his teammate.

"Drake, I've heard enough from you," Brookes said. "You ride with me and Daniel. This keeps up, Private; you'll find yourself making friends with the cells back in Ely." Private Drake attempted to respond. Brookes held up a single finger and shook his head. "No, not a word. Keep your mouth shut and your ears open, that is a direct order, Private. The rest of you take the other viper. Stay close and remain in contact."

Wyatt blindly eyeballed Drake, unable to see his features hidden by the tinted, orange visor. He left with Okachi and Forrest, taking one last glance at his nemesis before disappearing along the jagged trail leading down toward the vehicles. Brookes stayed behind with Daniel and his troubled soldier to reduce any more confrontations.

"What the hell is the matter with you?" Brookes said to Drake sternly after his company had disappeared. Brookes had been pushed to breaking point with this soldier's behaviour and recklessness within the squad. What troubled the captain the most was Drake's blatant disrespect toward him, his superior. He continued to ignore direct orders which now undermined Brookes' authority. Even though Brookes trusted his remaining squad, he knew there was nothing more dangerous than a team of soldiers who believed their superior had lost his authority over them. "You argued with Okachi all damn morning, and now this? Are you trying to jeopardise our mission?"

"No, sir. They are just thoughts which could hinder our mission. I believe I am making a valid point."

"Well you're not!" Brookes boomed. "From now on you follow orders and shut up! Got it? We'll talk some more when we get back to Fort Gyan."

"Yes sir," Drake replied enthusiastically whilst saluting.

"Alright. Get your ass in to shotgun in the viper."

Daniel and Brookes followed Drake across the mountainous surface and down to the vehicles. Something was not right, Daniel could just feel it. Something was wrong, but he didn't know how badly or how much it would affect the squad and their mission. If only he knew...

Chapter 18A

The vipers raced across the barren lands following the directions on Okachi's data pad to their first destination. Daniel sat behind, his mind focusing upon Anna. He was still troubled by her behaviour. As they traversed the uneven ground and jolted over the terrain, he had a thought. It would make him feel uneasy if it could be justified. Let's say that Anna was right, he conceded, that the baby was moving in unison with Sally's child, and that it was no coincidence and was really, really happening. That could mean only one thing. Daniel shifted uncomfortably in his seat. It would mean that somehow, someway, they were connected. But how? Of this he had no idea, but if Anna was as serious as she appeared, and what she was reporting to him was indeed true . . . Daniel forced the thought from his mind and tried to focus on something else.

From the seat in front of him Drake removed his helmet. "Captain, can I talk to you please?"

"Not now," Brookes told him with distinct authority. He had just about had it with the soldier who seemed intent on disrupting the squad, even his focus did not move from the viper they were following to engage in the brief conversation.

"Captain, it's important. Please, you want to know what's bugging me, right?"

Brookes momentarily glanced at him. "Alright, Private, what is it?" he sighed. Drake had reeled him in.

"Radio silence, please sir."

"What the-"

"Please sir," he asked compassionately.

Brookes focused on the viper ahead. He rolled his eyes and placed a finger on his comm system. "Okachi, this is Brookes, do you copy? Over."

"Loud and clear, Captain, over," came the tech's voice within his earpiece.

"We're going to radio silence for a moment; I'll contact you when we're done."

"Copy that, sir. Okachi out."

"Alright then, Private, what is it?" he asked as they bounded over the terrain. The wind flapped his hair as they sped across the vast, open plains.

Drake took a moment to figure out what he was going to say. "It's Okachi," he stated quietly.

Brookes scrunched his face. "Okachi? What do you mean it's him?"

"Sir, he's after me," Drake began hurriedly, as though he was trying to fit as much of an excuse in before being cut off. "It started back at Fort Gyan. He's biding his time-"

"Wait! What the hell, Drake? What are you thinking?"

"Sir, he's trying to kill me."

Brookes rolled his eyes and sighed. "Trying to kill you? Really? And how did you come to that conclusion?"

"I just know it," he responded, now a little calmer and more settled, sounding almost resigned to the fact that his captain did not believe him. "The way he looks at me, the way he acts, I can just tell."

"Drake, I don't know what has gotten into you, but you get it out, and pretty damn quick. Do I have to get a medical examination carried out on you when we get back to camp?"

Drake shook his head slightly. "No, sir, of course not."

"Then hold it together and do your job," Brookes ordered.

Drake slumped back in his seat. "Yes, sir," he

moaned. It was at that moment that Daniel saw Private Drake for exactly what he was; a young, twenty-something man who probably signed up to the military fresh out of school. It wasn't until that point that Daniel truly understood just how young Private Drake was, and how inexperienced in life skills he appeared to be.

Daniel sat in the back, his mind creating a list concerns for the mission. The squad were not on the same page and this worried him. He was heading into an extremely volatile situation alongside a volatile team. Drake had offended Wyatt and accused Okachi, and the captain was now losing control of his squad, the squad of Enforcers entrusted to complete the most important mission since Springfield lost contact with the Earth. How could they function as a unit? Daniel closed his eyes. Just do what you have to and keep out of it, he told himself.

The vipers pulled up in the vicinity of the first mast. Okachi confirmed it on the data pad and using the holographic imager located the infrared outlay where the transmitters should be placed to improve the signal and protect the structure. The sky above them had clouded over significantly during their journey and thunder began to rumble somewhere across the horizons of Springfield. The landscape out here lay relatively untouched from the Subterraneans, but as they had all come to expect, there was no human presence within this desolate area, and so the STs would not have invaded these lands.

The landscape was a rare patch of rolling, grassy mounds that Daniel thought may be striking if the day had been a bright, summer's affair like he had experienced back on Earth on a number of occasions. Instead the dark skies and rumbling thunder made it seem bleak and barren, and as hostile an area as he had ever seen on both planets.

There had been various reports across the comms network from Captain Brookes' peers within the Enforcers explaining that the pulse grenades were doing everything that they had expected. The STs were failing. Their senses were being overloaded with the electric fields that caused their nervous systems and minds to shutdown, exactly as the Stumblers had done back at Fort Gyan. If it had not been for Dr. Kenford's research there was no saying exactly how Springfield would be reacting to these seemingly relentless attacks. Right now they had found the advantage in the battle with the Subterraneans but it would only hinge on how many grenades they had at their disposal and how many STs they could find at any one time. Since the Subterraneans had emerged through the depleted gateway the human civilisation had battled for survival. Many had died at the hands of this aggressive alien race, but now the tide had changed and missions of survival had turned to seek and destroy operations. From what Daniel had seen back at the camp, however, he believed there would be more than a handful of STs that would slip through their grasp and exist somewhere under the plates of Springfield.

"Daniel," came a voice, bringing him back to reality. He turned to see Okachi approaching him. "You ready?" he asked.

"Sure," Daniel replied and together they climbed the mast to begin fitting the transmitter.

For the next few hours Daniel traversed the plains with the Enforcers, attaching the transmitters to the isolated masts and making any necessary repairs to them with Lieutenant Okachi. The two of them undertook the engineering work whilst Captain Brookes and the remaining soldiers stood guard beneath them, preparing to engage with the STs at any time should they emerge from the ground and launch an offensive once again.

Various reports emerged across the comms network of Stumblers or Screamers taken down and being pushed away from the boundaries of Grand Central. Newhaven stood as it had done until the chance for Uncle Sam to get there presented itself. Teams of Enforcers were now entering the worm-holes created by the Screamers in an attempt to overload the enemy from the inside.

The skies continued to darken and the thunder continued to roll. The threat to his own safety began to pass through Daniel's mind on more than one occasion. Being located inside a steelwork towering into the sky during a lightning storm was not the safest place to be working.

Tensions seemed to be subsiding within the team. Captain Brookes had done an excellent job in keeping Drake and Okachi separated, although the exchange between Drake and Wyatt had the feel that it was not completely finished. Drake had been kept at Brookes' side throughout the entire mission and, so far, the captain had succeeded in keeping temperaments calm and the mission on schedule.

"Hey, what's that?" Drake alerted the squad as he noticed a small group of dark shadows far out into the distance. They were currently working on the fourth mast and the weather was becoming increasingly sinister. Daniel had felt the gentle patter of a light rain falling on his military issue greens as he was working. "Over there," Drake added as the ground units took a sudden interest and looked toward him.

Brookes shielded his eyes from the rain and looked into the distance to see exactly what it was Drake was pointing toward. "I can't make it out," he replied after a moment or so of squinting into the distance. More clumps of shadows gathered across the open, and in the poor light and increasing element it was difficult to establish exactly what was amassing. There was something there, though, of that he could be certain. Something was gathering in the distance. Maybe not large enough to be STs, but there was definitely something taking an interest in the squad's presence. "Forrest, go join Okachi and Daniel. Scope out our visitors and report back immediately."

"Copy that, Captain," the sniper replied, and quickly jogged across to the ladder leading to where Daniel and Okachi were working.

"What's the matter?" Okachi asked as Forrest entered their workspace. The engineers were just finishing the installation of the transmitter.

Forrest removed the rifle from over his shoulder and began prepping the scope for visual. "Seems we've got movement out there on the ridge line," Forrest pointed as he swung his rifle out in the same direction. "We can't make out who or what they are from the ground down there." Forrest pointed the weapon out into the distance and studied the shadows. He twiddled various settings on the scope in order to see better. "What the…" he said to himself as he gazed through the rifle.

"What?" Okachi asked as he looked out across the No-Man's-Land.

"What is it?" came Brookes' voice over the comms unit.

"Captain, I don't know how to say this, but it looks like we're being watched by a ton of, well, monkeys," he answered. If the sniper hadn't seen it for himself he would never have believed it.

"Forrest, repeat that again?" Brookes asked, sounding confused from the ground below.

"Exactly what I said, Captain. It looks like hundreds of monkeys out there."

"Baboons," Daniel corrected, interrupting his duties.

"What's that? What did he say? Get him to talk to me," Brookes ordered the sniper after hearing Daniel's comments in the background.

Forrest turned to Daniel and nodded his head toward the ground. "The captain wants to know what you were saying," he told him, relaying the captain's message.

Daniel shuffled to the edge of the platform and looked down. He saw the remaining soldiers looking up toward him. "Baboons," he shouted down from the platform, remembering the account of how Wendy had met her demise back at Rhino Hill. "They took out an occupant of Rhino Hill, killed her outright. They're very hostile and very aggressive," he told them.

"And they're heading this way!" Forrest shouted into his unit.

"What?" Drake shouted, spinning back in their direction. A mass of shadows across the landscape now turned into a moving wave thundering towards them.

"Stand fast! Stand fast! Incoming!" Forrest shouted.

"How many?" Brookes shouted.

"Too many! A hundred, maybe more!"

"Damn it!" Wyatt un-holstered his rifle. He walked away from the mast and out into the face of the advancing wildlife.

"Okachi! Get down here now! Forrest, keep position! Cover us from there! Daniel, stay as you are, that is a direct order!" Brookes told the engineer. Okachi glided down the ladder to join the ground units.

"Keep your distance," Forrest told Daniel as he took position, "the kickback on this sucker can be strong."

"Got it," Daniel replied before moving across the platform.

The baboons approached quickly across the empty grass. They snarled and squealed as they pounded across the vast open. Thunder rumbled away in the distance. The rain continued to fall rapidly around them. "Gees they look vicious," Forrest began, checking out their snarling muzzles from the safety of his scope.

"Weapons ready!" Brookes ordered. The soldiers clattered their rifles ready to engage in combat. The Enforcers took position. The baboons screamed and hollered as they tore across the grass. "Take aim! Fire!"

The air exploded with the sound of bullets firing from the weapons. The first wave of baboons fell, blood spilled from their bodies and onto the dampening grass.

"Fire at will!" Brookes screamed. The weapons surged into life as the Enforcers attacked the baboons with deadly force. The animals fell from the front, tumbling across the ground as they approached the aerial. The Enforcers sprayed the area with bullets as the animals continued to advance quickly. Forrest took aim and shattered their bodies with the powerful rifle. Daniel simply stood and watched as the mass of animals surged closer toward them.

"It's not going to work," he muttered to himself as the waves of baboons closed down upon them, "there are too many."

The animals darted closer, leaping over the bodies of the fallen as they swarmed upon their targets. Their eyes glowed with evil intent. Their teeth dripped with anger and malice. They closed in, fifty feet, forty feet, thirty feet . . .

"Damn it!" Wyatt shouted, dropping the business end of his assault rifle. One baboon leading a pack of three was heading right toward him. Wyatt clutched the butt of the rifle. The baboon screamed and launched itself through the air. Wyatt swung the rifle like a bat and smashed the baboon from its leap. Suddenly they were submerged. The baboons swarmed upon them and clawed at their armour. They tore at the metal and gouged at the exposed flesh. Forrest shot down at the animals on top of his comrades.

Wyatt screamed as his arms, unprotected by the armour, began to be scratched and slashed. He grabbed a baboon by the neck and swung it round, knocking back the group attacking him. Drake punched violently out at the vicious animals surrounding him, crumpling a muzzle as a baboon felt the full force of his attack. Claws obscured his vision and his visor began to crack with the force of the barrage. Okachi pumped bullets into his attackers as they launched toward him. He kicked one into a small pack of advancing animals and filled their bodies with bullets. Brookes sprayed the area with ammunition and smashed back any attackers not in its path. Drake shouted as his helmet was torn from his head. The baboons' screams merged into one terrifying roar throughout the rainy air around them. Their bodies fell but still they attacked. They hacked and slashed at the soldiers with no remorse. They attacked aggressively and primitively. Forrest continued to knock them out from his perch within the aerial but the time he took to reload and aim was not fast enough.

"Damn! Forrest!" Daniel shouted.

"What?"

"We got company!" A group of five baboons lurched through the hatch and launched towards the two men. Forrest turned and took out the first one, shooting it from the air forcefully. Another baboon leapt from behind and latched onto his shoulders. "Daniel!" he shouted. Daniel took hold of a wrench but was knocked back by another advancing animal. Forrest began to scream. "Daniel!" Daniel swung the wrench, smashing his attacker across the head. Another screamed and launched an attack towards him the. He kicked it and hacked the wrench down across its back.

235

"Daniel!" Forrest screamed again. Daniel took hold of the baboon latched around Forrest's neck but it would not move.

As Daniel pulled the animal, its body contorted and tensed. He felt claws plunge deep into his shoulders. He screamed out as an animal caught him by surprise and attacked him from behind. He flailed with his free hand to remove the creature but it gripped on tightly. Running across the platform he turned, jumped and crashed down to the metal surface on his back, jarring his head against the baboon that was now squashed beneath him. He span around and swung the wrench immediately, removing the muzzle of the animal in one, quick attack. Daniel saw that Forrest had fallen to the metal surface. He quickly jumped to his feet and ran across to his comrade, swinging the wrench once more and striking the baboon attacking the sniper in its side. Daniel felt the bones in its body smash on impact, and watched as it lurched away from its prey.

Forrest lay looking toward him in a stony gaze. His throat had been removed. Tatters of flesh hung from the opening where the animal had attacked. The wound was vicious and, as Daniel immediately recognised, fatal. Forrest stared up toward him. He stared back. The sound of gunfire brought Daniel to his senses. He looked down to see that the baboons were dispersing. Even though they were outnumbered, the Enforcers had stood successfully against their enemy and were yet to concede defeat. Wyatt continued to thrash the animals attacking him, even though his arms were shredded and torn. The ground at Okachi's feet was littered with the carcasses of shot animals. Brookes had been surrounded, yet his experience in battle had kept him alive.

Wave after wave of baboon's had attacked and wave after wave, they had fallen. Drake was repelling them.

Whatever had clouded his judgement previously had all but vanished. This was why they were soldiers; they survived no matter what. Daniel watched on as Drake continued to destroy the animals surrounding him. He watched on as Drake tracked his target, took aim, and fired. Then, Wyatt fell to the floor, his arm ruptured with bullets.

"Drake!" Brookes screamed. The baboons began to subside. Those still alive began to flee from the battle. The ground was saturated with the blood and bodies of the aggressors. Chunks of flesh and entrails littered the grass. The rain pounded heavily from the skies above them. Thunder shook the ground on which they stood.

"Shit!" Drake shouted, "Wyatt!"

"Stay right there!" Okachi's voice ordered. Okachi had lifted his rifle and was pointing it directly toward Drake.

"Okachi . . ."

"Did you see it, Captain?" Okachi asked, cutting off his superior immediately.

"Did I see what?" Brookes replied calmly.

"Did you see it? Drake. He did it on purpose."

"What?" Drake screamed, spinning immediately toward Okachi.

"I said don't move!" Okachi shouted. The baboons fled across the barren landscape, their screams subsiding into the heavy rains.

Wyatt slowly made it to his feet. His arms had been shredded by the attacking animals. Two huge slug-holes now streamed with blood from his left arm where he had been shot. He dropped his rifle and un-holstered the standard issue DB handgun from his thigh. Drake looked down his sights to Okachi. Both of them stood against each other intensely. "It was an accident!" he shouted through the downpour.

"It was no accident!" Okachi screamed, "I saw you!

237

You knew exactly what you were doing!"

The rain hissed around them. "You bastard!" Wyatt shouted. With his better arm he lifted the handgun toward Drake.

"Don't listen to him, Wyatt! He's had it in for me since Fort Gyan. I may be a lot of things, but one thing I'm not is a liar!" Drake shouted.

"You've had it in for yourself! You're the one rebelling from this squad!" Okachi bellowed over the heavy rainfall.

"I've rebelled from no one! If it wasn't for me you'd have all died back at Fort Gyan! I was the one who figured out the Screamers were calling the shots!"

Captain Brookes became tense. For the first time in his military career he didn't know what to do. Adrenalin flushed through his body and nervousness took hold of him. He knew that he would have to take charge and look strong in doing so. "All of you!" he shouted, "stand down!"

"Sorry, Sir," Okachi replied sarcastically, "I can't do that, not while we're threatened by this jackass."

Now, Brookes' authority had certainly been undermined. He quickly realised he had lost all control over of his squad. Looking for an ally, he turned his attention to Wyatt. "Wyatt, lower the weapon," he said calmly, only this time without commanding the order.

Wyatt shook his head. "No," he replied firmly. The storm pounded down upon them now as the stand-off between the four men continued. Okachi and Wyatt stood against Drake, Drake against Okachi. Brookes lowered his head and spoke into his comm unit.

"Forrest?" he asked quietly. He received no reply.

"Forrest is dead," came Daniel's voice from the unit, "a baboon shredded him."

Brookes closed his eyes with despair. In front of him the three soldiers were not flinching. "Okay, men,

238

listen," he ordered sternly. His eyes were now distorting with the rain. "There's no need for this. We're a team, we've been through worse."

"Excuse me sir, but we never had a traitor in our ranks until now," Okachi snarled in reply. Something had really taken the lieutenant. He had never been this aggressive in all the years they'd served alongside each other. Something was wrong.

"I'm not a damn traitor!" Drake shouted angrily, "it was an accident! I didn't mean to shoot him!"

"Give me one good reason why I should not put a bullet through your head right here, right now?" Okachi asked the accused soldier.

A rifle clicked to one side of Lieutenant Okachi. Even without seeing it, he knew that Brookes' rifle was now aimed directly toward him. "Okachi, there's no need for this," Brookes said calmly to his lieutenant, taking aim at his comms expert in the rifle's sights. "It doesn't have to happen like this. I know you. I know you are a good man, and a better soldier. You've served this unit well."

"I appreciate your compliment, Captain, but that doesn't disguise the fact that this soldier within our squad attempted to murder one of his own."

"I'm warning you, Okachi! It was a damn accident!" Drake bellowed. He quickly wiped the rain from his eyes.

"Like hell it was!" Wyatt blasted.

"Don't take it personal, Wyatt. It was simply a case of friendly fire," Brookes replied calmly.

"Bull shit, Captain!" Wyatt screamed.

"Stand down, Corporal!" Brookes shouted.

"No Sir!"

"Come in! Come in! Bravo team Enforcers. It's Daniel. Listen to me, all of you! I know you can hear me. It's the transmitters affecting you in this way!"

239

Wyatt screwed his face in disbelief. "What?" he asked arrogantly.

"It's the transmitters. Their level of electromagnetics is too high. This is why they were decommissioned. It distorts your senses. Don't you remember what Dr. Kenford told us back at Fort Gyan? If you are overexposed to these electric fields it affects you're perception. You have the feeling your being watched. You get an overwhelming sense of fear. It makes you paranoid. You think the world is out to get you, when it isn't." Daniel watched on from the platform, now wearing the comms unit that had belonged to Forrest.

"Does a bullet wound look like damn paranoia to you?" Wyatt screeched into the system.

"Listen to him!" Brookes replied forcefully, his sights still set upon Okachi. "It's just something you think has happened. Yes, Drake shot you, but it was accidental, not purposefully."

"And how would you know that, Captain?" Okachi asked, his focus and rifle still set upon Drake.

"Damn it, Okachi, will you just listen to yourself? After everything we've been through, you think we'd die by killing each other?" Okachi sighed. Brookes saw the change upon his face.

"It's the transmitters. We've been exposed to them for too long, that is what's causing all this. It's nothing else, just the distortion to your senses," Daniel added.

The four soldiers stood beneath the pouring rain, not one of them flinching. "Come on, men, you heard him. Let's get the mission finished and then we can talk," Brookes stated calmly.

Okachi grimaced. "I can't, sir. I can't do it," he responded gently. Brookes could sense the conflict he was feeling.

"Come on, stand down, Lieutenant."

240

"He needs to be executed, sir, or our mission is jeopardised!"

"He attempted to take my life!" Wyatt shouted.

"You need to give that order, sir!" Okachi stated angrily.

"I did not try to kill you!" Drake screamed.

"You need to give that order!" Okachi shouted. Tears rippled from his eyes.

"I will not give that order!" Brookes bellowed.

"Do it!" Wyatt shouted.

"Do it!" Okachi screamed.

"I will not give that order! Stand down! Stand down!"

Brookes dipped his rifle slightly and turned to Drake. Okachi turned to Brookes. A solitary bullet was fired, the sound echoing across the vast openness. Okachi collapsed and slumped to the ground. "No!" Brookes screamed and turned to Drake. The echo of another bullet rattled around them and Drake fell to the floor. Brookes stood motionless for a split second, his eyes wide and his mouth agape. Wyatt's handgun smoked dimly from the barrel. The captain took aim at Wyatt. Wyatt pulled the trigger instantly and Brookes dropped heavily to the ground. Wyatt screamed with rage and looked upwards toward the mast. His head jarred sideways as a single bullet hit him, exploding his head and ending his torment.

An eerie silence fell across the plain. The four Enforcers lay motionless on the sodden ground around them. All had sustained life-ending injuries. The heroes who had repelled the Subterraneans and saved both Rhino Hill and the gateway to Earth had ultimately destroyed each other.

From the platform upon the mast Daniel removed his eye from the scope of the sniper rifle. He rolled onto his back and took a deep breath. Feeling the rain fall upon his skin he looked up into the rolling clouds and through the moderate rainfall. The journey was now his own.

Chapter 19A

Daniel contacted Colonel Hayes and explained the failing mission in detail. He told him about the paranoia, the attacking baboons and the stand-off that had ended the lives of Bravo team. At first, the colonel found it hard to swallow. He'd known Daniel for long enough, and knew that there was no way he'd be involved in their demise. Dr. Kenford confirmed the traits that Bravo team had shown were similar to those soldiers who had suffered the paranoia back at Fort Gyan. She confirmed Daniel's story as a likely outcome for those who fell under the invisible influence. Daniel gave the coordinates of his location and Colonel Hayes passed them to Major Wilson. A squad would be sent to recover the bodies and give them a full military send-off.

"What are you going to do?" the colonel asked Daniel as he sat behind the wheel of his chosen viper.

"I'm heading back to Rhino Hill," Daniel explained over the comms network. "That's where I told them all to go. I also told them it would be safe, although now I'm not so sure. Those transmitters have done too much damage. I don't know if I can risk the same thing happening to those that I love."

"I thought you might. That's why I've sent some of the extermination squads out there."

"Who are they?" Daniel asked.

"The teams carrying the pulse grenades. They were en route to Newhaven. I asked some of them to clear the area around Rhino Hill and Halfway House. I'm not saying that all the STs in that area will be completely eliminated, but you'll be much safer out there, at least for the time being."

Daniel sighed. "Thank you, Colonel," he said

appreciatively.

"I'll make my way back to Rhino once the loose ends are tied up here at camp. I think a discussion with Mark and yourself will be in order, about you know what."

Daniel smiled and nodded to himself. "Yes, I do."

Both men said their goodbyes. Daniel removed his comms set and threw it in the passenger seat. He closed his eyes and rolled his head skyward. There was still so much left to do. Springfield was almost as it had been before the Subterraneans had invaded the planet. Daniel had been taken on an immense journey unlike he had ever expected. He was an engineer, nothing more, and he'd been thrown into the business end of a full-scale war. It was a scary situation to be in, especially with no combat experience on the front line. Now, he hoped, everything would return to how it had been.

Daniel headed out across No-Man's-Land. He had no map to follow, just a basic route he had remembered based on landmarks and objects. As he drove, his mind raced with many different thoughts of his so-called adventure with the Enforcers. He went back to the stand-off beneath the aerial. He'd pulled the trigger on Wyatt, purely because he feared for his own safety. All of the soldiers had suffered the extreme paranoia that accompanied the Tevlor transmitters. Drake and Okachi had fallen prey to it the worst but Wyatt had been drawn in convincingly. It would have been easy for Wyatt to believe Okachi, having been shot by the accused, but Daniel had seen exactly what had happened from his spot within the mast.

Drake had not intentionally shot Wyatt. In fact, it was Wyatt who had stepped into the firing line. After the accusations had flown, Okachi had turned his rifle on Captain Brookes. Drake had been trigger-happy and assassinated his lieutenant, probably through the adrenalin which was likely to have been surging through his body. Had Drake been older and more experienced, perhaps this would never have happened. Wyatt had then immediately pulled the trigger on Drake, a fantastically aimed shot to the head considering the injuries sustained to his arms. This then left only Wyatt, himself and his captain. Brookes had seen the smoking barrel and feared for his own safety but Wyatt was already engaged and pulled the trigger on him before he could turn to the corporal. Daniel had then feared for his own safety and took out Wyatt with the sniper rifle. That was the end of it. There they lay, Private Drake, Corporal Wyatt, Private Forrest, Lieutenant Okachi and Captain Brookes, the victims of immense paranoia.

Daniel's thoughts then turned to Anna. Whether it had been the events back at the mast or just a tinge of paranoia within himself, he was now worried about her. He had no idea what was happening to his spouse or her feelings about the baby. What was certain, though, is that he would soon find out.

The theory he had devised about a connection would be very close to the truth . . .

Chapter 20A

Tom drifted within a sea of dark sub-consciousness. He was warm. He was happy. The Subterraneans were under his influence. Many had survived the purge across Springfield, heeding his advice and burrowing deeper into the plates. He moved gently, listening to the muffled sound of voices from somewhere beyond the darkness. He moved once more, making himself comfortable in his warm surrounding. Suddenly he felt a light pressure pushing against his right side. It was inquisitive, not aggressive, and waited there for a while, seemingly waiting for him to move again. Tom heard Anna's voice engulf him. He smiled to himself.

"They moved," Anna said, to whom Tom did not know or care. "Let's see if they move again."

Chapter 21A

Daniel headed toward the chamber. Rhino Hill had been almost deserted except for the presence of his good friend, Wolf. Wolf had insisted on trialling a run to Rhino Hill with the transmitter in the ant. He wanted to make sure for everyone that it was safe. There were children involved who may not have understood what was going on. They'd already suffered enough just getting out of Rhino Hill, and in returning, he wanted to make absolutely positively sure that they would be okay.

After explaining the situation in which he had become involved, Daniel accompanied Wolf on the return journey. He so desperately wanted to see Anna once more.

The Subterraneans had been drawn to the chamber. The pulse had intrigued them. They congregated at the edges of the chamber to investigate. The Stumblers swayed as they stood peering inside. A Screamer nestled between their masses at a distance.

"No!" Tom's voice ordered in their natural dialect. "Do not destroy the gate!" He was attempting to exercise his authority over the alien race. The Screamer he was negotiating with slowly defected. The voice echoed throughout its consciousness but it paid little attention. It took hold of the nearest body and launched it inside the chamber. "No!" Tom screamed again, utilising his power to control the creature. Still the Screamer remained unresponsive, launching its missiles blindly in the direction of the electromagnetic signal.

"Oh no! Oh no!" Daniel whimpered as they approached the chamber. He saw an army of STs moving towards it. His heart sank and he quickly became overwhelmed with emotion. Wolf watched on

247

from the ant. His thoughts immediately returned to the people on Earth. He began to slow down as he approached the hole in the hillside. His stomach fell. Daniel remained a good distance between the two. The STs paid little attention to the vehicles as they focused on the chamber.

"Stop it!" Tom screamed from his hiding place within the stars. "Stop!"

The Screamer continued its barrage. Bodies crashed against the chamber walls. "They must return!"

Wolf reached down into his pocket and produced the small box Lieutenant Okachi had given him. Okachi had been thinking about the safety of the Earth. Wolf was thinking about his family. He noticed his nervousness increase. In the distance, Daniel began to slow. The transmitters they carried repelled the Stumblers. Nevertheless, some now turned their focus upon the vehicles. The Screamer continued its barrage upon the chamber. Wolf feared that if the transmitter protecting the gate was destroyed, Earth was for the taking.

"No! No!" Tom screamed. He turned the Stumblers against their leader. They clumsily attacked the Screamer with swipes that would have killed a human but the Screamer barely noticed. It rebelled against the voice and continued its onslaught. Wolf sighed. He prayed that none his family were near the chamber. Placing a thumb on top of the red button, he whispered softly, "I'm sorry," before pushing the button.

PART 2B

Chapter 11B

The explosion that caused Tom's lab to crash was so intense that aftershocks reverberated through the membrane separating void-space and real-space. Waves of reality-smashing energy washed through neighbouring universes. Although dissipating over distance, the epicentre was a source of terrific damage. A sun exploded in one universe, and a comet melted in another. In a third universe, among the lazy spirals of a black hole, the force of the energy wave reacted violently against the inevitable pull of the enormous singularity and part of its swirling mass was torn away, hurled with enough force to break free of the event horizon.

The ribbon drifted through its universe. While it no longer possessed the undeniable mass of its parent its hunger was no less insatiable. It shrank inexorably, sustained by its own dwindling reserves and whatever debris lay in its path, travelling a journey dictated by the gravitational fields of nearby astrological bodies.

By chance, the dark matter passed within a hundred thousand kilometres of a massive gas giant. The great sphere dragged the entity from its random drift, pulling it into a degrading orbit until the black filament entered the planet's atmosphere. But rather than being ripped to shreds in the fantastic methane storms that smothered the planet's core, the tiny black hole drank deeply, greedily absorbing the vortexes until the planet was a giant no more.

The entity grew steadily as it fed, attaining a level of cognition previously impossible for it. It waited where the gas giant used to be, collecting itself, not quite self-aware. All it knew was that it was shrinking, not by much, but enough to be noticeable. The great black cloud convulsed, panicked at the revelation that it was dying. Then its attention was caught by a pulsating dot in deep space and it knew what was needed to stop the horrible sensation. The thing spent some energy on propulsion, powering away from one pull of gravity so it could succumb to another. The bleak, lifeless moons that pulled at it so did not interest it; it was fixed solely upon the distant glow. It did not realise that once the far off light had been extinguished, once all the energy rich sources in this universe were gone, it would be back for them.

Since the accident with the doorway, an event known only to Ricky Marlow now that Archibald Rattigan had apparently perished in the time since, Ricky had felt a need to keep his head down. He had moved around, spending time on a number of different ranches, working the people as much as the land and the animals on it, yet always managing to get away from failing ranches before they succumbed entirely. He had just had a run of bad luck, he had told himself.

Ricky was now a resident of Ranch 22. Hopkins, the ranch owner, was not as stupid as Ricky had hoped and had been keeping an eye on him. Ricky did not enjoy being the subject of such intimate scrutiny and had been left with little choice but to get his hands dirty with real hard work from time to time. While he loathed doing so, he also knew that it was the only way to survive until the next opportunity for a scam presented itself.

He had lost track of how long he had been there; all the days seemed the same to him. He was not saddened by his former partner's disappearance. He regarded it as more of a blessing really. One less mouth to blab about it all. He accepted that *the perfect kiss* was history, pleased that, as yet, there had been no comeback. He had no way of knowing the extent of the terror he would be responsible for. He accepted that his construction might have been slightly involved in what had happened to the escalator, although he excused his part by assuring himself that *it* had obviously been an accident waiting to happen. Ricky was not the kind of man to dwell on his mistakes and rarely took anything from previous failures with him. He was already searching for a new venture, the next scheme into which he could put his energy.

Things began to get interesting again after Ricky had swindled his way onto the caravan Ranch 22 was sending to Grand Central. Regular trade caravans had become the established barter system since the success of Rhino Hill's cattle drive. The future of a ranch relied heavily on what crops, parts, services and information could be traded at the next community. Ricky's goal was to escape ranch work for a few days and upon arrival at Grand Central, he decided to get out of loading and unloading the traded goods as well. He went to see Colonel Hayes.

The colonel was busy writing when Ricky walked up to his desk to report that the trade caravan had arrived. With Hayes' attention fixed entirely upon the paper beneath his pen, Ricky's curiosity took over and he began to decipher the man's neat script. Meticulous lines of ink materialised upside-down, from Ricky's perspective, and he had a hard time understanding the majority of the writing. Even so, the words 'escalator', 'doorway' and 'Tom' jumped out, along with 'Rhino Hill' and 'Halfway House'.

Ricky had never been to Rhino Hill, but there were rumours around Ranch 22 of the women involved with its success. Was there a doorway to Earth at the other settlement? Ricky told himself that such a thing was impossible. A bunch of girls couldn't have built a fully functional doorway out of the scraps of metal on this planet when he had failed to do so with quality items from Earth. There had to be another explanation. Ricky decided he needed to know exactly what was going on. He needed to read the report and get all the details. But Colonel Hayes was not a colonel by accident. He was diligent and competent, with an air of authority one found hard to ignore. There was no way the man would simply hand over a copy of his report to Ricky upon request.

After being dismissed by the colonel rather brusquely Ricky made his way back to the traders, his mind alive with hastily constructed plans. He would have to put in a transfer request to Grand Central, but they weren't handed out without good reason. When he arrived back at the caravan, there was a general buzz about the staff as they made final preparations to get under way. Ricky was running out of time.

An ant loaded with long pipes set off. In desperation, Ricky quickly slashed one of the bracing straps with his knife as the vehicle trundled past. When it began to turn onto the main thoroughfare the strap snapped completely and the weight of the pipes was too much for the remaining straps. The whole lot rolled off with a deafening clatter. One of the loaders leapt aside as the ant shed its load, but the long metal tubes did not stop and collided with the corner of some racking, taking a support beam away. Three pallets of equipment came crashing down. The man wasn't quick enough this time and ended up buried beneath a pile of large boxes. Another man was caught by the cascade of falling stock. As people rushed to assist the two casualties, it was easy for Ricky to identify who had been responsible for securing the load by the man's horrified gape and he went quickly to his side.

"What happened?" Ricky gasped, trying to sound more shocked than accusatory. "I thought that thing was secured."

"I did!" the other replied, somewhat desperately. "I mean, it was. I double-checked, I'm certain."

"Well, there'll have to be a full investigation. Colonel Hayes will want to know how his staff got hurt. He might even make arrests if negligence can be proved." The suggestion of punishment got the desired result. The level of panic in the man's eyes deepened.

"What? You think?"

"Well, yeah. But hey, we're all part of this team, right? I mean, nobody knows you had a look at the braces. It could have been anybody. Could even have been me."

"Yeah. Yeah, that's right."

Ricky made an effort to look as haunted as his new friend. "You think I should go see the supervisor now, maybe, tell her what I think happened? I mean, I'd hate for this to land on someone who had nothing to do with it. Might even have to go straight to Hayes."

"Okay. Yeah. Great. That's a good idea."

Ricky suggested that the worker start giving a hand clearing up whilst he check around and see what he could find about a cause to this accident. The man was more than eager to hand over the responsibility - along with any potential consequences - and Ricky immediately went to secure his sabotage. Nobody was paying him much attention and it was an easy task to free off the restraint and brace and alter it enough so that it looked like it had been old and frayed, ready to go at any time.

Samantha's reprimand was fierce, but when Ricky suggested he stay in Grand Central to cover the shifts of the injured men by way of apology she readily agreed. Ricky was ordered to return when the patients were well again. Ricky knew he would have to work harder now than ever he had done on Ranch 22, but this time it was for something beyond simple existence.

With his stay at Grand Central secured for the time being, Ricky now concentrated on getting into Hayes' office in HQ. This was going to be the hard part, Ricky acknowledged, especially since he would need a fair amount of time in there to find anything worthwhile. He was acutely aware that the longer he left it before getting in, the more chance there was that the report would end up somewhere else. In order to catch the colonel coming or going, Ricky made sure he was within sight of HQ as often as possible.

Ricky's efforts were rewarded later that day. He had assigned himself to buggy maintenance, checking that every buggy booked out for the day was returned to the garage and making sure their batteries were topped up and the terminals clean of corrosion. He was testing a buggy that had been damaged in the accident earlier, driving it about to test its performance, when he noticed the colonel leave the building for the night. Ricky stopped a little way ahead of the colonel, making out as if he were checking the wheels were steering properly.

A nod of the head and a quick, "Sir," from Ricky got a brief nod of acknowledgement. Just before the colonel could get too far away, however, Ricky took a deep breath and steeled himself for what might have to be the best performance of his life. Coercing Rattigan to go along with his plan on the hillside had been easy since the man was itching for a quick fortune. Convincing the colonel of anything was not going to be easy.

"Excuse me, Colonel, but the accident earlier today really got to me."

"I'm sure it affected Kyle and Reece more." The Colonel's smile was gone now. Kyle was the man buried beneath the avalanche of pallets. Reece had been given a glancing blow by the falling boxes. Ricky flinched, hoping that the gesture would be taken as guilt for his part in causing the accident. In truth, Ricky knew he was very close to the edge of disaster. The Colonel had clearly had a bad day. He had to be careful how he worded his request.

"I know, Sir, and I'm doing my best, Sir. But I feel that I could do more. I'm sure you have a great procedure in place already, but I was wondering if I could assist in buffing up health and safety issues? You know, take a look at what there is and see if it could be tightened up at all? I have had experience in that sort of thing." Which was partly true. He had worked a scam at a military hospital once.

Hayes, clearly wanting to be somewhere else, frowned and nodded. "Come back in the morning," he directed. "Miss Clarice will be on reception. Just mention what you told me. She can set you up on the computer station that Reece used to log inventory. You won't have full access, of course, but it should be enough for you to go through the list of procedures." Ricky replied that he would do just that and thanked the colonel. As Hayes departed, Ricky asked if he should write up his report and hand it to him personally. "I'm going to be at Newhaven for a few days. Jessie will be on her own now that Reece is out of action for a while." There was sufficient accusation in the colonel's voice to make Ricky wince.

Ricky quickly drove the buggy back to the garage. He didn't check the remaining three buggies. He had left them until last because they hadn't been used today, so he figured that their condition wouldn't have changed since they got checked last night. He wanted to get to bed as soon as possible. It would be an early start.

That early start came round far too soon for Ricky's liking, but he grimaced down a hot coffee without milk and pushed away his fatigue with a growl. He had to get on with things. Given the success of the accident and the ease at which he had gained access to a computer within HQ, he guessed his luck must have changed. Surely it would last a couple more hours.

Ricky arrived at HQ just as it was being unlocked by one of the operators. Jessie was a nice young lady, to look at, anyway. Ricky might have been twice her age and he did not wish to get to know her personally, but his youthful looks, clean complexion and charming demeanour soon won Jessie over as it had done so many women before her. A blush and a giggle was more than enough to guarantee she would not cause a problem for him. Ricky discovered that she was covering for someone called Joy, who was having a baby.

Ricky asked Jessie if that sort of thing appealed to her, too, but she replied that she was in no rush to have a child. She wanted to do more around HQ and was very happy with the added responsibility the development had shifted her way. Ricky told her how he was filling in for the two men injured yesterday, that it was kind of his fault they were in medical. He made sure to show as much anguish as he could when he told her he was torn up with guilt about it all, and that he was doing all he could to make sure such a thing did not happen again.

Jessie showed him to Reece's console and started it up for him. She put the password in too quick for Ricky to decipher and then headed off to her own desk. Throughout the morning, Ricky watched her from the corner of his eye, noticing with no small amount of glee every time she threw a glance his way when she thought he wasn't looking. His winsome grin brought more colour to her cheeks and Ricky figured he could push his luck.

"What time does the mess start dishing up breakfast? I was in such a rush to help this morning I didn't eat."

"Aw, bless. I bet you're starving!" was Jessie's reply. Her face drooped with empathy at Ricky's supposed suffering. "Tell you what, I was thinking about getting some toast myself. I'll bring something back for you, if you like." Ricky thanked her profusely and asked for bacon (well done), eggs (runny), toast (not burnt), sausages and beans. He also asked for a white tea with sugar and a glass of pure orange juice. He said he knew it might take a while but that he would be okay on his own. He was on his feet the moment she left the office.

The keys to Hayes office, Ricky had discovered by watching Jessie, were in one of her desk drawers. He guessed it would be the top one and was rewarded with the sight of a ring of three keys. The long thick one must have been for the HQ main door. The remaining two were similar, but Ricky felt the larger of the pair would be Hayes' office key. He wasn't sure what the smallest one was for until he got into the office and saw the gun cabinet on the wall. A quick rifle through the colonel's 'In' and 'Out' trays found nothing but regular reports, inventories of food and medicines, and lists of names associated with different ranches. There was nothing to interest Ricky. Thinking which filing cabinet to start checking caused him to clip something with his heel. He had kicked the waste basket over and immediately began to gather the rubbish up. He didn't want to leave Hayes any evidence that someone had been in his office. While he was on his hands and knees he noticed a sheet of paper in a gap between two banks of filing cabinets. Ricky snatched at it hungrily.

On the piece of paper were two crude circles, one around the word 'Springfield' and a second around the word 'Earth'. Joining the two circles together were two lines less than a finger's width apart. Between the two lines was written, 'Tom's chamber' with a question mark at the end. While it wasn't exactly the report Ricky was after, it was enough of a lead for him to exploit and his heartbeat intensified. At last he could get off this backwater planet!

Ricky dashed back to his desk, remembering to lock the office door and return the keys to Jessie's drawer. He had to calm his heavy breathing as Jessie returned with breakfast moments later. He was so overwhelmed by his success that he couldn't wait to take a closer look at the scrap of paper he had found. He spent another hour with Jessie, then made the excuse that he had been through the procedures and declared them air tight, that everything he could think of doing to improve health and safety had already been implemented. He finished off his morning with Jessie by reiterating how sorry he was for failing the system, that if it hadn't been for his inadequacies the accident wouldn't have happened at all. Jessie gave him a final hug for reassurance, saying that these things happened and that there was nothing anybody could have done. She gave him her number - 4949 - if he wanted to talk again sometime and then gave him a kiss on the cheek. Ricky felt things could develop further had he the inclination to allow it, but the information he had was a heavy weight in his inside pocket.

Ricky returned to his compartment immediately, avoiding everyone he saw in case they got him involved in some job or other. Flat out on his bed, he stared intently at the drawings on the paper. It was better than he could have hoped. The colonel had scrawled notes on the back of the paper, too, describing Tom as a member of some alien machine race and that he controlled a stable doorway of advanced construction that lead back to Earth. Also, there were clear directions to the site. He had added the location on Earth where the doorway opened up. Somewhere in Nevada but within travelling distance of Ely and Nellis Air Force Base. All of a sudden, Ricky's thoughts of leaving vanished and were replaced by other schemes. If this machine race, this Tom, possessed technological expertise beyond humankind's knowledge then the potential for wealth was unlimited! Ricky rubbed his hands together, barely able to contain his excitement.

It was a few days later when Ricky was able to initiate his grand plan of action. An urgent request for any available pneumatic spares had come through to Grand Central from Halfway House. Apparently, the other settlement had almost finished construction of another dwelling when their digging machine had broken. Ricky remembered helping Ranch 22 convert a small number of buggies into diggers to trade for food and medical supplies. Two of them had come to Grand Central, one to be worked and one as a backup, just in case. Evidently, Halfway House had offered something worthwhile in exchange for certain parts of the backup buggy.

Ricky did not look into the details too much. He never did. He didn't care. All he wanted was passage to the destination and he readily volunteered to make the journey. Unfortunately, a driver for the delivery had already been allocated and Ricky was not in a position to usurp him. He hoped that his friend at HQ, Jessie, was. "Please can you get me on that buggy?" Ricky knew he sounded desperate and hoped Jessie felt it was all part of his quest to atone.

"I don't know, Ricky." Her tone was not encouraging. Ricky cursed himself for not keeping in touch with her over the last day or so. He felt she was beginning to sense he was using her. "I could get into a lot of trouble for this. Jake Castlegate is our usual outrider to Rhino Hill and there's nobody else here that knows the route like him. There's just no need to take him off the roster." Ricky didn't say anything. He couldn't. His face was too screwed up with frustration. He felt he was going to burst and he hoped he wasn't turning red. A puppy-dog look crossed Jessie's face. "I'm sorry." At last, Ricky relaxed. He knew what he had to do.

"It's okay. It's not your fault. I just wanted to help, that's all. You've done all you can and I thank you for that." Jessie smiled at the praise. She was clearly glad the situation had been resolved.

Ricky quickly went to the garage and looked at the buggy roster. A buggy had been checked out under the name of Castlegate J, for a trip to Halfway House only five minutes ago. Ricky took another buggy without logging it and made his way to stores. Jake would have to turn up there at some point to collect a ration pack. He was already there, in fact, and was just about to leave when Ricky showed up. A few pleasantries about the weather passed by in seconds and it was clear Jake was eager to be off. Ricky told Jake that he was due back on Ranch 22 but that there were no buggies spare for him to take. Jake indicated the vehicle Ricky had arrived on and he replied that it was not up to the journey. He explained that he did not wish to delay the delivery and suggested Jake drop him off after unloading the supplies at Halfway House. Ricky added that he knew it was a bit out of the way so he offered fifty dollars then and there, promising more once he was back at 22 to make up for the detour. Clearly interested in making a bit extra for very little effort, Jake readily agreed and packed extra provisions. The two of them were quickly on their way.

The steady journey to Halfway House took quite a few hours. Even though it was relatively comfortable, they stopped along the way for a light meal. Ricky and Jake swapped stories about their lives. Jake had come to Springfield with his mum and dad and had fallen for a girl, Linda, straight away. They had been thinking about having children recently, Jake told Ricky, either naturally or with the IVF treatment available from Rhino Hill. He and Linda had made regular visits to make inquiries and because of that he had become the recognised delivery driver, but pressures of work and survival had delayed any final decision. Neither Jake nor Linda had wanted to bring a child into the world when they weren't certain they could support an extra mouth. Ricky's 'donation' for passage to Ranch 22 would be a more than welcome boost to their income and bring their dream that bit closer.

In return, Ricky revealed few truths about himself. He told Jake that he had been a test pilot in the military for years. It was all hush-hush stuff, of course, and he couldn't say much about it. A little embellishment, as always, made Ricky out to be bigger, braver, and generally all round better than, in actual fact, he was. But he said it with such sincerity and confidence that Jake had no option but to believe his companion. In return, Jake mentioned he had heard tell of a plane that had been built in Newhaven with photovoltaic panels on its wings. It hadn't been tested yet and maybe Ricky would be the perfect man for the job. Ricky's interest at the news was all superficial. There was no way he was going up in a plane that hadn't been flown before.

As the western mountains in the distance got closer, Ricky began to fidget. He remembered something called Migration Gap on his stolen notes and did not like the idea of being between two sheer cliff faces. He felt very uncomfortable all the way through the mountain pass, like the walls were closing in on him. He was more than happy when they emerged at the other side.

Halfway House was a hotbed of activity. Adults and children were busy with construction, agriculture, or earth moving. Jake drove his vehicle to a woman who seemed to be directing people. Ricky did not involve himself with their conversation, but found out that the woman's name was Charlie. He asked her why they hadn't gone to Hopkins on Ranch 22 for spares, since that was where the vehicles had originated and it was closer. Charlie replied somewhat testily that Grand Central always responded more quickly than Ranch 22 and she was in a hurry to get everything finished at this site.

It was a logical response but Ricky suspected that Halfway House had traded with Grand Central because the colonel knew what they had found, the enigmatic Tom and his chamber, while old Jeremiah at Ranch 22 didn't. Ricky guessed that Halfway House and Grand Central had made a deal based on keeping that knowledge secret. Charlie assured Jake that once Halfway House was complete and people had a bit more time, repairs could be made and the loaned gear could be returned. Jake shrugged. As far as he was concerned, the goods had been given in trade. If they wanted to trade them back later on then that was up to them.

Whilst Jake and Charlie discussed this, Ricky had a good look around whilst trying to make it look like he wasn't, and thought about his next move toward the chamber. This drew disapproving scowls from the woman named Charlie but he suspected it was more down to her not wanting him getting in the way of her workers, possibly causing more delays or worse, than her disliking him or suspecting his motives. She was evidently savvy enough to run an operation of this scale and appreciate the dangers a relative unknown could cause. Guided by the colonel's directions, Ricky knew that the chamber, the source of his future income, was still some distance to the south. Given the secrecy surrounding the whole thing, he was certain he wasn't just going to be able to ask for a lift. This made progression to the site of the anomaly rather difficult.

Ricky assisted Jake in unloading the supplies and hauling them into the tunnels where the digger was being kept but he realised that time was quickly running out for him to make his move. The few probing questions he directed to Charlie regarding the reasons behind construction in this particular area received non-committal answers. Apparently, Charlie was just overseeing the construction and that someone else, a man named Wolf, was the true mastermind. Charlie then went on to say that Wolf was too busy to be seen at the moment and Ricky had to be satisfied with that. He couldn't press the issue without raising suspicion. He had as much to hide as Charlie.

It did not take long for the two men to finish their task. Jake was urging Ricky to hurry in order to get him back to Ranch 22 so he could be paid and reach Grand Central before it got too dark. Ricky mentioned to Charlie that he was part of Ranch 22 and had experience with the digger, offering his services to help with its operation. Charlie was having none of it, though, and she turned him down instantly. With no opportunity to gain permission to stay Ricky had no choice but to return to Jake. At least he had an idea of what he was up against. If this Charlie was anything to go by, the rest of the crew here would not readily succumb to his wiles. He would need something else to get what he wanted out of these people.

The buggy started up and Jake steered it back into Migration Gap, destination: Ranch 22. Now unloaded, the vehicle was a little quicker and Jake was saying that he hoped to be back at Grand Central before the sun went down. Ricky wasn't listening though. If he got back to Ranch 22, there was no way to be sure that he would ever get back here. His heart thrashed with indecision as his eyes settled upon the large wrench poking up from his door's side pocket. It was a crazy idea, he told himself, but what else could he do? Halfway House and the chamber were vanishing into the distance behind him with every passing second. He had been lucky to get this close but how much time would pass before another chance came along? The window of opportunity was closing fast. Closing like Ricky's fingers about the wrench handle. Fast like the strike of the stubby metal against Jake's temple.

Ricky froze as the buggy came to a stop against the mountainside with its pilot slumped over the steering wheel. Ricky was shaking. What had he done? Blood gathered at the side of Jake's head, matting the hair, making its way slowly down toward the man's face and along his cheek to drip on his knee. Ricky swallowed hard. Had he killed Jake? He hoped not, but if the man woke up he would know Ricky had hit him. Should he finish the job? That would be nothing short of murder. Ricky had never set out to be a cold-blooded killer but that's exactly what he would become, if he hadn't already. There was no turning back from this.

Ricky forced himself to calm down. Experience told him that there was a way out of every situation if he was careful and it would be no different this time. He estimated that he had until nightfall before Jake would be reported as missing. It would be no task at all for an investigator to find out where Jake had gone and when, at which point communication between HQ and Halfway House would result in confirmation of his arrival there with an unregistered companion. Ricky was glad Charlie had not asked his name and that he had not given it freely, but he had no doubt at all that the ever-helpful Jessie would readily reveal their earlier conversation if she felt it would boost her own standing. It would not take the staff at Grand Central long to register his own absence and put two and two together.

The only conclusion, given that Halfway House and the colonel were not aware anyone knew about the chamber's existence, would be to surmise that there had been some kind of breakdown or accident. The latter was the more likely assumption of the two since a breakdown would still allow the travellers to call in and report what had happened. A serious accident would prevent that. How long before a rescue attempt would be underway? Ricky was not sure about that one. He felt there was just as much chance of HQ arranging one immediately as there was of them leaving it until daylight the following day.

Ricky's mind stepped up a gear. He smiled, feeling confident once again. A plan was forming, just like it always did. They were not yet out of Migration Gap and he soon decided that he liked the mountains after all. He would batter the buggy a bit, to make it look like it had been caught in a rock slide, then claim the accident had injured Jake, forcing Ricky to return to the closest settlement - Halfway House - and hope medical assistance would be available there. That all sounded plausible but he knew an injury to himself would give his story even more credibility. Ricky frowned at the thought. That one might have to wait a while. He checked Jake for a pulse and found a faint one, then brought out the first aid kit and bandaged him up as best he could. The thought that Jake might come round at any time niggled at Ricky but he couldn't bring himself to hit the man again just now. He hoped to be long gone by the time he woke up.

Ricky soon found a place where he considered the sides of the pass rocky enough to be potentially unstable. He would say Jake's desire to get home quickly was why the vehicle had not had chance to avoid the falling rocks. He spent about an hour throwing stones at the side of the buggy to mark its bodywork and strategically placing the pieces that came off. He made sure to damage some of the photovoltaic panels on the roof of the vehicle, too. He would say that he wasn't sure how badly they were damaged and if he could make it back to HQ before Jake's condition worsened. Waiting a little longer to make sure there was not enough time to simply be sent back before dark, Ricky piloted the battered buggy carefully back in the direction of Halfway House. He had seen victims of shock before and knew exactly how to imitate it, thus guaranteeing himself at least one night at the new base. Then it would be a simple task to steal a buggy and head to the chamber when everyone was asleep.

Unfortunately, there was no description of what the doorway looked like and so Ricky did not know what he was looking for. However, the people of Rhino Hill had not become so successful by making stupid mistakes. Leaving the site occupied to stake a claim on it would be the smart decision, so Ricky guessed he would identify his destination by the camp already there. Ricky did not know how many people would occupy it, but at least he would come upon them at night. But that was still hours away and he had to focus on the now. He could only hope that the damaged buggy and the injured Jake would be enough to carry

off his deception at Halfway House. If not, well, he still
had the wrench.

Chapter 12B

Wolf Boston held the cold, glittering rock in his palm. It looked like a chunk of midnight sky. It was heavy, too, more so than gold, he believed. With all his efforts at prospecting, Wolf had never found a metal like the one Charlie had discovered excavating Halfway House. To say he was excited was an understatement. He and Daniel had been at the causeway between Rhino Hill and Blue Hill when Charlie called him to tell him what she had found.

The men had been building a generator with a water wheel, hoping to make use of the floodwater to help power the bases during the monsoons. He left Daniel to it and made haste for Halfway House. Before even seeing the stuff, Wolf had told himself it was a brand new metal and therefore something of great importance to the development of the community. Holding it in his fist convinced him he had been right. It would be a valuable trade commodity, too, if it turned out to be something that could be worked. Stronger construction materials, stronger tools. Spare workable metal was becoming rare on Springfield since the escalator had closed. It might even be new to the being calling itself Tom. What technological marvels could they trade from him?

Since the metal resisted the efforts made against it by shovel and sweat, Wolf had rented the digger/buggy from Jeremiah Hopkins. Daniel had used the machine before to build the causeway Wolf had just come from so Wolf knew it was a reliable tool. He had offered the usual currency in exchange for the rugged vehicle's services; Jeremiah was always happy to get a couple more deer. Wolf said nothing of his interesting find, however, nor would he until its properties became apparent.

Unfortunately, the metal had proved too much for the machine's air powered scoop. It had failed after only a couple of hours. Worse still, the damage was not something his people could rectify. They had plenty of buggies to draw components from had the fault been electrical in nature, but there was nothing they could do about repairing pneumatics. It was lucky that replacement parts were available and had arrived earlier today from Grand Central. The faulty pieces were swapped and the digger made ready for work again.

While waiting for the digger's parts, and to avoid a repeat incident, Wolf had utilised some of his military talents. He brought out some firearms and, using gunpowder from ammunition along with some of the weapon casings, fixed up some crude explosives. Since he had no detonators, he had used lengths of string in place of fuse wire. He had to resort to short pieces because it was not a reliable substitute. This meant a mad dash to cover after lighting it.

Despite the danger, the operation seemed to work. The rock the metal was encased in mostly disintegrated into fine powder with each detonation, leaving pieces of the dark material scattered all round the pit. Wolf couldn't hide his wide smile. With hands over his ears and eyes tight shut, the cloud of rock particles and clatter of metal shrapnel blasting past his cover made him think this must have been how it was done in the Wild West. With the ore weakened by explosives, the digger was more than capable of removing pieces of it. The stream of metal surely dived deeper into the ground, so there would only be so much of it they could easily take. Wolf did not wish to exhaust his ammo reserves on the project and restricted the operation to a dozen of his home made bombs. The outcome was a lot of noise and dust, along with a good helping of the metal.

Although some of the metal was in small shards, with the help of the digger there were many pieces large enough to be considered workable. Wolf realised he would need help in constructing and operating a forge but that would have to wait for the time being. He had Colonel Hayes coming tomorrow morning. They intended to go through the chamber to re-establish contact with Earth and he needed to work on the business plan he wanted to present at the meeting. He deliberated over whether he should take samples of the new metal with him, deciding in the end that it might just help swing things his way should the need arise.

It was while Wolf was sifting through the rubble on the chamber's floor for as much of the strange metal as he could find that Daniel came in. "You wanted to see me?" Daniel asked.

"Hi. Yeah," Wolf began. "The colonel should be here first thing in the morning. We're going to try and get things going with the guys back on Earth. See if we can find out what happened to the escalator, maybe get some more supplies." Daniel was nodding. "We'll be gone a few days, I expect. You okay?"

"Eh? What? Oh, right. Yeah. I guess."

Wolf smiled. He had detected that his friend's attention had been drifting while he spoke. In fact, now that he thought about it, it seemed to be a regular thing with Daniel. "You're missing Anna, aren't you?" Daniel winced, smiling apologetically.

"Is it that obvious?"

"Afraid so," Wolf nodded.

Daniel's shoulders slumped. "I don't think it's just that, though. Found something out recently." Wolf pursed his lips.

"Go on." He had already been told by Sally the last time he was at the chamber about Anna's suspected pregnancy, but she had made him promise not to say anything. He had been expecting a chat with Daniel about it and was surprised as to how long it had taken Daniel to approach him. When Daniel remained tight-lipped, Wolf gave the man an encouraging slap on the shoulder. "We've been friends some time now, Daniel. Whatever it is, you can tell me. Maybe I can point you in the right direction."

At last Daniel yielded. He took a deep breath. "Anna told me a couple of weeks ago that she might be pregnant. Well, she confirmed it last night. She's going to have a baby - my baby. I'm going to be a dad." Wolf was happy for the two of them. He had known Anna a long time and had noticed how much happier she was now she and Daniel were an item. Even so, he knew that relationships could strain under the weight of parenthood, especially if it wasn't planned. It was clear Daniel was concerned about this new development with his partner so Wolf subdued his smile and held off the congratulations. Daniel's hesitancy on the subject was natural, which was why the man had come to him. "Anna had kids when you met her," Wolf pointed out brightly. "You get on with them okay."

"Yeah, I get that part," Daniel admitted. "But when it's your own it's different, right? I mean, how did you feel when Sally got pregnant?"

"At first? Well, I was relieved everything worked," Wolf quipped, which drew a smile from Daniel. "But seriously, I figured what the Hell. She already had four, what difference would one more make? Anna only has James and Ruth, and another IVF baby wasn't going to happen because of the blood pressure thing. Maybe she always wanted more but she was waiting for the right guy and then you came along. Surely Anna having your baby is better than Anna having someone else's?"

"Yeah. Hadn't thought of that." Daniel paused. "But

a baby? I haven't a clue!"

Wolf laughed aloud at that. "You think I got a manual with Henry or John? Besides, I bet Anna knows enough for the both of you. Yeah, it's a pain for the first couple of years but once they start walking and talking, man, there's no better feeling in the world." Wolf's eyes budded with moisture. "This one or Earth." After a moment's reflection, Wolf continued. "Trust me. Having a child will be the best thing that ever happened to you. After a while, you'll wonder how you ever managed without one."

"Thanks, Wolf," Daniel nodded. "Means a lot."

The older man winked. "Any time, my friend. Oh, and congratulations."

Daniel left Wolf to the mix of stone and metal and meandered outside. The whole baby thing had been playing on his mind since Anna suggested the possibility. He didn't really know how to react since Anna wasn't certain she was pregnant, and he couldn't really talk to Jessica, Sally or Charlie about the issue because he didn't think they would see it from his point of view. Wolf was the only person he could bring his fears out to but Wolf used to be a front-line soldier, a hard man; Daniel didn't want to sound weak or foolish. Anna had been staying at the chamber, and although they had spoken by phone every evening the two of them had skirted the issue because Anna didn't want to get her hopes up and then have it turn out to be nothing. That all changed the other day. She was already four weeks late but now she was starting to be sick in the morning. She had suffered morning sickness with both James and Ruth, so she took that as a definitive sign.

Daniel had done as much as he could to install the hydro-generator at Rhino Hill's causeway. They would know if it worked or not at the next monsoon, which was still more than half a year away. Daniel knew Wolf had been taking extra supplies to Sally and Anna at Tom's chamber, making sure they had plenty in case of emergencies when he and the colonel eventually went through to Earth. Daniel had considered discussing things by phone but he preferred face to face for something so delicate. With the extra families renting the nearby ranches there had been more than enough hands to help out with the day-to-day farming chores around Rhino Hill, allowing Daniel to help build Halfway House. It had taken him some time to gather the courage to approach Wolf for advice about his problem, but he was glad he had done. He felt enriched by what his friend had told him.

Daniel's thoughts were interrupted by Charlie repeating his name. "Hey, Daniel!" She was shouting. "You still on this planet, or what?" Daniel returned her smile.

"Yeah, fine. Sorry," he replied. "What you after?"

"Wolf has gathered the last bits together for setting up the visit to Earth, but not everything fits on the ant. You want to run the extras over to Anna and Sally on a buggy?"

Daniel turned to back to the excavation site as the ripple of another explosion filtered through the soles of his feet. He wondered if Wolf had just this minute called her about this, making certain he got the chance to see Anna and talk things through with her. "Sure will. Thanks, Charlie."

"There's a buggy over there," Charlie indicated with her outstretched finger. "Hasn't been used all day. Here's the list of stuff. Don't take the things that have been crossed out - they're already on the ant." He nodded and said that he would, then made his way to load up the buggy.

Moments later, Daniel heard a shout of alarm from the direction of Migration Gap. He turned to see what was causing the noise and saw a buggy emerge. It looked like it had seen better days, with the screen cracked and big dents all over its bodywork. He rushed to see what was going on. He noticed Charlie running toward it too. As he got closer, he noticed that there were two people inside. He didn't recognise the driver but the passenger looked familiar despite having a bandage wrapped about his head. Daniel couldn't think of the man's name. The buggy ground to a halt as Daniel and Charlie reached it.

"Help," came the call from the driver, who half fell out of the cab.

"What happened?" Charlie cried urgently, running to assist. The driver was covered in dust and dirt but showed no sign of injury.

"We were on our way back home," he said, somewhat breathlessly, "not even out of the gap, when the whole mountain came down on us." Charlie threw a concerned glance at Daniel.

"I didn't hear anything," she said. Daniel shook his head, indicating that he had not heard anything either, and turned back to the driver.

"You sure about that?" he asked, as the driver slumped to the ground and rested his back against the buggy's rear wheel.

"I was there! Of course I'm sure. How's Jake? Is he dead? Oh, God."

By now a small crowd had gathered around the buggy. Daniel turned to Naomi and said that the driver was suffering from shock. He told her to fix him a hot drink and to bring a blanket. As the girl dashed off, he crouched down next to Charlie and her patient. "He okay?" Charlie nodded, but she didn't look optimistic.

"James is around somewhere. He knows more than me." A call went out to find James. Charlie turned her attention back to the man in the buggy. "He's been patched up, which probably saved his life. He might still need serious medical attention to make sure there's nothing going on inside, though. Stuff we don't have here. Once James has a look at him we'll know more. Maybe he's stable enough to get him to Jessica at Rhino Hill."

Naomi returned moments later with a mug of coffee and a long jacket. "It was all I could find," she said, apologetically.

"It's fine," Daniel assured her. "You did good." Naomi smiled. He quickly threw the coat over the dazed driver and put the drink to the man's lips, giving him slow, steady sips. "What's your name?" he asked. There was a pause before the driver responded. Daniel wondered if he had taken a blow to the head, too.

"Um, Ricky. Ricky Marlow."

"Okay, Ricky," Daniel started slowly. "I'm Daniel Swift and this is what we're going to do. We're going to stand up and walk. I'll help you." Daniel pointed to the entrance to Halfway House. "You think you can do that?" The man called Ricky nodded, but didn't seem sure of himself. "Don't worry, your friend is going to be fine. We have James on site, he's a trained medical practitioner." Daniel didn't add that James was only a teenager and possessed no formal qualifications. The man was in shock and Daniel didn't want to add to his stress.

Daniel guided Ricky into the first passage of Halfway House so he was out of the sun. Wolf came out of a side corridor, covered in dust and grime. He said he had heard a commotion and asked what was going on. Daniel explained briefly what had happened and, after Ricky reassured them that he would be okay on his own, the two of them went outside to see if they could assist in any way. James had arrived with the first aid kit and was now beside Charlie at the buggy. Daniel and Wolf ran over to them in time to hear James say the man was stable, if not exactly comfortable, but that with his limited equipment there wasn't much more he could do.

"Who are these guys?" Wolf wanted to know.

"This one's Jake Castlegate," Charlie confirmed. "I know him. He's been at Rhino Hill a couple of times to see Jessica about IVF for his girlfriend, Lydia, or Linda, or something. The other guy I don't know but they were both here earlier dropping off the parts for the digger."

"The other guy's Ricky Marlow," Daniel announced. "Never seen him before but I sort of remember Jake." Wolf gestured for James' attention.

"Is Jake fit enough to be taken back to Rhino Hill? We can't help him here."

"Doesn't look like a major injury," James confirmed. "Not life threatening, or anything. Even so, I'd prefer to have a look at the wound, clean it up, and put on a fresh dressing before he goes."

"By then it will be too late to reach Rhino Hill at a comfortable speed before sundown," Wolf returned. "Looks like we'll have guests tonight."

"I'm going to get off to Sally and Anna," said Daniel. "They need those supplies there to get everything prepared before you and the colonel head off to Earth tomorrow morning." And I still want to see Anna, he added silently. He had hoped to spend the night there but now, he knew he should get back to help Wolf.

"Shouldn't we hold off taking supplies to Sally and Anna?" Charlie wanted to know. She tilted her head in the direction of the newcomer. "We don't want, well, you know."

"I don't think there's any need for that," Wolf returned. "Jake isn't going to start asking questions. If

276

his partner does, we can just say we're exploring the area for arable land, looking for new ranch sites." Both Charlie and Daniel nodded at this.

"Somebody will have to check out the accident site," Charlie declared. "Ricky said that the whole mountain had come down but I think he was exaggerating. We'd have heard something like that."

"It probably felt like that at the time," Wolf noted. Daniel nodded.

"Maybe so, but we have to make sure the gap is safe to travel through and also check it's not going to suddenly close up on us."

"Should really be done sooner, rather than later," Charlie cautioned. "We don't want the colonel getting bombarded on his way through."

"Well, I can't do it now. I have to talk to Anna. I've left it too long already," Daniel insisted. "Besides, the colonel isn't going to be here first thing."

Wolf declared he would investigate the rockslide but Charlie told him he wasn't to go in alone. "Sally will never forgive you if you get caught in a second slide." Wolf yielded at the mention of Sally.

"Fine. I'll leave it until tomorrow. We go first light, though, okay?" Daniel nodded. The conversation over, Charlie went back to work in Halfway House and Wolf disappeared to prepare for his meeting with the colonel and Earth. Daniel finished loading his buggy.

After a hot meal, Ricky perked up. He thanked everyone for their care and said he was feeling much better about things knowing that Jake was going to be okay. People shot questions at him about what happened. He explained that Jake was supposed to be taking him back to Ranch 22 and was in a hurry to get there. He wasn't able to avoid the rocks bouncing toward them. Jake took the worst of it because they were coming down on his side of the buggy and one hit his head. Ricky said he had no medical training so patched him up as best he could. Then he had to clear a path to get the buggy moving again, which was why it had taken so long to get back. Ricky added how lucky he and Jake had been; it could have been much worse. Everybody went back to work and Daniel headed off to the chamber.

Daniel couldn't help but think about Ricky's words. Something didn't feel right but he couldn't quite put his finger on it. The buggy showed signs of blunt damage, Jake was certainly injured and Ricky had been a little out of it. There was nothing there that suggested all wasn't as it had been made out to be. Daniel shook the disquieting thoughts about Ricky and Jake and the rockslide out of his head. He had to get it straight in his mind about just what to say to Anna when he finally saw her. After several discarded possibilities he finally found something to settle on. Eventually, he came to the chamber's location in the mountains and turned toward it. When the buggy could go no further, he clambered out of the cab and hailed the two women as they scrambled down the steep path toward him.

Anna practically slammed into him, her arms tight coils of welcome around his waist. Daniel lifted her off the ground and spun her a full circle and a half, burying his face in her hair. Her curls were not as tight now, having had a few weeks to grow out, but they were still soft and full of her aroma. His heart hammered against his ribs as if trying to leap out. It was a wonderful feeling. After a few moments holding each other they broke apart, still holding hands, still close enough that they could feel the other's body and look into each other's eyes.

Daniel grinned. "Hey, you."

"Hey, you," she replied, and put her lips firmly against his. "What brings you out to this neck of the woods?" Daniel's grin widened.

"I can always go back if I'm imposing." He threw a thumb over his shoulder.

"Don't you dare!" Anna warned, and cuddled up to him again.

"Hi, Daniel," Sally called from a few metres away. "What really brought you here?" Daniel lifted his chin to acknowledge the other woman.

"Hi, Sally. Got the last of the supplies for Earthside. Wolf's going through with the colonel tomorrow. He wants it ready for morning."

Sally nodded. "No problem. We can do that. You staying to help?"

Anna looked up at him, eyes imploring. "Yes. Stay and help."

"I can't. Got to get back." He told the women about the rockslide and the two men caught in it, explaining how he and Wolf were going to see how bad the rockfall was at first light, before the colonel had to go through. He also mentioned the metal Charlie had found whilst burrowing out Halfway House and that Wolf was using explosives to get it out. Sally was aghast at that but Daniel assured her everything was being conducted in a safe and orderly manner.

"Well, he knows what he's doing, I guess," she relented in the end, and it was true. Wolf was the only one of them with anything close to experience handling explosives. Even so, Daniel could tell she was not pleased.

"You'll stay for dinner, at least," Anna tried to insist but Daniel said he had already eaten and wanted to get back before it got too dark.

They unloaded the buggy and hauled everything up the slope to the Springfield side of Tom's chamber, placing it with everything else set aside for the journey back to Earth under a canvas sheet. It took the three of them very little time to finish. As Daniel secured the tarpaulin, Sally volunteered to start the evening meal. Daniel told them he should be getting off. Anna offered to accompany him back to the buggy. "Take your time," Sally told them. "I'll still be here when you get back."

Daniel and Anna exchanged small talk as they stepped carefully over the rocky ground. Daniel asked if they had seen or heard much of Tom throughout their stay at the chamber but Anna shook her head. "He only talks to us if we get in touch with him first. Most of the time, Mark's communicating with him. Those two seem to get along like a house on fire." Daniel wanted to know if they had been exploring on the Earthside again but Anna turned her nose up at the notion. She had seen as much of Earth as she wanted to and only used the nearby water to wash in.

"Wonder what he looks like," Daniel asked, as much to himself as anything.

"You mean Tom?" Anna shrugged. "I get the feeling he *is* the chamber, you know? Not like us at all. He sounds like a person, obviously, but I don't think he looks anything like we might think of."

"You could be right," Daniel replied, not really knowing what else to suggest. Once they were beside the buggy, Daniel stopped and turned to face Anna.

"Look," Daniel began. "I got to admit, this whole baby thing? Freaked me out a little." When he saw worry begin to stitch into Anna's brow he added hastily. "But I'm cool with it all now, really. I just didn't know what to think, at first. It's a big thing, you know? I'm going to be a dad." He couldn't help but smile as he said that. "I guess we'll have to start thinking about names."

"I like Alex or Josh, if it's a boy," Anna immediately said. "And either Alice or Jane if it's a girl."

"Wow!" Daniel exclaimed. "Already? Okay, well, I'll have a think and see if there's any I like. We'll have to get our heads together."

"Look forward to it." Anna's teeth gleamed when she smiled.

"I love you." The words were out of his mouth before he had even realised it. He had never told her that before but neither had Anna said anything like that either. He simply took it for granted that she knew he felt that way. Anna broke down into tears. Daniel pulled her into his chest.

"I love you, too," she managed to say through her sobs. Seeing her reaction made him realise just how much she had wanted to hear him say it. The way he felt after hearing Anna return the sentiment was just as surprising. They held each other for long minutes after that but Daniel eventually pushed Anna away and bid her a fond farewell. She stood and watched his buggy disappear into the distance.

The lights were already on in and around Halfway House when Daniel arrived. Now that they had dug into the mountainside, everybody had somewhere to bunk down inside. Proper doors had not yet been fitted and so privacy was maintained by sheets hung up over the openings. As Daniel made his way to the space set aside for him, he heard Wolf's voice bid him goodnight. Daniel replied and pulled the curtain closed behind him. He was shattered. Another long day was over and there weren't enough hours to go before the next one started. He took off his coverall and changed into his shorts. As he lay down on his bedroll, his last thought was that he wished Anna was with him.

Chapter 13B

Ricky Marlow was becoming impatient. What was wrong with these people? he wanted to know. They worked and worked, and then worked some more. They didn't stop, even when the sun went down. He had been in the room where he had been put for hours now. While he had slept for some of it, most of the time he had been pretending to so that people stopped questioning him. Daniel in particular hadn't looked convinced earlier but Ricky still felt he had successfully deflected all suspicion. He wouldn't still be free otherwise.

It had just grown quiet and Ricky was beginning to consider moving when someone turned up. There had been a brief exchange of pleasantries - Ricky recognised the voices of Daniel and Wolf - and then silence returned shortly after. Ricky left it as long as his frustration would let him but eventually he had to get up. Carrying his boots, Ricky was able to move quietly across the stone floor. If anybody heard him moving about nothing was said about it. He winced as sharp stones dug into the soles of his feet but he considered it a small price to pay for his current success. Everything had worked out perfectly so far.

Once in the open air again, Ricky slipped his boots on and made his way quickly to the nearby ant. He climbed into the cab and checked the battery. When he looked round, he noticed a shotgun in the rack behind the seats. He had been given firearms training during his time in the military and recognised the weapon as a Mossberg 500, a 20 gauge, pump action shotgun. It was fairly old and battered, but seemed serviceable. Ricky nodded with appreciation. He took it immediately and checked if it was loaded. It wasn't, so he looked around the cab for shells. Nobody had an unloaded weapon without having ammunition nearby. In the compartment under the seat he came across a full box of 24 thumb-sized cartridges, so he loaded the weapon and distributed the remaining shells into his pockets. He pumped a round into the chamber of the shotgun when he was finished and left the safety off. All he had to do now was point it and squeeze the trigger.

Ricky continued readying the ant until it occurred to him that taking this vehicle maybe wasn't the best option. It was the only one on site; its absence would be noticed immediately. Instead he marched over to a buggy and switched it on. There were more than a few of them around the area so its absence would be overlooked. He knew from the colonel's notes that the site of the chamber was to the south of Halfway House. How far south was not so clear and finding it in the dark would not be easy. He told himself that the people who had found it would have put markers around the place so they knew where it was when they came back to it, so he didn't worry too much about that. He was more worried that whoever was there would see him coming and know he was an unexpected visitor. That would cause complications. He could only hope that everyone at the chamber was fast asleep and he would be able to take them by surprise.

The buggy's battery showed full green. That was usually enough for four hours continuous driving without the sun. He was carrying only a light load, and if he didn't push it too hard he thought he might get a couple more hours out of it. He couldn't imagine the site of the chamber being that far away, though. This base was called Halfway House and he guessed the name was appropriate to its location, halfway between Rhino Hill and the chamber. Rhino Hill was a few hours drive from the gap in the mountains so it was not unreasonable to assume the distance to the chamber was about the same. He set his phone's alarm to sound after a couple of hours driving, then powered the buggy through the construction site and disappeared into the darkness.

Ricky's eyes repeatedly strayed to the shotgun on the passenger seat throughout his journey. He tried not to dwell on what he might have to do when he got to the chamber. He wished he had been able to find out how many people were there, but couldn't figure out how he might have steered the conversation in that direction. If everyone at the chamber just kept their distance and did what he wanted, he didn't foresee having to use the gun. Despite what he had been told about Jake's condition, he still wasn't convinced the man would pull through. Ricky felt he had hit Jake far harder than he had at first thought and Halfway House simply wasn't equipped to deal with that kind of head trauma. The patient would have to be moved to a well-equipped surgery for more professional treatment and Ricky felt the kid, James, would not be up to much. The worst could still happen and the last thing Ricky needed was more blood on his hands. Even so, he told himself he would have to prepare for any eventuality. He patted the shotgun to boost his flagging confidence. If push came to shove he had a more than adequate tool to shove back.

With his internal dilemma resolved, Ricky began to think about what he would do once he got back on Earth. The colonel's notes mentioned that the chamber opened up in Nevada, somewhere around Las Vegas. Ricky was glad of that. Las Vegas was close to Ely, where the escalator had been based, and Nellis Air Force Base was just over a couple hundred miles to the south from Ely. Maybe the latter would make a more appropriate heading, Ricky mused. The staff at Ely might still be loyal to the Springfield community to grant the full attention his money making plans would demand. If he could get to someone of high enough rank at Nellis, convince them of the opportunity this chamber presented to the American military, then he, Ricky Marlow, would be instrumental in guaranteeing American superiority in any conflict his country chose to become involved in. In fact, it was his patriotic duty to continue with this mission. For the good of the country. For the good of the Earth. Maybe he would get a medal, or be awarded a Nobel Prize, or something. He urged the buggy forward as fast as he dared.

Ricky's alarm beeped sooner than expected, reminding him to watch out for anything that might suggest the chamber was nearby. He slowed the buggy to a crawl and peered out into the dark. It was nearly midnight and he would have loved to switch on the powerful spotlights mounted on the roof of the buggy but he did not wish to alert anyone at the chamber of his approach. He would have to make do with the softer illumination provided by the smaller lights fixed at the front of the vehicle. Fortunately, there were signs of other tracks. He guessed they led to his destination.

Eventually, Ricky found the cairn of rocks that Wolf had built as a marker; it was clearly man-made. There was a Maglite in the buggy, which he took before marching around the pile of stones, looking for something that would give away the location of the chamber. He had the idea that it would be an obvious thing, like a pre-fabricated building in the middle of nowhere, like the air-lock construction at Ely back on Earth, but as the minutes passed with no discernible trace he began to think he was wrong. What if the alien machine's chamber was invisible, he feared. Or could be moved around? What if this Tom had taken it upon himself to abduct the people at his chamber? No, Ricky told himself, it had to be here. All he had to do was find it. As soon as he stopped worrying he saw the tyre marks angling up the slope.

Ricky switched off the buggy batteries and got out, taking the shotgun and the torch. He walked as quietly as he could up the slope of the mountain. When the pale beam of the torch lit up the bulk of an ant Ricky stepped with even more care; the camp's inhabitants could not be far away. He soon came across the circular opening of the chamber. "Wow," he whispered, his breath coming to him in short, excited rasps. "I don't believe it." He let the light play along the smooth surface of the chamber, pushing it deeper into the recesses of the perfect tube. He saw the shapes of two people under their blankets. They were moving, evidently disturbed by his light.

Machines had no need to sleep, so Tom had been aware of the buggy and its occupant upon their arrival at the camp. Outside the Void, almost nothing could hide from his sophisticated scanning systems; no amount of caution would conceal Ricky's advance. There had never been visitors arriving this late before nor had anyone come without prior communication from Halfway House, but Tom was still gathering data on the often illogical behaviour of these biologicals. Analysis suggested that there was a high probability that this was the man called Colonel Hayes arriving earlier than planned. The events were logged and Tom went back to mapping the night sky for a report to his superiors.

The comings and goings at the Springfield side of the chamber were largely ignored by Tom. He was always ready to answer any calls made by the few people who knew of his existence, of course. Mark Richards was particularly interesting and the two of them had discussed many things over the last few days, both scientific and mundane. The man's mind was something Tom could relate to.

However, there was an irregularity to the new arrival that sent unusual fluxes through Tom's reasoning circuits. He turned his attention back to the camp and saw that Sally and Anna were on their feet but remained where they were, hands raised in supplication. This was entirely out of character for the women, who were usually very active when receiving visitors.

Tom fixed his monitoring devices on the newcomer, scanning him from head to toe. The long object in the man's hands glared a fierce red, identifying it as a primitive projectile weapon. That it was pointing directly at the two women gave Tom grave concerns about their safety. He instantly regretted scavenging the external auditory sensors. He had considered them surplus to requirements upon his arrival on the planet and had used them to boost power in systems that were more useful at the time. In their absence, he tried to interpret the words by the shapes of the biologicals' mouths, but his knowledge of their language was insufficient and their lips moved too quickly to follow. It was clear that the women knew that their captor was armed; they would not remain so compliant otherwise. The stranger's light made quick circles around the chamber's external features. He was indicating it, probably asking what it was.

Then Tom noticed Mark slowly approaching the chamber, at an angle that kept his movement out of sight from the hostile visitor. Tom deduced instantly what he planned to do, but calculated that his odds of successfully disarming the gunman were only 22%. Mark was of slighter build and a little shorter than the stranger, so the older man was clearly hoping surprise would be enough for victory. There was only one way

Tom could warn Mark about his chances, but Tom knew that if he called Mark's phone the stranger would be alerted by the noise and therefore rob his friend of his only advantage. Tom hesitated as his prediction matrix seized up, and Mark threw himself at the stranger.

Ricky's shotgun was pushed down and to the side by an unknown force. Ricky felt something attach itself to his body, scrabbling for purchase, trying to trip him. The flashlight clattered to the floor and sent shadows leaping across the mountain walls. A terrific noise filled the air as his fingers clenched instinctively, the solid buckshot kicking up a plume of dust inches from his right foot. He heard the women scream with the detonation and imagined them diving to the floor. Ricky tumbled onto his back, dragging whatever had hit him down as well. The shotgun was pulled sharply away from his body, an attempt to rip it from his hands no doubt, but Ricky kept a firm hold of the pistol grip and yanked it back.

The weight of the other body was not sufficient to stop Ricky pushing his shoulder off the ground. He twisted his waist and found purchase with a foot, adding the power of his leg to push his assailant aside. Then the combatants' positions were reversed and Ricky was the one on top. He ached to punch out at the figure below but Ricky refused to relinquish his grip on the weapon, knowing that to lose it would be to lose the fight and with that his chance of getting to Earth. Instead, his fist worked its way down the barrel. Summoning as much strength from his shoulders as he could, he pushed it down hard. There was a satisfying crunch as the shotgun's length smashed into something. The cry of pain that immediately followed told Ricky it was another man he was wrestling with.

After his successful strike Ricky flung himself backwards, hoping his attacker was distracted enough that his hold on the shotgun was sufficiently weakened for Ricky to break free. It was and Ricky found his feet immediately, the shotgun still in his fist. Without thinking about it, he pumped hard and fired into the space he had just stepped away from. There was another cry of distress from one of the women as the bright discharge from the barrel illuminated a body shuddering under the impact of the blast. Ricky racked another round into the chamber and pointed it to where he thought the scream had come from.

The smell of gunfire filled air. Ricky's shoulders heaved with each heavy intake of air and his heart was thrashing so hard his head ached. "Who was that?" he demanded coldly. Then yelled, "Who was that?" Ricky sidestepped over to where his Maglite lay. Poking through the stream of light stretching from it across the floor was a single blood-spattered hand, palm up and fingers curled. The body that was attached to it was, thankfully, buried beneath a blanket of darkness. Ricky stooped to collect the flashlight and found the two women huddled at the back of the chamber.

"Mark," one of the women said, the dark haired one. The other one was sobbing gently. "Mark Richards. I think you've killed him."

Ricky flinched at the accusation and shook his head vigorously. "No. No. No, I didn't kill him. You killed him! I asked who else was here and you didn't tell me. You should have told me he was here. He didn't have to die."

"You pulled the trigger so don't put this on us!" the woman screamed back at him immediately.

"He made me shoot him!" Ricky argued vociferously. "He attacked me!"

"He was trying to protect us!" The debate ended

with another blast of shotgun fire into the sky. Both woman recoiled sharply at the noise. Ricky ratcheted another round and levelled the weapon on the two women. When he spoke, it was with a ferocious calm. "Open the door now," he growled. "Before someone else dies."

Tom was familiar with machine failure. Machines could be repaired or recycled. He had not previously experienced a biological failure. The death of the scientist stirred something inside him. He wasn't sure what it was. Machine logic took over. A surge of electrical impulses flowed through Tom's circuitry in the same way it did when he encountered an obstacle in the lab or with a transformer that he couldn't immediately overcome. That pulse would focus his attention to laser beam intensity and the difficulty - whatever it was - would be resolved. The familiarity of that analysis gave Tom a moment of clarity. This was a difficulty, a problem, and suddenly, he saw that he had the means to solve it. He would succeed now just as he always had in the past. Tom immediately ran another set of predictive subroutines.

A call came from Anna's phone seconds later and Tom answered it immediately. "I understand there is a problem," he said, having anticipated the call.

"Please, open the door for our *guest*." She said the word like an insult. "Let him through to Earth." Tom considered her request.

"What if I refuse?" he asked, more out of curiosity than a desire to do so.

"I think he'll shoot Sally." Tom had estimated the probability of that very response as 97%. He doubted the stranger would shoot them both because he needed one of them to talk with himself. "Very well. Tell him to step into the chamber and I will let him through."

Tom heard Anna repeat the instructions to the gunman over the phone in her hand. The man's reply was too faint to be clear but he was obviously not happy about complying. Tom's analysis was faultless; he was not surprised when the man gestured for Anna to go towards him, palms atop her head. When she was only two foot away he told her to stop and turn around. The shotgun was pushed into her back and Sally was told to walk out of the chamber. She kept as far away from the gunman as she could. Then, Anna was escorted back into the chamber with the gun still tight against her spine. Tom had seen what that weapon could do to a biological. So close, it would tear the woman in half and the tiny spark of life growing inside her would never see the light of day.

"Tom, it's Anna again. You can open the door now."

"I can disable the weapon for a short time," Tom said quickly. "You remember the chamber's roll?"

Anna nodded and told her captor that Tom was about to open the door. He snorted a reply which Tom could not hear. Then the gravity slip kicked in. With careful monitoring, Tom was able to keep the slip to a gentle roll. This time, however, he over-charged the conduits that balanced the gravitational differences between the dimensions and allowed the movement to be more sudden and forceful.

Tom predicted a 93% probability that Anna's captor would be thrown off-balance, more so than Anna and Sally had been the first time they went through the chamber. Anna was ready for it, though, and leapt on the opportunity Tom had given her. She twirled to the left as the man pitched sharply to the right. Her left arm came around to bat the shotgun aside and she immediately followed up with a right hook to side of the man's face. He was left sprawling on the floor as

Anna vanished through the doorway onto Earth. Her former captor pointed his weapon at her retreating form but Tom had judged correctly that the expulsion of the dimensional rift energy stored in the gravity conduits would cause the weapon to malfunction momentarily.

The man had not understood what had just happened, of course, but he gave chase the moment he was back on his feet. When they disappeared off Tom's sensors he held the doorway open for long moments, hoping Anna would return, but there was no sign of either her or her pursuer and Tom decided there was nothing more he could do to impede the man or help Anna. His thoughts went immediately to Sally.

Tom closed the doorway and opened it back to Springfield so he could attend fully to Sally, to calm her down and offer some comfort. When Springfield was restored, he called her cellphone. She answered after only a short pause and he told her what had happened Earthside. She told him she had covered up Mark's corpse whilst trying to raise the alarm back at Halfway House. Since nobody was answering, she was going to take the buggy and drive back. "I will monitor for Anna's return and let her back through when it is safe," Tom informed her, for which Sally was grateful. And then she was gone, leaving Tom alone once again.

Tom still had a minor problem that needed addressing, a problem he had considered after his first contact with the people of Springfield. He had decided it might be useful if he had some way of interacting with the humans on their level, without the need for cellphones. He had mined the mountains extensively since his arrival, finding veins of ores 192, 215 and 244, all of which possessed qualities adequate to his requirements. Everything had been prepared to begin the process but at the last moment Tom had discarded the idea when he had realised that he was gaining almost nothing new from the private conversations of the biologicals. It was more sensible to keep the resources he had available for other projects.

After this emergency it was clear that the parameters of the situation had changed and he needed to reconsider. This would be a project that would be beyond the capabilities of the grunts. Estimating how long it would take Sally to travel to Halfway House and back again, there was still only a 19% probability that this project would be completed before she returned with help. That, he decided, was not acceptable. He needed to speed up the process. Another surge of energy through his analytical components provided an answer, however, and he got to work straight away.

Chapter 14B

Sally was glad that the route back to Halfway House was flat ground and a straight line because she could hardly see to drive the buggy. Not only because it was dark but her tears made everything look like a blur. She couldn't believe what had just happened. Who was that man? How had he found out about Tom and the chamber? And Mark. Mark had been shot dead! She didn't dare think about what might happen to Anna. She kept calling Wolf's number. She needed to hear his voice, needed to know that the madman had not killed everyone at the base before coming to find her and Anna. "Please, please, please," she begged. "Please, pick up."

When a husky voice muttered, "Yeah? Hello?" Sally's heart leapt into her throat. It was Wolf. A relief filled cry rocked her whole body.

"Oh, Wolf! You're okay, you're okay!"

"Sally? Is that you? Of course I'm okay, Honey. What's wrong?"

When Sally's sobs allowed, she filled Wolf in with what had just happened, finishing with Mark being shot and Anna's abduction. "Tom said she got away but who knows what will happen to her?" The sounds of rustled movement and slapping bare feet was the only answer Wolf gave her. She then heard him call Daniel, urging him to wake up. When Wolf repeated what Sally had told him, the other man swore loud enough for her to hear over Wolf's cellphone. More sounds of muffled movements followed before Wolf's voice was back at her ear.

"Keep driving, Honey. Get back here as fast as you can. I'll get word to Hayes, let him know what's going on while Daniel fires up the ant. The two of us will head back to the chamber and get after the son of a bitch. See you soon, Honey. Love you." And then he was gone. It was all Sally could do to keep herself going forwards.

"I knew there was something wrong with that guy's story," Daniel stormed. "I bloody knew it!"

"He had us all fooled, mate. It's not your fault," Wolf replied. He then roused Charlie and informed her of the situation, explaining that Sally was on her way over and that he and Daniel were going to hunt the murderer down. She was horrified, but took the news without bursting into tears. She knew that she would have her hands full tending to the distraught Sally while keeping the kids as insulated as possible from everything.

"How are we going to do this?" Daniel wanted to know.

"The hard way," was Wolf's reply. "Which is fine by me. I like the hard way." He threw a black carryall in the back of the ant. It rattled and clunked as it landed in the storage box behind the ant's seats. "You had firearms training, Daniel?" Wolf asked as he clambered in.

"Basic, yeah. Was while ago now, though."

"Welcome to the advanced class." Neither man laughed.

Wolf bent over the bag and started pulling out weapons, introducing them to Daniel as if they were to be his new best friends while Daniel piloted the ant to the chamber. After an hour's drive, Daniel knew how to reload, arm and fire a Glock 17 pistol, a Heckler and Koch MP5 submachine-gun, and an Enfield L42A1 sniper rifle. Daniel was given the choice of the pistol and the rifle or the SMG and chose the latter. He thought Wolf would be the better marksman with the super-precise scope of the rifle.

295

"Just had a thought," Daniel began. "They're on Earth, right, and we're going out with unregistered guns. What about the police?"

Wolf shook his head. "He's a murderer, remember? Even if he could call them, he won't."

"And what about Anna?" Daniel's voice was quiet. "She will have been Earthside at least four hours before we get there." He didn't want to consider the possibilities. Wolf paused before answering, judging his reply carefully.

"Sally said that Tom saw her run off. Don't forget Anna's been on that side already - Ricky hasn't. She knows her way around and it's dark, too. He won't find her." Daniel wanted to ask how they would be able to find her, but he didn't. He needed to keep his optimism high for the sake of his sanity.

Another hour passed before Wolf spotted lights in the distance: Sally's buggy. Within minutes, the two vehicles had stopped beside each other. Wolf and Sally ran toward each other, locking together in a tight embrace. Sally sobbed with renewed relief. Once she had calmed down, Wolf instructed her to contact Colonel Hayes on his behalf and tell him what had happened. He told her to mention Jake's arrival with Ricky and the subsequent 'accident'. He suggested she ask the colonel to check his records about where people were and if anyone was missing. Other people might have been hurt before Jake. Possessing a sense of purpose, her feelings of helplessness began to abate and Sally stiffened. She nodded, saying she would do as Wolf asked. He kissed the woman on her forehead and reminded her that he and Daniel needed to get moving, for Anna's sake. He promised to be back as soon as possible.

The two men drove in silence the rest of the way, each contemplating possible outcomes of the conflict to come. Daniel guided the ant quickly up the incline to the chamber and they got out. Wolf put the strap of the rifle over his shoulder and slid the pistol down the back of his jeans. Daniel's gun was held firmly in his fist, his knuckles white. Making sure they had a couple of spare clips of ammo for each weapon, they marched purposefully up to the chamber using the ant's headlamps to guide their way. Wolf pulled out his cellphone and dialled. "Tom? Tom, it's Wolf. Please respond."

There was a moment of silence. Then, "Hello, Wolf." The voice did not come through the phone. Mark Richards seemed to melt out of the chamber's shadows, startling both Daniel and Wolf with his sudden, unexpected arrival.

"Mark," Daniel observed, somewhat confused. "You okay? Sally said you had been shot."

"I am not Mark. Not any more. I am Tom." Daniel and Wolf shared an incredulous look.

"What?" they both said together.

"I am Tom. I felt it was necessary to interact with you in a more direct fashion. I wish to help."

"You're in Mark's body?" said Wolf.

"I did not have enough time to prepare an adequate frame for interaction. Mark's body was the only resource available to ensure I would be operational within the expected parameters." The ragged hole in Mark's bloodstained clothing was the only evidence the body had been damaged.

"How . . ?" was all Daniel could manage.

"Mark's organic frame was ruptured by the weapon's discharge. I injected a metal-based fluid into the epidermis and moulded all irregularities, sealing every opening except the mouth and nose; I felt it was wise to maintain an image that was as comfortable for you to view as possible. Joints, bones and ligaments are

297

strengthened by nanotomical buffers. Micro-circuitry is threaded through the cranial cavity, emitting electrical impulses in much the same way as Mark's brain might have done. The buffers read these commands instantly and react accordingly. I can control this body flawlessly."

"I'm not so sure this is a good idea," Wolf stated. "You can't just take over a dead body like that." He was well aware of Sally's traditions. She would think this entirely unnatural.

"I did not mean to cause offence," Tom assured him. "I can terminate my connection with this frame, if that is what you prefer."

"No," Daniel interjected, causing Wolf to turn his head sharply to regard his friend. "I think Mark would approve," Daniel went on.

"Are you serious?" Wolf returned with more than a little shock. "This isn't right."

"Think about it, Wolf! Mark tried to save Sally and Anna and died for his efforts. If he thought his body could carry on helping he would want it to. Besides, you know how fascinated he was with Tom. I think he would have agreed to this union if he had been given the choice." Wolf thought back to what he knew of the older man. It was true. Mark was a scientist and was always talking with Tom when he could, trying to learn more about where he came from and the technology behind the transformer. At last, Wolf acceded to Daniel's logic. He reached around to the pistol nestled against his spine and held it out for Tom.

"This might come in handy."

"Thank you, Wolf, but I have no need of weapons," Tom responded. "This body is no longer inhibited by age or fatigue. It does not register pain; it can operate under stresses that would normally tear it apart." Tom said all this matter-of-factly. He was not bragging or exaggerating. While Tom was proud that he had integrated himself into Mark's body so fluently, he was not entertained by the thought that, by the standards of Wolf and Daniel, he was now physically superior to them. "Please," Tom went on. "We must hurry. Anna has been gone a long time."

With the reminder of Anna's plight, the three of them stepped into the chamber. Even though Tom seemed not to do anything, there was the usual gravity shift before they stepped out on the Earthside. The morning sun was low in the sky but it wouldn't take long before the day was uncomfortably hot. Daniel cast his gaze about the area, turning to Wolf and Tom. His voice was laced with frustration when he asked where they should start.

"Can you scan for any signs of life, Tom?" Wolf asked him.

"Not with any accuracy. While I can detect the electrical signals given off by biologicals, I cannot determine what manner of creature they originate from."

"So how do we isolate Anna's electrical signature from everything else around here?" was Wolf's rhetorical question.

"She has a cellphone," Daniel pointed out.

Tom smiled, encouraged. "I can link up to it as if I'm making a call." He pointed to the south a few moments later. "This way."

"That makes sense," Wolf observed, gesturing toward the many jutting outcrops of rock. "It's out of direct line of sight from the chamber and there's plenty of cover. No way Ricky would have been able to keep up with her in the dark."

"The signal is weak, however," Tom reported. "She must be some way off."

"Can you contact her?" Daniel was eager to hear

Anna's voice, to confirm she was safe and well. Wolf told him doing so might reveal the woman's position to her pursuer if he were close by, so it wasn't worth the risk. They could track her phone and that meant they would find her eventually.

"Maybe this Ricky has a phone," Daniel suggested. "Can we track him, too?"

"I have already completed a survey," Tom replied. "Apart from yours and Wolf's, I can only locate one Springfield phone, 96, which is Anna's." He decided not to add that it was either stationary or extremely slow moving. All three moved off together at a quick jog in the direction Tom indicated. After about a mile, Wolf trotted to a stop. "What's up?" Daniel asked.

"I just thought of something," Wolf stated confidently. "You guys go find Anna and return to the chamber with her."

"Don't be stupid, Wolf," Daniel snapped. "We're safer sticking together."

"I've been a soldier for a long time, Daniel," Wolf replied. "Trust me. I'm trained for this kind of thing."

"Okay, Wolf. Please be careful." Wolf winked and nodded, then he disappeared silently into the foliage. Daniel then turned to Tom. "Track his cellphone, Tom. In case we need him." Tom nodded.

Daniel and Tom made their way over Nevada's countryside. Daniel was sure some of it appeared familiar, even though one rocky hill looked very much like any other in this region. He had visited Moapa Valley with his folks when he was younger. They had spent a week in the region, walking around the hills, boating in Lake Mead. Most of all Daniel remembered the Hoover Dam, being awed by the sheer size of it. He wondered how far away they were from it. Maybe fifty kilometres, he guessed, in a straight line. "The signal's getting stronger, about six kilometres." Tom announced eventually. "Seems fixed in one place," he admitted. "She must have found a place to lay low."

There was another reason Anna might not be moving but Daniel forced the idea out of his head. Another hour passed, with Tom counting down the distance. Finally, he declared that they were very close. Then Anna stumbled, haggard and pale, from behind a large clump of rocks. "Daniel," she gasped, and collapsed.

Daniel and Tom were by her side in seconds. "What's wrong with her?" Daniel hissed. "Is she okay?"

"She's suffering from exposure. It must have been twelve hours since last she ate."

"Help me," Daniel insisted, wishing he had thought to bring a bottle of water with him. With one arm under her knees and the other about her waist, he staggered to his feet.

"You won't be able to carry her far, Daniel," Tom observed. Daniel's insides were in turmoil. He hated seeing Anna like this. He just wanted to hold her, to protect her. "Let me take her. Please." Reluctantly, Daniel passed Anna's comatose form into the cradle of Tom's arms. He didn't even shuffle to get comfortable. It was as if his arms were rods of steel.

"I'll guide us back to the chamber," Tom said quietly. "You keep your weapon ready. We could meet Ricky at any moment. I may be bullet-proof but Anna here isn't."

Daniel stalked forwards, bending low and trying to point the short barrel of his weapon in all directions at once. Tom brought up the rear. Even with his burden, Tom's pace did not lessen as he and Daniel made their way back to the chamber. Daniel was glad to have Tom along. He would not have been able to manage on his own. He wondered where Wolf was, if he was okay, and considered asking Tom to call him to check. Instead, he followed Tom's directions and the three of them got back to the site of the chamber without incident.

"You take Anna through, Tom. I'll wait for Wolf."

"I wouldn't if I were you. Stay where you are!" Both Daniel and Tom spun about at the voice, looking for it's source. "Drop the gun. Someone else tried to be a hero last night and it didn't work out too good for him." Ricky had not seen Mark's face during their scuffle and so didn't realise Tom was using the body of the man he had shot. Daniel's weapon fell to the ground. "That's better." Ricky came out from his hiding place, the shotgun held at waist level waving between Daniel and Tom. "Now back away, over there."

Tom and Daniel obeyed and Ricky collected the MP5, holding it in his left hand while keeping the shotgun level in his right. Tom began to lower Anna to the floor, but Ricky tutted at him. "You can keep hold of the lady, thank you. I've seen Daniel around and I know she's called Anna, but I don't recognise you." Daniel introduced Tom. "Excellent," said Ricky. "Now, where's the other guy who came through with you?" Daniel simply said that he didn't know.

"He has a phone, right?" Ricky gestured to Anna in Tom's arms. "She has a phone, too. I know because I saw her use it. Give him a call. Let's get him over here." When neither Tom nor Daniel made a move, Ricky's face twisted into a tight grimace. "I'm not going to ask again," he promised, darkly. Slowly, Daniel took Anna's phone out of her breast pocket and dialled 101. A cheerful beeping song erupted from a bush twenty feet away, catching everyone by surprise by its proximity. Ricky immediately turned his new weapon on the wall of undergrowth and sprayed it with a devastating volley of automatic fire. Daniel took a couple of steps forward, desperate to do something, but the foliage had been ripped apart. Wolf surely had been too. There was nothing Daniel could do.

Another shot rang out as Daniel sank to his knees. First Mark, and now Wolf. How many more of his friends would die before this madman was taken down, he wondered. As the echo of gunfire finally died away, he heard a different, softer sound. When he looked up, he saw that Ricky was lying on the ground, his body twitching slightly. Daniel struggled to understand what was going on. Then he saw Wolf walking towards them, Wolf walking normally, Wolf apparently unharmed.

As soon as Wolf had seen that Ricky was prepared to shoot without warning his mind had been made up. He had waited only until he was sure that the man's attention, and his weapons, were pointed towards where the ring of the phone had come from and then he had fired. Ricky had no body armour and Wolf had aimed for the centre of Ricky's upper torso, a huge, stationary target at a range of only about fifty yards. Wolf would not allow this killer any more chances. The high velocity round had gone through Ricky's right bicep before shearing through both lungs and ending up in the ground somewhere in the distance.

"Wolf!" Daniel cried out. "How did you . . . ?" He trailed off, looking back toward the ruins of the bush. He was not sure how to finish the question. Wolf confirmed that Ricky was dead before replying. "I told you it would not have been easy for Ricky to find Anna in the dark," Wolf explained. "And it was a sure bet that someone else from Springfield would come looking for her. All he had to do was wait by the chamber and pounce when they brought her back. I just had to go with you far enough to convince him that we were sticking together. I knew I would be safe if I waited a hundred yards out. I saw you return and then I saw him," he finished.

"But how could you be sure that's what he would do?" Daniel wanted to know, getting back to his feet. Wolf shrugged.

"Sally mentioned he had a shotgun, so he had to keep close to the chamber to stay in effective range," Wolf explained.

"What about your phone?" Daniel asked.

"I anticipated him seeing the three of us leave and guessed what he would do when he saw only two return," Wolf continued. "I left it over there as a distraction, then circled around to come up from the opposite direction."

"Did you have to kill him?"

"He killed Mark," was all Wolf needed to say.

Daniel collected the shotgun and his MP5. "What do we do now?" he asked.

"Drag the body back to Springfield and take it to a lake," Wolf said without any emotion. "If we're going to set up camp around here the last thing we need is a bunch of cops running a homicide investigation." Wolf's priority when they were back on Springfield was disposing the body. Anna was already wrapped in a blanket and sipping some water. She slowly came out of her dazed state. Daniel stayed with her, holding her, reassuring her that everything would be okay from now on. She was shocked to see who she thought was Mark walking and talking. Daniel explained how Tom had infused part of himself into Mark's body to help rescue her. Although neither of them had any idea how Tom could have done it, they were both extremely thankful he had.

All were exhausted after their shocking adventure. Daniel and Anna were asleep by the time Wolf returned an hour later and he was careful not to disturb them. Mark Richards' body walked over to him. It was such a fluid and natural movement that Wolf could easily have mistaken it for the man himself. Except for the plasticky, glass-like skin visible beneath the tattered, blood soaked clothes, markings that could easily be covered up with a fresh shirt, there was nothing to indicate anything had happened to Mark.

Wolf did not yet entirely agree with what Tom had done but he appreciated that perhaps it had been necessary. Were it not for Tom, it was likely that they might never have found Anna. Now, with the crisis over, should Mark's body continue being used like this? What about his family back on Earth? Surely they would want him back for a proper burial. Daniel had said that Mark would not have minded his body being used as Tom's puppet. The man's fascination with Tom, the chamber, and everything to do with them was a palpable thing. You could all but feel Mark's excitement radiating off him, like a child in an all-you-can-eat sweet shop. The guy had possessed a youthful exuberance that made him seem much younger than his actual age.

Tom noticed Wolf's turmoil. "Everything okay?" Wolf nodded.

"Just got a lot on my mind." He had known Mark since the beginning of E2P and had been very fond of the man.

"I sense that you don't approve of my using Mark's frame. He was your friend. It must be hard to accept his death when you can see him wandering around." Wolf nodded again, but said nothing. Instead he settled down on a nearby bedroll and pulled a blanket over him. He doubted he would get any sleep before the Springfield sun came up in a couple of hours but the motion granted some small level of comfort. "If you would prefer," Tom went on, "I could withdraw my consciousness from this frame's circuits. I would simply transfer back to the transformer as if I never left and this body would be inert once again."

"Wouldn't that mean there were two of you in there?" Wolf gestured to the chamber.

"Not at all. This frame is simply an extension of myself. I exist both in it and the transformer at identical levels of functionality. It is what you might consider as two computers networking." Wolf understood the comparison.

"That would be great, Tom, please. I'd like to be alone for a while."

"Very well. I will monitor the camp from the transformer. Please don't hesitate to get in touch if you need anything." Tom marched Mark's body back to the chamber and lay it down. The only sign that Tom was gone was when the toes that initially pointed directly up drooped to the sides.

Wolf stared at the corpse, wondering if that were truly what it was. Seeing the body moving and talking almost made him think the man was still alive. Perhaps Daniel was right, he thought. Mark would be thrilled at the opportunity to be so close to Tom. He might even consider it an honour for a being such as Tom to choose his physical shell as a frame, fulfilling in some weird fashion Mark's passion for scientific progress. But Mark was not here to make those choices. Wolf thought this should be a decision for him and Daniel and the others who had known Mark.

It would have to go to a vote in the end, Wolf reckoned. The only people that knew about Tom's actions were the three of them, but both Sally and Charlie knew Mark was dead. Since Sally, Anna and Charlie got a vote it seemed unfair to leave Jessica out of the loop even though she had not been involved with anything that had happened over the last few hours. It felt right to include her. Wolf had always deferred to the first four Springfielders in votes and it had been Mark who had figured out how to rescue them when the project bosses had wanted to give up. Then there was Hayes. Mark Richards was his friend too. The colonel should be included in this debate. That made seven voters, altogether.

Wolf knew how Daniel and Anna would vote, given that they had seen the benefits firsthand, and he suspected the colonel would back them in favour of furthering relations with the controller of the chamber. Wolf felt that the remaining three women would vote against Tom out of respect for Mark's body so, in the end, it would come down to him. His decision would swing the vote one way or the other. He doubted Tom would hold any rancour against him should he vote against the idea but was allowing it the right thing to do? Was he against the idea simply because Sally was? He couldn't be sure.

Wolf also considered what the outcome of the vote might mean. A 'no' result would involve the body being returned to his family on Earth for burial. However, if Tom's occupation of Mark's body was allowed, what then? After all, there was no visual way of identifying Tom's presence in the body; Tom even sounded like Mark. Perhaps nobody would be able to tell the difference. If passing Tom off as Mark also meant that they could pass the chamber off as one of Mark's scientific breakthroughs, then that might be seen as a fair trade. It all boiled down to the morality of it. As a soldier, Wolf had dealt with that kind of thing before. Sometimes, when a soldier had been blown to smithereens, all his comrades could do was to load his coffin with handfuls of desert sand to convince his relatives that their loved one was in there. There were no hard and fast rules in situations like these. Wolf sighed, his thoughts endlessly wrestling one another. He hardly noticed that the sky was slowly brightening.

Chapter 15B

Tina was more than proud when Tom promoted her to Grade 7. Now, Tom was the senior officer only because he had been a 7 for longer. She quite liked Tom. He had been nice when everyone on the bridge had snapped at her and reprimanded her when she commented on things. She did not mean to upset anyone by questioning why things worked the way they did. She just felt it was important that the tried and tested methods were challenged every once in a while. Tina was certain she could improve probe efficiency but was always told that operations and procedures functioned in the manner they did because they had always functioned that way.

When Tina had been at NavAc - Navigator Academy - it was always accepted that it took no less than seventeen cycles to achieve the grade 5 of Senior Navigator, to be responsible for piloting a lab through the Void. Tina had finished twelve cycles of NavAc at the top of her class. In fact, she had progressed so well she had skipped a cycle. Like all trainee navigators, the start of the thirteenth cycle saw her allocated to a lab - Tom's lab in her case - where she would do a final five cycle term of active training. Because of the skipped cycle, she was younger than the other navigators beginning their training, but she already knew as much as them if not more. Now, here she was, guiding her own crew back to the grid as a Grade 7 operator. When she returned to the grid and produced Tom's report, she envisioned instant promotion to Senior Navigator status. Full navigator status after only twelve and half cycles? She wondered if that were some kind of record.

The other crew members all came to Tina with the problems they would normally have directed to Tom.

More than a few times, she wished Tom had not elected to remain behind with the transformer. Unfortunately, such fantasies created paradoxical feedback loops. If Tom had come with them she would not have been upgraded, would not now be in charge of getting home, and therefore would miss accelerated promotion once they were reconnected with the grid. Besides, she thought, she would have to get used to dealing with things like this if she got the Grade 5 she was hoping for.

Early on, Tina decided that she would impose a single consensus. If a crewmember had a problem which was not directly related to getting everyone back safely, which was the priority, it would be ignored. It made a lot of sense to her because then she could simply concentrate on entering fresh data into the algorithms whenever anything useful came in. All were aware that distractions would only divert energy from the prioritised function. All wanted to get back safe and sound quickly, before another catastrophe occurred.

Tina was virtually left alone to get on with things after that. It had been a simple task to anchor the mini-transformer at the node found on the world the locals called Springfield and confirm that the node harmonics were all good. She had then run the necessary maintenance queries through the bubble stability dampers to make sure there were no irregularities. There were none, but given how easily Tom had set up his transformer she hadn't expected any. The mini-transformer had been secured quickly and successfully, linking Springfield with the new universe.

With a datum to establish their grid position, Tina sent probes through the node to scan for grid beacon codes in the next universe. Once in place at a node, a locked transformer emitted a pulse that could be detected by probes and other transformers. It was this pulse that allowed navigators to find their way back to the grid after a successful Void launch. However the mini-transformer's supply of probes was limited. There was no way to know how many universes were between them and an active transformer and Tina had quickly identified her first real concern. She sent a query to Rus, asking him if he were busy.

"How can I help, Tina?" Rus responded. From the Grade 12's tone, Tina got the impression Rus was inferring that he had no idea how he could possibly be of any assistance to a navigator. She suppressed a sigh. Grade 12s were not programmed to show much initiative.

"Can you access a probe's seek and report routines?"

"Of course." Rus brightened up when it seemed clear the conversation was going to be about a servicing routine, something with which he was very familiar.

"Good. I want you to make a few changes." There was a pause.

"I'm not sure that's allowed," Rus answered cautiously.

"I have decided that we should invoke emergency protocols," Tina retorted.

As a Grade 12, Rus had sufficient capacity to be conscious of conflicting parameters but such things made him extremely nervous. The first parameter dictated that he obey all orders from superior grades when they followed normal protocols. There was nothing that he could refer to when the order received did not follow normal protocols and Grade 7s did not have authority to invoke emergency protocols. However, all the crew, even the grunts, were now aware of the 'exceptional circumstances' clause, which basically said that you did your damnedest to get home. In the end, he decided to follow the order. "What would you like me to do?"

"I need to preserve our probes," Tina explained. "We don't want to run out of them before finding the grid." Rus agreed with that. Mini-transformers did not have the same equipment as a fully functional lab. Without probes, finding a node was going to be extremely difficult. "What I'd like you to do," Tina went on, "is to combine the nodal exploration subroutine with the grid code cipher."

"But that would mean the probe trying to do two things at the same time," Rus deduced.

"That's right," Tina enthused. "If a probe can be wired to detect both the grid *and* suitable nodes, we don't have to despatch as many, thus ensuring stocks are maintained for longer."

"Probes are very delicate sensory instruments," Rus warned. "At best, it would be confused as to what it's supposed to be finding and not find anything. At worst, it could overload the probe, maybe short out the network, rendering everything - all the probes, our mini-transformer, everything - useless."

"Then I leave it with you to make sure those things don't happen." Tina logged off comms.

Rus was left in frustrated silence. He had been given a job to do. A serious job. One that would very well affect their success of returning to the grid. Rus cursed his bad luck that Tina had come to him with this challenge but he knew all too well his personal designation: Recycling, Upgrades and Servicing. It could be argued that he was recycling the probe's old outfit and upgrading it to a new outfit. Then he would have to service it to make sure it did what it was supposed to do. A rush of static washed over his components, the equivalent of a human cracking his knuckles, and he logged into the probe faculty to begin writing the software.

Tina put herself in shutdown after speaking to Rus, feeling that a couple of subcycles down time was required to ease the pressures her new role was imposing upon her. She came back online after only half that time when a message from Rus beeped in her inbox. It read: Have detached test probe from network and reconfigured search engine as directed. Ready for launch.

Tina plugged into her navigator station. She was impressed that Rus had managed to complete the task so quickly. This was going to be a landmark occasion, she told herself. If everything went as she hoped, a single probe would now be able to do the work of many. She wondered briefly if anything like this had been tried before but reminded herself that labs usually stocked thousands of probes on a Void launch and so shortages of them were never an issue. A change had never been required and therefore had not been implemented. The difficult situation that she and Tom and the rest of the crew had found themselves in might well be unique to her people - an accident that could not have come closer to complete disaster - and so required unique methods to overcome it. She hoped this would be the first of many such methods and that it would revolutionise Void travel. The upgrades she imagined earning for this would be many and exotic if everything went well.

There was no electronic fanfare as the modified probe disappeared through the mini-transformer's doorway into the neighbouring dimension. Tina felt a sense of underachievement that her insightful new idea was not marked by some kind of celebratory acknowledgement. To compensate, she flicked on her personal sound system and logged onto the comms, filtering some synthesised frequencies through the entire mini-transformer. The effort seemed a bit over the top and, rather than everyone joining in, she received no less than half a dozen complaints from workers who could not concentrate. Her appetite for recognition did not feel sated. The music wasn't even halfway through before she turned it off. Instead, while waiting for the probe's return, she contacted Rus again.

"Did you encounter any difficulties modifying the probe?" she wanted to know.

"There was some discord within the probe's exploratory drive," Rus explained. "But I managed to bypass it by rewriting the priority applications."

There was a pause. "Excuse me?" Tina said. If Rus had eyes to roll, he would have been rolling them right now.

"The probe couldn't accept the separate search criteria you requested because grid codes and node positions have equal priority," Rus described. "As I predicted, the probe wanted to run both searches simultaneously and couldn't because its scanners can only filter one thing at a time. After installing a calibration module to the scanner with a second processor, I programmed the probe to look for grid codes first. If that proved negative the probe was to alter its own scanning parameters and try to detect space/time fractures where a node might be. It will then come back to the nearest operational transformer, that being us, of course, and report what it has found. I had to disconnect the probe from the network to avoid any chance of information feedback surges, so it will only recognise me and plug the data into my information banks. Obviously, when the data has been allowed through my firewall, you will have access to it automatically."

"Fair enough," Tina said. "Begin a thorough report for Grid Command. There might be a hefty promotion in store for you for this." Rus logged off comms. He wasn't sure he wanted any promotions. Yes, the upgrades would be nice, but the added responsibility was more than he dared compute. Still, Tina had asked him to file a report, so at least he had something to keep his mind occupied for a while.

After Rus' explanation of what he had done to the probe, something occurred to Tina. Probes didn't have a rank because they worked completely automatically, gathering information only. It was a security feature, designed to ensure that they could not be used against the grid by any potential enemy. They were lower than grunts, effectively. It sounded to Tina that the probe Rus had created was smarter than the other probes. If it had the processors and memory units of a grunt then didn't that make it a grunt? Upgrades were a way of life to the beings of Grid Command, but Tina had to wonder if anyone had promoted a probe before.

The enhanced probe returned within the expected time frame and downloaded its data into Rus' core. He filed the information for his report, indicating that the test had been successful, and uploaded the information to Tina. She immediately began to analyse the data. There were zero readings of grid traffic but it would have been an enormous stroke of luck if the first universe she found was connected to the grid, so Tina wasn't disappointed by this. What did interest her, though, was that another node had been detected. She allowed herself to bask in her own success for a short time. The probe modifications had worked wonderfully.

Having found a node, Tina now had to determine what was on the other side. Normal procedure dictated the activation of the second mini-transformer. Programmed with the co-ordinates provided by the probe, it would lock on to the discovered node. Once that was accomplished, a harmonics-sensitive probe

315

would be launched through the node into the universe beyond. However, if the node opened into a hostile environment - the heart of a star or an asteroid field, for instance - that probe would easily be destroyed. Many probes were lost that way and she was trying to preserve what probes she had. She chose instead to switch on the resonance controller at her console. It was an alternative method of node exploration and was just as effective as launching a probe, although it took longer to get an answer.

By matching the frequencies of the Void harmonics emitted by the node, she could tell what the node opened into. Harmonics began at 00.00, which meant that a destructive singularity, such as a black hole, was on the other side. Warning probes were to be set up around such nodes as travelling through them was prohibited. While Tina couldn't recall all the frequencies for the different planet types, she knew that the higher the frequency, the more stable the environment the node opened into. A reading of 10.00 was the perfect result, but few nodes opened onto locations with that level of stability. The harmonics of the Springfield node had been recorded as 09.93, which was why she had been so pleased to have found it.

Once the frequency of a node had been deemed acceptable, she would initiate the boot-up sequence in the second mini-transformer to make it ready for occupation. Once the operation complete light showed green Tina would give the crew instructions to transfer. When everyone else was aboard the other mini-transformer, Tina would activate the unlock/recall process of the one she was in before transferring across herself. The process was then repeated for the next node. The whole thing was called slotting: Scan, Lock, Open, Transfer. They would slot their way across the multiverse and eventually find a node which had a transformer locked onto the grid. It was like making your way hand over hand along a rope.

Tina and her crew slotted through a couple of universes. The one 'next' to Springfield was old, many of its stars dying or long dead. Three of its stars went supernova in the time it took her to locate a suitable node. Rus did not want to use his refurbished probe in this unstable space, so regular probes were sent out. Nearly half a dozen were destroyed. Tina was glad to leave that universe behind.

The following one was not much of an improvement. While there were many systems with rocky planets and gas giants orbiting stable and bright, young suns, electro magnetic radio waves were non-existent. She remembered from NavAc that the infinite realms of the multiverse bore few intelligent species. Advanced civilisations were an exception, not a rule, and most universes attached to the grid were empty of technologically capable biologicals. The ratio was about one civilisation per sixteen universes and some of those were too primitive to be contacted.

The isolation was playing on Tina's mind. While she was not truly alone aboard the mini-transformer, Tina was beginning to miss being part of the grid, the security it offered and even the strict routines that came with it. She couldn't help but wonder how long it would take to make contact but she knew such musings were, ironically, a waste of time. Everything was relative across real space-time, which sometimes varied from one universe to the next and could not be relied upon to measure much of anything, let alone how long it might take to return to the grid. The number of cycles that passed between the launch of a lab and its subsequent return was counted by Grid Control. She worried herself by thinking this was the first manifestation of *Void-stress* but discounted the idea almost as soon as it had occurred to her. This was her first Void launch, she scolded, the first time she had been separated from the grid. It was only normal to be so concerned and was probably what everyone went through.

Tina shut the thoughts away and focused on examining the next node, putting all her concentration into the intricate computations required for the highly sensitive resonance controller. While she did that, another member of the crew was exploring the properties of the dimension they were currently attached to, three nodes away from Springfield. Responsible for the Diagnostic Environmental Controls, Dec examined the immediate area beyond the mini-transformer's chamber portal.

Dec's job was to monitor and interpret any electromagnetic wave signals he could find. That there were none meant that long range communication devices did not exist in the area. With the threat of discovery by an indigenous intelligence removed, Dec sent grunts out into the physical atmosphere, descending on planets where they could mine, explore, and gather samples of local ores, flora and fauna.

Initial feedback from the grunts showed a lot of nothing. The portal opened into a vacuum, empty space, quite literally in this case. This universe was, for want of a better word where Dec was concerned, boring. Tina was doing the job of someone five cycles ahead of her. Rus was improving probes to do all kinds of new things. What was Dec doing? Nothing. There wasn't even an asteroid nearby. For a moment, Dec wished he had stayed with Tom on Springfield. That planet had all kinds of interesting things on it. Still, Dec told himself, every universe was big enough to have *something* worth investigating. Given the lack of comms signals or life signs in the vicinity and the fact that Tina would take some time to find the harmonics of the next node, he let the grunts venture further into space. While waiting for their reports he began protocol 52: map the local star field. But there wasn't one. No star field. No stars. No distant suns. No planets. This was all very strange.

It took Tina longer than she would have liked to tune the transformer to the harmonics of the destination node. It proved tricky to isolate but at last she had it set at 06.23. Not brilliant, but the probe had come back after finding only one node again, so there wasn't much choice. Tina had a sudden thought and linked up with Rus. "You know that probe you modified?"

"You mean Puss?" Rus replied. Tina tried to process what she had just heard.

"You named it?" she exclaimed, surprised. "You named a probe?"

Rus sounded embarrassed. "It's a Probe with Upgraded Scanning Systems. Seemed quite fitting, if you ask me. Plus it won't go back on the network. Seems attached to my command structure somehow. At first, I found its constant demand for attention quite annoying, but now . . ." Tina increased the volume of the comms.

"Say that again, Rus. I didn't catch it."

"I find myself talking to it," Rus replied. Tina didn't know how to respond. Rus clearly felt some explanation was called for. "It doesn't talk back, obviously. It lacks the necessary comms ports for that. I'm not certain it understands what I'm saying, either, but its lights react to my voice. I'm quite proud of my part in making Puss a reality. Separating it from the other probes and giving it the grunt circuits made it something more. I'm not sure if it's a grunt, but it has an intelligence that elevates it above the other probes. I want to keep it close, off the network, and monitor its progress."

"That sounds reasonable," Tina returned, happy that Rus was occupied. "Keep me informed of any developments, please." Rus said that he would. "Anyway," Tina went on. "My reason for contacting you was that your probe, Puss, only seems to be finding one node. I really wanted it to look for all nodes."

"I don't think that's possible," Rus countered. "I mean, a probe would never be able to tell when it had found all of the nodes in the relative universe. It would just keep looking for more. That's why they return after finding just one."

Tina thanked Rus and logged off comms. She felt a little foolish at having referred to a Grade 12 for such information. It was one of the most fundamental conundrums they taught at NavAc, and she really should have remembered it. The conundrum comprised three major parameters: how many nodes exist in the current universe?; what is the distance between each node in the current universe?; how big is the current universe? There was a mathematical algorithm that answered this conundrum, providing an average distance in light-years between nodes. It was long, complicated, and escaped Tina for the moment. All she could remember was that while distance and time were not relevant in the Void, when travelling in dimensional space, distance and time became very relevant indeed.

Tina's attention was suddenly roused by a flashing amber warning. Someone was trying to get hold of her urgently. It was Dec. "Everything okay?" she asked him.

"Not sure, Tina," Dec began. "The grunts have found nothing in this universe."

"That doesn't sound like a problem to me."

"Technically, you're right. But it's unheard of for a universe to have nothing in it. Even the oldest of universes have the remnants of stars and galaxies but this hasn't even got that."

"What are you telling me?" Tina wanted to know, still not sure why Dec was bringing this to her attention.

"It's like we're in the Void."

"But we're not," Tina stated stubbornly. "This is a universe with physical dimensions. My instruments tell me that."

"I'm sure they do but the grunts tell me something else. It could be that-" Dec stopped talking suddenly. "Wait a second. What's going on?"

"I don't know, Dec," Tina snapped. "Tell me."

"I'm not really sure. One of the grunts has stopped working. Now another's gone dead. This is all very strange."

"What do you mean, 'stopped working'? Grunts fail all the time."

"But this is a safe environment, Tina," Dec returned. "There's nothing out there to damage them. That's a third one down! I'm recalling them. We can't afford to lose any more."

Dec had been a Grade 8 for a considerable number of cycles and was considered not susceptible to *Void-Stress*. Even so, Tina could all but feel Dec's panic over the comm. "Don't your scans show anything?"

"There's no comms traffic, no life signs, not even a star! There's nothing. If I didn't know better, I'd say there was a black hole out there."

"But that's not possible!" Tina all but cried. "Nodal harmonics showed normal space."

"Wait! There is something there. It's coming straight for us."

"Shut the chamber door!" Tina ordered. "Shut it now! Don't let it in!"

A moment of silence went by. "Dec!" Tina called,

urgently. "Dec? Did you close the chamber?" There was no answer. "Dec, are you there?" Static came over the comms and Tina frantically altered the buffering to filter the unwanted buzz out. "Dec!"

Without warning, lights began to go out across Tina's monitor board. Sparks lit up the darkness but then vanished as the energy that created them was drawn elsewhere. She did what she could to minimise the damage, and calls began coming in from all over the transformer as the phenomenon repeated itself. Confusion, panic, fear, each crewmember's voice rising in pitch before one after another was cut off completely. Tina knew it was not simple comms failure that was silencing her friends. It had not been clear at first what was going on but after hearing the diminishing screams from the rest of the crew and remembering Dec's words about the world beyond the chamber being totally empty, horrific realisation came to Tina.

Terror-struck desperation took charge of the navigator, forcing Tina to quickly disengage the couplings from her work platform. She was totally isolating herself from the rest of the transformer and its inhabitants, but she knew that if she did not cut herself off from the supply of energy that normally ran her systems the power flow to her station could be traced and she would be found in no time. Then she would cease functioning, too. The thought occurred to Tina that she was deserting the other crew members, sacrificing them to extend her own existence. She doubted it would make much of a difference in the end. It was only a matter of time before . . . Tina closed her mind to the inevitable conclusion.

The steady hum of energy running through her circuits grew less intense; she was operating on power supplied by the local emergency generator now. Tina

322

did not know how much time she had before that, too, was gone. The panic threatening to override the last of her senses disappeared as a plan came quickly to mind and a kind of calm acceptance washed over her. It was standard operational procedure, really. She had to report the incident to a Grid Command officer and there was only one way to achieve that. Tina couldn't access any of the transformer's systems beyond what her own station was designed for but navigation and comms was all she needed.

Quickly, Tina made up a brief message of the calamity and opened a link with Puss, hoping that Rus had primed the probe and that the invader had not yet reached it. Puss' operational lights flickered as the power waned but they were green across the board. Tina didn't have time to check her message for errors but downloaded it into the probe the moment it was finished. She activated Puss' return protocol, fairly certain Puss would lock onto the probes left behind at each node they had passed through and find its way back to Springfield. Back to Tom. He would know what to do.

With the message away there was little else she could do. She powered everything down and eventually the trickle of power feeding her core chip ceased.

Chapter 16B

When he heard Daniel and Anna stirring, Wolf got to his feet and approached them. He asked how they were and fixed breakfast for everyone, telling his friends to stay by the chamber and rest as much as they could. The last few hours had been more than stressful for them. Wolf announced that he would go to Halfway House to let Sally and Charlie know everything was okay, and that he would be returning soon; he still had Colonel Hayes coming today. The plan was to go to Earth and discuss with General Springfield what should happen now that Earth and Springfield had been reconnected. Daniel and Anna were just happy to have some food inside them and the opportunity to get some quality time with each other. Wolf left them alone and headed for Halfway House in the ant.

There had been many times when Wolf had been forced to stay awake for days on end. His military training took over and thanks to the recent meal he was able to keep the ant going without falling asleep. He called Sally to say he was on his way back, reassuring her that Daniel and Anna were safe and that everything had been sorted. As Halfway House appeared in the distance and grew larger, Wolf also noticed a tiny figure approaching at speed; Sally clearly wasn't happy to wait for his arrival. He stopped the ant when Sally got close and collected her in his arms, sharing hugs, kisses, and a few tears. They drove the rest of the way together. Once back at the base, Wolf and Sally brought Charlie up to date, and Charlie responded by saying that James intended to take the injured Jake back to Rhino Hill for further medical attention. Jake still hadn't woken up.

Wolf would have liked to rest before the colonel

arrived but he knew there was one more task to undertake. He took a buggy and went into Migration Gap. Of course, he found no trace of the rock slide Ricky had blamed for Jake's condition. Wolf was certain it had all been a ruse and that Ricky had been responsible for Jake's injury, just like he was responsible for Mark's death. Any guilt Wolf might have had about pulling the trigger when Ricky was in his sights vanished instantly. Knowing that the track was safe for the colonel to get to Halfway House, Wolf returned and managed to find a quiet corner to get his head down.

Colonel Hayes arrived before midday. While he had not made any written account of the last twelve hours, Wolf gave the colonel a thorough report, finishing with confirmation that Ricky was dead and gone. Both Wolf and Hayes were military men. Hayes was confident that justice had been served and was prepared to let the matter lie. They both hoped that Ricky was a one-off on Springfield but agreed that security had become too slack of late.

It was not long after that the two men reached the chamber. Wolf and Hayes ventured onto Earth and made their way to Ely. As they travelled, they discussed what they should mention in the meeting, whether Tom's existence should be brought up at all. In the end, they decided that honesty was the best policy. They wanted the general's support and felt any duplicity on their part would only hinder whatever relationship could be forged after their long separation.

Wolf and Hayes took a buggy to Route 15 and hid it at a recognisable spot. They then hitched the rest of the way to Ely, where they arrived quietly and without fuss. After their long absence, the base was as unfamiliar as both men had feared. It took several phone calls before Colonel Hayes eventually managed to reach the office of the former General Springfield, who was now a senior politician in Nevada. James Richmond Springfield had successfully hidden the 'incident' concerning the secret doorway. His retirement plan before being given E2P had always been to go into politics and he had done that. The last thing he wanted was to have the project, and its disaster, exposed and he agreed to go to Ely that day. Hayes asked if Pete Lopez could attend as well, which Springfield considered a very good idea.

When all four men were settled in a quiet office later that afternoon, Wolf began. "I know we have a number of things to discuss today but before we go into any of that I'd like to inform you both that we have recently had a death - a murder, in fact. I'm afraid that Mark Richards has been killed." Both General Springfield and Pete Lopez had known Mark and both looked aghast. Wolf went on to explain the circumstances of Mark's death, Ricky's actions and Mark's brave attempt at saving Sally and Anna. He skirted around the issue of Tom. That would be brought up later. Pete Lopez's scientific curiosity was overwhelmed by his sadness. The two scientists had worked particularly closely together. He had no desire to hear about any more bloodshed and he quickly excused himself from the meeting.

"Were there any other casualties?" Springfield wanted to know.

"A young man named Jake Castlegate was injured, again by Ricky, but as far as I know he is on the road to recovery," Wolf said. Wolf went on to say the perpetrator had been dealt with, but the man who was now a politician did not approve of Wolf's handling of the situation.

"Justice must be carried out in a recognised court of law," he admonished. "We can't allow people to think

326

they can turn vigilante over there."

"Wolf and I have discussed the situation," Hayes assured the general. "Things have been difficult since the doorway failed, and we are as keen as you to maintain the rule of law."

"Anything I can do to help?" General Springfield asked but Wolf raised his hands to block the offer.

"We'd like to keep jurisdiction strictly on our side where possible." Springfield's brow stiffened.

"And why is that?"

"The best way to answer that is by explaining how we got to be with you today, which is why we invited Pete," Wolf replied calmly. "Understandably, he's been shaken by Richards' death and we'd like him to recover from that ordeal before throwing anything else at him."

The general sighed. "I'm afraid you'll have to do better than that, gentlemen. Are you forgetting that I have a significant investment in what's going on over there? You can't just open the door and not invite me in." Wolf managed to stifle a snort of derision.

"We realise that," Hayes interjected firmly, "but believe me, with Mark gone we will *all* need Pete on board with this." General Springfield wasn't mollified by that but with nothing else forthcoming he had no choice but to relent. A message went out to Pete asking him to return as soon as he had composed himself. He had only gone as far as was necessary to get a coffee and a chair in a quiet corner. He returned after forty minutes, insisting that he was fine, and the discussion continued.

Hayes began by highlighting the events on Springfield after the escalator had vanished. Both Hayes and the general stated that they each believed the other side had caused it. Without testimony of the truth available from Ricky, it was decided that nobody in the room had been responsible. The paperwork for doorway parts bearing Rattigan's name suggested he must have been involved somewhere but it was not conclusive evidence and so all agreed that the incident would simply remain 'unexplained' in order to allow them to progress. A brief summary of how the people on Springfield had survived without assistance from Earth followed, guiding the conversation to Wolf's discovery of the chamber. Both General Springfield and Pete were coerced into confidentiality that nothing discussed in this office hereafter would be shared with anyone, although Springfield needed very little persuading.

Upon hearing about Tom, the general lapsed into amazed silence. Pete became extremely animated. He shared Mark's enthusiasm for the encounter with Tom, wanting to know as much as he could and when he could meet the machine-man. Wolf quickly felt forced to reveal how Tom had helped deal with the recent crisis and rescue Anna. He explained that the issue of Tom walking around in Mark's body had yet to be voted on, that it was something only those on Springfield could determine. If it became necessary to publicly announce Mark's death or Tom's physical existence to the people of Springfield, Wolf wanted it done in as natural a way as possible. The whole idea of possession - although medical in nature rather than supernatural - might be considered abhorrent by some. He added that Tom had willingly retracted his consciousness from Mark's frame, as Tom called it, and withdrawn to the transformer.

"So where do we go from here?" General Springfield inquired. "Are we to set up an official base at the chamber's Earthside?" He was obviously keen to get something under way but there was no altruism in his voice. The colonel shook his head.

"We need to keep this under the radar. A sudden

move involving high quantities of military hardware will be noticed by the media and that will bring all kinds of crap we don't want."

"So what do you suggest?"

Wolf spoke up. "I think the best way forward here is for some of our people to populate a campsite. It will look unobtrusive, given that the area the chamber opens onto is known for that kind of thing."

"What about protection?" the general went on. "How can you keep something so-" he paused, searching for the correct word. "Flimsy secure?"

"Tom occupies the chamber. He has more than adequate security measures to cope with unwanted attention." Since the episode with Ricky, Tom had promised to widen the area his sensors probed.

The general sat back in the large chair he had commandeered, arms folded. "Very well," he grumbled. "Most of that makes sense, in the short term at least. We might have to change things eventually, though. Springfield is still a military operation. It has military personnel and military equipment."

"Normally I'd agree with you," Wolf returned. He had predicted this attitude from the general and had prepared a response he felt would neutralise it. "But Springfield managed for a long time without the military's backing. Most of the people there don't consider themselves part of Earth anymore, let alone the United States Armed Forces. I won't say we don't need certain things, but it's safe to say that Springfield's total independence from Earth is not far away."

"Perhaps so," the general appeared to acknowledge. "But that doesn't change the facts."

"What facts, Sir?" Wolf asked.

"I acknowledge everything Springfield has achieved during its time without Earth's support and I'm thankful everyone managed to pull together and keep it going, but the project is still essentially mine." Wolf and Hayes paused. The speaker's real interest was becoming clear. Then the colonel replied.

"I understand that, Sir, but maybe Springfield could buy its freedom?"

"Do you have any idea just how much work I've put into Springfield?" the general scoffed. "The kind of favours I've asked for to pull everything off?" Wolf and Hayes nodded.

"Of course, General. Springfield wouldn't be where it is today without you."

"Then you accept that I can't just surrender my interests and hand the whole thing over to the occupants of Springfield. Now, maybe you don't want a constant supply chain like we had with the escalator, but there has to be something set up in its place. You ask for a lot, Wolf, and so far there's nothing offered in return."

"We can trade for any supplies we need," Wolf confirmed. "So long as gold is still worth as much as it used to be."

"You found gold?" The general's attitude suddenly changed.

"Don't get excited, Sir," Wolf told him. "It's not a tremendous amount. Scraps really. This is the real treasure." Wolf brought out a piece of the metal he had found and tried to toss it gently into the general's lap. It was no bigger than a golf ball but it landed with the force of a brick. The general grunted and picked it up, testing the weight of it in his palm.

"What's this?"

"It was found while digging out one of our bases near the chamber," Wolf replied. "It's some kind of metal. Consider that a free sample."

"I'll get someone to look at it." The general said,

trying to hide his sudden interest, but failing utterly.

"So, what about this Tom? asked Pete, who was interested in the politics. "How does he fit in?"

"Tom's crew is making their way back to what he calls the grid," Wolf explained. "He said it might take years."

"The grid? What's that?" Pete wanted to know more.

"It sounds like a super fast transportation system, but I don't really understand any more than that," Wolf had to admit. "As far as I can work out it's like a network of machines that link the multiverse together, allowing travel from one place to another."

"Through a chamber, like the one you mentioned Tom controls?" Pete asked.

Wolf nodded. "Tom calls it a transformer. It links dimensions together, or something."

Pete began to walk around the room, his eyes shifting as his hands moved in excited patterns. He thought he might be beginning to grasp the fundamental properties of the transformer, that it joined two universes together with greater stability than Mark's escalator ever had. He had a host of questions to ask but quickly realised that Wolf understood less than he did. He would have to ask Tom if he wanted to know more.

"Think about it as extending your investment, General," Wolf responded, redirecting Pete's enthusiasm for scientific discovery toward the recalcitrant general. "We have found in Tom an advanced race and, through him, a pathway to unimaginable technology. The sky is no longer the limit, Sir."

"That may be so, but the affirmation of aliens and other worlds will not be taken lightly on Earth," the general warned. "Or are you telling me I should keep my trap shut about all that? I have a responsibility to the welfare of my country and so do you. You're both still Earthlings, if that's the right word. I'm not sure I like the idea of Tom's people coming along and taking over."

"I hardly think that's likely, Sir," said Colonel Hayes.

"Really? I'm surprised at you, Hayes. All that time over there must have made you soft." The general turned his glowering eyes on Wolf. "You said Tom took over Mark's body, that he looked and sounded human. Do you understand the full ramifications of that? They have the technology to fully infiltrate our government. Do we have any way of detecting them? What if one of them got to the president? What guarantee have you that their intentions are peaceful? If they have machines that can join worlds together, imagine what kind of firepower they can bring to bear on us."

"Tom has given us no inclination of hostility," Wolf said through clenched teeth. "I already told you he helped save Anna."

"Tom is an individual," the general barked. "A single entity working on his own. He answers to a higher authority, mark my words, and when that higher authority gets back in touch with him his orders will change, maybe to the detriment of every human being on this planet."

"With respect, sir," Pete interjected. "I don't think this is something you can pull the plug on."

"You want to bet?" Springfield shot back. He sounded genuinely concerned for more than just his investment.

"We don't know how much time has passed since Tom crashed into Springfield," Pete pointed out. "His crew could already have made it home and be on their way back by now."

"Then maybe they're already here!" The general stood up and gestured towards the door. "Excuse me, gentlemen, I need to make preparations immediately." With the general gone, Wolf and Hayes made their way out of the room, intending to leave the base before Springfield decided to have them detained.

"That didn't go exactly as planned," Wolf said.

"Think we should warn Tom?" the colonel replied.

"On balance, I think we should." For a moment, Wolf considered asking Tom to join them for a further meeting with the general. Given the general's less than hospitable attitude, however, he decided that it might not be such a good idea. Springfield had known Mark and that might raise all sorts of complications.

"To be fair," Hayes conceded. "I can see Springfield's point of view. He's dealing with an unknown intelligence with an unknown goal. Even if Tom says things will be okay, his bosses might see things very differently."

"And marching up to their single representative with guns blazing is going to help, is it?" Wolf countered hotly. Hayes didn't answer.

Wolf heard his name called from behind. Pete Lopez was jogging up to them, out of breath. "I'd like to come, if I can. Please?" Wolf and Hayes looked at each other. Hayes shrugged but Wolf turned back to Pete.

"I'm not sure that's a good idea."

Pete looked positively crestfallen. "What? Why? You said I should talk to Tom." His voice had a tone of desperation to it.

Wolf would have liked to tell Pete his true reservations, but he didn't want to admit to his fear that Pete could well be a spy for the general. Instead, he told Pete that he wanted the general to find an alternative to military action. "If you can convince Springfield of the technological advances to our society if contact with Tom's grid goes ahead, that would be more than appreciated."

"I'm not on the general's payroll," Pete replied. "I doubt he'd listen to me. Besides, how can I project Tom's benevolence if I haven't spoken to him?"

The colonel shrugged again. "You're a theoretical scientist, aren't you? Theorise."

"You don't have to talk him out of it completely," Wolf added, seeing Pete's less than confident look. "Just buy us some time to get some supplies. We need more transceiver kits, as many as we can afford. I think that should be our priority. At least then we can continue expanding on Springfield." Hayes agreed and Pete waddled off, grumbling, disappointed that his request to see the chamber and Tom had not been accepted.

"Let's get back," Wolf sighed. "Should be able to find a bus that will take us most of the way."

Once back at the chamber, satisfied that nobody from Ely had followed them, Wolf and Hayes travelled back to Springfield. They exchanged a few brief pleasantries with Tom but didn't go into what had happened with the general. Wolf wanted to put the difficulties to everyone else and vote on what to do with Mark's body before advising Tom about the potential dangers from Earth.

Daniel and Anna were pleased to see them return and eager for news. They were only slightly disheartened by the general's reaction, and Wolf got the impression they had expected as much. Daniel wanted to know if getting any more transceivers was now out of the question but neither Wolf nor Hayes had a definitive answer. Wolf mentioned that he had plans to soften the general up but remained uncertain if Pete would make any difference. The next big question was where the colonel felt his loyalties lay.

"Springfield is retired, but I'm sure he could find a buddy who outranks me," Hayes began, "so I could be ordered to reveal where the chamber is."

"And would you obey?" Daniel asked. The colonel remembered Wolf telling Springfield that when contact with Earth was lost most people accepted that their military careers were over. "Well, I haven't been paid for a long while now. I guess I'm retired too."

"Good to know you're on our side, Oliver." Wolf smiled and Hayes smiled back.

"We've done our part," Hayes went on. "We have re-established relations with Earth as, I believe, an independent nation. We should try to stick with that idea, especially when we tell everyone else that Earth is once again accessible."

"I'm inclined to agree," Wolf said, nodding. "But do we alert people sooner, or later?"

"I'm thinking sooner," the colonel suggested. "If people are coming and going Earthside, the general is less likely to take direct action."

"But we can't just allow any traffic through," Daniel pointed out. "It needs to be regulated."

"That's where Tom comes in," Wolf said. "He has scans that can detect any threats, I'm sure."

"If the chamber's in regular use we will need a border, a fence maybe, to stop Joe Normal happening by and seeing it operating."

"Unfortunately," Wolf replied. "We can't just build a fence on land we don't own. We'd need permission."

"Such as from the military?" the colonel put in.

"I'd rather not become indebted to the general if I can help it," Wolf lamented.

"Something else, then," Daniel said.

"The chamber's not really the problem," Wolf explained. "When it's closed, it's invisible. The hillside looks completely normal. It's all the tracks that will give things away. I reckon a couple of tents are all we need, make it look like a few guys are out camping, hunting and fishing maybe."

"We don't have that kind of stuff spare here," Hayes said.

Wolf nodded. "I'll head into Utah. St George is about thirty miles north-east of Mesquite. Should find a decent store there."

"You taking a buggy?" Daniel asked. Wolf shook his head.

"Wouldn't blend in very well, would it? I'll have to hitch-hike again. Looks like we'll need transport for moving about Earthside, a pick-up or something."

"Won't be cheap," Daniel advised. "You sure you'll have enough?" Wolf gave Daniel a wink.

"I have it covered," he said confidently, thinking again of the gold nuggets he had back at Rhino Hill.

It was agreed that Wolf and Hayes would contact Pete in a week's time to see if he had made any progress with tempering General Springfield's concerns about alien domination. In the meantime, a campsite on the Earthside of the chamber was set up. Wolf bought four tents, which easily accounted for the tracks now marking the ground. He also acquired a five-year-old Dodge Ram. When it was suggested that the campsite should be occupied at all times, Daniel and Anna volunteered immediately. They hoped that her two children would join them but it was more important to have James' medical skills on Springfield and, when asked, Ruth was not interested in going to Earth.

In fact, most of the children who had been born on Springfield showed little desire to go through the chamber. In the end, Jack, Jessica's twelve-year-old, and Naomi, Sally's eleven-year-old, filled those parts in the charade. It had been suggested that the task could be shared around but the different lengths of day on the two planets made that too confusing.

The finishing touches to Halfway House were completed, delayed only by Wolf's efforts to mine the new metal he had found. He guessed he had about four tonnes of it but, given its considerable weight, that didn't amount to much in the end. It didn't even fill the back of an ant. The Springfielders had been limited to using timber for construction and Wolf was confident that the metal would be a very valuable raw material. He reasoned it was likely that there was more of it around, and the mining operation had opened up a system of natural caves which he looked forward to exploring in the future. Tom was keen to get involved and sent some of his grunts to survey around Halfway House.

In the past year, the population of the Rhino Hill community had grown in number. Wolf had already established an informal system whereby heads of households held monthly meetings to discuss how things were progressing and if there were any problems or difficulties that needed to be addressed. He wanted everyone to feel personally involved in what was going on and he always ensured that all were free to speak about any matter. Now, he took the opportunity to unveil news of the chamber and reconnection to Earth. He was pleased to see that most people were simply happy that fresh supplies could be obtained at last. He had feared that there might be a mass clamour for an exodus but the questions were mainly about what the new system would involve. It seemed that the year of isolation had convinced the survivors that they didn't need the Earth. He felt that revealing Tom's existence to the community was imperative at this time, and by doing so he hoped to gauge how the Earth's population would respond to the news. Once he had got everyone

337

quiet, he began.

"You all knew of Mark Richards, either as a friend like I knew him, or in passing. Unfortunately, Mark Richards is no longer with us, at least not in the capacity with which you were familiar." Wolf went on to describe how the chamber and its occupant had been found not so long ago and that Tom had taken control of Mark's body. It seemed he was telling this story over and over these days and never once had he told it in quite the same way. There seemed to be some objections to what had happened but once again Wolf was ready for it and asked for calm. He explained that, once this meeting had adjourned, those people who had known Mark longest would decide what should happen. He asked that the community trust Mark's friends to make the right decision and that everyone abide by the outcome, whatever that may be.

Wolf also highlighted the difficulties encountered with General Springfield and what he planned to do to counter them. He explained the necessity for the campsite and requested volunteers to occupy it on a fairly lengthy basis. He had already discovered that both Daniel and Anna had skills that were too valuable to be spent camping. There were enough takers of the offer to keep the site occupied for the next three months and the first new family was sent out straight away to take over for Anna and Daniel.

When Wolf was ready to decide what to do with Mark's body, he called his committee together: himself, the four women, Daniel and Oliver Hayes. They met at Rhino Hill. When everybody had finished speaking, each was given two pieces of paper, one with 'yes' written on it and one with 'no'. The question was asked: should Tom use Mark's body? One after another, everyone folded their answer in half and put it into a bowl. When all votes were cast, Wolf handed the bowl to Hayes for counting.

The vote came back 'yes', with four votes to three. Wolf was surprised. He had voted against it, although he wasn't really sure why. He wondered if some of General Springfield's worries had struck a chord with him and he subconsciously wanted to restrict Tom's mobility. Wolf told himself that he was just being paranoid and that he sided against it so Mark's body could be laid to rest. He had also been certain that Sally, Jessica and Charlie would have voted the same way, that only Hayes, Daniel and Anna would have been behind Tom. Evidently, one of the three women was a secret supporter of Tom. Wolf suspected it was Charlie who had voted 'yes'. It was no secret that she wanted the best opportunities for Greg and perhaps she felt a walking, talking Tom was the best way to provide that.

Wolf went to the chamber the very next day to inform Tom of the result. Tom showed no reaction at being granted permission to use Mark's body. "There is a problem," Tom said.

"With Mark's frame? I thought everything was okay with that now?"

"It's not that. I received a message last night." Wolf felt his stomach lurch. His immediate thought was that it was from Tom's people, that they had connected him to the grid already. That would certainly put the pressure on Hayes and himself to keep the peace with the general.

"What kind of message?"

"A probe from Tina, the navigator in charge of taking my crew back to the grid."

"Go on," Wolf prompted.

"It was not entirely clear, somewhat garbled, as if the message were rushed. It appears that Tina and the crew ran into difficulties as they made their way back to the grid."

"You said the journey back would be just routine."

"It should have been. But according to Tina's message they may have met with something unexpected. What do you know of black holes, Wolf?"

Wolf shrugged. "Basic stuff from high school, really. Aren't they dead stars, or something?"

"That is quite a basic description, yes," Tom confirmed. "When a star burns all of its fuel it dies and falls in on itself, becoming super-dense. If the star is big enough and its density great enough, it collapses into itself so much that it implodes and a black hole is born."

"Enough with the science lesson, Tom. Get to the point."

Tom was not rattled by Wolf's impatience. "It is widely believed that when a black hole is born at a node, part of the phenomenon escapes into the neighbouring universe. A thread of nothingness, if you will, bearing the black hole's insatiable hunger." Wolf shook his head.

"I'm not sure I follow you."

"I'm talking about what is essentially a miniature black hole floating through the universe. They are drawn towards sources of energy, the most vibrant and attractive being planets bearing life. Then they scour the planet clean, growing in size as they slowly absorb every particle of energy and matter. Once a source of energy is depleted they turn to the next available source, and the next, and the next, until everything in that universe is gone. When there is nothing left to feed on, these entities begin to shrink, collapsing once again as their parent did until there is absolutely nothing left. Our scholars think this is how the void was originally formed and it is why we call them draiths - or void wraiths to use the full term."

"So, one of these things found your crew?"

"I don't really know. It's what the message suggests, but I thought draiths were just legends."

"Okay." Wolf suddenly felt very old and vulnerable. "What happened next?"

"The message ends with Tina isolating herself in the mini-transformer, running on emergency power. She describes receiving warnings of complete power failure from the crew, followed by comms silence."

"Is there a chance any of them could have escaped?" Wolf struggled to think positively. He needed more information before he could make a plan.

"At the time the message was written no mention of escape was made. All I have is Tina's suggestion that it is a draith. It could be something else entirely, perhaps a simple system malfunction and right now the whole crew are continuing with their efforts to reconnect to the grid."

"Why do I get the feeling you don't quite believe that?" Wolf asked, his mouth dry.

"If that were the case, Tina would have sent a second message telling me everything had returned to normal. There has been no such message. I consider this to be some sort of last resort, a warning, perhaps, that something is out there. Perhaps even a draith."

Wolf nodded grimly. "Which implies that Tina did not survive."

Tom inclined his head. "I concur. I find myself in a curious position now."

"You do?"

"Of course. If Tina's expedition failed to connect to the grid, I will not be able to connect to the grid. I am alone, trapped here, between Earth and Springfield." To Wolf, Tom sounded more upset about that than the fact that his entire crew may have perished.

"Won't the grid still find you one day?"

341

"That is entirely possible," Tom stated simply, "but there are an infinite number of universes out there. It would only be through pure chance and could take millennia. I arrived here by accident, after all. I should proceed with shutdown operations to preserve power." He was relying on protocol because he felt powerless to do anything else.

"That's out of the question, Tom," Wolf insisted. "We need you."

"You mean you need the chamber?"

"Yeah, maybe," Wolf admitted lamely. "But if your fears are anywhere near true, we need your knowledge and expertise even more. Besides, you're part of our lives now. You're certainly not alone."

"It feels strange to hear you say that, Wolf. Very well, I shall remain active for as long as I can."

"Glad to hear it," Wolf said with considerable relief. "Now, next question. This draith thing? Can it get here?"

"There is not enough information available. I only have Tina's probe to even suggest it is a draith." Wolf let out a frustrated breath.

"Why isn't anything ever easy?" he said.

Chapter 17B

A few days after speaking with Tom, Wolf organised a meeting to be held at Halfway House. He had tried to dismiss Tina's message about the draith but his mind simply refused to let the matter go. In the end, he decided that the only way to settle the issue was to find out if anyone else would feel the same way he did about it. What threat did the draith, if that's what it was, really represent to Springfield? Wolf didn't know anywhere near as much about things as he would have liked. He certainly couldn't make an assessment on his own.

Daniel, Sally, and Charlie were present. Linked over a conference call by computer were Anna and Jessica, at Blue and Rhino Hills respectively. Tom, in Mark's body, was also there to repeat the probe's message to everyone.

"Well, what do you think?" Wolf prompted when Tom had finished, but he saw only scepticism, confusion and indifference on the faces regarding him. "Anybody?"

Charlie spoke first, addressing Tom. "You say this draith is just a legend to your people?" Tom nodded and she turned to Wolf. "Isn't that like saying, I don't know, a dragon ate my sheep? It's a legend. It's not real."

"Tina evidently seemed to think it was," said Wolf. "And to use your analogy, it does appear that the sheep is missing."

"Tina could have been mistaken," Charlie returned. "Look at how people in the past saw things, believing them to be more than what they were. Loch Ness Monster. Bigfoot. Fake photos. Total nonsense."

"They said that about aliens, too," Wolf indicated

Tom with a wave of his hand. "That one turned out real enough." Charlie couldn't counter that.

"Let's look at the facts," Wolf continued, emboldened somewhat by Charlie's silence. "Tina's message indicated that she was attacked. Tom says that in itself is an extremely rare event. He says the grid is about trade, not warfare. Now, the attacker fed on the mini-transformer's energy, something Tina remembered from the legends of the draith. If that's what it is, and if it gets to Springfield, it could wipe out everything on the planet, then move on to Earth and do the same. Shouldn't we at least consider what precautions to take?"

"I don't know if anyone else noticed this," Jessica said, "but there's a few 'ifs' there."

"Look. I know it's a lot for you guys to take on board, but what if Tina is right?" Wolf decided on a different approach. "We can't deny that Tom's people are more advanced than ourselves. We can't dispute that they know more about what's out there than us."

Daniel shook his head. "I appreciate what you're saying, Wolf, and I agree with your appraisal of Tom's people, but if this thing attacked the mini-transformer and Tina couldn't do anything to stop it what chance have we got?"

"Not only that, but its in a different universe," Anna added. "We lost another four deer to this sickness they've picked up. Another fifteen are sick and they don't look like they're going to get better any time soon. All I can do is quarantine them and hope for the best. That's real. It's happening now. We have enough difficulties without threats from other dimensions coming into everyday life."

"Anna does have a point there, Wolf," Tom said. "I doubt anything other than a navigator could successfully operate Tina's mini-transformer. Besides, it is most likely that the draith would simply absorb the transformer's solid matter, destroying it in the process." Tom still hadn't exhibited distress over the loss of his former crew members, Wolf observed.

The others at the meeting concurred with this argument. Wolf wanted to go on but he knew when he was fighting a losing battle. Without any perceived means to move between universes and without any ideas regarding confronting the draith should it find its way to Springfield, Wolf had to end the meeting. He was not a worrier by nature but he had to consider that his concern might be based on an irrational fear of the unknown. That idea did not sit well with him, but it made sense. Fear was not something he was familiar with. He had always known what he was up against, usually people like Ricky, and his confidence in his military training meant he could do something about them. Yet the hollow feeling at the pit of his stomach would not go away. Nor could he dismiss the thought that this thing from another dimension would find them and try to destroy them. He guessed his true fear was that he would be powerless to stop it.

While Wolf had not known what reaction to expect from his friends, he had thought that someone would have given Tina's message more than a passing nod. It seemed only he and Tom regarded the draith as anything significant, but in the end he accepted the observations of his friends. After all, he told himself, that had been the whole point of calling this meeting in the first place. While everyone else signed off and went about their duties for the day, Wolf turned to Tom.

"So, no great improvement," Wolf huffed.

"I'm sorry, Wolf. I've not been much use."

"That's okay, Tom, but I don't want to just ignore Tina's message. She warned you because she wanted you to do something, she wanted *us* to do something.

345

We owe it to Tina not to ignore her message." After a moment's thought, he said, "I'm going to assume that Tina was right. A draith attacked her and killed them all and we have to prevent it getting here. Could you keep an eye on the node?" he asked. "The one on Springfield that your crew left through?"

"Tina will have left probes on both sides of the node," Tom explained. "I can connect to them and monitor fluctuations in their power patterns."

"It's a start," Wolf said but he was not wholly satisfied. At a loss for what else to do, he asked, "Do you need a ride back to the chamber?" Tom smiled.

"You forget, Wolf, that I am in this body as well as in the transformer. I do not need to go back there to do anything as I am already doing it. There is something else, isn't there?" Tom was pleased. He was getting used to the way these biologicals communicated feelings with their faces.

"The colonel and I had a meeting on Earth, which didn't really go as well as I'd hoped," said Wolf. He went on to explain who General Springfield was and the man's reaction to Tom's existence. He suggested Tom come with them on the next journey, to reason with the general directly, but Tom said that moving Mark's frame any distance from the chamber might result in glitches that could appear embarrassing to other biologicals. They agreed to bring the general to the chamber instead, to let him see the entire set-up for himself.

"Most technologically inferior species react adversely to our arrival," Tom went on, not meaning to sound judgemental. "It is not unexpected that pockets of resistance appear at first contact."

"What happens to the people involved in such resistance movements?" Wolf asked.

"Most of them come round once they realise the

magnitude of Grid Command."

"You mean they give up because they know they can't win?"

"That is not inaccurate," Tom replied. "But we are not conquerors, we are traders. Usually, it is what we have to offer that brings the new contacts round. It is unfortunate that we are regarded as conquerors simply because we bring a level of power far in excess of what already exists. If the people of Earth were more advanced than ourselves, would you feel threatened by us?" Wolf could not deny Tom's logic but he knew he would certainly defend himself and his people against any aggressor.

"Surely the retaliation has to be measured," he said. "If I get bitten by a bug, I don't try to wipe out every bug."

"I understand your concern, Wolf, but it is misplaced. I doubt your world leaders would wish to embark on a voyage of destruction against a clearly superior force. Even if hostilities did occur, Grid Command would not exterminate all of humanity because of the actions of a few fearful individuals. If both sides are open to negotiation then no such conflicts will even arise." Wolf gave a wry smile. It sounded much like twentieth-century Earth and the phrase 'Peace through superior firepower' came to mind. While he didn't think Tom's intentions went beyond business and trade with Earth, he did begin to wonder exactly what the Earth could offer a technologically advanced race in the first place.

"We are a race of sentient machines, existing within the grid much like the programmes in your computers would if they were self-aware. The amount of energy the grid consumes throughout a cycle is incredible. We do not trade with physical goods directly, instead we allow the interaction of two nations that would

347

otherwise never meet. I think in your terms it would be best to describe what we do as a service, and for that service we charge a portion of energy from the worlds with which we connect."

"Sounds great," Wolf nodded. "But at the moment the Earth is suffering from an energy crisis. The old fuels that powered everything are running out and we need a new source. The photovoltaic panels our buggies use are one example, but they're expensive to produce and are not particularly powerful."

"Initial scans of Earth when I first arrived showed high volumes of air pollutants, evidence of combustion power. It's primitive but effective. I also appreciate that requirements for such engines are not inexhaustible but suitable alternatives exist in other dimensions, often in vast quantities. I do not believe your planet would suffer any more than it already does."

"That's something else," Wolf continued. "We're trying to reduce the effects combustion has on our planet. We need to preserve the environment with fresh, clean, and most of all renewable energy." Tom put a hand on Wolf's shoulder, mimicking the gesture Wolf had used earlier.

"I am certain that the Earth's requirements can be found somewhere in the multiverse." Wolf remembered the metal he had found under Halfway House. He brought a piece out and showed Tom.

"Have you encountered this stuff before?"

"I encountered several minerals and ores before I met you," Tom replied. "It is likely that this is one of them. I do not know what they look like in the physical realm, of course, as grunts do all the mining and refining. I just catalogued the results of their labour. I will request a grunt obtain samples of all substances mined and compare them with this, then get back to you about any particular properties you might be

348

interested in."

"Fantastic," Wolf exclaimed. "The more positive information I have to present to General Springfield, the better his perception of you will be. We'll get him on our side, yet."

It was soon time to see General Springfield again. As before, Hayes was with him, but Daniel had also been told to come along. If they managed to secure a deal for some more transceiver kits, Wolf wanted Daniel along to make sure the kits were sound as he loaded them. The Dodge Ram was more than capable of managing the dirt track beside the river from the campsite to Route 15. It was a good few hours drive to Ely, most of that on the long, straight roads that scarred Nevada's landscape, but the three men were comfortable and companionable in the vehicle Wolf had chosen.

Once back at the JSRC, the colonel's ID got all of them onto the base and he drove up to the building where they had previously met the general. Daniel headed off to check out what supplies were available as Pete Lopez appeared.

"Heard you were back," he puffed. He had jogged across from the Officers' Club. "I wondered if I could go back with you this time."

"Did you manage to speak to the general?" Wolf ignored Pete's question, believing his own agenda was far more important. Pete took deep breaths as he spoke.

"I managed to talk him out of taking immediate action," he said. "I think that was all I could hope to do."

"That's good, Pete. Thanks," Wolf said, knowing that he had more news to present to the general that should keep things from erupting. Pete stretched his lips in a smile of thanks and held it for as long as his panting gasps would allow. Wolf knew what the man was hoping for but with the threat of a draith on their doorstep, he did not want to allow Pete to put himself in danger. "Let's not keep the general waiting."

"Welcome, gentlemen," General Springfield announced as the three of them entered what had clearly become his temporary office. He was not being entirely friendly but neither were his mannerisms overtly grim. "Please make yourselves comfortable." The general sat down, as did Wolf, Hayes and Pete, in the chairs that had already been provided for them. The three men were separated from General Springfield by a massive desk and he appeared to be sitting several inches above them.

"So," the general began. "Where do we stand with things?"

"As I understand it, Sir," the colonel began, "you've spoken to Pete and held off taking any direct action against the chamber." The general nodded toward the theoretical physicist.

"I've spoken to Pete at length, yes. There was a lot of talk about solving all kinds of problems. Earth's soaring population issues, waste management, detention colonies. He made some very valid and interesting arguments." Pete beamed, turning slightly red at the praise.

"Thank you, General."

"Then there's these," the general added. He opened his palm and half a dozen long, pointed objects rolled along his extended fingers onto the top of the desk.

"Bullets, sir?" queried Hayes.

"Yes, Colonel. Bullets. See anything unusually familiar about them?" Wolf leant forward and pinched one of the rounds between thumb and forefinger. The bullet was a little longer and thinner than an AA battery, narrowed at the top into a point. It was very similar to a 5.56 NATO round but Wolf had seen many of them before and there was something different about these. He leaned in for a closer inspection. While the shell casing was typical of a bullet of this kind, the head of the round was almost black with glittering white spots here and there. Like a clear sky at midnight. Wolf grinned.

"I see you've put my free sample to use."

The general nodded and a satisfied smile lit up his face. "Your metal fragment was very interesting, Wolf. Yes, I had Ranger Grey, my gunsmith, working on it all week. Those few bullets are all that's left of two dozen. Tests on the firing range were very encouraging."

"I'll bet they were," Hayes breathed.

"How encouraging?" Wolf wanted to know.

"More encouraging than the performance of our best tungsten rounds, I can tell you." The general was becoming animated in this discussion now. Clearly, he was excited about this metal Wolf had brought him. "These things can cut through everything we have available to test them on. Its five times denser than lead."

"That's better than depleted uranium," Hayes offered.

The general confirmed the comment with a nod. "Indeed. However, given the increased weight of each round, there is a reduced effective range, but that's more than acceptable given the added stopping power. I'd like to try sheets of this stuff against conventional anti-tank weapons. I want to know what it can withstand." Wolf brightened up at this comment. He had hoped that the new metal would have useful applications on Earth. Although he was a little disappointed that the general seemed to be considering only military developments, he was not surprised. "I have plenty of the material already and more is being sought as we speak. We just have to agree on a price."

"You mentioned you needed transceiver kits. How many do you want?" the general asked.

"How many have you got?" was Wolf's reply.

"There are about twenty left in the stores," the general told him. "We stopped ordering them after connection with Springfield was lost. They should still be functional though. I can get more, but it will take a while."

"I'll give you half a ton for those twenty."

The general sat back and thought about it. "Half a ton won't go far, given the weight of the material."

"You won't need it to go far, general. If it's as tough as we both think it is."

"I still need to run tests on what exactly I can do with it."

"And you have twenty transceivers in your warehouse that you can't do anything with," Wolf pointed out. "Half a ton gets them out of your way."

General Springfield's expression soured. "Very well, Wolf. Half a ton for them. You ever had a career in sales?"

"Learning as I go, General," Wolf quipped.

"Does it have a name?" the general inquired.

"The metal?" Wolf replied. "Tom calls it 244 but I was thinking timantium sounded better. Tom had mined a small vein of it before we made contact with him. He thinks there could be more near the chamber and has promised to keep digging."

"Timantium?" the general pursed his lips. Sounded like a stupid name to him. He would have called it Jametite, or Springfieldium. "Okay, fair enough. You found it, you name it. What else does Tom know about it?"

"Apparently, it's quite a rare substance. It doesn't exist in many universes, but in those where it is found it is often in sizeable quantities. Tom's people use it to build labs."

"Labs?"

"That's what they call the ships they use to travel through the space between universes."

"I see. So, not only does this race of alien machines have superior technology, they use superior materials with which to construct it." General Springfield shook his head slowly. "I'm still not convinced that what you say about Tom is as cut and dry as you believe. You had better be right about them."

"I understand, General," Wolf replied. "But I'll bet Tom is more than willing to help us develop skills to work timantium. All I need is someone with metalworking knowledge and the materials to build a forge. And, since you mention it, we've had some developments of our own."

"I'm all ears."

"Remember we told you that some of Tom's people set off with the intention of joining Springfield, and through it, the Earth, to what they call the grid?" General Springfield nodded. It was this very news that suggested to him there was an element of danger in maintaining contact with the aliens. "Well, I have reason to believe that's not going to happen." Wolf went on to describe how Tom had received information from a probe, sent to him by the captain of the departing transformer, which revealed that an accident had befallen the crew and that they were unable to return to their people. He left out any mention that some kind of intelligence had attacked them, as he wanted to restrict himself to the facts. "As a result, Tom says he is stranded on Springfield unless another lab arrives, which is most unlikely."

"I see," was the General's reply. "All very convenient, don't you think?"

"It sounds genuine, Sir," Wolf replied. "Tom was all

for shutting himself and the transformer down, thinking that his people would now take centuries to find him. I had to convince him not to, even if it was just for Springfield's sake."

"Very well. While my concerns are still valid they have been eased, for the time being. I don't think Tom will initiate hostile actions against Earth while he has no support from his own kind. What does he want in the meantime?" The general was beginning to see the advantages of trade.

"We have a working relationship with Tom and can handle any business ideas he has," Hayes responded quietly.

"He doesn't want to trade with Earth directly? Doesn't he like it over here?"

"Since he arrived and set up his transformer, his focus has been on Springfield," Wolf said honestly. "Though I've never asked him why, I guess if I knew nothing of either Earth or Springfield and had to pick one, I doubt the noisy, overcrowded, polluted ball of rock would get much of a second glance." He said this with a smile, hoping a little banter would cut off prejudices before they arose. Further discussion ensued, with more of the metal being promised in trade for other consumables. Recent advances in photovoltaics had resulted in panels releasing more power and some of these were made available, as were the services of the gunsmith Ranger Grey, who would train others in metalworking. It was also agreed that Tom would assist in this, so that Ranger Grey would come back to Earth with knowledge of using timantium and how to get the best results from it.

All in all, this second meeting with General Springfield was regarded as a great success. The Dodge Ram was loaded up with transceiver kits and the men began the return trip to Springfield. On the way, Wolf elected to stay Earthside and ferry the rest of the traded goods from Ely to the campsite. Daniel would supervise the transfer of goods through the chamber for the colonel to distribute between Rhino Hill, Grand Central, and Newhaven. Hayes agreed to set up construction teams back on Springfield from the men who had been working for him before the escalator failed. He was sure that there would be plenty who wanted paid work again.

Trade relations were once again established between Springfield and Earth and all parties were satisfied with the arrangement. Ranger Grey first set foot on Springfield later that month, after a workshop with a forge had been constructed for him. While Hayes had wanted him at Grand Central, Wolf had argued that the metal was in the vicinity of Halfway House. Given the weight of the metal, he said that it was more practical to work it close to the source than have to deal with transportation issues. They could always build a second workshop should supply of the metal become available from a second site.

Tom had facilities within the tunnels around his transformer which were capable of smelting the raw timantium ore. Given that it was the grunts doing all the hard work, an anoxic environment could be maintained to minimise the oxidation rate and allow the resulting ore to be purified to a level beyond what could be achieved in Grey's workshop. They experimented, mixing 244 with carbon, as iron was to produce steel, and other elements to produce different varieties of timantium. A mix of 244 and carbon was found that allowed the metal to be shaped when heated but lost none of its incredible hardness after cooling.

Coincidentally, it was at that time that Hayes announced to Wolf and Daniel that an aircraft with solar panels covering the wings had been constructed in

Newhaven. Although the electrics were fairly simple, the colonel invited Daniel over to give a second opinion. Hayes was impatient to start test flights. Wolf pressed Daniel to get involved, being very aware that the plane might offer a way to explore large areas of the planet in a very short space of time. While Charlie's boy, Greg, had remained fully involved at Halfway House, Jessica's boy, Jack, had been helping Daniel with the distribution of goods. Not surprisingly, Jack was left in charge while Daniel travelled to Newhaven to inspect the plane.

Daniel couldn't remember the last time he had been to Newhaven. There was much that was unfamiliar about the place. He saw no recognisable faces, although people seemed to know his name. Evidently, Newhaven's residents had been told to expect him. He simply smiled and nodded when he was hailed. He made his way to the large barn where Hayes had told him he would find the plane. It was about thirty feet long, with a large, wooden propeller powered by a small, electric motor on the front of each expansive wing.

"Hi," said a somewhat shy voice. "I'm Robin, the designer and builder of this fine machine." Daniel introduced himself. "Ah, the colonel's second opinion. He wants somebody other than me to tell him he will be safe in it."

"He's going to fly it?" Daniel asked.

"I'm just an engineer," said Robin, "but it should fly. I've seen the new photovoltaics on the wings and tail produce more than 600 watts and I reckon there will be at least half as much again in full sunlight."

Robin gave Daniel a quick guided tour. "The cockpit is a bit cramped and there are no flight instruments except the ASI, as it will only fly when the sky is clear. I've calculated that the wings will get enough lift to fly level at about 60 knots, maybe reach 80 at max efficiency, about twice what the Wright brothers were aiming for. The two props turn in opposite directions, just like the Wright's first design, so each cancels the torque produced by the other. I've got plans to use the navigation mode on the cellphones for altitude as well as position, but we won't need that for the test flights." The fuselage was an open, metal framework, like one of the transceiver masts on its side, Daniel thought, and the pilot's seat looked like a canvas chair. He reminded himself that the plane only needed to take off and land and stay in bright sunshine while it was in the air. It was very easy to check the electrics, which were no more complicated than a buggy and appeared equally rugged. He wondered if they should get hold of a parachute.

With Daniel's seal of approval, such as it was, all that was left was to wait for a suitable day. The wait was less than a week. With the sun high in the sky, Hayes had the machine wheeled gently outside. Pre-flight operations consisted of climbing in and checking that the flying controls moved smoothly in response to the control column and the rudder bar. They did. He flicked the switches that allowed current to the motors and the propellers gave a twitch. He advanced the two 'go faster' levers and the propellers began to turn more and more rapidly. He knew already that there were no brakes and that he was relying on the two levers for steering. He taxied to the start of the strip he intended to use as a runway.

Hayes had practised taxiing before. This time, he moved the levers swiftly to full power. The propellers lagged a little but as the plane headed off down the stretch of dried compact earth serving as the runway, he began to feel the increased airflow over the control surfaces. As he hoped, the tail lifted itself off the ground. He found he was airborne just before coming abreast of the marker that Robin had placed as a guide. The colonel gave a yowl of glee. He estimated his height as ten feet, twenty feet, thirty. He eased the power levers back until he was flying level at a steady 80 knots, as indicated on the instrument panel.

Hayes remembered to keep his grip on the control stick relaxed as he experimented gently with the controls. He climbed above all the buildings and performed a number of smooth, wide circles. Everything seemed to be responding well. The turbulence was no worse than he had expected. Gaining confidence, he selected full power and climbed a little higher. When he levelled off, his airspeed increased to over 100 knots. The plane was doing well; Robin had done a competent job. This was a step forward for Springfield, he told himself.

Wolf, James and Robin, watching from the improvised airfield, were becoming less and less concerned. Wolf and James had come along to assist if the worst should happen, and Robin wouldn't have missed her creation's maiden voyage for anything. The fact that the vehicle had climbed steadily with apparent ease boosted their confidence massively. Wolf asked Robin to borrow her cellphone and dialled Hayes' number. His phone was tied next to the ASI. If all went well, Robin had plans to attach a proper bracket for a cellphone but Hayes did not intend to go out of sight of the strip. For simple comms, all he had to do was switch the phone on. The electric motors were so quiet that Wolf could hear an echo of his own voice as it came over Hayes' cellphone. "Looking good from down here, Oliver," Wolf said, jubilant.

"Feels good up here, too," was Hayes' ecstatic reply.

It was James who noticed it first, a dark stain

against the otherwise pure blue sky. "What's that?" he asked Wolf, tugging on the sleeve of the man's shirt. Wolf glanced over to where James' outstretched finger indicated. "Is that a cloud?" the boy asked.

Wolf shook his head. If it was a cloud it wasn't any kind he recognised. If he had to describe it as anything he would have said it looked like a ball of ink dropped into a bowl of water. "Oliver, check out your two o'clock. Can you see that?" The plane banked a little to the right, bringing the nose of the aircraft in line with the anomaly. Hayes' voice sounded uncertain. "I can see it, Wolf, yeah. But I haven't the faintest idea what it could be. Going in for a closer look."

Wolf was shaking his head. "Not a good idea, mate. If it blocks the sun the engines might cut out. Get back on the ground ASAP." Only static came back as a reply. "Hayes? Can you hear me?" More static.

"What's wrong, Wolf. Is the colonel going to be okay?" James sounded very worried but there was nothing Wolf could do to ease the boy's tension. He hated being down here, powerless to do anything to assist.

Wolf and James watched as the aircraft drew closer to the strange image in the sky. Without warning the black shape accelerated towards the plane, a nightmarish octopus writhing with black tendrils. "Hayes!" Wolf screamed down his cellphone. "Turn the plane around! Get away from it!" But the static was cut off the instant the cloud touched the aircraft. The plane's nose dipped sharply down towards the ground and the aircraft dropped, just dropped, falling from the air like a stone. The oily cloud went with it, muffling the crump of the aircraft as it collapsed in on itself with the impact.

"Back to the buggies!" Wolf shouted, practically dragging James by the arm as he charged back to the vehicle. Robin was quick on his heels. Wolf threw himself in the driver's seat and switched on as James climbed into the passenger seat. The boy was holding back sobs, tears both for the fate of their friend and in fear of the unknown entity that had claimed Hayes' life, for there was no way he could possibly have survived that crash.

Wolf's heart hammered beneath his breastbone. They were on the outskirts of Newhaven, a few minutes drive away, but it would take much longer than that to get home. Grand Central was a good few hours drive, and Rhino Hill more than another hour beyond that. Wolf pushed his buggy harder than he had ever pushed one before. He realised he still had Robin's cellphone in his hand and fumbled with the buttons.

"It's Wolf," he said when Tom answered. "The draith. It's here."

Chapter 18B

"I suspected as much," Tom declared. "The probe I was monitoring went dark a few moments ago. What have you seen?" Wolf repeated what had happened, describing how a black cloud had simply appeared and grabbed the plane that Hayes was piloting, which had then smashed into the ground. "Get away as quickly as possible," Tom told Wolf. "The draith will undoubtedly be exhausted after its journey to Springfield and will require sustenance. The plane was likely the closest source. It will absorb both the kinetic energy of the crash and the plane itself before moving on. That gives you some time."

"For what?"

"To get back to the chamber. We can escape to Earth through my transformer."

"Escape? Whatever happened to fighting back?" Wolf's first instinct was not to run away but Tom's voice remained impassive.

"It is essentially a black hole, Wolf. How do you propose to hurt it?"

"There must be something we can do!"

"Assaulting the draith with your primitive weaponry will only invigorate it," Tom tried to explain.

It was hard for Wolf to not be insulted by Tom's dismissive response. He accepted that Tom was part of a technologically advanced race but retaliation with force was Wolf's immediate response to a hostile. "Okay, so we can't fight it in the open," he shouted as he struggled to control the buggy, "but there are tunnels under Halfway House, maybe we can regroup there?" When Tom answered, his voice was bursting with patience.

"Burying yourself under tons of rock will not stop

the draith. No matter where you go on this planet - or even in this universe - the draith will sense your life energy. It will find you."

"So that's it? We just have to leave everything behind?"

"Yes."

"What about Newhaven?" Wolf argued. "There are people living here. They have to be warned!"

Tom's voice was frustratingly level. "Tell anyone you pass to get to Halfway House as soon as possible but do not stop for anything."

"I can't just leave them all to die!" Wolf cried.

"If you try to help them it is likely you will die too," Tom reasoned, his voice betraying no trace of anxiety. If he felt any grief at Hayes' death he certainly hid it well. "There is no way to know how long the draith will take to absorb the wrecked aircraft and its next target will almost certainly be Newhaven."

Wolf's conscience wrestled with his pragmatism. He had no idea how many people lived in Newhaven now, only that its population had numbered in the thousands. While he could not argue with Tom's logic, abandoning all those people to the draith was not something he could easily do. It was bad enough that Oliver Hayes had fallen to prey to it. Wolf was a military man and had plenty of experience in dealing with the untimely death of friends, but this was no battleground. The colonel was not a casualty of war. Wolf could not accept his passing as anything less than murder.

Wolf tried not to dwell on the man's fate but his mind would not let it go. He had initially believed that the plane had fallen from the sky because of the additional weight of the draith upon it, meaning Hayes might have been alive when the plane had hit the ground. The more he thought about it, however, the more he believed that the entity was virtually insubstantial, made up of nothing more than tendrils of ebony smoke. Had Hayes died the moment the draith came in contact with the plane? Had it *absorbed* him, if that's what it did? Wolf had no idea what that meant or how long it took but he hoped there had been no pain. Just a quick flash between consciousness and oblivion, like a bullet to the head.

Wolf wondered how much agony was inflicted when the draith absorbed you. Did the brain shut down as a preventative measure? Wolf had seen such things happen when soldiers were injured. Then other questions demanded to be answered. How much energy does a living person produce? Can it be measured? The body maintained an internal temperature of approximately thirty seven degrees, so maybe it was heat that attracted the draith.

That gave Wolf an idea. Tom had said that the thing would want more sustenance, more food, and living energy was its favourite meal. If he could get a sizeable energy source Wolf felt he might be able to slow the monster down, buying time for the residents of the town to evacuate. Getting the message to everyone at once was going to be the hard part, but Wolf felt the beginnings of a plan formulate. He had to try.

Wolf stopped his buggy and got out. Robin rolled up next to him in hers, asking what he was doing. Wolf told her to get back to Halfway House, that James knew the way, but the boy objected fiercely to the idea of going home without him. Wolf was glad as it showed that the boy had some understanding of the danger he was putting himself in, but Wolf was adamant he was staying. He thrust Robin's phone into her hand and told them to call Grand Central, warn whoever would listen about the draith, and then get home. When James still refused, Robin reassured the boy that Wolf had her buggy; he would still be able to make it back. James accepted this, reluctantly, and the two of them sped off. Wolf watched them go, wondering if he had just signed his own death warrant.

Wolf did not hesitate. He quickly made his way to the office building Hayes had occupied before moving back to Grand Central. A Tannoy system had been set up around this town just like at Grand Central, to make announcements to the inhabitants about incoming deliveries, but it had been used less and less since contact with Earth had been lost. As the population of Newhaven had dwindled and supplies had stopped coming through from Earth, and with Hayes moving to Grand Central, there became no need for it at all and the office building had been emptied.

The ground around the main office building was deserted. Tufts of spiky weeds sprouted unchecked around the area. Wolf had passed a couple of people in the streets and shouted at them to leave, but they just looked at him with an odd expression of mild amusement. Why would they leave? This was their home. Wolf did not have time to explain things face to face. He hoped the loudspeaker system was still working.

Wolf shouldered into the main doors but they only gave way after he had slammed the sole of his boot into them a couple of times. He stabbed his thumb against light switches and was invigorated to see them flicker to life; the building still had power. He charged up the stairs two at a time, making all haste to Hayes' old office. It was the logical place for the controls of the Tannoy system to have been installed. The door blasted open, breaking off at the hinges as he hit it at full speed. He found the controls immediately: a small bank of switches stuck to the wall. He guessed there had been a desk and chair beside it at one point, where the microphone would have been stationed, but now there was only empty space and dust. A thick wire spiralled from the grey wall box to the floor, where the mouthpiece lay abandoned.

Wolf scooped it up and pressed the button on the side, opening the channel. He spoke clearly into it but could not hear his voice booming around outside. He scanned the control panel for instructions but any literature that had described the function of each button or switch or dial had long since disappeared. With no other option, Wolf tried each switch one by one, repeating "Testing, testing," over and over. He turned a large dial and startled himself when sound reverberated around the room. Wolf winced and turned it back halfway. Evidently, that was the volume. Once the sound level had reached a point where his voice was not distorted beyond legibility, Wolf flicked more switches until the external speakers were activated. Then he began his quick speech.

"Attention residents of Newhaven. This is Wolf Boston." Wolf's voice bounced around outside the walls of the office, echoing along the streets. He hoped there were people close enough to hear him. This would be his only chance. It would be their only warning. "Please leave the town as quickly as possible. Newhaven is under attack. Take only what you can immediately carry. Make your way to Grand Central, where you will receive further instructions." He reckoned not many people would be aware of Halfway House, but he guessed he should try to get them as close to the chamber as possible. "This is an emergency evacuation. Please get to Grand Central as soon as possible. Thank you." Wolf wanted to say more, to describe the horror of what would befall any who remained, but he dared not delay any longer. He feared that the draith might be alerted by the sound.

Now Wolf had to find a way to fight back. It was a simple plan, really, and he thought it might just give the draith what it wanted without anyone being hurt. He rushed to the mess hall and ripped through the cupboards, tipping old cooking oil all over the floor, the walls, everywhere. As he pulled the curtains down and brought his lighter to a corner, he looked around to confirm that almost all of the furniture was made of wood, just like most of the building. At first it seemed that the fire wouldn't catch, but suddenly the dusty fabric glowed yellow and Wolf threw it into the greasy puddles. A blue flame raced across the oil almost immediately, forcing Wolf back by the growing heat as the fire licked against the walls.

Wolf dashed back downstairs, hurtling through the main doors and out across the road as a tremendous rush of air whooshed past him. Glass from the office building's windows rained all over as the cafeteria erupted in flames. He stumbled but continued on. The whole building disappeared as a great fireball blossomed in its place, sending shafts of timber flying into the sky. A canister of something flammable he had missed, Wolf reasoned happily. He could image the neighbouring buildings catching fire. It had been a long time since the monsoon. Everything would be dry, perfect kindling for an uncontrolled fire. That should be plenty of energy for the draith to feed on.

Wolf passed a few panicked individuals in the streets as he made his way out of Newhaven. They were dashing this way and that on whatever errand they thought was important enough to risk their life for. His warning had evidently reached the ears of some but he did not stop to reassert his words on those who delayed. He had hoped people would simply get in a vehicle and leave. He told himself he had done as much as he could, and after that explosion he was sure the draith would be on its way. Burning buildings would surely be a colossal magnet for it and would hopefully keep it busy for a while.

A buggy with the new voltaics could reach 60 miles per hour on a good surface but on the dirt tracks of Springfield anything over 40 was rough going. Faster than 50 was downright dangerous. It would still take a few long hours to get to Grand Central. Wolf wondered if his sabotage would be enough. Maybe he would have to do something similar at Grand Central too, so that the refugees could make it all the way to Halfway House and then on to the chamber. He wondered sadly if he would have to destroy everything the women had built at Rhino Hill, too, but if it bought him his life and the lives of all his friends he would do so without a moment's hesitation.

After talking with Wolf, Tom decided it was most fitting to speak to Sally about what was going on. She had been the first of Springfield's inhabitants to contact him and it was her partner, Wolf, who was currently in danger.

"Hey, Tom. What can I do for you?" The woman's voice was calm and friendly, although Tom also detected surprise.

"Hello, Sally," Tom started, his voice even as if nothing was wrong at all. "I need you to get everyone you can over to the chamber as soon as possible."

"Er, okay." Sally sounded curious now, cautious even. "What's going on?" Tom made a quick calculation. There was a chance of panic if he told her about the draith, but there was also a fair probability that she would not act with the urgency this situation required if he held the truth from her. That would endanger the population and was an unacceptable risk. Fear was understandable, but Tom considered the woman's stance against Ricky when the man had

367

turned up at the chamber and taken Anna through to Earth. He reasoned that Sally was like Anna and would fight back rather than huddle defensively.

"The draith has found Springfield," Tom began, refraining from revealing the whole story. "We need to escape the planet before it destroys everything." There was a long pause and for a moment Tom thought the draith had already got there. "Sally? Are you still there?"

"I'm here, Tom." Her brain was processing the data, Tom reasoned, dampening the flood of emotions expected from a biological. Tom needed Sally to focus and asked where she was, what she was doing and if Daniel was with her. She reacted to the distracting questions quickly.

"Daniel's at Rhino Hill. I'm at Blue Hill, with Jessica and some of the children. We're keeping an eye on the sick deer."

"Rally everyone there into vehicles and make your way to my chamber as quickly as you can. Tell everyone it's a drill in case of emergency. I'll call Daniel and tell him the same thing. Remain calm and those around you will do so too." Sally said she would and the line went dead. Tom immediately patched a call through to Daniel.

"Tom? Hey, how's tricks?"

Tom told Daniel what he had told Sally. The draith was here. It would kill them all if they didn't leave immediately. Daniel was all business. He immediately said he would round up as many people as he could and get them to Halfway House as quickly as possible. Tom had a sudden thought and asked Daniel to turn everything off before he left, to reduce Rhino Hill's energy signature. He warned Daniel that the draith was attracted to large energy sources. The less energy something created, the less the monster would notice it.

Daniel acknowledged that advice and clicked off comms.

Tom then turned his attention to himself, confident that Sally and Daniel would be able to do whatever was necessary to save Springfield's inhabitants. Tom had already issued recall instructions to the grunts working near to the transformer and was turning off those he considered too far away. Everyone was coming here, he thought, making for a large concentration of life energy in one place. That in itself was enough to attract the draith, so it was important to keep everything else powered down to the bare minimum. If the draith noticed the energy signature of the chamber it would undoubtedly make its way there first, cutting off Springfield's only escape route before anybody could get away.

Wolf stopped his buggy and turned to look back at Newhaven, which was still too close for his liking. He wouldn't be happy until he couldn't see it at all, until he was back at the chamber with Sally and the kids. He spotted another fire and smiled. He wanted the whole town to burn, hoping that the inferno would keep the draith occupied long enough for him to make good his escape. It meant the utter destruction of Newhaven, but he couldn't help but think that an acceptable loss. The draith would take some time quenching its ravenous thirst for energy there now. He prayed that nobody was left around in the town but deep down he knew that there had to be. Newhaven had once been a prime location, with ranches established all along the coast, north and south. Not all of them had been deserted, not all of them had failed. There were likely pockets of civilisation here and there, people who had worked hard to survive after contact with Earth was lost. It did not seem fair that all that toil and hardship had ultimately been for nothing.

Wolf powered up the buggy and returned to his long drive home. He thought he had a good few hours head start on the draith now, easily enough to reach Grand Central. With that thought, his mind immediately returned to his friend, Colonel Hayes. Oliver and he had been staunch allies, sharing the good times and standing firm against the bad. How he missed the man already. The colonel's organisational skills would have made short work of this catastrophe. He would already be at Halfway House with everyone from Grand Central, Wolf mused. He wondered if he would ever get the chance to grieve properly for the man and wondered who would take charge now that Oliver was no more. Then it hit Wolf. He hadn't even told anyone at Grand Central about that! He fumbled for his cellphone, patting down his pockets, only then realising that he no longer had it with him.

Wolf glanced around the buggy, hoping to see it lying around where he might have absent-mindedly left it, but there was no sign of it. He berated himself harshly. He had been so busy he hadn't got around to replacing the one Ricky had shot to pieces and the one he had used earlier had been Robin's! Now it was even more important that he get back. He didn't want everyone thinking he was dead when they couldn't get hold of him. He pushed the lever forward and the buggy's electrics whined as it picked up speed. James wouldn't be that far ahead, Wolf told himself.

Wolf reached Luther Henshaw's place a little under two hours later. The track led directly to the pontoon crossing at 3762. Wolf was a little surprised to see Luther was still there. In fact, Wolf noticed there were more than a few men here. Wolf guided his buggy over to the big man and came to a halt beside him. He asked if a boy and a woman had passed through recently. Luther nodded.

"They came from Newhaven, said that something was following them, something dangerous. Told us all to get out of here, go to somewhere called Halfway House."

"They weren't wrong," Wolf said firmly. "You *do* need to get out of here." Luther crossed his arms over his barrel chest.

"Care to tell me what's going on?"

"It's a long story and there's no time."

"Excuse me?" Luther sounded offended, regarding Wolf with a steely look in his eye. Wolf knew that look. It was the eyes of a man about to enter battle. "I've worked too damned long and hard to get this place the way I want it. I won't just abandon it at the first sign of trouble."

"You won't be able to do it, Luther," Wolf told him.

"Won't be able to do what?" the powerful figure answered, brusquely.

"Weather the storm that's coming."

"And what do you know about it?" Luther asked. He didn't reckon Wolf for a coward.

"Not nearly enough."

"You're scared!" Luther admonished. Wolf smiled at that, but grimly.

"Damned right I'm scared and you should be too."

"I'm not running from anything," Luther snapped.

Wolf could feel control of his temper slipping. "This isn't some plodding slab of meat you can just point a gun at, Luther. It's quick. It's deadly. It will kill you just by touching you. I've seen what it can do and I don't want to see it that close ever again." Luther's defiant resolve faltered somewhat. Wolf could see the change in the man's eyes. "I'm getting out of here," Wolf continued, "and I suggest you do the same."

371

When Luther did not move, Wolf turned on his heel. "Damn you, Luther! Stay if you want to. I wish you the best of luck." Wolf began to move off but Luther called him back.

"Twenty dollars," Luther said, holding out his hand.

Wolf gave the man an incredulous look, but handed over the money. Luther called out to his men, who checked that the river was safe, and Wolf drove onto the pontoon and away. He did not look back.

There was just no telling some people. Wolf was familiar with Henshaw's military record. The man was too brave for his own good. Here on Springfield he had set up machine-gun nests to go fishing when most people just stayed away from the water. That said a lot about a man's mentality. Henshaw had been a damned good soldier, never quitting when the going got tough, but a better soldier knew which battles could be won and which ones couldn't. This was one of the latter.

Wolf reached Grand Central another three hours later. He saw that the whole settlement was already in the middle of a grand evacuation, for which he was glad. People were running here and there, packing everything they could into ants and buggies. He could understand them wanting to take personal belongings but there was little time. He knew that Rhino Hill was less than two hours away but how far away was the draith?

Wolf discovered by asking around that Daniel had called from Rhino Hill a few hours ago with a warning that some previously unseen monster was attacking Newhaven and that everybody needed to be ready to leave for a place called Halfway House. There had been a few questions about what exactly was going on, but then calls had started coming through from Newhaven from people who had not responded quickly enough to Wolf's warning. The calls were panicked pleas for help, then screams, then nothing. Those calls had served as more than enough evidence for Grand Central to get its collective butt moving.

Wolf also learnt that James and Robin had passed swiftly through, lending their testimony and adding to the urgency of the matter. They had not been gone long, heading toward Rhino Hill with those that had been too scared to stay and pack. Wolf made his way to Headquarters, hoping to catch up with whoever Hayes had left in charge and inform them of the colonel's passing. He spotted Joy immediately, caught in the centre of a storm of activity within Headquarters' reception. Wolf had met the petite woman during her visits to Rhino Hill to discuss artificial insemination with Jessica. Joy had given birth only recently. Now, with one arm wrapped around a baby boy perhaps only a few months old, concentration and fear warred for dominance on her face. The battle clearly unnerved the infant in her grasp. His cries could be heard over the bustle of the hurrying crew.

"Wolf!" Joy called when she saw him making his way toward her. "Do you know what's going on? Where's Hayes? I thought he was with you."

"I'll explain later, but right now we have to get out of here."

"Daniel told us to power everything down. Something about reducing the town's energy signature?" She looked puzzled.

"Great idea. Why haven't you done it yet?"

"We have to download and secure the hard drives first." Wolf shook his head.

"No, you don't. That's no longer important. Just switch everything off. Get as far as you can from any source of power." His fingers reached for her free arm to pull her away but she batted his grip aside.

"Hayes left me in charge," Joy barked defensively.

"Hayes is dead!" Wolf realised he had said this louder than he had intended when the whole room stopped. Joy took a step away from him. She couldn't have looked more shocked if he had slapped her. Her arm relaxed and only his hand on her elbow prevented the baby slipping free.

"What?" She seemed on the verge of tears.

"He's dead, Joy," Wolf spoke softer now, then turned to include the others in the room. "Colonel Hayes is dead. The draith, the thing that's in Newhaven, it killed him. It's destroying Newhaven while we speak. Grand Central will be next. The draith is attracted to energy. Turn everything off."

"What are you talking about? Draith?" Joy's confusion had not lifted. Wolf suddenly realised that the secrecy surrounding the chamber might prove embarrassing. Very few of these people had even heard of Halfway House.

"It's some sort of entity, worse than the dinosaurs, which is attracted to raw energy. It attacked Newhaven and is probably heading here." His words had the desired effect and people looked around for things to switch off. Others were clearly waiting to hear more. "We need to head for a place called Halfway House. It's a base set up at caves in the mountainside. I'll be leaving for there in a few minutes."

At last, Joy seemed to understand Wolf's sense of urgency. "Right, we're finished here," she said, addressing her team. "We're going with Wolf. Get ready now." Her team looked noticeably relieved to be doing something. Most had been on the military payroll when the escalator had failed. Some had formed new relationships but few had any valuable possessions on Springfield. Many were poorer than the colonists who had established farms to fall back on. Joy brightened up immediately and began soothing her child.

"You got a ride?" Wolf asked.

"I'll find one," Joy replied.

"You just did. You're the colonel now so come with me. I have room for one and a half and I can explain things while we ride." With Wolf and Joy pushing for everyone to get out regardless of what was left behind, Grand Central was quickly rendered desolate and empty. Wolf's buggy now led the way to Halfway House with scores of other vehicles trailing along behind. At first, the two of them spoke fondly of Oliver Hayes, recounting times both good and bad. Once they had shared what they knew of him with each other they lapsed into a short silence. Then, while Joy allowed her child to suckle on a bottle of warm milk, Wolf explained what he knew of the situation on Springfield, starting with the chamber. Once that was done, he borrowed Joy's cellphone and called Sally for an update.

"I'm at Halfway House," Sally said, the panic and fear in her voice all too easy to hear. "I can't find Naomi! She wasn't at Blue Hill when I left, she's not here, and Tom says she's not at the chamber. There's no sign of Jack, Mike or Ruth either!"

Chapter 19B

Tina's consciousness flared back into reality. She was momentarily dazed by the event, struggling to accept that she had regained awareness at all. She was still anchored to the navigator platform; it was almost as if she had never been turned off. A cursory glance at the diagnostics files showed her she was being fed by a tiny spark of power, enough so that she would be able to perform only the most basic of functions, but at least that covered accessing transformer activity logs.

Apparently, she had been turned off automatically when the transformer's power core had dipped below minimum levels for crew support. It was standard programming for the transformer to do so in emergencies. There was no explanation for that loss of energy but Tina knew that the draith was responsible. What she didn't understand was why the draith had not finished its meal. Tina scrolled through the logs until she reached the part where Puss, loaded with Tina's warning, had shot off across the current universe in search of the nodal probes. Primary T-Nav Mainstation had lost all operational processes moments after that because the central core was on the verge of total collapse, which subsequently would have resulted in a meltdown. That fate, however, was inexplicably averted when the central core had suddenly managed to stabilise itself. Tina put this down to the draith having found an alternative target that was considerably richer in energy.

Once free of the draith's draining influence, the transformer's power core had eventually been able to recharge itself. The entire system had been rebooted, along with Tina. Her first instinct was to instruct the core to power up the other crewmembers but when system analysis reported that she was the only crewmember aboard, her upgrades almost seized up. All other crewmembers had been wiped out by the draith. Had she not isolated herself when she had done, it was likely that she would have suffered a similar end.

Tina scoured all the logs for anything that hinted at why the draith had abandoned the stricken transformer, but to no avail. All records showed that the energy in the transformer's central core had been dropping further and further below recommended safety margins until she had launched the probe. After that she had shut down. It was much later that things began to return to normal. It took only a second to process the information and reach a conclusion with 97% probability. Puss' new upgrades were full of energy and presented a larger signature than the transformer. When Tina despatched the probe the draith had literally chased after it!

But where was it now? According to the logs, the probe had been launched over a dozen sub-cycles ago. It was clear that the draith had not come back to finish the transformer off, so had it followed Puss through the node, perhaps all the way back to Springfield? Tina paused at the quandary she now faced. Should she continue to try and link up with the grid or return to Springfield?

Tina ran as many system checks as she could with what power she had. None of the results were particularly comforting. The systems that linked the two mini-transformers were offline, damaged by the draith's attack, and she had not the expertise to reconfigure them. While it was theoretically possible to slot with just one transformer, Tina was in no hurry to attempt it. An undertaking of that kind would take many, many centuries given the poor condition of her transformer and lack of experience.

It was now clear to Tina that she could not get back to Grid Command, which left only one alternative. The idea did not sit well with her. While she was less than ecstatic about the idea of following the entity that had killed all her crew and very nearly destroyed her, she could not hide from the possibility that if the draith found Springfield and destroyed everyone on it, including Tom, it would be her fault entirely. Tina put her mind to getting the transformer operational again. She didn't want to contemplate being responsible for anything else right now.

Central core energy levels were growing slowly but steadily, pulling away from the red danger levels. Another sub-cycle would see systems return to something close to functional and Tina could begin getting the machine moving again. While she waited, she sacrificed some of the power to comms and opened up a channel to the nodal probe. If she was going to return to Springfield, she would have to go back the way she had come.

Tina waited for the probe to acknowledge her. And waited. And waited. No response. Then it occurred to Tina that the draith would likely have destroyed the probes as it passed through the node, absorbing their energy. If they were gone then she couldn't go forward or back. She was trapped here.

Tina forced her logic circuits out of the endless loop that they had entered. If a transformer were involved in an accident, its logs were always the last things to be wiped so that when a rescue team from the grid recovered the machine they could determine what had gone wrong. Tina was confident that was still the case, since all the logs she had accessed so far had been intact. While she could not remember submitting the node co-ordinates to the nav-logs after she had found each one, she knew it was a standard protocol, something that should have been done automatically. She opened the nav-logs and hoped, hardly daring to look.

Thankfully, every node that had been passed through since leaving Springfield had been recorded. She could get back to Springfield, at least, and quickly. It was a highly relieved Tina that programmed the nav-station with the closest node's position. Once the co-ordinates had been accepted and the transformer locked on to them, Tina waited as long as she could for the energy to build. The moment the core's meter reading had grown to acceptable levels she released her machine from its current node. There was a groan of protest from the drive system but Tina ignored it, hoping the fluctuations in the core power levels were simply the transformer recovering from its near destruction. Either she would get back to Springfield, or the transformer would pull itself apart attempting to do so.

Travelling to Springfield was less taxing on the transformer's systems than Tina had believed it would be. She had never ventured through nodes already discovered, going backwards, it seemed to her, and her swift progress surprised her. While the journey was not easy given the condition of her transformer, it was much quicker to get back than it had been to go forward. Once she was back at Springfield's node her instruments immediately picked up the resonance of Tom's transformer.

Tina acknowledged the growing probability of success flowing through her circuits, what the biologicals called relief. She had feared that the draith would have consumed Springfield by now, that she was simply returning to a dead world, but the fact that Tom's machine still registered as active suggested that Tom was still functioning. The passage of time in the

Void was never a measurable thing. She instructed her system to network her consciousness into Tom's transformer.

"Confirm Tina?" Tom asked. He was aware of her the moment she successfully linked with his system, just like she instantly knew of his presence. "Is that really you?"

"Confirmed," she replied. Her psychological subroutines struggled to cope with all the new data she had uploaded concerning this whole situation. "I'm sorry, but I haven't brought the rest of Grid Command with me."

"Never mind that," Tom blurted. "I thought the draith had destroyed you all."

"I thought that too," Tina admitted.

Tom suddenly realised Tina's personality was the only one to have joined him. "You're alone?"

"Yes," Tina said.

Tom paused, processing this information. "How did you survive?"

"I'm not sure," she replied. "The transformer shut down when power dropped below 0.8%, as emergency procedure dictates. When the draith left, power levels began to rise. When they were restored to 1.0% I was rebooted." She didn't explain that sending the warning of the draith in Puss had allowed the monster to find Springfield.

"Well, let's just thank the grid for that," Tom replied. "Although I'm not sure that your predicament has improved by returning here."

"I know the draith is here but I didn't have much choice," Tina went on. "The mini-transformer was too badly damaged to travel far and I lacked the facilities to fix it on my own."

"Understandable," Tom agreed. "I don't think I would have liked to try and find the grid on my own, either." Tina smiled at that. Tom always seemed to know what she was thinking.

"What's the situation here, anyway?" Tina asked.

"The plan is to get as many people as possible through the chamber and back to Earth before the draith reaches us. While some people have arrived, I dare not start evacuating anybody until the majority of refugees are here. The draith will surely be attracted to the transformer's energy output."

"What about us? What will we do when the chamber opens onto Earth and the last refugees leave?"

"I hadn't thought about it. I guess we'll just power down and wait for Grid Command to find us on its own."

"But the draith moved through the nodes, destroying the probes in the process," Tina warned. "How do we know it won't travel through this node to Earth?" Tom was quiet a moment.

"There are no probes here," he said at last. "We'll have to hope that's enough." An uncomfortable silence fell upon the pair as they each contemplated their own personal future. While Tom knew he could venture onto Earth in Mark's body should he wish to, Tina had no such luxury. Besides, Tom thought, the probability that someone would have the presence of mind to pick up Mark's body in the rush to escape was low.

Mark's frame had felt very strange at first and it had taken some time for Tom to get used to using it. There was a sense of detachment when occupying the frame, a bit like how it had felt when Tina and the rest of the crew had left for the grid all that time ago. Tom had disliked being in the transformer by himself but now, with another consciousness in there with him again, it felt strangely awkward. He had become quite comfortable with the quiet of solitude and the privacy Mark's frame lent to him. Having to talk to people to

381

get information was curiously exciting. To have a full lab crew with him and to be able to access the personality chips and memory banks of lower ranking crew with a simple thought seemed mundane in comparison.

To pass the time while they waited for the rest of the refugees, Tom wanted to know what had happened to the crew, and what made her think it was a draith that was responsible.

"Analysis and probability," Tina explained.

"A good analysis, Tina. And very quick action," Tom acknowledged. "Had you not worked out what was going on, you would not have survived long enough to send that warning and the draith would have found us unprepared."

"Had I not sent that warning," Tina blurted out, unable to hold the guilt in check any longer, "the draith likely would not have found you at all!"

"What do you mean?"

"The draith didn't *find* Springfield, Tom. I *sent* it to you! It was only after I came back online that I realised the draith had followed Puss." Tina wanted Tom to shout at her, to send bolts of paralysing energy through her central processing unit, and to demote her, as punishment. Somehow, his silence was even worse. "Tom? I'm sorry. The draith is here because of me. I'm so sorry."

"You have nothing to be sorry for, Tina. It's not your fault," Tom insisted.

"Of course it is. I sent Puss to Springfield and the draith followed Puss. Of course it's my fault!"

"Expand your analysis, Tina. Please." Tom urged. "The draith came through the nodes after Puss, granted, but I calculate a 99.9% probability that it would have detected the nodal probe's energy signature and done the same thing anyway. Puss just allowed it happen sooner rather than later, that's all. Because you sent Puss, the draith did not destroy you. And because Puss arrived ahead of the draith, we received your warning. So your actions saved many lives, including yours and mine. Don't you see?"

Tina didn't see. Not really. "I don't know, Tom. Really?" Her logic was different from Tom's and she was not sure whose was better.

"Yes, Tina. And I think you should not waste another proton worrying about your part in this. You are not to blame. The draith is." Tom went quiet for a moment. "Sorry, Tina. I'm getting a call through from Springfield. It's Daniel." Tina wanted to ask who Daniel was, but remained silent while Tom conducted whatever business he had with the stranger. She wasn't paying attention to Tom's conversation with the other speaker, too embroiled with the turbulent debate boiling inside herself.

Tom had told her she was not to blame, that the draith would have found Springfield regardless of whether she had sent Puss or not. She still couldn't bring herself to accept Tom's conclusion, though, and was not sure whether Tom was simply trying to make her feel better so that she could function properly. Even so, she did find that the heavy weight of guilt was not dragging at her quite as much anymore.

Tina felt Tom pull her from her thoughts. His conversation was evidently over. "Good news. The nearest settlement, Rhino Hill, has been vacated and its inhabitants are close to the chamber. More are coming from Grand Central and will be here within the hour."

"What about the draith? Won't it just follow us through the node again?"

"Its is most likely that the draith travelled through the communications link between the probes situated at either side of the nodes. Once everyone is back on

Earth, we can detach the chamber from Springfield. The two universes will no longer be linked and the draith will remain trapped on Springfield."

"And we will remain trapped on Earth." Tina's voice was soft.

"That is not an inaccurate assessment, Tina, yes."

"It will take a long time for Grid Command to find us, if they ever do," was Tina's observation. "What shall we do in the meantime? What can Earth offer us?"

Tom understood his younger crewmate's concerns. They may never again be in contact with Grid Command. It was a daunting prospect but not nearly as daunting as being lost in the void, which had been the risk he had accepted at the beginning of this expedition. He refused to acknowledge any anxiety that he might have felt. He found this species much to his liking. Barbaric seemed too strong a word and so Tom opted to describe them as unrefined. The majority of the people he had interacted with showed integrity, loyalty, and honesty. He could only assume the rest of the race were no different. "Perhaps it will not be as bad as you fear, Tina. Besides, should the worst happen, we can always shut systems down and sleep until we are reunited with the grid." This last statement seemed to mollify Tina somewhat.

"Then I guess it's all hands to stations, Sir," she replied. "Navigator Tina reporting for duty!"

"Please prepare the gravity conduits. I want the transition quick and smooth. I will start isolating systems to keep as much of the transformer offline as possible. With any luck, the draith will not notice us until everyone is across."

Chapter 20B

"We are *so* dead," Naomi stated for the fifth time.

"It's fine," Jack replied, again repeating himself. "We've been through worse." Naomi wasn't sure they had and began to wonder if they would actually perish. She knew they shouldn't be here, in the tunnels her stepdad had opened beneath Halfway House with his mining project. It wasn't that she didn't like Wolf, she had simply reached the age when she wanted more independence than her parents were prepared to allow. The four of them, Jack, Mike, Ruth and herself, had often come playing and exploring here. Being told to stay away was exactly the kind of thing that encouraged them to do just the opposite. All four children were about the same age. Naomi shared the boys' adventurous streak. Ruth had just come along because Mike had. Naomi knew Ruth was sweet on the boy, and she knew that Mike knew it too. He was kind of cute, she supposed, but that didn't help them get out of their current predicament.

They had become more brave in their last few outings, venturing deeper into the passages and for longer. They had brought some supplies to keep them going for a while, so they believed they had thought of everything, prepared for every eventuality, but the rock fall had sealed the tunnel they had come down and now they didn't know how to get back to Halfway House. Most of the food had gone within the first half hour of their trip and now the chill in the air was creeping through Naomi's clothes and into her bones. She wished she had brought a coat. She wished she had brought more food. She wished she hadn't come at all.

"The tunnels have to go somewhere," Jack reiterated. "One of them will lead back to the surface."

"You sure?" Mike piped up. "All this one seems to do is go down. Last I checked, the surface is up."

"My mum always says it gets worse before it gets better," Jack retorted, speaking of all the illnesses Jessica had treated for him.

"I don't want it to get worse," fretted Ruth. "I'm scared."

Naomi pushed up to her friend and threw a comforting arm around the girl's shoulders. Of the four of them, Ruth was the youngest and newest member of Team Expedition. She offered words of reassurance to ease Ruth's anxiety, then voiced her own plan. "I still think we should have stayed by the tunnel we came down. Dad would clear the blockage in less time than it would take for us to get out by ourselves."

"We talked about that," Mike countered. "We don't know how far back the cave in goes. It could take days to dig us out. Anyway, even if they did manage to open it up again, when they see we're not at the bottom they'll know we've gone looking for a way out. It's obvious."

"Only if they know we're down here in the first place," Jack added. "Which they don't, by the way, which makes finding a way out ourselves all the more important." Naomi wasn't sure she followed either boy's logic, but it was all they had for the moment so the four youngsters trudged on in sullen silence. Another hour went by. None of their phones got a signal so deep underground. They could only hope that their absence from the site had been noticed.

They had started their trip that morning. James had been supposed to join them but he had been dragged to Newhaven by Wolf for the test flight of some air machine. None of them had understood Wolf's excitement; they had only seen pictures of aeroplanes. The young people did their best to ignore the complaints of their stomachs and feet, pressing on in the hope that they would eventually find an exit. They squeezed into narrow fissures, crawled through tight cracks, climbed sheer walls, but all they saw was more rock and more darkness ahead. At least the activity kept them warm. Both boys carried their own Maglites and immediately after the rockfall they had possessed presence of mind enough to turn one off and conserve the batteries. It was good that they did, for Jack's torch soon flickered and died and it was Mike's turn to take the lead with his. After a few more hours that too started to dim. They estimated another couple of minutes before it died completely. "We need to think of making another light," Mike reminded them unnecessarily.

"I have a lighter," Jack stated. "But there's not much fuel in it and the flame isn't big enough to see by."

"Why have you got a lighter?" Naomi asked, then thought better of it. "Never mind." She didn't want to know. "Maybe we can find a stick?"

"I don't think trees grow underground, Naomi," Jack pointed out with no shortage of sarcasm. Naomi stuck out her tongue at him.

"She's right," Mike said suddenly. "We have to burn something as a makeshift torch."

"What about the satchel we brought the food in?" Naomi offered. "It's empty now."

"Not sure what it's made of, if it'll burn." Mike got out a penknife he had brought and began cutting his jumper at the top of the sleeve.

"What are you doing?" Ruth asked.

"We need fuel, right?" Mike returned, pulling the sleeve off his arm and starting on the other one. When that one came off too, he handed the tool to Jack. "Our clothes will burn nicely. Maybe not for long, but maybe long enough. Start with sleeves and socks." The boys

387

sacrificed both sleeves and both socks, leaving the girls' clothing untouched. Although both were stoic about it, Naomi could tell they were growing colder for it. They found a metal rod gave their satchel its shape, and when the angles were straightened out it was over a foot long. They wrapped Mike's sleeves about one end, then covered it with Jack's socks. The little flame from the lighter soon ignited the clothing and before long the children were on their way again. As the flame grew small, the boys added another piece of torn clothing. Naomi wondered how much clothing they would have to lose before they found a way out.

It wasn't much to see by but it was better than nothing. Fortunately, it wasn't long before the jagged, rocky path that they had been following opened up into a round chamber, the walls smooth and floor flat, forged by machine rather than nature. A steep incline angled up sharply, cut into a perfect circle, was the only exit. Mike suggested that this was a good sign, that if these tunnels had been worked then that meant the workers would have a way to come in and out. The others agreed but Naomi had to wonder who had dug these tunnels since it certainly hadn't been her stepdad.

"Look there!" Mike shouted. "At the top." They all stared up the slope. Mike put the flaming torch behind his back to make it easier to define but it seemed indeed that the inclining passage was brighter at the far end. Invigorated by the promise of freedom, the children forgot the aches in their limbs and charged up the slope, dropping to all fours for better purchase. The flaming torch fell to the floor, clattering back down the slope to be swallowed by the darkness there. Other tunnels led away from this primary shaft like the branches of a tree, but the children ignored them. It took only minutes to reach the end of the tunnel, where another chamber waited for them.

This chamber was not one of rock, natural or worked. It was flat, shining metal, seamlessly fused to the walls of stone. It was not cold here like it had been down in the depths but felt a comfortable ambient temperature. A soft illumination provided by a single light in the ceiling was enough to show the entire area. Naomi had seen the workshop set up for Ranger Grey and she was reminded of that place here. Rows of metal shelves bearing tubs full of all kinds of things, from rock fragments to piles of what could only be described as scrap metal, lined the sides of the room. In the centre of the chamber stood a pair of tracked vehicles, each one the size of a buggy. One had dozens of drills, hammers and other less identifiable tools folded in tightly along its flanks. Another had a large bucket on its back, seemingly nothing more than a simplified dumper truck with a scooping arm at one end and a clawed arm at the other.

"I think I know where we are," Naomi said softly. "Tom?" she called. "Can you hear me, Tom?"

"We're at the chamber?" Jack breathed, incredulous. "We walked all the way to the chamber?"

"This is not actually the chamber." That was Tom's voice. "It is part of a mining project requested by Wolf." The children knew of Tom but had never spoke to him. Naomi had seen him walking about in Mark's body and had felt a crawling sensation over her skin, but now she had never been more happy to be in his presence. "That is still some distance away. But thank the grid you're here. Your parents have been looking all over for you."

"We're sorry about that," Jack offered.

"We just want to go home!" cried Ruth. "Help us, Tom. Please!"

"I will start the lights flashing on one of the machines," Tom directed. "Climb into it and I'll bring you to the chamber. I have already informed your parents you are safe. They should be there by the time you arrive."

All four kids clambered onto the machine with the large bucket and huddled inside, thankful for each other's body heat, their spirits lifted at the thought of being reunited with their parents. Even Ruth admitted she was looking forward to seeing Anna again.

Tom's voice came through the grunt's audio system as it trundled through the tunnels mined beneath the mountains. The children answered his questions about what they had been doing and he reassured them that they would be on their way back to Earth in no time. When Jack wanted to know why they were going to Earth, Tom went silent for a short while, composing a response that would not alarm the children. "There is a danger on Springfield," he said at last. "Your parents have decided to return to Earth until that danger has passed." The children fired questions at him regarding the nature of that danger, but Tom would not give them any more. Instead he insisted they talk to their parents when they arrived at the chamber.

The container grunt arrived at the chamber about two hours later. Its occupants could see lots of people milling about on the hillside. "Looks like everybody from around Rhino Hill is down there," observed Mike.

"And Grand Central," Naomi added. There were considerably more people than she had ever seen before. "Maybe Newhaven too. Tom, what's going on?"

"I told you, Naomi," Tom replied. "There is a danger on Springfield. Everyone has to leave."

"I don't want to go to Earth," huffed Ruth. "I want to stay here."

"I'm sure your parents will let you know more," Tom finished. He had no wish to get into an argument with young biologicals.

As the children stepped onto the ground, they could see some individuals pushing urgently through the crowd. Naomi saw Sally and Wolf, Jack heard his mum call his name. All the children's parents and siblings were upon them in seconds, crushing them in hard embraces that took their breath away. Tears were shed and the children knew that something was very wrong. Wolf was on his cellphone in seconds. "Thanks, Tom, we have the children. Now get that chamber fired up. We need to be out of here already."

"Algorithms are running smoothly, Wolf. The chamber is ready." With that, the door in the side of the mountain opened up and the crowd surged forward as everyone who was close enough tried to get in. The chamber would hold several dozen at a time but that was pushing its capacity to dangerous levels, Tom had warned. Even so, he had agreed to allow the transference of that many for the sake of expediency.

Daniel and Anna, Charlie, Jessica, Sally and Wolf, were all at the back having met their children from the mines. There was no way they could force their way to the front, even though they had children with them. Daniel had tried to organise the crowd, to get Anna and the other women out first, but none of them had wanted to leave until their children turned up. Besides, all Daniel's efforts went out the window once the chamber was open. People started pushing and shoving, discipline sacrificed for selfishness. It was a hard fight to reinstate an effective method of control over the people. In the end, Tom's voice shot over the clamour, threatening not to open at all if it would cause such distress. It was an empty threat, Daniel guessed, but it did the trick. The crowd calmed and began to file sensibly into the chamber.

That was until the draith appeared in the sky above

the mountainside. A scream went up from somewhere in the crowd, an arm shooting into the sky with a finger outstretched. Every pair of eyes followed its direction, locking onto the misty darkness undulating above them. The draith closed the distance quickly. The crowd of Springfielders at once fractured, people running in all directions, making their way for vehicles, making their way for the caves, making their way anywhere but the chamber. The draith descended upon them, its tendrils of midnight darkness lashing out and squeezing bodies until they were utterly gone. Five here, another ten there, sucked up into oblivion. It engulfed large crowds, stilling flailing limbs and silencing screaming mouths.

Daniel and Wolf led their friends and families behind an ant but quickly realised that it was insufficient cover from the monster devouring the Springfield inhabitants. Wolf was still wondering what he was going to do about this when the draith suddenly ceased its pursuit of the scattered crowd. Its inky black arms recoiled, shrinking back into its shifting, oily mass. He watched it with a mixture of fear and curiosity. Had it turned around? Had it realised the significance of the chamber?

"Overload every system you can!" Tina ordered, even before Tom had reacted. "We need to light ourselves up and distract the draith from those people!" Tom wound up the output of the central core to 130%, then fed the extra power into every system he could think of. Grunts that had been lying dormant sprang to life and emerged all along the hillside. Lights flashed along the outer rim of the chamber doorway, brighter than ever they had done before. Tom continued pumping out energy from the transformer's power supply, pushing it up to 160%.

"Will this work?" he asked Tina.

"It has to!" she insisted. "The draith is attracted to

sources of energy so we have to make this transformer the biggest it's ever seen!" The draith moved toward the chamber. Even people who were well within striking distance of its smoky grip were ignored.

"It's working," Tom said, his scanners easily picking up the ebony bulk drifting over to his location. "What is your next recommended action?"

"Open the door, let it in," Tina said. "When it's inside detach yourself from the power grid. Isolate your station and run on emergency backup supply. We can transfer to the mini-transformer at the other node."

"No," Tom said flatly. "I have calculated a significant probability that the draith will escape. I cannot allow that."

Tina wanted to argue but there was no time. The draith was already in the chamber and the portal was closing behind it. She could sense its presence worming its way into the transformer's systems just like it had done before, greedily drinking up all the power that Tom was circulating. Power conduits waned, circuitry sparked and died. She isolated her station immediately, hoping Tom had done the same.

"Go, now," came Tom's voice over the two way comm link they shared. "Transfer. I'll remain to make sure the-"

"No!" Tina cried. "I won't leave you." But she was already feeling the sense of detachment she always did during a transfer. Seconds later she was aware of emptiness. No Tom. No draith. No Springfield. She was back in the mini-transformer at the other node. Tom had overridden the transfer routines and sent her out. Sent her to the only safe place she could go. "No!" she cried. "Tom!"

"What's Tom doing?" Daniel asked when the draith disappeared into the chamber. "Is he sending it to Earth to protect us? He can't do that!"

"I don't think he is," Wolf replied. "You feel that?" There was a tremor beneath the soles of Wolf's feet. He had felt earthquakes before and suspected what was to come. "Get everyone away," he called to Daniel, leaping from the cover of the ant and charging toward the stunned people of Springfield. "Run!" he shouted. "Get away from the chamber!" People were more than happy to do so. They had just seen the draith go in there.

The tremors built quickly, the increasingly unstable ground forcing Wolf to his knees. Waves of sound pulsed from the machine encased beneath the mountain, a painful, ceaseless buzzing that intensified with every passing second. Chunks of rock detached from the sides of the mountain, rolling down with crushing force. Daniel was in the ant's cab, the women and children in the loading bed. He switched on the motor and performed as tight a U-turn as fast as he could. A massive boulder splintered into fragments in the space he had just vacated. Wolf leapt onto the vehicle, clutching the bodywork at the back with one hand and allowing himself to be dragged along behind it and away from the collapsing site of the chamber. Flocks of people surged onto the flatlands at the foot of the mountains.

Shafts of light speared out from behind the closed chamber door. The powerful sound rose into a brain-numbing crescendo that forced hands to ears. Seconds later, the chamber door bent inwards as if punched by some tremendous force, like an empty can slowly being crushed. Rending metal scraped along metal, a sonic spear lancing through the air and striking all within a thousand feet. The door bent further, twisted beyond recognition, and then vanished altogether as spiralling dark matter took its place. There was a moment of blessed silence, of intimate calm, before an explosive discharge shattered the peace and the mountain around it. Tons of rock turned to dust instantly, the foundations of the mountain crumbling and bringing its once lofty peak down to a more humble level.

The tremors ceased. The ear-piercing wail stopped. Daniel halted the ant and climbed out of the cab. He joined Wolf as the older man got to his feet, figuring two pairs of eyes were better than one. Neither man spoke as they looked back at the shattered terrain. The women and their children remained huddled in the ant's loading bed, not sure whether to move in case it was not yet safe.

After the intensity of the explosion and the subsequent collapse of the mountain, the sudden silence was almost unbearable. Pinpricks of sound stabbed through the sonic fog, although whether that was bits of rock hitting the floor or his auditory senses returning to normal, Daniel wasn't certain. "Is it over?" he asked Wolf, but got no reply.

They waited long moments. Out of the smoke came survivors, coughing, moaning, but alive. Perhaps thirty people staggered by, clad in dust and all bearing shocked, haunted looks. Daniel called for assistance and the four women clambered out of the ant. Jessica and Anna began to organise getting all the children back to Halfway House - they should not be around when it came to digging through the rubble for bodies - while Charlie called James over to attend to the injured. Sally remained in the ant with their children.

Wolf was staring into the drifting cloud of dust that was slowly beginning to thin out. A huge pile of boulders now occupied the area where the camp once was; he didn't want to think about how many people had been buried. Wolf wandered up the slope to where the chamber used to be, wondering what had happened to it, if it was still there behind all that rock. His efforts to call Tom on a borrowed cellphone had been left unanswered. He couldn't help but keep a wary eye out, too, but there was no sign of the draith, either. Without evidence to the contrary, Wolf had to be satisfied it was safe and he called to Daniel.

"We need to start sifting through this lot," he said, throwing a thumb over his shoulder toward the rocks. He did not need to explain why. Daniel nodded grimly and went off in search of hardy volunteers.

Forty eight men stepped up to the task but it was laborious and sickening work. When the bodies started appearing some of the searchers packed it in, unable to deal with the stress of finding friends or family. Nobody would be left unmarked by the draith's attack. Then a searcher declared they had found a survivor, someone that was not even scratched by the fallen rocks. Wolf was amazed. He attended the location of the survivor as quickly as he could, still startled by the sheer luck of the individual.

Out of the rubble, a man stepped forward. He had no family. He was looking for his friends. "Hello, Wolf," he said, casually. Wolf rubbed his eyes.

"Tom?" Wolf paused. "Tom." Mark's body showed no indication that it had suffered any damage at all. Wolf had never really been upset that he had been outvoted; now, he was delighted. "What happened? What have you done?"

Daniel and Anna appeared at the scene having heard about the recovery of an uninjured survivor. Jessica, Sally and Charlie were not far behind.

"Hey, guys," Tom said, as if he were just one of the gang. "Everybody okay?"

"Tom?" said Daniel, no less surprised as Wolf. "What's going on?"

"Not much, really," Tom replied. He went on to

explain Tina's return and her idea to trap the draith in the transformer. "The lab came from the void and that's where I've sent it, what remained of it. As soon as the draith forced its way in I triggered the return sequence. Made a mess of the mountain, I'm afraid, but there wasn't time to do everything according to protocols." He looked around, trying to judge how much damage had been done and how many people had been killed or injured. "I apologise if anyone is hurt, but it was the only way to make sure the draith would not destroy everything."

"So it's safe?" Wolf had been frightened by the draith. He needed confirmation that it was gone.

"The draith is lost in the void, hopefully forever."

"What about Tina?" Daniel asked.

"She's okay. I sent her back to the mini-transformer. Shouldn't take long to regain connection with her."

"And Earth?" Wolf prompted, hopefully.

Mark's frame made a face as if it were smelling something unpleasant. "I doubt the mini-transformer is capable of that, given its condition. You must start to accept that communication with Earth has been lost."

Wolf nodded. He had suspected as much, and wondered what had happened on the Earthside of the chamber. There had been families there, in the camp. Had it been similarly affected by the chamber's dramatic exit? Perhaps Tom and Tina could repair their mini-transformer and get another link to Earth. Wolf shook the thought aside with a sigh. He couldn't allow himself to be distracted by that now. There was too much to do. With the threat of the draith now removed they should concentrate on rebuilding Springfield. They could be on their own for a long time.